D0208340

WOMEN ON WOMEN

Here are 28 superb works of lesbian short fiction gathered in one volume for the first time, including:

"Tommy, the Unsentimental" by Willa Cather—the story of a young woman's coming of age that shows, in its sublety and reserve, how the "free" lesbian voice has emerged since its publication.

"Don't Explain" by Jewelle Gomez—a nostalgic tale of love and longing in a roadside diner during Boston's hot summer of 1959.

"In the Life" by Becky Birtha—a sentimental story of an older woman remembering her lover.

"A Lesbian Appetite" by Dorothy Allison—a southern tale of food, sex, and love.

Plus 24 more stunningly crafted works of short fiction. . . .

JOAN NESTLE is the co-founder of the lesbian Herstory Archives and the author of *A Restricted Country*. NAOMI HOLOCH is a professor of French at SUNY Purchase.

WOMEN
on
WOMEN

An Anthology of American Lesbian Short Fiction

Edited by Joan Nestle and Naomi Holoch

A PLUME BOOK

PLUME
Published by the Penguin Group
Penguin Books USA Inc., 375 Hudson Street,
New York, New York 10014, U.S.A.
Penguin Books Ltd, 27 Wrights Lane,
London W8 5TZ, England
Penguin Books Australia Ltd, Ringwood,
Victoria, Australia
Penguin Books Canada Ltd, 2801 John Street,
Markham, Ontario, Canada L3R 1B4
Penguin Books (N.Z.) Ltd, 182-190 Wairau Road,
Auckland 10, New Zealand

Penguin Books Ltd, Registered Offices:
Harmondsworth, Middlesex, England

First published by Plume, an imprint of Penguin Books USA Inc.
Published simultaneously in Canada.

First Printing, May, 1990
10 9 8 7 6 5 4 3 2 1

Copyright © 1990, Joan Nestle and Naomi Holoch
All rights reserved

Permissions and Acknowledgments

Excerpt from the novel *The Cook and the Carpenter* © 1975 by June Arnold. Reprinted here by permission of the Estate of June Davis Arnold. All rights reserved.

"When It Changed" by Joanna Russ. First published in *Again Dangerous Visions*, edited by Harland Ellison. © 1972, Doubleday. Reprinted by permission of the author.

"Lover" by Bertha Harris. © 1976, Daughters Publishing Co., Inc. Reprinted by permission of the author and the publisher.

"Eat" by Sapphire. First published in *Conditions* 15, 1988. © 1988, Sapphire. Reprinted by permission of the author.

"With Love, Lena" by Teya Schaffer. Previously published in *Shmate, Common Lives/ Lesbian Lives* and *Sinister Wisdom*. © 1989, Teya Schaffer. Reprinted by permission of the author.

"In the Life" by Becky Birtha. Published in *Lovers' Choice*. © 1987, The Seal Press. Reprinted by permission of the author and the publisher.

"Liberties Not Taken" by Joan Nestle. Published in *A Restricted Country*. © 1987, Firebrand Books. Reprinted by permission of the author and the publisher.

"The Rosy Medallions" by Camille Roy. Published in *Deep Down: The New Sensual Writing by Women*. © 1989, Faber & Faber. Originally appeared under the title *Oct. 8*. Reprinted by permission of the author.

(The following pages constitute an extension of this copyright page.)

"Don't Explain" by Jewelle L. Gomez. First published in *Love, Struggle and Change*, Crossing Press. © 1987, Jewelle L. Gomez. Reprinted by permission of the author.

"A Long Story" by Beth Brant. Published in *Mohawk Trail*. © 1985, Firebrand Books. Reprinted by permission of the author and the publisher.

"A Life Speckled With Children" by Sherri Parris. Published in *Politics of the Heart*. © 1987, Firebrand Books. Reprinted by permission of the author and the publisher.

"Aqua" by Jess Wells. Published in *Two Willow Chairs*. © 1987, Jess Wells. Reprinted by permission of Library B Books.

"The Juliette Low Legacy" by Judith McDaniel. © 1989, Judith McDaniel. Published by permission of the author.

"My Lesbian Imagination" by Leslie Lawrence. First published in *Sojourner*. © 1987, Leslie Lawrence. Reprinted by permission of the author.

"Trespassing" by Valerie Miner. Published in *Trespassing and Other Stories*. © 1989, Crossing Press. Reprinted by permission of the author and the publisher.

"Letting Bode" by Kristina McGrath. From *Last House on January Road*. © 1989, Kristina McGrath. Reprinted by permission of the author.

"Causes" by Jacqueline Woodson. First published in *Out/Look*. © 1988, Jacqueline Woodson. Reprinted by permission of the author.

"A Letter to Harvey Milk" by Lesléa Newman. Published in *A Letter to Harvey Milk*. © 1988, Firebrand Books. Reprinted by permission of the author and the publisher.

"Fruit of the Loom Undershirts" by Cathy Cockrell. Published in *Undershirts and Other Stories* by Cathy Cockrell. © 1982, Hanging Loose Press. Reprinted by permission of the author and the publisher.

"Our Life in Iowa" by Margaret Erhart. Originally published in *Common Lives/Lesbian Lives*, Winter 1984, issue #14. © 1984, Margaret Erhart. Reprinted by permission of the author.

The Gloria Stories by Rocky Gámez. First published in *Conditions*. © 1980, Rocky Gámez. Reprinted in *Cuentos: Stories by Latinas* and in *Wayward Girls and Wicked Women*. Reprinted by permission of the author.

"Cruz" by Ida Swearingen. © 1989, Ida Swearingen. Published by permission of the author.

"Upstate" by Naomi Holoch. © 1989, Naomi Holoch. Published by permission of the author.

"The Swashbuckler" by Lee Lynch. Published in *Sinister Wisdom*, © 1985. Reprinted in *The Swashbuckler*. © 1985, Naiad Press. Reprinted by permission of the author and the publisher.

Lyrics from the song "Don't Explain" are by B. Holiday and A. Hefzog, Jr. Northern Music Co. (ASCAP). Used by permission.

"Dead Heat" by Willyce Kim. Published in *Dead Heat*. © 1988, Alyson Publications. Reprinted by permission of the author and the publisher.

"The Penis Story" by Sarah Schulman. Published in *On Our Backs*. © 1986 by Sarah Schulman. Reprinted by permission of the author.

"A Lesbian Appetite" by Dorothy Allison. Published in *Trash* by Dorothy Allison. © 1988, Firebrand Books. Reprinted by permission of the author and the publisher.

Lyrics from the song "Sad-Eyed Lady of the Lowlands" are by Bob Dylan, copyright 1966 by Dwarf Music. Used by permission.

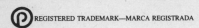REGISTERED TRADEMARK—MARCA REGISTRADA

Library of Congress Cataloging-in-Publication Data

Women on women : an anthology of American lesbian short fiction / edited by Joan
  Nestle and Naomi Holoch.
      p.   cm.
    ISBN 0-452-26388-3
    1. Lesbians—Fiction.   2. Lesbians' writing, American.   3. Short stories,
  American—Women authors.   I. Nestle, Joan, 1940–
  II. Holoch, Naomi.
  PS648.L47W66   1990
  813'.01089287—dc20   90-5714
                                                                    CIP

Printed in the United States of America
Designed by Nissa Knuth

Without limiting the rights under copyright reserved above, no part of this publication may be reproduced, stored in or introduced into a retrieval system, or transmitted, in any form, or by any means (electronic, mechanical, photocopying, recording, or otherwise), without the prior written permission of both the copyright owner and the above publisher of this book.

PUBLISHER'S NOTE
This is a work of fiction. Names, characters, places, and incidents either are the product of the authors' imagination or are used fictitiously, and any resemblance to actual persons, living or dead, events, or locales is entirely coincidental.

BOOKS ARE AVAILABLE AT QUANTITY DISCOUNTS WHEN USED TO PROMOTE PRODUCTS OR SERVICES. FOR INFORMATION PLEASE WRITE TO PREMIUM MARKETING DIVISION, PENGUIN BOOKS USA INC., 375 HUDSON STREET, NEW YORK, NEW YORK 10014.

Contents

*"Listen, Faith, why don't you tell my story?
You've told everybody's story but mine."*
—Grace Paley, "Listening"

Introduction

Naomi Holoch

One of our goals as we undertook this anthology was to introduce "new" lesbian writers to the public at large by including in this collection a large number of previously unpublished works. A number of the authors included here have been writing for years and are familiar with the long, difficult process of criticism and self-criticism that is part of the struggle of refining one's narrative voice. For many reasons, ranging from an author's timidity to the controversial nature—in conventional terms—of some of the material, the work of many of these authors has remained within the lesbian community, known only to other lesbians through readings, writing workshops, or informal requests for feedback. In this manner, the writing of lesbians still mirrors the traditions that have informed women's writing for so long: It is part of a literature that has often excused itself for existing by insisting on its "private" use. As in the keeping of a journal, the writing is only meant "for oneself." If, over the last decade, women's fiction has effectively changed its image of itself, recognizing its need, its desire, and its right to a general public, lesbian writing, which represents "the extreme outsiders among the outsiders,"[1] has had a still more complicated battle to wage. Those selections included here that have appeared before—both short stories and excerpts from novels—have, with one exception, been published by small gay and/or feminist presses that have not had the financial means to distribute and bring them to the attention of the public at large. NAL's interest in this anthology highlights the relatively new process and possibility of redefining the relationship between lesbian literature and the general reader.

We have structured this collection of lesbian fiction around major themes that unite lesbian lives. We have, at the same time, looked for stories and styles that truly represent the extraordinary diversity that underlies our common concerns. The choices we had to make were difficult: In order to create an anthology that would give voice to the variety of experience rising out of ethnic, race, class, and generational differences as well as out of the simple, irreducible fact of individual histories, we were not able to include all the well-crafted manuscripts we received.

The issues raised in these stories are of course basic to the human condition: Intimacy, loneliness, death, anger, ambition, and desire thread their way through this collection explored now with an eye for the comic, for the absurd, now with a sense of poignant sadness and longing. Desire appears at moments as an exuberant appetite, at others as a desperate hunger. Yet in all these stories, the experience and its expression is shaped by the lesbian identity of the author. It is critical to recognize that to live, to observe, to write as a lesbian is to live, observe, and write from a position of difference. Belonging to a minority group that has behind it a long history of oppression and invisibility—one of oppression's pernicious manifestations—the lesbian writer must in some manner attend to her lesbianism. As a gay woman, it is rarely possible to step into the street

[1]Bonnie Zimmerman, "Exiting from Patrimony: The Lesbian Novel of Development," from *The Voyage In, Fictions of Female Development,* eds. G. Adel, M. Hirsch, E. Langland (Hanover, NH, University Press of New England, 1983) p. 245.

without remembering who one is; what one sees and how one is seen are constant reminders of difference. The lesbian writer cannot set aside such a strongly enforced self-consciousness as she goes about her business. To do so would isolate her art from her existence, mutilating both the writing and the writer.

These are stories that surely have been told before, but they have not been heard. When the narrator-writer of Grace Paley's story "Listening" records the complaint of her lesbian friend Cassie that heterosexual writers have created their worlds as if the lesbian never existed, Paley is marking a turning point by giving literary form to the complaint. As Cassie goes on to say, however, whoever wants their story truly told must, in the end, go ahead and do it themselves: "You've told everybody's story but mine. I don't mean my whole story, that's my job. You probably can't."[2]

In this volume, lesbian writers have come together to tackle the job that only they can do. Given the diversity of background already present in an American context of the 1970s and 1980s, we have limited this volume to American writing of this period, with the exception of the opening selection. Willa Cather's "Tommy, the Unsentimental," written in 1899, presents a tomboyish figure, her traditional ambiguity only slightly muted by her protective attachment to an inept young man. Interestingly, she is the darling of her community, although the community sees her clearly: "The Old Boys said it was a bad sign when a rebellious girl like Tommy took to being sweet and gentle to one of her own sex, the worst sign in the world." But it is the turn of the century, and Cather does not allow Tommy to push her community too far; she leaves Tommy musing affectionately about men, even if it be about their limitations. Selections from the 1970s reflect the enormous distance covered toward self-acceptance and the influence of the women's move-

[2]*Later the Same Day* (New York: Viking Penguin, 1986), p. 210.

ment on lesbian life, as well as a willingness to experiment with form. Gender is viewed as a concept to be consciously challenged, as in June Arnold's *The Cook and the Carpenter*. Arnold confronts our dependency on gender as a point of reference by removing all feminine and masculine pronouns and replacing them with the invented term of "na." Joanna Russ brings science fiction into the realm of lesbian feminist writing as she creates a territory that has been free of men but is about to be colonized. Bertha Harris plays with style, constructing a work out of a series of vignettes that evoke a mixture of myth, Gertrude Stein, and surreal fantasy culminating in images that turn traditional symbols topsy-turvy. A baby becomes something to be eaten rather than fed and names become a magic tool by which women may invent each other.

The themes of loss and attachment unite a number of the stories in this collection. In two separate stories, a Holocaust survivor and an old black woman continue to struggle with the death of a lover after more than a decade, each in her own voice, each unmistakably rooted in her different culture yet joined by a delicate balance of humor and pathos. In another story, the untimely and sudden death of a lover evokes at once a sense of loss and commitment to life, culminating in an image that interweaves separation and adventure as the author evokes the wagon trains of the last century. Elsewhere, a woman confronts yet one more loss as she sees her connection to an ex-lover's child fade; a lesbian mother loses her child to the courts with a sense of tearing mutilation rooted in the historical memory of a Native American woman one hundred years earlier. A tough, hard-drinking woman relives her mother's betrayal as she celebrates her birthday with a stranger stranded on her porch because of car trouble.

Women approach each other across generational lines, sometimes tentatively, obeying the constraints of our culture, as in Joan Nestle's "Liberties Not Taken," sometimes with greater freedom in their very marginality, as in Sapphire's "Eat," yet always with the same longing for human warmth and nourishment. Intimacies among women are hampered, crippled, sometimes prevented by fears of the consequences of stepping "out of bounds" as in "My Lesbian Imagination"; the social constraints and expectations of the "straight" world undermine the already fragile contemporary sense of solidarity and safety in "The Juliette Low Legacy" and take on an explicitly menacing form in "Trespassing."

But if protagonists are caught up in the conventions of heterosexual society, they also find ways to reach out to each other, as all these stories attest. And there are other presences in these stories: the voice of Billie Holiday brings two women together; a widowed elderly Jewish man relives painful but intensely alive memories as he does writing exercises for his young lesbian writing teacher, for whom he has almost become family. In every instance, the narrative voice reflects an intense sensitivity to the "other," to the delicacy—though not necessarily the fragility—of connections among individuals, an almost obsessive awareness of difference even as intimate ties are formed. The Paul Bunyan-like figure of "Letting Bode" remains more a part of the earth than of her lover, and the breaking down of physical boundaries in "The Rosy Medallions" does nothing to diffuse the elusiveness of the narrator's lover.

Protagonists may sidestep, defy, and in some cases ignore the constraints and prohibitions of "straight" society. Rocky Gámez's Gloria believes herself capable of fathering a child with the woman she loves; Frenchie, "The Swashbuckler," leads her pirate existence every Saturday night, even if she must hide her boots and her identity the other six days of the week. With less poignancy, and greater liberty, Cathy Cockrell claims and redefines a basic and ordinary article of men's clothing, the undershirt, as it molds a woman's breasts and torso while retaining its suggestion of power and freedom. Rebellion may be obscure; it may take a paradoxical form, as it does in the angrily defiant gesture of the Sergeant in "Upstate." It may be direct, confrontational, and self-affirming as it is in "Cruz."

In the end, marginality may mean freedom as well as oppression. Writers such as Willyce Kim and Sarah Schulman infuse their characters with a style and energy that suggest a new sense of ease in their identity as lesbian writers. Irreverence and exuberance are perhaps at last becoming integrated into the lesbian experience in a manner that will help give still more varied forms to lesbian lives and literature. The dream of Bertha Harris's Veronica of rooms filled with art but no food may be slowly dissipating. Instead, we can dream Dorothy Allison's dream: "For the first time in my life I am not hungry, but everyone insists I have a little taste. I burp like a baby on her mama's shoulder. My stomach is full, relaxed, happy, and the taste of pan gravy is in my mouth. I can't stop grinning. The dream goes on and on, and through it all I hug myself and smile."

Tommy, the Unsentimental

Willa Cather

"Your father says he has no business tact at all, and of course that's dreadfully unfortunate."

"Business," replied Tommy, "he's a baby in business; he's good for nothing on earth but to keep his hair parted straight and wear that white carnation in his buttonhole. He has 'em sent down from Hastings twice a week as regularly as the mail comes, but the drafts he cashes lie in his safe until they are lost, or somebody finds them. I go up occasionally and send a package away for him myself. He'll answer your notes promptly enough, but his business letters—I believe he destroys them unopened to shake the responsibility of answering them."

"I am at a loss to see how you can have such patience with him, Tommy, in so many ways he is thoroughly reprehensible."

"Well, a man's likeableness don't depend at all on his virtues or acquirements, nor a woman's either, unfortunately. You like them or you don't like them, and that's all there is to it. For the why of it you must appeal to a higher oracle than I. Jay is a likeable fellow, and that's his only and sole acquirement, but after all it's a rather happy one."

"Yes, he certainly is that," replied Miss Jessica, as she deliberately turned off the gas jet and proceeded to arrange her toilet articles. Tommy watched her closely and then turned away with a baffled expression.

Needless to say, Tommy was not a boy, although her keen gray eyes and wide forehead were scarcely girlish, and she had the lank figure of an active half grown lad. Her real name was Theodosia, but during Thomas Shirley's frequent absences from the bank she had attended to his business and correspondence signing herself "T. Shirley," until everyone in Southdown called her "Tommy." That blunt sort of familiarity is not unfrequent in the West, and is meant well enough. People rather expect some business ability in a girl there, and they respect it immensely. That, Tommy undoubtedly had, and if she had not, things would have gone at sixes and sevens in the Southdown National. For Thomas Shirley had big land interests in Wyoming that called him constantly away from home, and his cashier, little Jay Ellington Harper, was, in the local phrase, a weak brother in the bank. He was the son of a friend of old Shirley's, whose papa had sent him West, because he had made a sad mess of his college career, and had spent too much money and gone at too giddy a pace down East. Conditions changed the young gentleman's life, for it was simply impossible to live either prodigally or rapidly in Southdown, but they could not materially affect his mental habits or inclinations. He was made cashier of Shirley's bank because his father bought in half the stock, but Tommy did his work for him.

The relation between these two young people was peculiar; Harper was, in his way, very grateful to her for keeping him out of disgrace with her father, and showed it by a hundred little attentions which were new to her and much more agreeable than the work she did for him was irksome. Tommy knew that she was immensely fond of him, and she knew at the same time that she was thoroughly foolish for being so. As she expressed it, she was not of his sort, and never would be. She did not often take pains to think, but when she did she saw matters pretty clearly, and she was of a peculiarly unfeminine mind that could not escape meeting and acknowledging a logical conclusion. But she went on liking Jay Ellington Harper, just the same. Now Harper was the only foolish man of Tommy's acquaintance. She knew plenty of active young business men and sturdy ranchers, such as one meets about live western towns, and took no particular interest in them, probably just because they were practical and sensible and thoroughly of her own kind. She knew almost no women, because in those days there were few women in Southdown who were in any sense interesting, or interested in anything but babies and salads. Her best friends were her father's old business friends, elderly men who had seen a good deal of the world, and who were very proud and fond of Tommy. They recognized a sort of squareness and honesty of spirit in the girl that Jay Ellington Harper never discovered, or, if he did, knew too little of its rareness to value highly. Those old speculators and men of business had always felt a sort of responsibility for Tom Shirley's little girl, and had rather taken her mother's place, and been her advisers on many points upon which men seldom feel at liberty to address a girl.

She was just one of them; she played whist and billiards with them, and made their cocktails for them, not scorning to take one herself occasionally. Indeed, Tommy's cocktails were things of fame in Southdown, and the professional compounders of drinks always bowed respectfully to her as though acknowledging a powerful rival.

Now all these things displeased and puzzled Jay Ellington Harper, and Tommy knew it full well, but clung to her old manner of living with a stubborn pertinacity, feeling somehow that to change would be both foolish and disloyal to the Old Boys. And as things went on, the seven Old Boys made greater demands upon her time than ever, for they were shrewd men, most of them, and had not lived fifty years in this world without learning a few things and unlearning many more. And while Tommy lived on in the blissful delusion that her role of indifference was perfectly played and without a flaw, they suspected how things were going and were perplexed as to the outcome. Still, their confidence was by no means shaken, and as Joe Elsworth said to Joe Sawyer one evening at billiards, "I think we can pretty nearly depend on Tommy's good sense."

They were too wise to say anything to Tommy, but they said just a word or two to Thomas Shirley, Sr., and combined to make things very unpleasant for Mr. Jay Ellington Harper.

At length their relations with Harper became so strained that the young man felt it would be better for him to leave town, so his father started him in a little bank of his own up in Red Willow. Red Willow, however, was scarcely a safe distance, being only some twenty-five miles north, upon the Divide, and Tommy occasionally found excuse to run up on her wheel to straighten out the young man's business for him. So when she suddenly decided to go East to school for a year, Thomas, Sr., drew a sigh of great relief. But the seven Old Boys shook their heads; they did not like to see her gravitating toward the East; it was a sign of weakening, they said, and showed an inclination to experiment with another kind of life, Jay Ellington Harper's kind.

But to school Tommy went, and from all reports conducted herself in a most seemly manner; made no more cocktails, played no more billiards. She took rather her own way with the curriculum, but she distinguished herself in athletics, which in Southdown counted for vastly more than erudition.

Her evident joy on getting back to Southdown was appreciated by everyone. She went about shaking hands with everybody, her shrewd face, that was so like a clever wholesome boy's, held high with happiness. As she said to old Joe Elsworth one morning, when they were driving behind his stud through a little thicket of cottonwood scattered along the sun-parched bluffs, "It's all very fine down East there, and the hills are great, but one gets mighty homesick for this sky, the old intense blue of it, you know. Down there the skies are all pale and smoky. And this wind, this hateful, dear, old everlasting wind that comes down like the sweep of cavalry and is never tamed or broken. O Joe, I used to get hungry for this wind! I couldn't sleep in that lifeless stillness down there."

"How about the people, Tom?"

"O, they are fine enough folk, but we're not their sort, Joe, and never can be."

"You realize that, do you, fully?"

"Quite fully enough, thank you, Joe." She laughed rather dismally, and Joe cut his horse with the whip.

The only unsatisfactory thing about Tommy's return was that she brought with her a girl she had grown fond of at school, a dainty, white, languid bit of a thing, who used violet perfumes and carried a sunshade. The Old Boys said it was a bad sign when a rebellious girl like Tommy took to being sweet and gentle to one of her own sex, the worst sign in the world.

The new girl was no sooner in town than a new complication came about. There was no doubt of the impression she made on Jay Ellington Harper. She indisputably had all those little evidences of good breeding that were about the only things which could touch the timid, harassed young man who was so much out of his element. It was a very plain case on his part, and the souls of the seven were troubled within them. Said Joe Elsworth to the other Joe, "The heart of the cad is gone out to the little muff, as is right and proper and in accordance with the eternal fitness of things. But there's the other girl who has the blindness that may not be cured, and she gets all the rub of it. It's no use, I can't help her, and I am going to run down to Kansas City for awhile. I can't stay here and see the abominable suffering of it." He didn't go, however.

There was just one other person who understood the hopelessness of the situation quite as well as Joe, and that was Tommy. That is, she understood Harper's attitude. As to Miss Jessica's she was not quite so certain, for Miss Jessica, though pale and languid and addicted to sunshades, was a maiden most discreet. Conversations on the subject usually ended without any further information as to Miss Jessica's feelings, and Tommy sometimes wondered if she were capable of having any at all.

At last the calamity which Tommy had long foretold descended upon Jay Ellington Harper. One morning she received a telegram from him begging her to intercede with her father; there was a run on his bank and he must have help before noon. It was then ten thirty, and the one sleepy little train that ran up to Red Willow daily had crawled out of the station an hour before. Thomas Shirley, Sr., was not at home.

"And it's a good thing for Jay Ellington he's not, he might be more stony hearted than I," remarked Tommy, as she closed the ledger and turned to the terrified Miss Jessica. "Of course we're his only chance, no one else would turn their hand over to help him. The train went an hour ago and he says it must be there by noon. It's the only bank in the town, so nothing can be done by telegraph. There is nothing left but to wheel for it. I may make it, and I may not. Jess, you scamper up to the house and get my wheel out, the tire may need a little attention. I will be along in a minute."

"O, Theodosia, can't I go with you? I must go!"

"You go! O, yes, of course, if you want to. You know what you are getting into, though. It's twenty-five miles uppish grade and hilly, and only an hour and a quarter to do it in."

"O, Theodosia, I can do anything now!" cried Miss Jessica, as she put up her sunshade and fled precipitately. Tommy smiled as she began cramming bank notes into a canvas bag. "May be you can, my dear, and may be you can't."

The road from Southdown to Red Willow is not by any means a favorite bicycle road; it is rough, hilly and climbs from the river bottoms up to the big Divide by a steady up grade, running white and hot through the scorched corn fields and grazing lands where the long-horned Texan cattle browse about in the old buffalo wallows. Miss Jessica soon found that with the pedaling that had to be done there was little time left for emotion of any sort, or little sensibility for anything but the throbbing, dazzling heat that had to be endured. Down there in the valley the distant bluffs were vibrating and dancing with the heat, the cattle, completely overcome by it, had hidden under the shelving banks of the "draws" and the prairie dogs had fled to the bottom of their holes that are said to reach to water. The whirr of the seventeen-year locust was the only thing that spoke of animation, and that ground on as if only animated and enlivened by the sickening, destroying heat. The sun was like hot brass, and the wind that blew up from the south was hotter still. But Tommy knew that wind was their only chance. Miss Jessica began to feel that unless she could stop and get some water she was not much longer for this vale of tears. She suggested this possibility to Tommy, but Tommy only shook her head, "Take too much time," and bent over her handle bars, never lifting her eyes from the road in front of her. It flashed upon Miss Jessica that Tommy was not only very unkind, but that she sat very badly on her wheel and looked aggressively masculine and professional when she bent her shoulders and pumped like that. But just then Miss Jessica found it harder than ever to breathe, and the bluffs across the river began doing serpentines and skirt dances, and more important and personal considerations occupied the young lady.

When they were fairly over the first half of the road, Tommy took out her watch. "Have to hurry up, Jess, I can't wait for you."

"O, Tommy, I can't," panted Miss Jessica, dismounting and sitting down in a little heap by the roadside. "You go on, Tommy, and tell him—tell him I hope it won't fail, and I'd do anything to save him."

By this time the discreet Miss Jessica was reduced to tears, and Tommy nodded as she disappeared over the hill laughing to herself. "Poor Jess, anything but the one thing he needs. Well, your kind have the best of it generally, but in little affairs of this sort my kind come out rather strongly. We're rather better at them than at dancing. It's only fair, one side shouldn't have all."

Just at twelve o'clock, when Jay Ellington Harper, his collar crushed and wet about his throat, his eyeglass dimmed with perspiration, his hair hanging damp over his forehead, and even the ends of his moustache dripping with moisture, was attempting to reason with a score of angry Bohemians, Tommy came quietly through the door, grip in hand. She went straight behind the grating, and standing screened by the bookkeeper's desk, handed the bag to Harper and turned to the spokesman of the Bohemians.

"What's all this business mean, Anton? Do you all come to bank at once nowadays?"

"We want 'a money, want 'a our money, he no got it, no give it," bawled the big beery Bohemian.

"O, don't chaff 'em any longer, give 'em their money and get rid of 'em, I want to see you," said Tommy carelessly, as she went into the consulting room.

When Harper entered half an hour later, after the rush was over, all that was left of his usual immaculate appearance was his eyeglass and the white flower in his buttonhole.

"This has been terrible!" he gasped. "Miss Theodosia, I can never thank you."

"No," interrupted Tommy. "You never can, and I don't want any thanks. It was rather a tight place, though, wasn't it? You looked like a ghost when I came in. What started them?"

"How should I know? They just came down like the wolf on the fold. It sounded like the approach of a ghost dance."★

★ The ghost dance, a ritualistic worship of Wovoka, a self-appointed Indian Messiah, was associated with the so-called Sioux Uprising in 1890, which culminated in the battle of Wounded Knee, in South Dakota near the Nebraska border, on December 29, 1890.

"And of course you had no reserve? O, I always told you this would come, it was inevitable with your charming methods. By the way, Jess sends her regrets and says she would do anything to save you. She started out with me, but she has fallen by the wayside. O, don't be alarmed, she is not hurt, just winded. I left her all bunched up by the road like a little white rabbit. I think the lack of romance in the escapade did her up about as much as anything; she is essentially romantic. If we had been on fiery steeds bespattered with foam I think she would have made it, but a wheel hurt her dignity. I'll tend bank; you'd better get your wheel and go and look her up and comfort her. And as soon as it is convenient, Jay, I wish you'd marry her and be done with it, I want to get this thing off my mind."

Jay Ellington Harper dropped into a chair and turned a shade whiter.

"Theodosia, what do you mean? Don't you remember what I said to you last fall, the night before you went to school? Don't you remember what I wrote you—"

Tommy sat down on the table beside him and looked seriously and frankly into his eyes.

"Now, see here, Jay Ellington, we have been playing a nice little game, and now it's time to quit. One must grow up sometime. You are horribly wrought up over Jess, and why deny it? She's your kind, and clean daft about you, so there is only one thing to do. That's all."

Jay Ellington wiped his brow, and felt unequal to the situation. Perhaps he really came nearer to being moved down to his stolid little depths than he ever had before. His voice shook a good deal and was very low as he answered her.

"You have been very good to me, I didn't believe any woman could be at once so kind and clever. You almost made a man of even me."

"Well, I certainly didn't succeed. As to being good to you, that's rather a break, you know; I am amiable, but I am only flesh and blood after all. Since I have known you

I have not been at all good, in any sense of the word, and I suspect I have been anything but clever. Now, take mercy upon Jess—and me—and go. Go on, that ride is beginning to tell on me. Such things strain one's nerve. . . . Thank Heaven he's gone at last and had sense enough not to say anything more. It was growing rather critical. As I told him I am not at all superhuman."

After Jay Ellington Harper had bowed himself out, when Tommy sat alone in the darkened office, watching the flapping blinds, with the bank books before her, she noticed a white flower on the floor. It was the one Jay Ellington had worn in his coat and had dropped in his nervous agitation. She picked it up and stood holding it a moment, biting her lip. Then she dropped it into the grate and turned away, shrugging her thin shoulders.

"They are awful idiots, half of them, and never think of anything beyond their dinner. But O, how we do like 'em!"

First published in *Home Monthly*, VI (August 1896), 6–7.

From *The Cook and the Carpenter*

June Arnold

In most groups there are whispers, a term that has little to do with the volume of the speaking voice but refers rather to the peregrinations of what is said: phrases wander from ear to mouth to ear, during a walk across grass, down a hall to work, behind a door in the bathroom, at varying distances from the people or events which are their subjects, leaving a trail of uneasy excitement throughout the routine. Words are passed along like hasty pats, the person speaking making no more serious commitment to them than the recipient, sometimes with a laugh, sometimes with a future aimed frown, always with the meaning though that we should wait and see.

By the time the carpenter ran across the trail, several verbal days had gone by.

Na was working in the garage, making two bookcases for money. Na had also agreed to remodel a garage into a studio for money. Na was singing a half-voiced, half-mouthed song on the first October day that was slightly cool—seventy-two—a break in the temperature of summer which whispered that the heat was essentially over. But the carpenter was really listening to the whispers of the wood by which a board suggested that it be laid this way not that. Na stood now stroking with nan eye the incredible curves of the grain.

The time before beginning to make any structure, the minutes after the wood is in front of you but before you take any tool to it, was to the carpenter a period of pure happiness and nan body felt sprung from the earth like a tree itself in joy.

Therefore na was angry that someone should choose those minutes to intrude the trail of the whispers, and the anger produced a useful deafness.

"Stubby is leaving," the one called Tracy said, the one who drove a taxi for a local fleet but who was only really interested in writing. Because na wrote, na wandered around the group when na was not working, trying to find out who everyone was. Na had not gotten to the carpenter before.

The carpenter said, "Good." Na had misunderstood.

Stubby was not going to leave just like that. Na had told everyone including people who shared the group's politics in Chicago, Boston, New York and Berkeley. Na had written a statement, detailing nan position and enemies, and intended to read it tonight at a meeting. Na had sent a copy of the statement to Chicago, Boston, New York and Berkeley.

There were two main charges in the statement: that Stubby was being treated as if na were a pig and that personal dislike of na was infiltrating the movement.

That night they got word that one called Three was coming down to pay their group a visit. From Chicago. A change came over everyone; their faces showed that they were straightening out their politics as if they were cleaning up the house for a visitor. It was very unreal.

"Na is leaving because of you," the cook said. A large number of the whispers had passed by the stove and across the chopping table. "Everybody knows that you don't like Stubby—after Saturday night no one could miss knowing it. And you have a lot of influence here."

"I don't want that kind of influence—to be 'followed.' " The carpenter had once wanted that, and even now experi-

enced as a kiss the cook's admiration when na spoke of nan
lover's influence. But the chill followed so fast that the kiss
was cold before it reached the brain: the carpenter knew
that to be followed was the prerequisite for being dumped
and na wanted more than anything to belong.

"What you say is important to people, that's all. There's
nothing you can do about it. People have learned to value
your mind because it is clearer than most of ours, and
usually fair. So then the rare time it is not completely fair
. . . those who don't know you all that well value what you
say then too."

"I'm going to have to be perfect, then."

"You could apologize."

"Godammit, everybody gets to say what na is feeling
except me. I have to hold everything in until I'm sure I'm
not just reacting emotionally to my own hang-ups—no one
else had to do this, just me. I have to be a goddamn holy
parent. An editor. A spokesperson for the movement. Stubby
had more time than I did to tell everyone how wrong I
was."

"Stubby needed even more time. Na doesn't understand
naself or you well enough to explain how na was right. And
besides," the cook grinned, "na has that irritating way of
saying anything."

The carpenter was sitting in the center of an energy field
of anger and stood up, sat down, stood up, turned and
turned back. The cook could light a cigarette but the carpenter would not; na forced nan brain to carry the anger
until it exploded.

"I have marvelous choices," na said, the words pushing
each other out very fast and clear. "I can apologize to
Stubby and whoever else wants to listen—I can say that I
am clearer-headed than na is and should not take advantage
of this gift of mine; I should instead grow muddled to give
na a fair chance. If I force myself to grow muddled, na
might feel that I am the patronizing parent crawling on the
floor with the children. If I remain silent to allow Stubby

plenty more time to say what na needs so much time to say,
the whole group may feel that they are getting to hear only
one person and then doesn't Stubby become the one with
too much influence? If I scream and complain about na in
private, to you, to let off steam so I can be cool in the
meetings, I am being private and talking about people behind their backs not to their faces. However, if I tell na
exactly what I think of na, everyone else might be influ-
enced to get rid of na absolutely. Stubby naself might be
crushed beyond the repair of those most dedicated to we-
have-to-support-each-other. So if it's impossible for both of
us to co-exist in one group, one of us will have to leave, and
it'll be me since I'm the one who cares too much about the
group to let it collapse beneath Stubby's and my mutual
antagonisms. And that's always the way—the group loses
the one person who is most dedicated to it. I'm going to go
out and get drunk."

Paralyzed from habit, from the past when na was impo-
tent to stop the child who screamed and ran away, the lover
who raged and slammed the door, the parent who cursed
and drank and stayed away, the cook sat stone still and
trembling while the carpenter moved toward the door, checking nan pockets for money and keys. Na was not moving
fast, the cook saw. "Wait," the cook said, barely audibly.

"Wait." The cook took nan arm, nan shoulder, held nan
face with nan own. "I love you. Don't go."

For a moment the carpenter's body began to cry, hold
me, hold on, hold, hold. But na abruptly let go and stepped
back. Na was furious, too angry to feel the love that nan
mind said was there. "I can't stay here and rave at you.
That's no help and unfair to you. I'm going out to get
drunk." Na did not move toward the door, however. "Why
can't Stubby just go—leave, storm out, walk out, run away,
stamp nan feet, slam the door and be done with it! Godammit,
na leaves but na won't leave. We're going to be tied up in
nan leaving for days and then na'll stay so na can leave
again next week. I should have let na handle that belligerent

one they call Tiny all by naself and let na get the shit beaten out of na and then na could leave because no one stepped in to help na."

The cook said quickly, "You didn't hate na before that night though. I did."

"You're smarter than *I* am."

"I never felt I had to like na in the first place. Na was here and I accepted that, but I didn't think I had to like na too. But you did. You spent all that time understanding the point na might have had. It's like what the moon said to the dough: you're not doing anything but rising, you just look different when you do it."

The carpenter's frown slipped away and nan voice which had been flat as tin, softened. "Okay, you're a fucking poet, you are."

"Come here." The cook reached out and held the carpenter urgently close. "You are my child, my own precious child, come here and let me hold you."

"I'm here," the carpenter murmured through a mesh of hair.

"Now I'm going to get you something to eat," the carpenter said after a timeless period of time, an acting love that had swamped and filled them both coming as it did onto their already spinning emotions—the carpenter's rage and the cook's fright that na would not be quick enough to turn the rage around. "I'm going to feed the world's feeder. Then you can tell me the best thing to do, the choice I haven't thought of."

"I'll tell you a story," the cook said, before starting the second half of nan sandwich but keeping the beer nevertheless resting close on nan knee, because it was a surprise. "I thought I knew everything that was anywhere in that refrigerator. I didn't know we had beer. You know Stubby has gotten to know a lot of people who have power in this town, because na speaks Spanish and works in the Center and likes to talk politics. Na thinks that if we're careful—if we let Stubby do our talking—that the people who run this town can be won over to support us, or at least to accept the fact that we're here. Na said yesterday that it looks like they want a favor from us in return, if we took in a certain number of homeless people and children and helped obliterate that blot on their town's shining surface. Stubby said, 'If we run a refuge for blots.' "

The carpenter laughed out loud. "Good. I didn't know na had a sense of humor."

"That's arrogant, too, of course—to accept na for that."

"I'm arrogant. It's also using na, to accept na for a front."

"What choice do we have?"

"Or maybe it's not. The two things we are trying to do—set up a counterculture and make a revolution . . . it's hard to do both things at the same time. So people like Stubby who are devoting all their energies to one thing, who aren't sidetracked by looking for personal happiness—we need people like that. And it's easier for Stubby too in a way, since na is only interested in the revolution part."

"Easier? But na also has no personal world. . . ."

"Simpler."

". . . to live in, no sustenance or comfort. Na is not in love and doesn't even have friends na loves. We should be able to understand how lonely na must feel, how left out and jealous of those who are in love. Darling, we should feel sorry for the rest of the world."

"Na is in love with you! Fuck it, I'm sure of it."

"Na isn't."

"Of course na is. Everyone is." The carpenter stood up and towered above the cook, who was sitting cross-legged like a child on the bed. "This whole display is for you— writing letters and making speeches and calling meetings and getting that person down here from Chicago . . . Three. Na is creating a storm to get your attention, to force you to choose nan side, to make you notice na and see how much na loves you and to what great lengths na would go for you."

"That's really unfair. You're saying nan politics is motivated by that old desire to win love and approval and that's all."

"Wait a minute." The carpenter sat back down. "That is what I'm saying . . . let me think a minute. Aha! I know. Look, I really don't believe that anyone can work for a revolution separate and distinct from nan own personal happiness or love-needs. Such a person wouldn't have any way of knowing the difference between what is true and what false. It isn't that we're trying to do two things at once—set up a counterlife and work for a revolution; the two are halves of the same whole and the absolutely essential thing is to keep juggling them. If we concentrate on either one and forget the other we produce a monster. That's Stubby's definition; na is a monster and nothing na says, even when na is 'right,' is really right."

"Stubby is not a monster," the cook said firmly.

"You don't understand what I mean by monster. I mean na does everything by thinking and analyzing and reasoning, and na doesn't pay attention to who na is and what na is feeling. I think that *is* a monster. Or becomes or produces or might as well be a monster."

"You don't mean the term as an insult . . . but it *is*."

"So then it is. I'm going to get us another beer."

"I have to go to sleep. It's very late."

"Do you?"

"I have to get up early."

"You do. I'll go back to my room."

"How can you?"

"You're right. I can't." The carpenter crawled into the mattress on the floor and lay close to the cook. "I'll sleep here with you, crowded and beerless." Na put nan arm under the cook's shoulders and held na close. "Because we love each other. Don't we?"

Why despair? The carpenter moved gently away from the cook's sleeping arm curved across nan lover's back, stopped still when the cook tightened nan grip on the carpenter's hand, waited until the grip loosened and then slipped the hand away, leaving the cook's hand to reach in sleep and settle finally into a fist pushed under nan own belly. The carpenter stood by the window, breathing deeply, quickly awake with the feeling that na had escaped. At once na sat back down on the mattress on the floor and put nan hand lightly on the cook's extended leg, loving na through that symbolic touch and ashamed na had thought, escape.

But why despair? The carpenter's whole mind and body longed for another beer, na total consciousness was irritable and diffused and craved alcohol to drop nan mind into its patterns or apparent patterns which served the same purpose as real ones could have done. After several minutes spent talking naself into and out of the trip to the kitchen, na decided that the argument was the real waste of time and went to the kitchen for another beer.

The trip, the new room empty and dark, the different light through different windows, caught nan imagination and fed it briefly with visual patterns; then na sat at the kitchen table with nan beer and asked again why despair?

The burden the cook is putting on me—of being strong—is throwing me back into that intolerable position again: parent. Na tells me I am strong so na can sleep easily wrapped in the knowledge that na has told me. Na even tells me I am so strong I don't need to go out and drink myself out from under the burden and leaves me awake and ashamed of myself for now unjustifiably doing just that.

Clarity came with the last swallow of this beer hastily drunk. Since I weaken my reason with drink, I can no longer be expected to understand that I am too strong to need a drink.

The next beer na took to the back porch and the carpenter sat on its edge in the moonlight thinking about nan own edge.

In alcoholic catalogue, na found naself listing the reasons for joy; most of them concerned the cook and that love found. But the more na listed, the longer the list, the more it became clear that, like a devious taxpayer's return, the same thing was being counted many times: the cook, one person, one love, was in truth only one joy. The carpenter was forced to concede to the nagging feeling of despair that other platitude: the same food which can drive a person to obsessive lengths to obtain is, once eaten, accepted by the mind as well as the belly and little thought of. Now what? despair wanted to know and the question rang with the undertone of, so what?

So the questions were back, the questions na had thought forever past had only been on a little trip, away less than a month and full of renewed health and vigor after their vacation. To attack now in the moonlight a mind gentle with beer. Na thought of gin: the sharp bite of that stronger cold whiteness could speed nan mind to deal with the questions in five minutes and then obliterate them. There was one hotel where na might be able to buy gin at this hour, for a huge cost both in money and to nan own mind now open and soft. Na finished the beer and went inside for another, but na knew that nan stomach could not hold enough of its volume to benefit from its minor alcohol.

Na took this beer across the moonlit backyard which stretched back an eighth of a mile, to a large willow whose tears reached to the ground. Inside that umbrella, na curled nan back into the angle where the trunk met the earth. Na gripped the beer can which bent easily; it was as weak and temporary as its contents.

I held and adored my lover earlier this same night and now I feel nothing of love; verbal memory only remains. I know that I love na but I feel nothing. I know that I have never loved anyone as much as I love the cook but I feel nothing. I only know love from my own loving, which tells me that loving someone completely more than anything ever on earth means sometimes feeling nothing, not one ounce of love for na. Feeling nothing but remembering that one did feel two hours ago is to feel something after all—the pain of the difference between the two.

My bones are dissolving, the frame which supports my flesh is melting and I will soon be the shape of dumped wet cement which will harden uselessly. My teeth are clenched and my mouth contracted and there is no room for food inside it at all. My eyes are open to no purpose except that when they close the darkness is confusion pounding dark against my eyelids. I am curled into the past because it is only there that I can breathe so shallowly that consciousness fades, because the past is so far back because I am so old, too old, much too old to dare to go wake the cook and shout, how dare you go to sleep and leave me old and dareless?

The carpenter woke the next morning as the first light came through the glistening green of the willow threads. Na neck was stiff and would not turn and na knees ached like a tired child's. Na laid naself on the grass and wept, nan mind furry and vulnerable. The greatest love na had ever known was not enough.

When It Changed

Joanna Russ

Katy drives like a maniac; we must have been doing over
120 km/hr on those turns. She's good, though, extremely
good, and I've seen her take the whole car apart and put it
together again in a day. My birthplace on Whileaway was
largely given to farm machinery and I refused to wrestle
with a five-gear shift at unholy speeds, not having been
brought up to it, but even on those turns in the middle of
the night, on a country road as bad as only our district can
make them, Katy's driving didn't scare me. The funny thing
about my wife, though: she will not handle guns. She has
even gone hiking in the forests above the 48th parallel
without firearms, for days at a time. And that *does* scare
me.

Katy and I have three children between us, one of hers
and two of mine. Yuriko, my eldest, was asleep in the back
seat, dreaming twelve-year-old dreams of love and war:
running away to sea, hunting in the North, dreams of strangely
beautiful people in strangely beautiful places, all the wonderful guff you think up when you're turning twelve and the
glands start going. Some day soon, like all of them, she will
disappear for weeks on end to come back grimy and proud,
having knifed her first cougar or shot her first bear, dragging some abominably dangerous dead beastie behind her,

which I will never forgive for what it might have done to my
daughter. Yuriko says Katy's driving puts her to sleep.

For someone who has fought three duels, I am afraid of
far, far too much. I'm getting old. I told this to my wife.

"You're thirty-four," she said. Laconic to the point of
silence, that one. She flipped the lights on, on the dash—
three km. to go and the road getting worse all the time. Far
out in the country. Electric-green trees rushed into our
headlights and around the car. I reached down next to me
where we bolt the carrier panel to the door and eased my
rifle into my lap. Yuriko stirred in the back. My height but
Katy's eyes, Katy's face. The car engine is so quiet, Katy
says, that you can hear breathing in the back seat. Yuki had
been alone in the car when the message came, enthusiasti-
cally decoding her dot-dashes (silly to mount a wide-frequency
transceiver near an I.C. engine, but most of Whileaway is
on steam). She had thrown herself out of the car, my gangly
and gaudy offspring, shouting at the top of her lungs, so of
course she had had to come along. We've been intellectually
prepared for this ever since the Colony was founded, ever
since it was abandoned, but this is different. This is awful.

"Men!" Yuki had screamed, leaping over the car door.
"They've come back! Real Earth men!"

We met them in the kitchen of the farmhouse near the
place where they had landed; the windows were open, the
night air very mild. We had passed all sorts of transporta-
tion when we parked outside, steam tractors, trucks, an I.C.
flatbed, even a bicycle. Lydia, the district biologist, had
come out of her Northern taciturnity long enough to take
blood and urine samples and was sitting in a corner of the
kitchen shaking her head in astonishment over the results;
she even forced herself (very big, very fair, very shy, always
painfully blushing) to dig up the old language manuals—
though I can talk the old tongues in my sleep. And do.
Lydia is uneasy with us; we're Southerners and too flamboy-
ant. I counted twenty people in that kitchen, all the brains

of North Continent, Phyllis Spet, I think, had come in by glider. Yuki was the only child there.

Then I saw the four of them.

They are bigger than we are. They are bigger and broader. Two were taller than me, and I am extremely tall, 1m, 80cm in my bare feet. They are obviously of our species but *off*, indescribably off, and as my eyes could not and still cannot quite comprehend the lines of those alien bodies, I could not, then, bring myself to touch them, though the one who spoke Russian—what voices they have!—wanted to "shake hands," a custom from the past, I imagine. I can only say they were apes with human faces. He seemed to mean well, but I found myself shuddering back almost the length of the kitchen—and then I laughed apologetically—and then to set a good example (*interstellar amity,* I thought) did "shake hands" finally. A hard, hard hand. They are heavy as draft horses. Blurred, deep voices. Yuriko had sneaked in between the adults and was gazing at *the men* with her mouth open.

He turned *his* head—those words have not been in our language for six hundred years—and said, in bad Russian: "Who's that?"

"My daughter," I said, and added (with that irrational attention to good manners we sometimes employ in moments of insanity), "My daughter, Yuriko Janetson. We use the patronymic. You would say matronymic."

He laughed, involuntarily. Yuki exclaimed, "I thought they would be good-looking!" greatly disappointed at this reception of herself. Phyllis Helgason Spet, whom someday I shall kill, gave me across the room a cold, level, venomous look, as if to say: *Watch what you say. You know what I can do.* It's true that I have little formal status, but Madam President will get herself in serious trouble with both me and her own staff if she continues to consider industrial espionage good clean fun. Wars and rumors of wars, as it says in one of our ancestors' books. I translated Yuki's words into *the man's* dog-Russian, once our *lingua franca,* and *the man* laughed again.

"Where are all your people?" he said conversationally.

I translated again and watched the faces around the room; Lydia embarrassed (as usual), Spet narrowing her eyes with some damned scheme, Katy very pale.

"This is Whileaway," I said.

He continued to look unenlightened.

"Whileaway," I said. "Do you remember? Do you have records? There was a plague on Whileaway."

He looked moderately interested. Heads turned in the back of the room, and I caught a glimpse of the local professions-parliament delegate; by morning every town meeting, every district caucus, would be in full session.

"Plague?" he said. "That's most unfortunate."

"Yes," I said. "Most unfortunate. We lost half our population in one generation."

He looked properly impressed.

"Whileaway was lucky," I said. "We had a big initial gene pool, we had been chosen for extreme intelligence, we had a high technology and a large remaining population in which every adult was two-or-three experts in one. The soil is good. The climate is blessedly easy. There are thirty millions of us now. Things are beginning to snowball in industry—do you understand?—give us seventy years and we'll have more than one real city, more than a few industrial centers, full-time professions, full-time radio operators, full-time machinists, give us seventy years and not everyone will have to spend three quarters of a lifetime on the farm." And I tried to explain how hard it is when artists can practice full-time only in old age, when there are so few, so very few who can be free, like Katy and myself. I tried also to outline our government, the two houses, the one by professions and the geographic one; I told him the district caucuses handled problems too big for the individual towns. And that population control was not a political issue, not yet, though give us time and it would be. This was a delicate point in our history; give us time. There was no need to sacrifice the quality of life for an insane rush into industrialization. Let us go our own pace. Give us time.

"Where are all the people?" said that monomaniac.

I realized then that he did not mean people, he meant *men*, and he was giving the word the meaning it had not had on Whileaway for six centuries.

"They died," I said. "Thirty generations ago."

I thought we had poleaxed him. He caught his breath. He made as if to get out of the chair he was sitting in; he put his hand to his chest; he looked around at us with the strangest blend of awe and sentimental tenderness. Then he said, solemnly and earnestly:

"A great tragedy."

I waited, not quite understanding.

"Yes," he said, catching his breath again with that queer smile, that adult-to-child smile that tells you something is being hidden and will be presently produced with cries of encouragement and joy, "a great tragedy. But it's over." And again he looked around at all of us with the strangest deference. As if we were invalids.

"You've adapted amazingly," he said.

"To what?" I said. He looked embarrassed. He looked inane. Finally he said, "Where I come from, the women don't dress so plainly."

"Like you?" I said, "Like a bride?" for the men were wearing silver from head to foot. I had never seen anything so gaudy. He made as if to answer and then apparently thought better of it; he laughed at me again. With an odd exhilaration—as if we were something childish and something wonderful, as if he were doing us an enormous favor—he took one shaky breath and said, "Well, we're here."

I looked at Spet, Spet looked at Lydia, Lydia looked at Amalia, who is the head of the local town meeting, Amalia looked at I don't know who. My throat was raw. I cannot stand local beer, which the farmers swill as if their stomachs had iridium linings, but I took it anyway, from Amalia (it was her bicycle we had seen outside as we parked), and swallowed it all. This was going to take a long time. I said, "Yes, here you are," and smiled (feeling like a fool), and wondered seriously if male Earth people's minds worked so very differently from female Earth people's minds, but that couldn't be so or the race would have died out long ago. The radio network had got the news around-planet by now and we had another Russian speaker, flown in from Varna; I decided to cut out when *the man* passed around pictures of his wife, who looked like the priestess of some arcane cult. He proposed to question Yuki, so I barreled her into a back room in spite of her furious protests, and went out on the front porch. As I left, Lydia was explaining the difference between parthenogenesis (which is so easy that anyone can practice it) and what we do, which is the merging of ova. That is why Katy's baby looks like me. Lydia went on to the Ansky Process and Katy Ansky, our one full-polymath genius and the great-great-I don't know how many times great-grandmother of my own Katharina.

A dot-dash transmitter in one of the outbuildings chattered faintly to itself: operators flirting and passing jokes down the line.

There was a man on the porch. The other tall man. I watched him for a few minutes—I can move very quietly when I want to—and when I allowed him to see me, he stopped talking into the little machine hung around his neck. Then he said calmly, in excellent Russian, "Did you know that sexual equality has been re-established on Earth?"

"You're the real one," I said, "aren't you? The other one's for show." It was a great relief to get things cleared up. He nodded affably.

"As a people, we are not very bright," he said. "There's been too much genetic damage in the last few centuries. Radiation. Drugs. We can use Whileaway's genes, Janet." Strangers do not call strangers by the first name.

"You can have cells enough to drown in," I said. "Breed your own."

He smiled. "That's not the way we want to do it." Behind him I saw Katy come into the square light that was the screened-in door. He went on, low and urbane, not mocking me, I think, but with the self-confidence of someone who has always had money and strength to spare, who doesn't know what it is to be second-class or provincial. Which is very odd, because the day before, I would have said that was an exact description of me.

"I'm talking to you, Janet," he said, "because I suspect you have more popular influence than anyone else here. You know as well as I do that parthenogenetic culture has all sorts of inherent defects, and we do not—if we can help it—mean to use you for anything of the sort. Pardon me; I should not have said 'use.' But surely you can see that this kind of society is unnatural."

"Humanity is unnatural," said Katy. She had my rifle under her left arm. The top of that silky head does not quite come up to my collar-bone, but she is as tough as steel; he began to move, again with that queer smiling deference (which his fellow had showed to me but he had not) and the gun slid into Katy's grip as if she had shot with it all her life.

"I agree," said the man. "Humanity is unnatural. I should know. I have metal in my teeth and metal pins here." He touched his shoulder. "Seals are harem animals," he added, "and so are men; apes are promiscuous and so are men; doves are monogamous and so are men; there are even celibate men and homosexual men. There are homosexual cows, I believe. But Whileaway is still missing something." He gave a dry chuckle. I will give him the credit of believing that it had something to do with nerves.

"I miss nothing," said Katy, "except that life isn't endless."

"You are—?" said the man, nodding from me to her.

"Wives," said Katy. "We're married." Again the dry chuckle.

"A good economic arrangement," he said, "for working and taking care of the children. And as good an arrangement as any for randomizing heredity, if your reproduction is made to follow the same pattern. But think, Katharina Michaelason, if there isn't something better that you might secure for your daughters. I believe in instincts, even in

Man, and I can't think that the two of you—a machinist, are
you? and I gather you are some sort of chief of police—
don't feel somehow what even you must miss. You know it
intellectually, of course. There is only half a species here.
Men must come back to Whileaway."

Katy said nothing.

"I should think, Katharina Michaelason," said the man
gently, "that you, of all people, would benefit most from
such a change," and he walked past Katy's rifle into the
square of light coming from the door. I think it was then
that he noticed my scar, which really does not show unless
the light is from the side: a fine line that runs from temple
to chin. Most people don't even know about it.

"Where did you get that?" he said, and I answered with
an involuntary grin, "In my last duel." We stood there
bristling at each other for several seconds (this is absurd but
true) until he went inside and shut the screen door behind
him. Katy said in a brittle voice, "You damned fool, don't
you know when we've been insulted?" and swung up the
rifle to shoot him through the screen, but I got to her before
she could fire and knocked the rifle out of aim; it burned a
hole through the porch floor. Katy was shaking. She kept
whispering over and over, "That's why I never touched it,
because I knew I'd kill someone, I knew I'd kill someone."
The first man—the one I'd spoken with first—was still talking inside the house, something about the grand movement
to re-colonize and re-discover all that Earth had lost. He
stressed the advantages to Whileaway: trade, exchange of
ideas, education. He too said that sexual equality had been
re-established on Earth.

Katy was right, of course; we should have burned them
down where they stood. Men are coming to Whileaway.
When one culture has the big guns and the other has none,
there is a certain predictability about the outcome. Maybe
men would have come eventually in any case. I like to think
that a hundred years from now my great-grandchildren could

have stood them off or fought them to a standstill, but even that's no odds; I will remember all my life those four people I first met who were muscled like bulls and who made me—if only for a moment—feel small. A neurotic reaction, Katy says. I remember everything that happened that night; I remember Yuki's excitement in the car, I remember Katy's sobbing when we got home as if her heart would break, I remember her lovemaking, a little peremptory as always, but wonderfully soothing and comforting. I remember prowling restlessly around the house after Katy fell asleep with one bare arm flung into a patch of light from the hall. The muscles of her forearms are like metal bars from all that driving and testing of her machines. Sometimes I dream about Katy's arms. I remember wandering into the nursery and picking up my wife's baby, dozing for a while with the poignant, amazing warmth of an infant in my lap, and finally returning to the kitchen to find Yuriko fixing herself a late snack. My daughter eats like a Great Dane.

"Yuki," I said, "do you think you could fall in love with a man?" and she whooped derisively. "With a ten-foot toad!" said my tactful child.

But men are coming to Whileaway. Lately I sit up nights and worry about the men who will come to this planet, about my two daughters and Betta Katharinason, about what will happen to Katy, to me, to my life. Our ancestors' journals are one long cry of pain and I suppose I ought to be glad now but one can't throw away six centuries, or even (as I have lately discovered) thirty-four years. Sometimes I laugh at the question those four men hedged about all evening and never quite dared to ask, looking at the lot of us, hicks in overalls, farmers in canvas pants and plain shirts: *Which of you plays the role of the man?* As if we had to produce a carbon copy of their mistakes! I doubt very much that sexual equality has been re-established on Earth. I do not like to think of myself mocked, of Katy deferred to as if she were weak, of Yuki made to feel unimportant or silly, of my other children cheated of their full humanity or turned into strangers. And I'm afraid that my own achievements will dwindle from what they were—or what I thought they were—to the not-very-interesting curiosa of the human race, the oddities you read about in the back of the book, things to laugh at sometimes because they are so exotic, quaint but not impressive, charming but not useful. I find this more painful than I can say. You will agree that for a woman who has fought three duels, all of them kills, indulging in such fears is ludicrous. But what's around the corner now is a duel so big that I don't think I have the guts for it; in Faust's words: *Verweile doch, du bist so schoen!* Keep it as it is. Don't change.

Sometimes at night I remember the original name of this planet, changed by the first generation of our ancestors, those curious women for whom, I suppose, the real name was too painful a reminder after the men died. I find it amusing, in a grim way, to see it all so completely turned around. This too shall pass. All good things must come to an end.

Take my life but don't take away the meaning of my life. *For-A-While.*

From *Lover*

Bertha Harris

Macrina the Younger, a dedicated maiden, was assailed by her foes for unswerving ambition, exertion of influence, opportunism and silver-tongued wit. Suspicious rumors were also cast abroad regarding the successive untimely deaths of five wealthy husbands. She endured her enemies' spite, however, with cheerful forebearance and unflagging piety; and, in her middle age, established by the River Iris a small but luxurious school-cum-community for the daughters of aristocrats. Her fame as a successful educatrix spread far and wide, and she died, surrounded by her devoted students, at the age of ninety-nine.

A week after Veronica and Samaria had moved themselves and their dependents into the same house, Veronica broke through that silence with which sex had overwhelmed speech and began to talk all the time to Samaria. From early in the morning until bedtime, she talked; the subject was always herself. Somehow, however, her words sounded like documentations of the past or prophecies of the future. *Eternal passion, eternal pain*, Samaria had learned to quote in response, as if it were a nightingale she was learning to hear.

Listening, Samaria could hear the spell break—or a new

spell each day begin to weave: she had always wanted someone to talk to her, she realized, as that thing began to
happen. Whatever she had wanted before, she could not
now remember. Now, she felt she had always wanted only
what she at last had. Always within range of the voice, she
spent those days fixing, painting, shaping her new home.
And memorizing all Veronica told her; and being glad at
what was new.

Veronica would begin to speak after oatmeal and her first
swallow of coffee. Her first words would swarm out with the
first burst of smoke from the first Lucky of the day. She
would begin with whatever dream she had had just before
waking.

"The dreams I have just before I wake up always start
inside some extraordinary piece of scenery—some places
I've visited, some I have not. The Grand Canyon, the coast
of Cornwall, the canals of Venice, the Gobi Desert, the
interior of a pyramid. I am always happy, but hungry; and,
in an utterly unalarming manner, I am always exactly the
work I am presently engaged in painting—I mean, there is
no difference between me and my painting during my dream,
and I am not afraid of that. This morning I was a medium-
sized, late Soutine, a painting of a red side of beef. Why, I
don't know. I have never made much money painting
Soutines, although it is a pleasure. Such flesh . . . better
than a Rubens nude."

"Maybe there is no difference," Samaria walked past her
with a tomato in each hand. She was thinking of finding the
sunniest sill for ripening. But Veronica made her stop and
let her run her hands across her breasts. Samaria leaned into
the caress but was careful to keep the tomatoes at a distance.
She held her arms wide and apart above her head. Her
hands held the tomatoes. She could have been diving from a
great height if there had been water beneath her. But it was
only that her breasts lay in the cups of Veronica's palms;
and Samaria's breasts in Veronica's hands far below were
the same as the tomatoes in Samaria's hands high above.

There was no difference. One pleasure seemed to be causing the other; and there was no difference. Then it was over, and all was separate.

"But thinking about money was not part of the dream," Veronica continued. "I am adding that part." Samaria, released, did not move away. She stood and watched Veronica's mouth move as it talked. "And hungry. Always, at the beginning of these dreams, I am convinced that the end of my journey through the landscape—or the artifacts or the furniture, whatever it is—will take me to a delicious meal. This morning I smelled pork roast and applesauce sprinkled with fresh cinnamon."

Samaria found a window sill good for tomatoes. She began to unwind a bolt of blue velvet. She was going to measure the kitchen windows and hang blue velvet for curtains.

"And endive salad, vinaigrette dressing; and brussel sprouts with cheese sauce. But as I am coming to this place where I'll be given something to eat, the dream is over—all but for the smell of the food. I never get anything to eat, and I wake up."

"You are my darling, my darling."

"There was nothing to eat this morning but oatmeal."

Samaria closed her eyes and said it only once again: "You are my darling."

"And so this morning—throw me those matches—I was walking through 27 Rue de Fleurus, trudging in back of Gertrude Stein's coat-tails. She was being a goddamned bore—all talk and no food. But I was behaving myself because she was a client. I had, I understood, painted every picture on her walls, but all the Matisses had already been carried off by the brother. But everything else was there, and she was showing it all to me as though I were some tourist clod—room after room of it—showing me my own stuff and not a bite to eat. Miss Moneybags herself pointing out the endless virtues of her Picassos—*my* Picassos, if you know what I mean. And a Soutine, an uncooked slab of beef, coming up behind her: me.

"But then she stopped talking and started doing another thing. She started rubbing her hands and arms across the paintings and she gestured for me to follow suit; and I did. We rubbed away all the Picassos in the whole house. When we'd finished, she was covered with the Blue and Rose periods and I with all the angles of *cubisme*.

"Then she said, 'After dinner (which I hope you'll share with us) Miss Toklas and I will immediately move into the new house you've built for us." I panicked. I was covered with wet paint—but I was not a forger of houses. I had no house for her. But she stood there and endlessly described all the stairways and landings and porches and dining rooms she *said* I had built! But suddenly I realized it was all a trick, the sly bastard. She knew I could not eat her food if I had not built her house. She knew that. It was all a ruse to keep me starving to death."

"Will you hold this end of the tape measure for me, darling?" Samaria's huge length of hair was held up by an ivory comb and tortoise shell pins; and she was dressed all in dark green. But Veronica was still in her flannel robe— the mornings were sharpening—and the odors of warm bed rose up out of it when she moved to the window; and other smells so poignant they made Samaria close her eyes as though she were being visited by some bright memory of a never-never girlhood. Veronica scattered her cigarette ash behind her, and she held her end of the measure; but this did not stop her from spreading her mouth, lightly, for a moment against Samaria's neck. Vampires, thought Samaria; but still she measured space and unfolded cloth.

Veronica sat down again, with more coffee. "Then," she said, "I got proof that I was right: suddenly there was Alice appearing all dim in a doorway holding a tray set with two dinners, one for each of them. For just a second it crossed my mind that maybe Alice wasn't eating with us, but I was fooling myself. Alice was eating, and I was not. Alice was already chewing."

"Then you woke up." The dark blue velvet was spreading across the red tiles.

"You know that? Yes I did. How did you know?"

"Because just then you felt my tongue and woke up. Because I was going down on you. Sleep is never so wonderful." She chose long-bladed scissors and slashed the air above the cloth. The earth turned; sun flashed all at once through the window glass and blinded both of them. "And then you went back to sleep. And then what?"

"When I went back to sleep I was sitting on an onyx throne at the head of a banquet table so long I could not see the end of it. It was covered with pots, pans, tureens, bowls, platters, dishes, saucers—and all of these were full of food. And a naked woman midway down the table's length wafting the smells to my nose with a peacock fan—*naked* but for solid gold pantaloons, and a red satin turban, a pearl necklace; and her nipples and mouth painted with red rouge. Then naked women were all around me; I could hardly breathe, they were feeding me from all the food, taking turns ladling it into my mouth, caressing my head while they waited for me to chew and swallow. In each of my hands was a golden goblet—from one hand I drank red wine, from the other I drank white. I ate everything. I ate lobster their tiny fingers plucked from the shell; bits of creamy beef, partridge, one hot soup—and a cherry tart!

"Then, at the bottom of my banqueting table, there was suddenly a door, and the door opened, and a woman eleven feet tall came through it; and she was naked, too. She carried a great silver platter, and on the platter was a roast baby; it was an infant human being with an apple in its mouth, and ringed with parsley and done to a turn. The room was full of a thousand burning candles, but I woke up before I could eat the baby. It was broad daylight. That's all."

"Veronica, you are a thin person who never seems to eat enough. The seeds from everything we eat, from now on, I'm going to plant in clay pots, then transplant into the ground all around this house. I am going to make a garden for you to eat—that is what they meant when they thought

of Eden—and then the seeds from that food and then the
seeds from those foods. I will plant all there is to eat, and
you will eat it. And I'll keep pigs, I'll cut their throats with a
long knife, and you will have hams all winter long. I'll wring
my chickens' necks; I will have laying hens—and when one
doesn't lay I'll take her out and shoot her in front of all the
others: I will terrify everything I grow into becoming food
for you."

"None of that will ever happen," Veronica answered. She
stood up and reached to take the bright, dangerous blades
from Samaria's hand; and she began to unwind the blue
cloth, thumping the bolt against the floor; and, once it was
all unwound, she rewound it, this time around and around
Samaria until Samaria had become a tall blue wand Veronica could bend and lift: only the face was free of the blue.

"Do you believe," Veronica said finally, "that your daughter is going to have a baby? And if we asked her, would she
know if that is true?"

Veronica could not make herself care at all. "If it's true,"
she answered, "it won't matter whether she knows or not
that it's true. . . . It grows inside you. It happens to you . . .
it happens *on* you. You can't say no to it. Touch me."

Veronica dropped her robe to the floor and began to
stroke her naked self against velvet Samaria. She pulled the
wrapping from Samaria's head; she unfastened the comb
and hairpins from Samaria's hair.

"If I called you by other names sometimes—and the names
sounded real enough," she whispered, "would you answer
to them?"

"I am willing to listen," said Samaria.

Eat

Sapphire

"You too good to eat my pussy?" she snorted.

I don't believe it, I thought.

Sunlight strained through deep purple velvet curtains, breaking through the white lace which was draped in front of the velvet. She sat at the head of the big comfortable bed surrounded by her dusty finery. Her body seemed like a series of alabaster poles wrapped loosely inside blue denim.

"Cough syrup?" she queried.

I nod.

"It's from China," she informs me, "high opium content."

"Really," I murmur. "I thought they weren't into that anymore."

"It's not from *that* China," she spit out.

"Oh scuze me," I said apologetically.

Bob Dylan poured aquamarine and indigo from the stereo.

with your mercury mouth in the missionary times

"Did ya hear what I said?"

"Yeah bout China."

"No," she said emphatically, "bout eating my pussy."

Wow, this was deep. I wanted the cough syrup but I wasn't gonna fuck for it.

"Here," she shoves me a dark amber bottle in a crumpled paper bag, I hand her a twenty. I look down at my string bag on the floor, filled with bread, cheese, and sweet, gold-flecked green grapes. The sounds of the street seep in through the window. I'd forgotten about Fontaine the six years I'd been away. The week after my aunt's funeral I'd found myself walking from one end of the city to the other. My feet had stopped in front of the old hotel remembering what I'd forgotten—the music: Jimi, Janis, Buddy Miles, water pipes, syringes, acid and strawberry incense, and Fontaine. I couldn't imagine she still lived here. I couldn't imagine her living any place else though, I'd thought as my feet padded across the faded maroon carpet, my nose taking in the odor of old wood, perspiration, and cigarette smoke.

"Miss Fontaine please, room 522," I had asked the faded little man behind the desk.

"Go right up," his voice limped softly.

It seemed like years now since I had stepped out of the elevator. Fontaine gaunt and emaciated stared at me with hard eyes.

"You just got here!" she wailed.

Dylan crooned:

with your sheets like metal and your belt like lace
and your deck of cards missing the jack and the ace

She was dying and I was leaving as fast as I could get up and get out of there. But I didn't go. I sat there staring at her quilt, astrological symbols on blue velvet squares juxtaposed with red roses on yellow. I looked at her shiny black leather riding boots. She looked at me looking.

"Brand new," she shrugged gesturing to the boots. "Never wore 'em before."

My knees felt like they had rusted but somehow I got up. I moved away from the curtains fighting the light, away from the red roses on their yellow squares. The door was not far. I would get there.

sad-eyed lady of the lowlands
where the sad-eyed prophet says that no man comes

I look back at Neptune on blue velvet and her long white arms coming out of her denim jacket.

Against the deep purple drapes she is whiter than the white lace.

oh sad-eyed lady, should I wait?

Bones are revealed in stark relief as she strips away her clothes. Her body is an elongated tear. I am standing. My feet move, but not where I told them. I am kneeling beside her now, helping her slide the hard boots off her feet, one, then the other. Now the jeans. I gasp at the cavern between the two pale flares of her pubic bones. I pull her pants off, dropping them beside the bed. Her arm goes around my neck like a hook.

"Wait," I plead. Her smell is harsh—fear, nicotine, perfume. No heat, no sex-odor.

My breasts drop from my bra warm with the heat of my body. Opening my jeans I am aware of the roundness of my brown belly as I slide my pants down. Dropping my pants on the floor next to hers I pull back the quilt, pull up the wrinkled sheet, and slide under the covers like a little girl. My hand on her arm tells her to do the same. Her eyes are silent beggars. I pull her on top of me. She seeps into me like sand. My hands move slowly over the psychic battlefield that is her body, over the war she is losing. Sadness fills me. My hand spans her thigh, her buttocks. Hold her, hold her, *hold her* my soul screams. And it feels so good to hold someone I stop being horrified at what she has lost and marvel at what she has—life, breath, her legs between my opening thighs.

"Turn over," I whisper. Prayerfully my hands begin to move over her body like the wind, everywhere, finding armpit, shoulder, neck, lips, thighs, knees, breasts, stom-

ach, buttocks, eyebrows, hair. I am putting a shell to my
ear, trying to hear the sea. She begins to talk like the sea
does, in whispers, moans, churnings. I move down in the
bed and pull her vagina to my mouth. My tongue searching
for life between her legs. One orifice pressed to another, to
suck. First thing we know to do when we born, suck—or
die. My tongue beats her clitoris, joy spreading over my
face as the sea begins to flow in my mouth.

"Please," she whispers.

I keep on, my mouth a warrior in a pink battlefield
pushing back death. Feel, feel, *feel*, I willed. Her body
begins to rock in the old time rhythm, and I know it won't
be long. I keep on and on, her body mine, mine hers. I feel
the soft moans coming from her throat before I hear them.
My will is transformed to power. I pull her on top of me and
we press our bodies together, rocking like Naomi and Ruth
musta rocked. She pulls my head back down between her
legs, the taste is alive in my mouth. She comes again and
again. We hold each other quiet, long. She laughs like a
warm soft bird in my arms. Stroking my face she whispers,
"Momi, what can I do for you?"

I hesitate for a second, then reach for the string bag on
the floor, pull out the sweet grapes. Holding them to her
mouth I say, "Eat."

With Love, Lena

Teya Schaffer

Dear Sadie,

It's a long time already and it could be longer since last I wrote but as you can see by the crooked letters I am here again. The arthritis is as usual but better it is to write to Sadie than not, so behind my complaints let it be our secret that my joints uncurl for you.

Sadie, Sadie, am I crazy for writing? After so long what should I tell you? The government gives to the bank, the bank gives to the landlord, and the rent is paid for another month; something's going up in the lot, I don't know what, only that it requires a lot of noise; Mr. Issacson's wife was mugged not two blocks from the hardware and he had a heart attack from it . . . is this what you want to hear? As if you didn't know 9th street.

I got a letter from your Norma: everyone's fine, her Laura's baby is walking already, David is making *aliyah* to Israel this summer. You did well Sadie. Meanwhile life continues. I drink my tea, the Senior Citizens sends up a hot lunch, every bone hurts, you know how it is Sadie.

Sadie. I could write your name for a whole page. What did they say about names? My Joseph, may he rest in peace, would have known: "Lena, the sages tell us that the numbers of a name reveal the fate of its owner." But what did he know of names or numbers, names and numbers all that is left of those he named. Sadie, I don't

47

cry any more for them. Now that you are gone there is no
one to receive my tears.

Remember how we cried the first time we cried together like animals, like cows, as if our throats were not
designed for emoting, the funny ugly sounds that finally
made us laugh. And when we could talk I touched the
place where Norma was growing in you and asked, "Sadie
why did we never cry for our dead before?" and you said,
"Because we refused to water the void." Sarah, my
princess. . . .

I pick up the pen again, I am not in the habit of writing
anymore and you, you are so finally gone after your
bits-and-pieces departure. True the fat from your bones
and the hair from your head flew quickly away as if from
disaster but the rest . . . a slow dream-like quality to
those days and then, suddenly, gone, to the home . . .
and your letters, little notes of love encoded in the pages
you dictated.

Sadie I am as foolish as you said I'd be. I never told
you the truth about your apartment—it's been taken: a
family, four of them, poor as poor, crucifix on the wall. I
didn't want you to know that you were gone from 9th
street. I didn't want to know that I was all that was left of
you. One day the new woman put curtains in your window. When I saw them I felt faint like an undergarment
had come undone and was sinking down in a pile around
my feet—Sadie today nobody reads your mail—remember
my princess the day we put up curtains . . .

. . . It was so hot, we stripped to our brassieres and still
our breath was short. It was like a movie, wasn't it? The
hot day a year before that when you met me on the
stairway, my one sleeve rolled up and the other sleeve
down, and you said "Excuse me," lightly touching the
cloth over the numbers, "Excuse me but I think we can
survive differently." And I learned to roll up both sleeves,
the way you did, and a year later our bare arms touched
hot and sticky with July and we rolled ourselves together—
just like that.

*   *   *

It is two days since I've begun this letter . . . well, I won't make excuses, there is no rush. I know it wasn't "just like that" our loving, it had been coming and coming, but when it arrived—it seemed a gift from nowhere, Sadie—Nowhere. Shall I call you that? but it is me who feels without a home while you are a spirit, or a scattered aura . . . or only my memory—SadieSadieSadie according to the teachings of the Mothers of the Dead as long as I can pen your name you will not leave this world, my Sadie, my Princess Sarah. . . .

I'll tell you: in the morning, when I awake, sometimes I am disappointed, but at night before my eyes close I pray for the next day. Remember what we worried? that we would be discovered and shamed, that we would in old age regret and repent . . . well we outlived those fears . . . Sadie . . . Sadie: there is a reason I write to you. Do you notice my Sarah my gift that I am still here on 9th street? I mean my Sadie that I am still not dead, that I am once again left alive . . . there grows a fist in my throat, a hand squeezes tight about my heart. . . . I write this letter, I bind you to it with your names Sadie Sarah Princess my gift, I call and hold you by the writing of your names Sadie Sarah because my Princess, my gift, I refuse to water the void.

In the Life

Becky Birtha

Grace come to me in my sleep last night. I feel somebody presence, in the room with me, then I catch the scent of Posner's Bergamot Pressing Oil, and that cocoa butter grease she use on her skin. I know she standing at the bedside, right over me, and then she call my name.

"Pearl."

My Christian name Pearl Irene Jenkins, but don't nobody ever call me that no more. I been Jinx to the world for longer than I care to specify. Since my mother passed away, Grace the only one ever use my given name.

"Pearl," she say again. "I'm just gone down to the garden awhile. I be back."

I'm so deep asleep I have to fight my way awake, and when I do be fully woke, Grace is gone. I ease my tired bones up and drag em down the stairs, cross the kitchen in the dark, and out the back screen door onto the porch. I guess I'm half expecting Gracie to be there waiting for me, but there ain't another soul stirring tonight. Not a sound but singing crickets, and nothing staring back at me but that old weather-beaten fence I ought to painted this summer, and still ain't made time for. I lower myself down into the porch swing, where Gracie and I have sat so many still summer

51

nights and watched the moon rising up over Old Mister
Thompson's field.

I never had time to paint that fence back then, neither.
But it didn't matter none, cause Gracie had it all covered up
with her flowers. She used to sit right here on this swing at
night, when a little breeze be blowing, and say she could tell
all the different flowers apart, just by they smell. The wind
pick up a scent, and Gracie say, "Smell that jasmine, Pearl?"
Then a breeze come up from another direction, and she turn
her head like somebody calling her and say, "Now that's my
honeysuckle, now."

It used to tickle me, cause she knowed I couldn't tell all
them flowers of hers apart when I was looking square at em
in broad daylight. So how I'm gonna do it by smell in the
middle of the night? I just laugh and rock the swing a little,
and watch her enjoying herself in the soft moonlight.

I could never get enough of watching her. I always did
think that Grace Simmons was the prettiest woman north of
the Mason-Dixon line. Now I've lived enough years to know
it's true. There's been other women in my life besides Grace,
and I guess I loved them all, one way or another, but she
was something special—Gracie was something else again.

She was a dark brownskin woman—the color of fresh
gingerbread hot out the oven. In fact, I used to call her
that—my gingerbread girl. She had plenty enough of that
pretty brownskin flesh to fill your arms up with something
substantial when you hugging her, and to make a nice background for them dimples in her cheeks and other places I
won't go into detail about.

Gracie could be one elegant good looker when she set her
mind to it. I'll never forget the picture she made, that time
the New Year's Eve party was down at the Star Harbor
Ballroom. That was the first year we was in The Club, and
we was going to every event they had. Dressed to kill.
Gracie had on that white silk dress that set off her complex-
ion so perfect, with her hair done up in all them little curls.
A single strand of pearls that could have fooled anybody.

Long gloves. And a little fur stole. We was serious about
our partying back then! I didn't look too bad myself, with
that black velvet jacket I used to have, and the pleats in my
slacks pressed so sharp you could cut yourself on em. I
weighed quite a bit less than I do now, too. Right when you
come in the door of the ballroom, they have a great big
floor to ceiling gold frame mirror, and if I remember rightly,
we didn't get past that for quite some time.

Everybody want to dance with Gracie that night. And
that's fine with me. Along about the middle of the evening,
the band is playing a real hot number, and here come Louie
and Max over to me, all long-face serious, wanting to
know how I can let my woman be out there shaking her
behind with any stranger that wander in the door. Now they
know good and well ain't no strangers here. The Cinnamon
& Spice Club is a private club, and all events is by invitation
only.

Of course, there's some thinks friends is more dangerous
than strangers. But I never could be the jealous, overprotec-
tive type. And the fact is, I just love to watch the woman. I
don't care if she out there shaking it with the Virgin Mary,
long as she having a good time. And that's just what I told
Max and Lou. I could lean up against that bar and watch
her for hours.

You wouldn't know, to look at her, she done it all herself.
Made all her own dresses and hats, and even took apart a
old ratty fur coat that used to belong to my great aunt
Malinda to make that cute little stole. She always did her
own hair—every week or two. She used to do mine, too.
Always be teasing me about let her make me some curls this
time. I'd get right aggravated. Cause you can't have a proper
argument with somebody when they standing over your
head with a hot comb in they hand. You kinda at they
mercy. I'm sitting fuming and cursing under them towels
and stuff, with the sweat dripping all in my eyes in the
steamy kitchen—and she just laughing. "Girl," I'm telling
her, "you know won't no curls fit under my uniform cap.

Less you want me to stay home this week and you gonna go
work my job and your job too."

Both of us had to work, always, and we still ain't had
much. Everybody always think Jinx and Grace doing all
right, but we was scrimping and saving all along. Making
stuff over and making do. Half of what we had to eat grew
right here in this garden. Still and all, I guess we *was* doing
all right. We had each other.

Now I finally got the damn house paid off, and she ain't
even here to appreciate it with me. And Gracie's poor
bedraggled garden is just struggling along on its last legs—
kinda like me. I ain't the kind to complain about my lot, but
truth to tell, I can't be down crawling around on my hands
and knees no more—this body I got put up such a fuss and
holler. Can't enjoy the garden at night proper nowadays,
nohow. Since Mister Thompson's land was took over by the
city and they built them housing projects where the field
used to be, you can't even see the moon from here, till it get
up past the fourteenth floor. Don't no moonlight come in
my yard no more. And I guess I might as well pick my old
self up and go on back to bed.

Sometimes I still ain't used to the fact that Grace is
passed on. Not even after these thirteen years without her.
She the only woman I ever lived with—and I lived with her
more than half my life. This house her house, too, and she
oughta be here in it with me.

I rise by six o'clock most every day, same as I done all
them years I worked driving for the C.T.C. If the weather
ain't too bad, I take me a walk—and if I ain't careful, I'm
liable to end up down at the Twelfth Street Depot, waiting
to see what trolley they gonna give me this morning. There
ain't a soul working in that office still remember me. And
they don't even run a trolley on the Broadway line no more.
They been running a bus for the past five years.

I forgets a lot of things these days. Last week, I had just
took in the clean laundry off the line, and I'm up in the

spare room fixing to iron my shirts, when I hear somebody pass through that squeaky side gate and go on around to the back yard. I ain't paid it no mind at all, cause that's the way Gracie most often do when she come home. Go see about her garden fore she even come in the house. I always be teasing her she care more about them collards and string beans than she do about me. I hear her moving around out there while I'm sprinkling the last shirt and plugging in the iron—hear leaves rustling, and a crate scraping along the walk.

While I'm waiting for the iron to heat up, I take a look out the window, and come to see it ain't Gracie at all, but two a them sassy little scoundrels from over the projects—one of em standing on a apple crate and holding up the other one, who is picking my ripe peaches off my tree, just as brazen as you please. Don't even blink a eyelash when I holler out the window. I have to go running down all them stairs and out on the back porch, waving the cord I done jerked out the iron—when Doctor Matthews has told me a hundred times I ain't supposed to be running or getting excited about nothing, with my pressure like it is. And I ain't even supposed to be *walking* up and down no stairs.

When they seen the ironing cord in my hand, them two little sneaks had a reaction all right. The one on the bottom drop the other one right on his padded quarters and lit out for the gate, hollering, "Look out, Timmy! Here comes Old Lady Jenkins!"

When I think about it now, it was right funny, but at the time I was so mad it musta took me a whole half hour to cool off. I sat there on that apple crate just boiling.

Eventually, I begun to see how it wasn't even them two kids I was so mad at. I was mad at time. For playing tricks on me the way it done. So I don't even remember that Grace Simmons has been dead now for the past thirteen years. And mad at time for passing—so fast. If I had my life to live over, I wouldn't trade in none of them years for nothing. I'd just slow em down.

The church sisters around here is always trying to get me

to be thinking about dying, myself. They must figure, when you my age, that's the only excitement you got left to look forward to. Gladys Hawkins stopped out front this morning, while I was mending a patch in the top screen of the front door. She was grinning from ear to ear like she just spent the night with Jesus himself.

"Morning, Sister Jenkins. Right pretty day the good Lord seen fit to send us, ain't it?"

I ain't never known how to answer nobody who manages to bring the good Lord into every conversation. If I nod and say yes, she'll think I finally got religion. But if I disagree, she'll think I'm crazy, cause it truly is one pretty August morning. Fortunately, it don't matter to her whether I agree or not, cause she gone right on talking according to her own agenda anyway.

"You know, this Sunday is Women's Day over at Blessed Endurance. Reverend Solomon Moody is gonna be visiting, speaking on 'A Woman's Place In The Church.' Why don't you come and join us for worship? You'd be most welcome."

I'm tempted to tell her exactly what come to my mind— that I ain't never heard of no woman name Solomon. However, I'm polite enough to hold my tongue, which is more than I can say for Gladys.

She ain't waiting for no answer from me, just going right on. "I don't spose you need me to point it out to you, Sister Jenkins, but you know you ain't as young as you used to be." As if both of our ages wasn't common knowledge to each other, seeing as we been knowing one another since we was girls. "You reaching that time of life when you might wanna be giving a little more attention to the spiritual side of things than you been doing. . . ."

She referring, politely as she capable of, to the fact that I ain't been seen inside a church for thirty-five years.

". . . And you know what the good Lord say. 'Watch therefore, for ye know neither the day nor the hour . . .' But, 'He that believeth on the Son hath everlasting life. . .' "

It ain't no use to argue with her kind. The Lord is on they

side in every little disagreement, and he don't never give up. So when she finally wind down and ask me again will she see me in church this Sunday, I just say I'll think about it.

Funny thing, I been thinking about it all day. But not the kinda thoughts she want me to think, I'm sure. Last time I went to church was on a Easter Sunday. We decided to go on accounta Gracie's old meddling cousin, who was always nagging us about how we unnatural and sinful and a disgrace to her family. Seem like she seen it as her one mission in life to get us two sinners inside a church. I guess she figure, once she get us in there, God gonna take over the job. So Grace and me finally conspires that the way to get her off our backs is to give her what she think she want.

Course, I ain't had a skirt since before the war, and I ain't aiming to change my lifelong habits just to please Cousin Hattie. But I did take a lotta pains over my appearance that day. I'd had my best tailor-made suit pressed fresh, and slept in my stocking cap the night before so I'd have every hair in place. Even had one a Gracie's flowers stuck in my buttonhole. And a brand new narrow-brim dove gray Stetson hat. Gracie take one look at me when I'm ready and she shake her head. "The good sisters is gonna have a hard time concentrating on the preacher today!"

We arrive at her cousin's church nice and early, but of course it's a big crowd inside already on accounta it being Easter Sunday. The organ music is wailing away, and the congregation is dazzling—decked out in nothing but the finest and doused with enough perfume to outsmell even the flowers up on the altar.

But as soon as we get in the door, this kinda sedate commotion break out—all them good Christian folks whispering and nudging each other and trying to turn around and get a good look. Well, Grace and me, we used to that. We just find us a nice seat in one of the empty pews near the back. But this busy buzzing keep up, even after we

seated and more blended in with the crowd. And finally it
come out that the point of contention ain't even the bottom
half of my suit, but my new dove gray Stetson.

This old gentleman with a grizzled head, wearing glasses
about a inch thick is turning around and leaning way over
the back of the seat, whispering to Grace in a voice plenty
loud enough for me to hear, "You better tell your beau to
remove that hat, entering in Jesus' Holy Chapel."

Soon as I get my hat off, some old lady behind me is
grumbling. "I declare, some of these children haven't got no
respect at all. Oughta know you sposed to keep your head
covered, setting in the house of the Lord."

Seem like the congregation just can't make up its mind
whether I'm supposed to wear my hat or I ain't.

I couldn't hardly keep a straight face all through the
service. Every time I catch Gracie eye, or one or the other
of us catch a sight of my hat, we off again. I couldn't wait to
get outa that place. But it was worth it. Gracie and me was
entertaining the gang with that story for weeks to come.
And we ain't had no more problems with Cousin Hattie.

Far as life everlasting is concerned, I imagine I'll cross
that bridge when I reach it. I don't see no reason to rush
into things. Sure, I know Old Man Death is gonna be
coming after me one of these days, same as he come for my
mother and dad, and Gracie and, just last year, my old
buddy Louie. But I ain't about to start nothing that might
make him feel welcome. It might be different for Gladys
Hawkins and the rest of them church sisters, but I got a
whole lot left to live for. Including a mind fulla good time
memories. When you in the life, one thing your days don't
never be, and that's dull. Your nights neither. All these
years I been in the life, I loved it. And you know Jinx ain't
about to go off with no Old *Man* without no struggle, nohow.

To tell the truth, though, sometime I do get a funny
feeling bout Old Death. Sometime I feel like he here
already—been here. Waiting on me and watching me and
biding his time. Paying attention when I have to stop on the

landing of the stairs to catch my breath. Paying attention if I
don't wake up till half past seven some morning, and my
back is hurting me so bad it take me another half hour to
pull myself together and get out the bed.

The same night after I been talking to Gladys in the
morning, it take me a long time to fall asleep. I'm lying up
in bed waiting for the aching in my back and my joints to
ease off some, and I can swear I hear somebody else in the
house. Seem like I hear em downstairs, maybe opening and
shutting the icebox door, or switching off a light. Just when
I finally manage to doze off, I hear somebody footsteps
right here in the bedroom with me. Somebody tippy-toeing
real quiet, creaking the floor boards between the bed and
the dresser . . . over to the closet . . . back to the dresser
again.

I'm almost scared to open my eyes. But it's only Gracie—in
her old raggedy bathrobe and a silk handkerchief wrapped
up around all them little braids in her head—putting her
finger up to her lips to try and shush me so I won't wake
up.

I can't help chuckling. "Hey Gingerbread Girl. Where you
think you going in your house coat and bandana and it ain't
even light out yet. Come on get back in this bed."

"You go on to sleep," she say. "I'm just going out back a
spell."

It ain't no use me trying to make my voice sound angry,
cause she so contrary when it come to that little piece of
ground down there I can't help laughing. "What you think
you gonna complish down there in the middle of the night?
It ain't even no moon to watch tonight. The sky been filling
up with clouds all evening, and the weather forecast say rain
tomorrow."

"Just don't pay me no mind and go on back to sleep. It
ain't the middle of the night. It's almost daybreak." She
grinning like she up to something, and sure enough, she say,
"This the best time to pick off them black and yellow

beetles been making mildew outa my cucumber vines. So I'm just fixing to turn the tables around a little bit. You gonna read in the papers tomorrow morning bout how the entire black and yellow beetle population of number Twenty-seven Bank Street been wiped off the face of the earth—while you was up here sleeping."

Both of us is laughing like we partners in a crime, and then she off down the hall, calling out, "I be back before you even know I'm gone."

But the full light of day is coming in the window, and she ain't back yet.

I'm over to the window with a mind to holler down to Grace to get her behind back in this house, when the sight of them housing projects hits me right in the face: stacks of dirt-colored bricks and little caged-in porches, heaped up into the sky blocking out what poor skimpy light this cloudy morning brung.

It's a awful funny feeling start to come over me. I mean to get my housecoat, and go down there anyway, just see what's what. But in the closet I can see it ain't but my own clothes hanging on the pole. All the shoes on the floor is mine. And I know I better go ahead and get washed, cause it's a whole lot I want to get done fore it rain, and that storm is coming in for sure. Better pick the rest of them ripe peaches and tomatoes. Maybe put in some peas for fall picking, if my knees'll allow me to get that close to the ground.

The rain finally catch up around noon time and slow me down a bit. I never could stand to be cooped up in no house in the rain. Always make me itchy. That's one reason I used to like driving a trolley for the C.T.C. Cause you get to be out every day, no matter what kinda weather coming down—get to see people and watch the world go by. And it ain't as if you exactly out in the weather, neither. You get to watch it all from behind that big picture window.

Not that I woulda minded being out in it. I used to want to get me a job with the post office, delivering mail. Black folks could make good money with the post office, even way back then. But they wouldn't put you on no mail route. Always stick em off in a back room someplace, where nobody can't see em and get upset cause some little colored girl making as much money as the white boy working next to her. So I stuck with the C.T.C. all them years, and got my pension to prove it.

The rain still coming down steady along about three o'clock, when Max call me up say do I want to come over to her and Yvonne's for dinner. Say they fried more chicken than they can eat, and anyway Yvonne all involved in some new project she want to talk to me about. And I'm glad for the chance to get out the house. Max and Yvonne got the place all picked up for company. I can smell that fried chicken soon as I get in the door.

Yvonne don't never miss a opportunity to dress up a bit. She got the front of her hair braided up, with beads hanging all in her eyes, and a kinda loose robe-like thing, in colors look like the fruit salad at a Independence Day picnic. Max her same old self in her slacks and loafers. She ain't changed in all the years I known her—cept we both got more wrinkles and gray hairs. Yvonne a whole lot younger than us two, but she hanging in there. Her and Max been together going on three years now.

Right away, Yvonne start to explain about this project she doing with her women's club. When I first heard about this club she in, I was kinda interested. But I come to find out it ain't no social club, like the Cinnamon & Spice Club used to be. It's more like a organization. Yvonne call it a collective. They never has no outings or parties or picnics or nothing—just meetings. And projects.

The project they working on right now, they all got tape recorders. And they going around tape-recording people story. Talking to people who been in the life for years and years, and asking em what it was like, back in the old days.

I been in the life since before Yvonne born. But the second she stick that microphone in my face, I can't think of a blessed thing to say.

"Come on, Jinx, you always telling us all them funny old time stories."

Them little wheels is rolling round and round, and all that smooth, shiny brown tape is slipping off one reel and sliding onto the other, and I can't think of not one thing I remember.

"Tell how the Cinnamon & Spice Club got started," she say.

"I already told you about that before."

"Well tell how it ended, then. You never told me that."

"Ain't nothing to tell. Skip and Peaches broke up." Yvonne waiting, and the reels is rolling, but for the life of me I can't think of another word to say about it. And Max is sitting there grinning, like I'm the only one over thirty in the room and she don't remember a thing.

Yvonne finally gave up and turn the thing off, and we go on and stuff ourselves on the chicken they fried and the greens I brung over from the garden. By the time we start in on the sweet potato pie, I have finally got to remembering. Telling Yvonne about when Skip and Peaches had they last big falling out, and they was both determine they was gonna stay in The Club—and couldn't be in the same room with one another for fifteen minutes. Both of em keep waiting on the other one to drop out, and both of em keep showing up, every time the gang get together. And none of the rest of us couldn't be in the same room with the two a them for even as long as they could stand each other. We'd be sneaking around, trying to hold a meeting without them finding out. But Peaches was the president and Skip was the treasurer, so you might say our hands was tied. Wouldn't neither one of em resign. They was both convince The Club couldn't go on without em, and by the time they was finished carrying on, they had done make sure it wouldn't.

Max is chiming in correcting all the details, every other breath come outa my mouth. And then when we all get up to go sit in the parlor again, it come out that Yvonne has sneaked that tape recording machine in here under that African poncho she got on, and has got down every word I said.

When time come to say good night, I'm thankful, for once, that Yvonne insist on driving me home—though it ain't even a whole mile. The rain ain't let up all evening, and is coming down in bucketfuls while we in the car. I'm half soaked just running from the car to the front door.

Yvonne is drove off down the street, and I'm halfway through the front door, when it hit me all of a sudden that the door ain't been locked. Now my mind may be getting a little threadbare in spots, but it ain't wore out yet. I know it's easy for me to slip back into doing things the way I done em twenty or thirty years ago, but I could swear I distinctly remember locking this door and hooking the key ring back on my belt loop, just fore Yvonne drove up in front. And now here's the door been open all this time.

Not a sign a nobody been here. Everything in its place, just like I left it. The slipcovers on the couch is smooth and neat. The candy dishes and ash trays and photographs is sitting just where they belong, on the end tables. Not even so much as a throw rug been moved a inch. I can feel my heart start to thumping like a blowout tire.

Must be, whoever come in here ain't left yet.

The idea of somebody got a nerve like that make me more mad than scared, and I know I'm gonna find out who it is broke in my house, even if it don't turn out to be nobody but them little peach-thieving rascals from round the block. Which I wouldn't be surprised if it ain't. I'm scooting from room to room, snatching open closet doors and whipping back curtains—tiptoeing down the hall and then flicking on the lights real sudden.

When I been in every room, I go back through everywhere I been, real slow, looking in all the drawers, and under the old glass doorstop in the hall, and in the back of the recipe box in the kitchen—and other places where I keep things. But it ain't nothing missing. No money—nothing.

In the end, ain't nothing left for me to do but go to bed. But I'm still feeling real uneasy. I know somebody or something done got in here while I was gone. And ain't left yet. I lay wake in the bed a long time, cause I ain't too particular about falling asleep tonight. Anyway, all this rain just make my joints swell up worse, and the pains in my knees just don't let up.

The next thing I know Gracie waking me up. She lying next to me and kissing me all over my face. I wake up laughing, and she say, "I never could see no use in shaking somebody I rather be kissing." I can feel the laughing running all through her body and mine, holding her up against my chest in the dark—knowing there must be a reason why she woke me up in the middle of the night, and pretty sure I can guess what it is. She kissing under my chin now, and starting to undo my buttons.

It seem like so long since we done this. My whole body is all a shimmer with this sweet, sweet craving. My blood is racing, singing, and her fingers is sliding inside my nightshirt. "Take it easy," I say in her ear. Cause I want this to take us a long, long time.

Outside, the sky is still wide open—the storm is throbbing and beating down on the roof over our heads, and pressing its wet self up against the window. I catch ahold of her fingers and bring em to my lips. Then I roll us both over so I can see her face. She smiling up at me through the dark, and her eyes is wide and shiny. And I run my fingers down along her breast, underneath her own nightgown. . . .

I wake up in the bed alone. It's still night. Like a flash I'm across the room, knowing I'm going after her, this time. The carpet treads is nubby and rough, flying past underneath my bare feet, and the kitchen linoleum cold and smooth. The back door standing wide open, and I push through the screen.

The storm is moved on. That fresh air feel good on my skin through the cotton nightshirt. Smell good, too, rising up outa the wet earth, and I can see the water sparkling on the leaves of the collards and kale, twinkling in the vines on the bean poles. The moon is riding high up over Thompson's field, spilling moonlight all over the yard, and setting all them blossoms on the fence to shining pure white.

There ain't a leaf twitching and there ain't a sound. I ain't moving either. I'm just gonna stay right here on this back porch. And hold still. And listen close. Cause I know Gracie somewhere in this garden. And she waiting for me.

Liberties Not Taken

Joan Nestle

Mac was a big man, a square-jawed engineer who built bridges and looked like he could shove them into place. He was laying stretched out on our couch with my mother sitting alongside him, as if he were ill. I could tell she was impressed that a person such as he—what she called a professional—was listening to her. Standing quietly before him, answering his questions and looking mainly at the soles of his shoes, I realized I had been summoned to pass some unknown test. His questions seemed to come from far away, and he barely moved his head to acknowledge that my voice was reaching him. I understood then that he was not ill, but that it was his power over us, the two women, that kept him so regally immobile. I did not know who he was or why he had this power, but I had learned by this, my thirteenth year, that men were my mother's secret.

After the interrogation, he asked me if I would like to spend a summer in the country helping his wife, Jean, care for their five children, "a mother's helper" he said. I knew then some of the talk that had gone on between the two of them: the sad tale of our circumstances, my mother's worry that I was getting into trouble. I had already been in a fight at school. Here was a chance for me to see what a real

family was like. I accepted and prepared for a journey into
other people's lives.

Early the next week, we left for the cottage in a battered
blue station wagon. I was packed in among the twins and
the older boy and could barely hold my own among the
tumbling duffle bags filled with T-shirts and sneakers. Mac
and Jean were invisible to me, and I was not sure how I
could help make some order out of this family chaos. The
house was flat with small rooms, musty and bare. Somehow
it swallowed all of us up each night and then in the day
turned us loose on its screened-in porch and shaded lake
front.

The first day Jean and I were alone with the children, I
learned quickly that she knew exactly what she wanted from
me. I was to help with the cooking and cleaning, and in the
afternoons watch the kids as they played on the lake's edge.
All of this was told me in a quick crisp voice while she never
took her eyes off me, and then she said, "Want to swim?"

I followed her down to the lake, walking behind her tall
lean body and quietly wondered at what was to come. She
strode into the water, swam powerfully out to the floating
raft, and ignoring the wooden ladder, hauled herself up. I
was still knee-deep in the lake's shallows, frightened by the
muddy bottom. This was the first time I had felt dying
leaves, soft sticks, and small shelled creatures under my
feet. I kept my eyes on her as she looked toward me, and
then she walked across the raft until she was balanced on
the extreme edge, facing the water. She raised her arms
straight above her head, stood perfectly tall and still, a long
unbroken line, and then almost too quick for me to be sure
I had seen it, she sprang high up into the air and did a deep
dive into the grey water. So clean, so sharp, so strong. I had
never before seen a woman do such a thing, except for
Esther Williams in the movies. I had known only the tired
women of the cities, women who like my mother dragged
their bodies to work, stuffed them into too-tight shoes and
full-line bras. I knew women's bodies were for sex, but I did

not know they could cut through the water or leap straight
up into the air. Jean surfaced not far from me, waved me
on, and then walked quickly out of the water up the hill and
back to the house. I stood silently, knowing I had seen a
wonderful thing, knowing that a woman brave enough to do
that was going to teach me things I would never forget.

As the days went by, I washed the dishes, cleaned the
little square rooms, tended the four boys and the little girl
who all had a California enthusiasm for the outdoors that
left me exhausted, and most of all, listened to Jean talk. I
learned that she had met Mac when she was in the WAVES
and he was in the Navy. Even after their marriage, her
favorite nights out were with her women buddies, spending
long weekends in San Francisco bars. She had a special
girlfriend, a woman who delighted in dropping her glass eye
into her Scotch and watching other patrons turn away in
disgust. The eye would sit there in the amber water, staring
up at them as the evening wore on. Eventually Mac would
storm into the place, drag Jean out, and fuck her hard that
night as if he could drive their deep women's laughter out of
her belly. But Jean would keep returning to the bars and to her
one special friend. Five children later, to save her from
herself, Mac got a new job in New York, moved the family,
and for a short time ended up in the same square, desolate
housing development as we had.

She told me these things as if I would understand them,
and I did. She taught me to play poker and got angry when I
made a mistake, but it was anger that made me feel proud.
She let me drive the car down the dirt roads, and one night
she took me to a drive-in and let me lie with my head in her
lap and dangle my feet out the window. She made me laugh
until I couldn't stop and looking down at me, she started
laughing too. I felt it deep in her bones; she had no belly,
just taut skin stretched over her bones. My head rolled with
her laughter. Then I felt her hands on my face, on my hair,
and a sweetness overcame me. I wanted never to take my
head out of her lap, wanted her laughter pouring out over

me for always because with it came a caring and indulgence too sweet, too grand to let time take away.

She introduced me to her gay nephew who visited irregularly throughout the summer. Mac hated this young man who wore his suit jacket over his shoulders, smelled of perfume, and read Anaïs Nin. She arranged a date between us, and we sat in the borrowed car for a respectable amount of time before returning, aware that we were thrown together for a purpose but not yet having words to share our longings. I didn't call myself gay yet. For three years I had been making love to my best friend Roz Rabinowitz with my mouth, and I knew the word *Lesbian*, but I was terrified of its implications and could not say it.

With Jean it was different; I was not afraid of being anything she was—except Mac's wife. We spent the long weekday nights playing cards with the older women who shared a cabin down the road. Every night before we went to bed she asked me to massage her back. I would straddle her, marveling at her body that was her ally, the muscles lying lean on the bones. I longed to slip my hands around her, to catch her small pointed breasts in my hands, to extend the travel of my fingers down the small of her back to her buttocks, to slip gently into her, and to give her all the pleasure there was in my thirteen-year-old imagination to give. I wanted to lie beside her, hoping that she would wrap her long legs around me and carry me with her in her leaps for freedom. I never had the courage to do these things. I just whispered "I love you," as she stretched under my hands.

When Mac arrived for the weekends, they would move into the double bed on the porch, and I would hear their arguments, hear Jean saying, "I don't want to, leave me alone." Then I would hear her being fucked, a hard rushing sound that silenced her. I wondered where the strength went that I saw all week until I pictured Mac, a huge man who was sure he knew what was good for her.

One weekend after they had fought particularly hard, we

were all in the lake together. I was out over my head, but I wasn't afraid because Jean was there. All of a sudden Mac, whose head was only a few feet away from me, said, "You have never been kissed by a father. I will show you what it is like." And he swam toward me, a large moving head with an open mouth and a power hidden beneath the surface. I tried to swim to land, but he grabbed me and held my head while he pushed his tongue deep into my mouth. I churned my arms and legs to keep from drowning, and finally he let me go. I swam desperately for shore, not wanting to see Jean's face, not wanting to see her failure.

I had been kissed like this before, by the lonely fireman whose wife had just brought home their new baby. While she was upstairs showing it off to the other little girls, he sat beside me on the sofa, showing me a picture of a naked Hawaiian woman. Then he kissed me, pushing his tongue into my mouth. I was ten years old. And two years later, my mother's lover forcing me to give him a "real kiss good night," the same tongue this time joined with a knee between my twelve-year-old legs and his hand squeezing my breasts. And it was to happen many years later when a renowned young doctor kissed me in front of my woman lover to show me what I really needed. Always it was done to save me, to show me something I did not know, and always it resulted in near drowning. It was not that I lacked desire; I longed for Jean's lips. But because I did not tell her clearly that it was my yearning, my choice, my passion that wanted her, a thirteen-year-old knowledge that was deep and fine, she and I did nothing, and Mac kissed me and fucked her.

As the summer wore on, Jean gave me more freedom from my chores, and I made friends with the teenage counselors who worked in the Jewish socialist camp a few yards down the beach. I quickly found myself in their world of summer camp romances. The summer was dying and Stanley, the City College freshman who had become my half-hearted pursuer, convinced me to have a party on the beach near our cabin. It started late, a late summer night, a night of teenage scents—beer, cigarettes, Scotch—of wet kisses, fumblings, twisting in the blankets, the fire blazing up; couples, the young men laying on the young women, rubbing their swollen needs. I did not want it and retreated from my young man to sit in the gently rocking canoe, knowing the summer was going to end and wondering if my deliverance would come. He followed me, angry that I had deserted our chance to open mouths to each other. I sat still in the night air, seeing his lips move but not hearing his words.

My whole body was tuned for another sound. I knew she would come, and I wanted to show her I recognized my difference. I will bide my time until she touches me. I want her hands on me, her tongue in my mouth. I want to hold her head against me and throw my legs around her. And then I heard her canoe coming, the slow dipping of the paddle. I saw her flashlight search for me among the coupled bodies. Sooner than I thought possible she shone the light full on me, her eyes dark in her small face. The others in the canoe sat in the shadows behind her, but she forgot they were there. I answered her before she spoke, "I am here. I am only talking, waiting."

"I would have killed you if you were there," she said, flashing her light over the entangled bodies as if she were a general surveying a field of fallen opponents.

No, Jean. You gave me the freedom to choose, but you feared that freedom more than you knew. I showed you in the best way I could that it was your touch I sought, and in the end all you could give me was the suspicion that I had not listened, had not heard your stories, not recognized your gifts of woman difference. You heard their voices, not mine, because I was a girl-woman and it was a dangerous thing to touch me, and yet I had been touched so many times before by men who did not pause to think of innocence. Your touch would have healed me. But we had been judged unclean, and you would not harm me with the power of what they called our sin.

The summer ended. My mother lost the apartment, and I went back to live with my childless aunt and uncle in their grey rooms. I never saw Jean again, but my mother must have because she told me five years later that Jean was dead of breast cancer. My high deep diver, I would have touched you so.

From "The Rosy Medallions"
Camille Roy

October 6, 1983

The day I first saw her was a day the fog didn't clear.
Whiteness everywhere, a kind of extinction. In the dim
climate hardly anything could move. My first impression
was vague: a tall slim figure with dog walking through the
tangled groves of eucalyptus by an oily lake. I had been
spending my days off wandering aimlessly; that day I'd gone
to the park to watch the ducks. I'd stopped on a footbridge
which crossed the lake where it was as narrow as a small
river when she drew close to me. Seeming oblivious, staring
at the still water under the bridge, she gave me a chance to
study her. Displaying herself, I wondered? Not at all. A
perfect unselfconscious disdain was settled into that face.
Her clothes were fine and understated—the expensive
trenchcoat, Italian shoes, closely cropped gray hair. An obvious pervert, remote as a vampire who is no longer young.
Shock settled into my shoes; I had never seen anyone like
her before. She obviously had money. The thought made
my teeth hurt, but filled me with modesty. I wanted to drag
along in a white pinafore, to show how dreamy I was; it was
the only quality of mine I could think of which might be
attractive to her. The inadequacy of this idea filled me with

sorrow and rage. I was staring at the water with a twisted expression when she spoke to me.

"The poor dog has arthritis. This damp weather doesn't agree with him."

I looked at the small white poodle at her feet. He had three legs and a grim expression.

"What happened to his leg?"

"Claude had an accident with a bear trap."

Nothing about her encouraged leading questions; rather the opposite, and caution affects all my senses. This is not unpleasurable; I remained still and silent, staring at the still and silent water, in part to measure my own apprehensions.

"How far do you think the dollar will fall?" she said finally, in a soft voice.

"Has it fallen?"

"It's lost twenty-five percent of its value against the European currencies."

"Oh," I said, feeling rich disdain myself, "the capitalist economies will all go to rot."

"Yes. Things have gotten out of hand," she said with interest.

"The profit motive!" I said dismissively. When she didn't respond I added, "What can you expect but slime and corruption!" I felt so sure of myself I spoke ridiculously, and laughed out loud. Then a few moments of silence passed when I was afraid our conversation had ended. I felt ashamed for using the word "slime." Finally she turned to me with a quizzical expression.

"I know I've sold myself short, and in ways I should be ashamed of. But I find it impossible to remember how, exactly, I did this."

October 7, 1983

I knew you would never be wholehearted, instead evasive, putting your sly face on an expectation of disappoint-

ment. With anyone else this would have meant no sex, I
sense these things from the start. But with you I was im-
pelled, awkward, even grabby, and I feel at fault, tho all
this also seems somehow entirely your fault.

October 8, 1983

"I followed you. I think you're interesting". At her doorway I suddenly acquired my mother's clear bony pronuncia-
tion, an embarrassment. She took my shoulder, gently steered
me into the house, and shut the door.

"I noticed you."

I followed her through a dark hall, though the rooms on
either side seemed full of light. It led to a library, or living
room. She seemed clear and unworried, picking up a few
things, laying her coat over a chair. Her disdainful expression had shifted to amusement. I thought, I'm going to have
to do most of the talking, felt fatigued. I leaned back cautiously on a brown velvet sofa.

"You caught us by surprise". This in a wry, but friendly,
tone.

Writing this, a sharp sense of visibility decreasing. The
literalness of my desire becomes disjointed, slides off from
the target. All this breath between myself and the pleasure.
You invited me in. The shock of that image disconnects me.

She became suddenly tense, but I knew I had only to let
her know it was too late to get out from under it. Her
caustic frown, the weary sliding away of her eyes made me
pushy. When she asked, "Why are you here?" I was lighting
a cigarette.

"I don't know, you asked me."

She shook her head irritably.

"Sorry. I get annoyed when I don't know what I'm doing."

I leaned back on the couch and put my feet on her coffee
table.

"Oh, you know what you're doing".

She smiled sideways, a sharp smile of recognition not directed at me. "OK, sure". She swung around to the chair next to the couch. Sat down, leaned forward, and nudged my leg with her finger.

"So what's your name?"

"Tanya."

"Hah, like Patty Hearst."

Just as quickly she got up to pour drinks. For some reason this struck me as really funny and I smiled foolishly for a long time.

One thing I like about her is she makes me feel inexperienced. A relief. The room was warm, the books against the far wall seemed vague but secure in their built-in bookcases. Suddenly I wanted to talk for a long time, or else be very quiet on that soft brown couch, leaning back and studying the layer of whiskey in my glass.

When she came back she lifted my hair off my neck as if it were very heavy, gently grazed my neck with her lips, then her teeth.

The glass was in my hand.

She leaned against the back of the couch, looking serious, swirling the ice in her glass with her finger.

"How you doing? You ever done anything like this before?"

Have I ever—that's funny, I thought. "Yes" I said. The word felt weak, I sounded like a liar.

She shrugged and traced the outline of my lips with her finger, ran her hand down my throat.

"Whatever."

Leaning back, she draped her hand across my lap. That shift on her face I thought must be a smile, perhaps an ironic imitation. A sexual flare had followed her hand across my face, I wanted to cover myself. I thought of striking her, the interesting sparks off that hard, long life.

"Anything special I should know about?"

"No, of course not."

It was a good time to get up and walk around the couch, get myself between her legs. But I seemed to move slowly, couldn't get used to the speed.

"No, of course not" she said gently, mocking me. Hand on my shoulder, the slow approach was beginning to make me suffer. "We'll see."

October 9, 1983

Her mountainous perversity is like buckets of hair. Buckets of finally hair, at a time of night when I get my pronouns confused. It's the kind of image or scene you want to describe to your friends, but it's so weird that no openings come up in regular conversation.

Overheard on the street:

Y: She's a sadomasochist. And that's a new one, I'm telling you. But what's appealing to me is that she's been doing it for so long that her style and attitude about it are completely immune to fashion.

X: . . .

Y: Very hot. But I mean she has a pure attitude. And a kind of macabre seriousness, that reminds me of that writer's party we went to.

October 10, 1983

Her hand on my shoulder, that first gesture of invitation, was so characteristic of her. Circular as a huge conscience, something to follow indefinitely. Her fingered good-byes marked my body, a sexual technique. Even this story, its thin crust, marks her evasions.

So the room was either dark or light, or was two rooms. There were implements beyond my consciousness. Sharp cravings make narratives, also subjects. So it was easy to let her carve it, warble wobble. Only by turning on her with all my teeth bared could I regain ground already lost. Of course I did it. Of course yearning made it impossible. Pleasures of the rupture, rack and screw.

All over her, squall. Green rose wet, puff of smoke.

She had a collection of crops framed and under glass. Each one had a name under it: Lady Fastbuck, Mary Mountbatten. She said these were mementos of the days when she rode in steeplechases. "It is hard to do this," she said, kneading my breast in the rhythm of her breath.

My moment in the hallway: I wanted to sit on the French inlaid bureau under the crops and get fisted. Marks rise to the surface of my neck. She looks like her leather jacket is causing long prickly emotions down the back. The bedroom is a place to die I think, shiny and submissive death. Pulling her shirt off is attacking the decency of white cotton, is attaching myself via red lines I draw in her flesh.

She's pushing me toward the next room. I'm reluctant, want to say "SHUT UP" though she is silent. Instead I twist out of her grasp and lean against the window. Cool glass against my cheek and hardening nipples, then a grassy sloping garden. Her hands are on my hip bones, they slide down slow and firm as if following a groove. "Slow down" I say. "No." Her voice is calm and flat, then her teeth graze my neck. I laugh, breath fogs the glass. What slides up my cunt is a smooth genital pain, it unfolds. "Please baby" I say. "What?" I twist around to look at her face. A slight smile but her eyes are wide and full with desire. Slipping my arm beneath her shirt I run my lips along her jaw line. I whisper "Fist me." Her hands tighten on my breasts, so hard they hurt. "Alright" she says, and leans back into the doorway, hips cocked.

Dropping item by item on the rug, I'm oddly comfortable with my body. "Display item." Content to sink into this wordless stomach she runs her fingers across. There's a curious sense of touching the thick carpet only with my heels, perfect rounds of skin. She is rubbing her crotch, she says "Let me see your tits."

If I'm going to abandon the real world, the one made up solely of dressed people, I want her to, also.

I drop the shirt for her, push my breasts together hard enough to feel their resistance.

Her hand disappears in my fur and I tighten my thighs around her leg to grasp it. Sliding down, riding her knuckles, the juices of my cunt crease her expensive pants. Hand on my shoulder, she looks down at the wet streak and laughs. I suddenly like her; this new affection streaks thru my body like aggression. I undo her pants and push them down; her clit is warm and wet under my tongue. She slides down the wall into a heap, leans her head to one side. "What do you think you're doing?" she says quizzically.

"Making advances" I say. She makes a little leap forward and we're rolling on the floor like dogs. Democratic cacophony. What orders the flow is a modulation of aggression, hers. Unlike bathing. She's not a sadist really, rather, possessive. That's the deepest thickest point. Working this, I could draw out desire even when she's unwilling. I twist over guilty as a yawn (timid gesture). But she's grasping buttocks with both hands, hardly lingering. Bent over the edge of the body, lattice handiwork, the roseate palm smacking my tin flesh.

I'm getting rosier and rosier. There's no telling where we are. These large sensations come and go. I want to be a star, I want to be adorable. Instead the larger sensations, so open there is a sense of leveling. What is inside slips out and vanishes. So when I am finally on my back again she fists me with her total possessiveness, I am wholly (not) there having left (come), fucked to heaven.

November 1, 1983

There it is, a dark house on the corner, curled up. Fistlike, not aggressive, but holding something. A padded representation. Brown with darker window frames, the house gives a mindful impression. Light streaks in through the library windows, through the many small square panes that face the park, the row of cypresses standing there. Grim trees, I think. It's an especially clear light because we are above the

street, on the second floor. The Bonnard on the wall gives
the room a watery sheen. It's a room no one can peer into,
a room you pad about in, casual, as if privacy were nothing.

You treat me like "daring youth in sweet decay." One of
your miscalculations, hovering among the appliances and the
gleam of brass. It wears thin, like the kitchen, this table
also, even the blush after three drinks.

My argument is simple: your tender face is a place to sleep.

Presenting myself so bluntly becomes a more or less hu-
miliating mistake depending on the level of your sexual
interest. Days pass in your kitchen, you make soup, a sour-
ish chicken soup with gelatinous noodles, a beef barley with
red wine and rosemary. You boil whole tiny red potatoes,
we eat them with butter. You are tender, rub my shoulders,
lightly season the trout before sautéing.

Today I want to move into the small dark room in the
back of the house—a maid's room probably. I want to go
grocery shopping. You go off to watch football. Here the
phone never rings, no paper arrives. You live in the half-
light of some shrewd investments, tell me I'm young, I
should live in Paris. That's a hint, of course. Still the maid's
room sits in the back of my mind. With a few things arranged, it's a place I could vanish in.

Don't Explain

Jewelle L. Gomez

Boston 1959

Letty deposited the hot platters on the table, effortlessly.
She slid one deep-fried chicken, a club-steak with boiled
potatoes and a fried porgie platter down her thick arm as if
removing beaded bracelets. Each plate landed with a solid
clink on the shiny Formica, in its appropriate place. The last
barely settled before Letty turned back to the kitchen to get
Bo John his lemonade and extra biscuits and then to put her
feet up. Out of the corner of her eye she saw Tip come in
the lounge. His huge shoulders, draped in sharkskin, barely
cleared the narrow door frame.

"Damn! He's early tonight!" she thought but kept going.
Tip was known for his generosity, that's how he'd gotten his
nickname. He always sat at Letty's station because they
were both from Virginia, although neither had been back in
years. Letty had come up to Boston in 1946 and been
waiting tables in the 411 Lounge since '52. She liked the
people: the pimps were limited but flashy; the musicians
who hung around were unpredictable in their pursuit of a
good time and the "business" girls were generous and always willing to embroider a wild story. After Letty's mother
died there'd been no reason to go back to Burkeville.

Letty took her newspaper from the locker behind the
kitchen and filled a large glass with the tart grape juice
punch for which the cook, Mabel, was famous.

"I'm going on break, Mabel. Delia's takin' my station."

She sat in the back booth nearest the kitchen beneath the
large blackboard which displayed the menu. When Delia
came out of the bathroom Letty hissed to get her attention.
The reddish-brown skin of Delia's face was shiny with a
country freshness that always made Letty feel a little warm.

"What's up, Miss Letty?" Her voice was soft and saucy.

"Take my tables for twenty minutes. Tip just came in."

The girl's already bright smile widened, as she started to
thank Letty.

"Go 'head, go 'head. He don't like to wait. You can thank
me if he don't run you back and forth fifty times."

Delia hurried away as Letty sank into the coolness of the
overstuffed booth and removed her shoes. After a few sips
of her punch she rested her head on the back of the seat
with her eyes closed. The sounds around her were as familiar as her own breathing: squeaking Red Cross shoes as
Delia and Vinnie passed, the click of high heels around the
bar, the clatter of dishes in the kitchen and ice clinking in
glasses. The din of conversation rose, levelled and rose
again over the juke box. Letty had not played her record in
days but the words spun around in her head as if they were
on the turntable:

". . . right or wrong don't matter
when you're with me sweet
Hush now, don't explain
You're my joy and pain."

Letty sipped her cool drink; sweat ran down her spine
soaking into the nylon uniform. July weather promised to
give no breaks and the fans were working overtime like
everybody else.

She saw Delia cross to Tip's table again. In spite of the

dyed red hair, no matter how you looked at her, Delia was still a country girl: long and self-conscious, shy and bold because she didn't know any better. She'd moved up from Anniston with her cousin a year before and landed the job at the 411 immediately. She worked hard and sometimes Letty and she shared a cab going uptown after work, when Delia's cousin didn't pick them up in her green Pontiac.

Letty caught Tip eyeing Delia as she strode on long, tight-muscled legs back to the kitchen. "That lounge lizard!" Letty thought to herself. Letty had trained Delia: how to balance plates, how to make tips and how to keep the customer's hands on the table. She was certain Delia would have no problem putting Tip in his place. In the year she'd been working Delia hadn't gone out with any of the bar flies, though plenty had asked. Letty figured that Delia and her cousin must run with a different crowd. They talked to each other sporadically in the kitchen or during their break but Letty never felt that wire across her chest like Delia was going to ask her something she couldn't answer.

She closed her eyes again for the few remaining minutes. The song was back in her head and Letty had to squeeze her lips together to keep from humming aloud. She pushed her thoughts onto something else. But when she did she always stumbled upon Maxine. Letty opened her eyes. When she'd quit working at Salmagundi's and come to the 411 she'd promised herself never to think about any woman like that again. She didn't know why missing Billie so much brought it all back to her. She'd not thought of that time or those feelings for a while.

She heard Abe shout a greeting at Duke behind the bar as he surveyed his domain. That was Letty's signal. No matter whether it was her break or not she knew white people didn't like to see their employees sitting down, especially with their shoes off. By the time Abe was settled on his stool near the door, Letty was up, her glass in hand and on her way through the kitchen's squeaky swinging door.

"You finished your break already?" Delia asked.

"Abe just come in."

"Uh oh, let me git this steak out there to that man. Boy he sure is nosey!"

"Who, Tip?"

"Yeah, he ask me where I live, who I live with, where I come from like he supposed to know me!"

"Well just don't take nothing he say to heart and you'll be fine. And don't take no rides from him!"

"Yeah, he asked if he could take me home after I get off. I told him me and you had something to do."

Letty was silent as she sliced the fresh bread and stacked it on plates for the next orders.

"My cousin's coming by, so it ain't a lie, really. She can ride us."

"Yeah," Letty said as Delia giggled and turned away with her platter.

Vinnie burst through the door like she always did, looking breathless and bossy. "Abe up there, girl! You better get back on station. You got a customer."

Letty drained her glass with deliberation, wiped her hands on her thickly starched white apron and walked casually past Vinnie as if she'd never spoken. She heard Mabel's soft chuckle float behind her. She went over to Tip who was digging into the steak like his life depended on devouring it before the plate got dirty.

"Everything alright tonight?" Letty asked, her ample brown body towering over the table.

"Yeah, baby, everything alright. You ain't workin' this side no more?"

"I was on break. My feet can't wait for your stomach, you know."

Tip laughed. "Break! What you need a break for, big and healthy as you is!"

"We all gets old, Tip. But the feet get old first, let me tell you that!"

"Not in my business, baby. Why you don't come on and work for me and you ain't got to worry 'bout your feet."

Letty sucked her teeth loudly, the exaggeration a part of the game they played over the years. "Man, I'm too old for that mess!"

"You ain't too old for me."

"Ain't nobody too old for you! Or too young neither, looks like."

"Where you and that gal goin' tonight?"

"To a funeral," Letty responded dryly.

"Aw woman get on away from my food!" The gold cap on his front tooth gleamed from behind his greasy lips when he laughed. Letty was pleased. Besides giving away money Tip liked to hurt people. It was better when he laughed.

The kitchen closed at 11:00 p.m. Delia and Letty slipped out of their uniforms in the tiny bathroom and were on their way out the door by 11:15. Delia looked even younger in her knife-pleated skirt and white cotton blouse. Letty did feel old tonight in her slacks and long-sleeved shirt. The movement of car headlights played across her face, which was set in exhaustion. The dark green car pulled up and they slipped in quietly, both anticipating tomorrow, Sunday, the last night of their work week.

Delia's cousin was a stocky woman who looked forty, Letty's age. She never spoke much. Not that she wasn't friendly. She always greeted Letty with a smile and laughed at Delia's stories about the customers. "Just close to the chest like me, that's all," Letty often thought. As they pulled up to the corner of Columbus Avenue and Cunard Street, Letty opened the rear door. Delia turned to her and said, "I'm sorry you don't play your record on your break no more, Miss Letty. I know you don't want to, but I'm sorry just the same."

Delia's cousin looked back at them with a puzzled expression but said nothing. Letty slammed the car door shut and turned to climb the short flight of stairs to her apartment. Cunard Street was quiet outside her window and the guy upstairs wasn't blasting his record player for once. Still, Letty lay awake and restless in her single bed. The fan was

pointed at the ceiling, bouncing warm air over her, rustling
her sheer nightgown.

Inevitably the strains of Billie Holiday's songs brushed
against her, much like the breeze that fanned around her.
She felt silly when she thought about it, but the melodies
gripped her like a solid presence. It was more than the
music. Billie had been her hero. Letty saw Billie as big, like
herself, with big hungers, and some secret that she couldn't
tell anyone. Two weeks ago, when Letty heard that the
Lady had died, sorrow enveloped her. A refuge had been
closed that she could not consciously identify to herself or to
anyone. It embarrassed her to think about. Like it did when
she remembered Maxine.

When Letty first started working at the 411 she met Billie
when she'd come into the club with several musicians on her
way back from the Jazz Festival. There the audience, curious to see what a real, live junkie looked like, had sat back
waiting for Billie to fall on her face. Instead she'd killed
them dead with her liquid voice and rough urgency. Still,
the young, thin horn player kept having to reassure her:
"Billie you were the show, the whole show!"

Once convinced, Billie became the show again, loud and
commanding. She demanded her food be served at the bar
and sent Mabel, who insisted on waiting on her personally,
back to the kitchen fifteen times. Billie laughed at jokes that
Letty could barely hear as she bustled back and forth between the abandoned kitchen and her own tables. The sound
of that laugh from the bar penetrated her bones. She'd
watched and listened, certain she saw something no one else
did. When Billie had finished eating and gathered her en-
tourage to get back on the road she left a tip, not just for
Mabel but for each of the waitresses and the bartender.
"Generous just like the 'business' girls," Letty was happy to
note. She still had the two one dollar bills in an envelope at
the back of her lingerie drawer.

After that, Letty felt even closer to Billie. She played one
of the few Lady Day records on the juke box every night

during her break. Everyone at the 411 had learned not to bother her when her song came on. Letty realized, as she lay waiting for sleep, that she'd always felt that if she had been able to say or do something that night to make friends with Billie, it might all have been different. In half sleep the faces of Billie, Maxine and Delia blended in her mind. Letty slid her hand along the soft nylon of her gown to rest it between her full thighs. She pressed firmly, as if holding desire inside herself. Letty could have loved her enough to make it better. That was Letty's final thought as she dropped off to sleep.

Sunday nights at the 411 were generally mellow. Even the pimps and prostitutes used it as a day of rest. Letty came in early and had a drink at the bar and talked with the bartender before going to the back to change into her uniform. She saw Delia through the window as she stepped out of the green Pontiac, looking as if she'd just come from Concord Baptist Church. "Satin Doll" was on the juke box, wrapping the bar in cool nostalgia.

Abe let Mabel close the kitchen early on Sunday and Letty looked forward to getting done by 10:00 or 10:30, and maybe enjoying some of the evening. When her break time came Letty started for the juke box automatically. She hadn't played anything by Billie in two weeks; now, looking down at the inviting glare, she knew she still couldn't do it. She punched the buttons that would bring up Jackie Wilson's "Lonely Teardrops" and went to the back booth.

She'd almost dropped off to sleep when she heard Delia whisper her name. She opened her eyes and looked up into the girl's smiling face. Her head was haloed in tight, shiny curls.

"Miss Letty, won't you come home with me tonight?"

"What?"

"I'm sorry to bother you, but your break time almost up. I wanted to ask if you'd come over to the house tonight . . . after work. My cousin'll bring you back home after."

Letty didn't speak. Her puzzled look prompted Delia to start again.

"Sometime on Sunday my cousin's friends from work come over to play cards, listen to music, you know. Nothin' special, just some of the girls from the office building down on Winter Street where she work, cleaning. She, I mean we, thought you might want to come over tonight. Have a drink, play some cards . . ."

"I don't play cards much."

"Well not everybody play cards . . . just talk . . . sitting around talking. My cousin said you might like to for a change."

Letty wasn't sure she liked the last part: "for a change," as if they had to entertain an old aunt.

"I really want you to come, Letty. They always her friends but none of them is my own friends. They alright, I don't mean nothin' against them, but it would be fun to have my own personal friend there, you know?"

Delia was a good girl. Those were the perfect words to describe her, Letty thought smiling. "Sure honey, I'd just as soon spend my time with you as lose my money with some fools."

They got off at 10:15 and Delia apologized that they had to take a cab uptown. Her cousin and her friends didn't work on Sunday so they were already at home. Afraid that the snag would give Letty an opportunity to back out Delia hadn't mentioned it until they were out of their uniforms and on the sidewalk. Letty almost declined, tempted to go home to the safe silence of her room. But she didn't. She stepped into the street and waved down a Red and White cab. All the way uptown Delia apologized that the evening wasn't a big deal and cautioned Letty not to expect much. "Just a few friends, hanging around, drinking and talking." She was jumpy and Letty tried to put her at ease. She had not expected her first visit would make Delia so anxious.

The apartment was located halfway up Blue Hill Avenue in an area where a few blacks had recently been permitted to rent. They entered a long, carpeted hallway and heard the sounds of laughter and music ringing from the rooms at the far end.

Once inside, with the door closed, Delia's personality took on another dimension. This was clearly her home and Letty could not believe she ever really needed an ally to back her up. Delia stepped out of her shoes at the door and walked to the back with her same, long-legged gait. They passed a closed door, which Letty assumed to be one of the bedrooms, then came to a kitchen ablaze with light. Food and bottles were strewn across the pink and gray Formica-top table. A counter opened from the kitchen into the dining room, which was the center of activity. Around a large mahogany table sat five women in smoke-filled concentration, playing poker.

Delia's cousin looked up from her cards with the same slight smile as usual. Here it seemed welcoming, not guarded as it did in those brief moments in her car. She wore brown slacks and a matching sweater. The pink, starched points of her shirt collar peeked out at the neck.

Delia crossed to her and kissed her cheek lightly. Letty looked around the table to see if she recognized anyone. The women all seemed familiar in the way that city neighbors can, but Letty was sure she hadn't met any of them before. Delia introduced her to each one: Karen, a short, round woman with West Indian bangles up to her pudgy elbow; Betty, who stared intently at her cards through thick eyeglasses encased in blue cat-eye frames; Irene, a big, dark woman with long black hair and a gold tooth in front. Beside her sat Myrtle who was wearing army fatigues and a gold Masonic ring on her pinky finger. She said hello in the softest voice Letty had ever heard. Hovering over her was Clara, a large red woman whose hair was bound tightly in a bun at the nape of her neck. She spoke with a delectable southern accent that drawled her "How're you doin' " into a full paragraph that was draped around an inquisitive smile.

Delia became ill-at-ease again as she pulled Letty by the arm toward the French doors behind the players. There was a small den with a desk, some books and a television set. Through the next set of glass doors was a livingroom. At the record player was an extremely tall, brown-skinned woman. She bent over the wooden cabinet searching for the next selection, oblivious to the rest of the gathering. Two women sat on the divan in deep conversation, which they punctuated with constrained giggles.

"Maryalice, Sheila, Dolores . . . this is Letty."

They looked up at her quickly, smiled, then went back to their preoccupations: two to their gossip, the other returning to the record collection. Delia directed Letty back toward the foyer and the kitchen.

"Come on, let me get you a drink. You know, I don't even know what you drink!"

"Delia?" Her cousin's voice reached them over the counter, just as they stepped into the kitchen. "Bring a couple of beers back when you come, OK?"

"Sure, babe," Delia went to the refrigerator and pulled out two bottles. "Let me just take these in. I'll be right back."

"Go 'head, I can take care of myself in this department, girl." Letty surveyed the array of bottles on the table. Delia went to the dining room and Letty mixed a Scotch and soda. She poured slowly as the reality settled on her. These women were friends, perhaps lovers, like she and Maxine had been. The name she'd heard for women like these burst inside her head: bulldagger. Letty flinched, angry she had let it in, angry that it frightened her. "Ptuh!" Letty blew air through her teeth as if spitting the word back at the air.

She did know these women, Letty thought, as she stood at the counter smiling out at the poker game. They were oblivious to her, except for Terry. Letty remembered that was Delia's cousin's name. As Letty took her first sip, Terry called over to her. "We gonna be finished with this game in a minute Letty, then we can talk."

"Take your time," Letty said, then went out through the foyer door and around to the livingroom. She walked slowly on the carpet and adjusted her eyes to the light, which was a bit softer. The tall woman, Maryalice, had just put a record

on the turntable and sat down on a love seat across from the
other two women. Letty stood in the doorway a moment
before the tune began:

"Hush now, don't explain
Just say you'll remain
I'm glad you're back
Don't explain . . ."

Letty was stunned, but the song sounded different here,
among these women. Billie sang just to them, here. The
isolation and sadness seemed less inevitable with these women
listening. Letty watched Maryalice sitting with her long legs
stretched out tensely in front of her. She was wrapped in her
own thoughts, her eyes closed. She appeared curiously disconnected, after what had clearly been a long search for this
record. Letty watched her face as she swallowed several
times. Then Letty moved to sit on the seat beside her. They
listened to the music while the other two women spoke in
low voices.

When the song was over Maryalice didn't move. Letty
rose from the sofa and went to the record player. Delia
stood tentatively in the doorway of the livingroom. Letty
picked up the arm of the phonograph and replaced it at the
beginning of the record. When she sat again beside Maryalice
she noticed the drops of moisture on the other woman's
lashes. Maryalice relaxed as Letty settled onto the seat
beside her. They both listened to Billie together, for the
first time.

A Long Story

Beth Brant

Dedicated to my Great-Grandmothers
Eliza Powless and Catherine Brant

> *"About 40 Indian children took the train at this depot for the Philadelphia Indian School last Friday. They were accompanied by the government agent, and seemed a bright looking lot."*
>
> The Northern Observer
> *(Massena, New York, July 20, 1892)*

> *"I am only beginning to understand what it means for a mother to lose a child."*
>
> Anna Demeter, Legal Kidnapping
> *(Beacon Press, Boston, 1977)*

1890

It has been two days since they came and took the children away. My body is greatly chilled. All our blankets have been used to bring me warmth. The women keep the fire blazing. The men sit. They talk among themselves. We are frightened by this sudden child-stealing. We signed papers, the agent said. This gave them rights to take our babies. It is good for them, the agent said. It will make them civilized, the agent said. I do not know *civilized*.

95

I hold myself tight in fear of flying apart in the air. The others try to feed me. Can they feed a dead woman? I have stopped talking. When my mouth opens, only air escapes. I have used up my sound screaming their names—She Sees Deer! He Catches The Leaves! My eyes stare at the room, the walls of scrubbed wood, the floor of dirt. I know there are people here, but I cannot see them. I see a darkness, like the lake at New Moon. Black, unmoving. In the center, a picture of my son and daughter being lifted onto the train. My daughter wearing the dark blue, heavy dress. All of the girls dressed alike. Never have I seen such eyes! They burn into my head even now. My son. His hair cut. Dressed as the white men, his arms and legs covered by cloth that made him sweat. His face, streaked with tears. So many children crying, screaming. The sun on our bodies, our heads. The train screeching like a crow, sounding like laughter. Smoke and dirt pumping out of the insides of the train. So many people. So many children. The women, standing as if in prayer, our hands lifted, reaching. The dust sifting down on our palms. Our palms making motions at the sky. Our fingers closing like the claws of the bear.

I see this now. The hair of my son held in my hands. I rub the strands, the heavy braids coming alive as the fire flares and casts a bright light on the black hair. They slip from my fingers and lie coiled on the ground. I see this. My husband picks up the braids, wraps them in cloth; he takes the pieces of our son away. He walks outside, the eyes of the people on him. I see this. He will find a bottle and drink with the men. Some of the women will join him. They will end the night by singing or crying. It is all the same. I see this. No sounds of children playing games and laughing. Even the dogs have ceased their noise. They lay outside each doorway, waiting. I hear this. The voices of children. They cry. They pray, They call me. *Nisten ha.* I hear this. *Nisten ha.**

*mother

1978

I am wakened by the dream. In the dream my daughter is dead. Her father is returning her body to me in pieces. He keeps her heart. I thought I screamed . . . *Patricia*! I sit up in bed, swallowing air as if for nourishment. The dream remains in the air. I rise to go to her room. Ellen tries to lead me back to bed, but I have to see once again. I open her door. She is gone. The room empty, lonely. They said it was in her best interests. How can that be? She is only six, a baby who needs her mothers. She loves us. This has not happened. I will not believe this. Oh god, I think I have died.

Night after night, Ellen holds me as I shake. Our sobs stifling the air in our room. We lie in our bed and try to give comfort. My mind can't think beyond last week when she left. I would have killed him if I'd had the chance! He took her hand and pulled her to the car. The look in his eyes of triumph. It was a contest to him, Patricia the prize. He will teach her to hate us. He will! I see her dear face. That face looking out the back window of his car. Her mouth forming the words *Mommy, Mama*. Her dark braids tied with red yarn. Her front teeth missing. Her overalls with the yellow flower on the pocket, embroidered by Ellen's hands. So lovingly she sewed the yellow wool. Patricia waiting quietly until she was finished. Ellen promising to teach her designs— chain stitch, french knot, split stitch. How Patricia told everyone that Ellen made the flower just for her. So proud of her overalls.

I open the closet door. Almost everything is gone. A few things hang there limp, abandoned. I pull a blue dress from the hanger and take it back to my room. Ellen tries to take it from me, but I hold on, the soft blue cotton smelling of my daughter. How is it possible to feel such pain and live? "Ellen?!" She croons my name. "Mary, Mary, I love you." She sings me to sleep.

1890

The agent was here to deliver a letter. I screamed at him and sent curses his way. I threw dirt in his face as he mounted his horse. He thinks I'm a crazy woman and warns me, "You better settle down Annie." What can they do to me? I am a crazy woman. This letter hurts my hand. It is written in their hateful language. It is evil, but there is a message for me.

I start the walk up the road to my brother. He works for the whites and understands their meanings. I think about my brother as I pull the shawl closer to my body. It is cold now. Soon there will be snow. The corn has been dried and hangs from our cabin, waiting to be used. The corn never changes. My brother is changed. He says that *I* have changed and bring shame to our clan. He says I should accept the fate. But I do not believe in the fate of child-stealing. There is evil here. There is much wrong in our village. My brother says I am a crazy woman because I howl at the sky every evening. He is a fool. I am calling the children. He says the people are becoming afraid of me because I talk to the air and laugh like the raven overhead. But I am talking to the children. They need to hear the sound of me. I laugh to cheer them. They cry for us.

This letter burns my hands. I hurry to my brother. He has taken the sign of the wolf from over the doorway. He pretends to be like those who hate us. He gets more and more like the child-stealers. His eyes move away from mine. He takes the letter from me and begins the reading of it. I am confused. This letter is from two strangers with the names Martha and Daniel. They say they are learning civilized ways. Daniel works in the fields, growing food for the school. Martha cooks and is being taught to sew aprons. She will be going to live with the schoolmaster's wife. She will be a live-in girl. What is a *live-in girl*? I shake my head. The words sound the same to me. I am afraid of Martha and Daniel, these strangers who know my name. My hands and arms are becoming numb.

I tear the letter from my brother's fingers. He stares at me, his eyes traitors in his face. He calls after me, "Annie! Annie!" That is not my name! I run to the road. That is not my name! There is no Martha! There is no Daniel! This is witch work. The paper burns and burns. At my cabin, I quickly dig a hole in the field. The earth is hard and cold, but I dig with my nails. I dig, my hands feeling weaker. I tear the paper and bury the scraps. As the earth drifts and settles, the names Martha and Daniel are covered. I look to the sky and find nothing but endless blue. My eyes are blinded by the color. I begin the howling.

1978

When I get home from work, there is a letter from Patricia. I make coffee and wait for Ellen, pacing the rooms of our apartment. My back is sore from the line, bending over and down, screwing the handles on the doors of the flashy cars moving by. My work protects me from questions, the guys making jokes at my expense. But some of them touch my shoulder lightly and briefly as a sign of understanding. The few women, eyes averted or smiling in sympathy. No one talks. There is no time to talk. No room to talk, the noise taking up all space and breath.

I carry the letter with me as I move from room to room. Finally I sit at the kitchen table, turning the paper around in my hands. Patricia's printing is large and uneven. The stamp had been glued on halfheartedly and is coming loose. Each time a letter arrives, I dread it, even as I long to hear from my child. I hear Ellen's key in the door. She walks into the kitchen, bringing the smell of the hospital with her. She comes toward me, her face set in new lines, her uniform crumpled and stained, her brown hair pulled back in an imitation of a french twist. She knows there is a letter. I kiss her and bring mugs of coffee to the table. We look at each other. She reaches for my hand, bringing it to her lips. Her hazel eyes are steady in her round face.

I open the letter. *Dear Mommy. I am fine. Daddy got me
a new bike. My big teeth are coming in. We are going to see
Grandma for my birthday. Daddy got me new shoes. Love,
Patricia.* She doesn't ask about Ellen. I imagine her father
standing over her, coaxing her, coaching her. The letter
becomes ugly. I tear it in bits and scatter them out the
window. The wind scoops the pieces into a tight fist before
strewing them in the street. A car drives over the paper,
shredding it to garbage and mud.

Ellen makes a garbled sound. "I'll leave. If it will make it
better, I'll leave." I quickly hold her as the dusk moves into
the room and covers us. "Don't leave. Don't leave." I feel
her sturdy back shiver against my hands. She kisses my
throat, and her arms tighten as we move closer. "Ah Mary,
I love you so much." As the tears threaten our eyes, the
taste of salt is on our lips and tongues. We stare into
ourselves, touching the place of pain, reaching past the fear,
the guilt, the anger, the loneliness.

We go to our room. It is beautiful again. I am seeing it
new. The sun is barely there. The colors of cream, brown,
green mixing with the wood floor. The rug with its design of
wild birds. The black ash basket glowing on the dresser,
holding a bouquet of dried flowers bought at a vendor's
stand. I remember the old woman, laughing and speaking
rapidly in Polish as she wrapped the blossoms in newspaper.
Ellen undresses me as I cry. My desire for her breaking
through the heartbreak we share. She pulls the covers
back, smoothing the white sheets, her hands repeating the
gestures done at work. She guides me onto the cool material. I watch her remove the uniform of work. An aide to
nurses. A healer of spirit.

She comes to me full in flesh. My hands are taken with
the curves and soft roundness of her. She covers me with
the beating of her heart. The rhythm steadies me. Heat is
centering me. I am grounded by the peace between us. I
smile at her face above me, round like a moon, her long
hair loose and touching my breasts. I take her breast in my

hand, bring it to my mouth, suck her as a woman—in desire, in faith. Our bodies join. Our hair braids together on the pillow. Brown, black, silver, catching the last light of the sun. We kiss, touch, move to our place of power. Her mouth moving over my body, stopping at curves and swells of skin, kissing, removing pain. Closer, close, together, woven, my legs are heat, the center of my soul is speaking to her, I am sliding into her, her mouth is medicine, her heart is the earth, we are dancing with flying arms, I shout, I sing, I weep salty liquid, sweet and warm it coats her throat. This is my life. I love you Ellen, I love you Mary, I love, we love.

1891

The moon is full. The air is cold. This cold strikes at my flesh as I remove my clothes and set them on fire in the withered corn field. I cut my hair, the knife sawing through the heavy mass. I bring the sharp blade to my arms, legs, and breasts. The blood trickles like small red rivers down my body. I feel nothing. I throw the tangled webs of my hair into the flames. The smell, like a burning animal, fills my nostrils. As the fire stretches to touch the stars, the people come out to watch me—the crazy woman. The ice in the air touches me.

They caught me as I tried to board the train and search for my babies. The white men tell my husband to watch me. I am dangerous. I laugh and laugh. My husband is good only for tipping bottles and swallowing anger. He looks at me, opening his mouth and making no sound. His eyes are dead. He wanders from the cabin and looks out on the corn. He whispers our names. He calls after the children. He is a dead man.

Where have they taken the children? I ask the question of each one who travels the road past our door. The women come and we talk. We ask and ask. They say there is nothing we can do. The white man is like a ghost. He slips in and out where we cannot see. Even in our dreams he comes to take away our questions. He works magic that resists our medicine. This magic has made us weak. What is the secret about them? Why do they want our children? They sent the Blackrobes many years ago to teach us new magic. It was evil! They lied and tricked us. They spoke of gods who would forgive us if we believed as they do. They brought the rum with the cross. This god is ugly! He killed our masks. He killed our men. He sends the women screaming at the moon in terror. They want our power. They take our children to remove the inside of them. Our power. They steal our food, our sacred rattle, the stories, our names. What is left?

I am a crazy woman. I look to the fire that consumes my hair and see their faces. My daughter. My son. They still cry for me, though the sound grows fainter. The wind picks up their keening and brings it to me. The sound has bored into my brain. I begin howling. At night I dare not sleep. I fear the dreams. It is too terrible, the things that happen there. In my dream there is wind and blood moving as a stream. Red, dark blood in my dream. Rushing for our village. The blood moves faster. There are screams of wounded people. Animals are dead, thrown in the blood stream. There is nothing left. Only the air echoing nothing. Only the earth soaking up blood, spreading it in the four directions, becoming a thing there is no name for. I stand in the field watching the fire, The People watching me. We are waiting, but the answer is not clear yet. A crazy woman. That is what they call me.

1979

After taking a morning off work to see my lawyer, I come home, not caring if I call in. Not caring, for once, at the loss in pay. Not caring. My lawyer says there is nothing more we can do. I must wait. As if there has been something other than waiting. He has custody and calls the shots. We must wait and see how long it takes for him to get tired of being a mommy and a daddy. So, I wait.

I open the door to Patricia's room. Ellen and I keep it dusted and cleaned in case my baby will be allowed to visit us. The yellow and blue walls feel like a mockery. I walk to the windows, begin to systematically tear down the curtains. I slowly start to rip the cloth apart. I enjoy hearing the sounds of destruction. Faster, I tear the material into strips. What won't come apart with my hands, I pull with my teeth. Looking for more to destroy, I gather the sheets and bedspread in my arms and wildly shred them to pieces. Grunting and sweating, I am pushed by rage and the searing wound in my soul. Like a wolf, caught in a trap, gnawing at her own leg to set herself free, I begin to beat my breasts to deaden the pain inside. A noise gathers in my throat and finds the way out. I begin a scream that turns to howling, then becomes hoarse choking. I want to take my fists, my strong fists, my brown fists, and smash the world until it bleeds. Bleeds! And all the judges in their flapping robes, and the fathers who look for revenge, are ground, ground into dust and disappear with the wind.

The word *lesbian*. Lesbian. The word that makes them panic, makes them afraid, makes them destroy children. The word that dares them. Lesbian. *I am one*. Even for Patricia, even for her, I *will not cease to be*! As I kneel amidst the colorful scraps, Raggedy Anns smiling up at me, my chest gives a sigh. My heart slows to its normal speech. I feel the blood pumping outward to my veins, carrying nourishment and life. I strip the room naked. I close the door.

Thanks so much to Chrystos for the title. Thanks to Gloria Anzaldúa for encouraging the writing of this story.

A Life Speckled with Children

Sherri Paris

Sabra had been, as they say, unlucky—meaning foolish—in love. Out of this foolishness had come a life intermittently speckled with children. Now in her continuing role as friend or mother, she identified, in truth, more with the children who clutched at her with moist open hands than with their cool, ambivalent mothers who came and went. Everyone assumed that Sabra adored children because she was kind, because she played at the beach in a certain way. This assumption had grown into the legend that she was somehow especially adept with children and irrevocably bonded with them. Well, maybe. . . .

Gayle, the first woman she had sworn to spend her entire life with, now arrived twice monthly with a joint in her mouth, a Halston briefcase clamped to her side, and Richard trailing sullenly along behind her. Sabra and Gayle had parted just over four years ago. During those years, Richard had turned from a sly balding three-year-old to a stodgy man of seven-and-one-half. He was certain and systematic in his movements, with a dim-eyed stubbornness which looked—from a great distance—like some sense of purpose. He was not, Sabra felt, all that different from Gayle's husband, Bryan, who had promptly adopted the boy after their marriage three years ago. Since then, Gayle had never alluded to the life she and Sabra had shared, but maintained instead an easy affection for Sabra, kissing her chastely on the cheek and daintily patting her back whenever they hugged.

Sabra's second eternal love, Diana, still an avowed lesbian, had become so politically inspired in the ensuing years that she had cut off all her hair. Now, she and her son Thaddeus both sported bristling crew cuts, and Diana worked relentlessly to shape him into a feminist man, hopefully gay, and earnestly encumbered with the appropriate modes of guilt. Diana consistently needed child care while she attended her weekly co-op meetings, her committee in sympathy with the women of Nicaragua, her incest survivors' support group, and her network for adult children of alcoholics. Thaddeus, at eleven, was as critical of Sabra's lifestyle as her mother had been, pointing out to her that coffee and television were both addictions which Sabra could rid herself of by turning her life over to a higher Power. Sabra was considering it.

And now, Grace, her most recent lover, had left her for their best friend, Lisa, and Sabra found herself picking up Jewel, Grace's five-year-old daughter, for a Sunday afternoon drive in the park.

"Hello," called Grace, smiling fiercely, as she approached the locked car door. Without looking up, Sabra worked on adjusting Jewel's seatbelt. Jewel fidgeted, cheerfully unscrewing the legs from the Barbie doll she had just acquired for her birthday.

Off the tapedeck, Emmy Lou Harris flipped a melodic line, "Lou, you gotta start new and the first thing you gotta do is get some white shoes."

"Are you going to get white shoes?" Jewel asked Sabra.

"Should I?"

"Sure. Why not?"

Grace leaned forward to blow Jewel a kiss. Sabra gunned the engine loudly. As they drove off, Jewel tugged at Sabra's arm. "How come my mommy always pretends to say hello to you when you never answer?"

"She's not pretending exactly," said Sabra. "Not *exactly*."

"Sure she is. When you first moved out, I used to come downstairs with my blanket and pretend to say good morning to you. Now I don't though. Now I can't even see you with my eyes closed. Look what Lisa bought me."

She held up her hand, showing a gold and ruby bracelet.

"That's very petty."

"I know," said Jewel, taking the bracelet and placing it on her head like a tiny crown.

"I think Mama pretends to say hello to you because she kisses you. Why don't you answer her?"

"I can't." Sabra stared down the street aware of the passing homes with unfolding families tucked into their living rooms. "Maybe I'm just not a very nice person."

Jewel stroked her arm softly. "Yes," she said. "You are a *very* nice person."

The two rode together in silence for a while.

"I miss you," Sabra finally said.

"I used to miss people. You and papa. But then, my misser broke. Now I don't miss anyone at all."

"Your misser broke?"

"Yes, I used to have a strong misser, but then it broke. Like the E.T. clock Grandma bought me on Christmas. My misser just ran down."

Sabra pulled the car to the curb alongside a tiny park with swings.

"Push me, Sabra. I want to go up high."

"I can't push you, because my body is hurt." Sabra had been disabled for years by rheumatoid arthritis, a difficult thing for a sunny-minded five-year-old to grasp. "Remember?"

"Yes. I remember, but I keep thinking that one day you'll be all better. Like my knee. I skinned it last week, but now—look. It's perfect." She offered her pale, bald knee for Sabra's inspection.

Sabra kissed it. "Indeed, a completely perfect knee."

Jewel giggled. "That's not where you kiss, silly. Kissing is like this." She scrunched her eyes shut tightly, grabbed Sabra's head, and kissed her fiercely on the lips.

"Whew! Where'd you learn that?"

"From Mama and Lisa, of course. I learned everything from Mama. Except for about Jesus. Papa teaches me that."

Sabra walked around the car and unbuckled Jewel's seatbelt.

"You're certainly learning a lot these days."

"Yes, about kissing. Only women do it. Men hardly kiss at all. They do like this." She leaned forward and gave Sabra a dry, papery brush on the cheek. "That's what men do. I learned that from Papa."

Sabra lifted her from the car. As she did so, a twisting blade of pain shot down her spine. "How about if you and I go feed the ducks?" Taking Jewel's hand, she reached into her shirt pocket and popped a pain pill.

"Hey, is that candy? Can I have one?"

"I'll buy you candy later. This is medicine."

"Will it make you well?"

"Not exactly. But it makes me feel better."

"Oh," said Jewel, hopping on one foot, "what kind?"

"Huh?"

"What kind of candy will you buy me later?"

"Well, I don't know. That's a very serious question."

"What's serious?"

"It's when you care about something so much you don't even smile."

Jewel scowled. "I'm *very* serious. Do you think we could have chocolate?"

"Yes."

"Good." Jewel hugged her and ran down a shallow hill to the duck pond.

Sabra slumped down on the grass and lay on her back,

looking up at the clouds which brooded over the playground
like anxious and tangible spirits. It seemed that much of her
life had been spent looking up at clouds. Shortly, Jewel
returned, flushed with exertion. In her hand she gripped an
absolutely undistinguished grey stone.

"Sabra. Look what I found. It was just laying there on the
ground. Can you *believe* it? Someone must have lost it or
something—huh?"

Sabra picked up the rock and peered under it as if looking
for what she couldn't see.

"A fine rock."

"I love this playground. You can find incredible stuff
here. It's *amazing*, Sabra."

"Yes," said Sabra, "amazing."

By the time they were ready to leave the playground,
Jewel had collected eight rocks, one sneaker, and a yellow
plastic squeeze-top with the voluptuous odor of slightly spoiled
honey.

She assigned Sabra to carry the squeeze top and two of
the larger rocks.

"I don't know about the sneaker, honey. The little boy
who lost that sneaker might come back to look for it."

"I *want* it, Sabra, I *want* the sneaker."

"But some little boy will be walking around with just one
shoe on."

"Yes. He has one and I have one. That's *fair*. My teacher
taught us about that. It's called sharing."

Sabra shrugged. Often these days, because she had so
little time with Jewel, because she felt their relationship
slowly slipping away, she chose not to argue. Chose to give
in. Trying to protect a bond between them which seemed
incredibly fragile.

Children, Sabra knew, were not creatures of memory.
They loved you when you were there. Once Jewel's and
Sabra's hearts had joined through daily hugs and hurts,
through afternoon baths and far-fetched stories. Now their

lives had separated. And Sabra was attempting to hold that heart with trips to the park and pieces of candy.

So Sabra tended to let Jewel have her way. Not that Jewel had ever been easy to say no to. She stuck out her heart-shaped chin and argued with a dead certainty which had always left Sabra feeling awed and hopeless. Jewel had been unshakable—certain of her right to the universe even as a wobbly toddler. How, Sabra had often wondered, could a *child* be so certain. Sabra's own early years had been dim and cramped, permeated with the smells of the Jewish ghetto: a blend of chicken and cabbage cooking, of floor wax and smoke, and old, frayed sheets, ironed again and again. It was a world ruled by old people; grandparents and widowed aunts, so unlike California which was ruled by the sun, the sea, by the young. By children.

"Now Jewel, suppose we put these rocks in the trunk of the car."

"No. I want them where I can see them. Because they are so bee-yew-tee-ful."

"O.K." Sabra piled the rocks and the plastic squeeze-top on the floor of her car and buckled Jewel's seatbelt. Jewel insisted that Sabra tie the gym shoe to her rearview mirror, the way she had seen people do with bronzed baby shoes.

"That looks *good*, Sabra. You know what? I lost my Barbie doll."

"Oh dear. Should we go back to the duck pond and look for her?"

"Uh, uh. I don't like her anymore. Her legs wouldn't come off. They were stuck. It was too much work. I don't want her."

"Oh, O.K. Well, where should we go then?"

"Nowhere."

"Nowhere?"

"Yes, Sabra. I just want to sit in the car and *be* with you."

"Just stay here?"

"Yes, because you're here and my rocks are here now and I can look at them and you too, Sabra. Tell me a story about you and my mama. O.K.?"

Sabra stared at the small, dangling gym shoe. Her relationship with other children had always been distant and indulgent. Sabra used their presence as an excuse to do things off the beaten path of adulthood, things she enjoyed, like devouring pizza to the dance of predictable puppets at Chuckie Cheese. Or wading at the beach or rollerskating at the Discorama rink in Scotts Valley. Or watching strange monsters reenact a classic morality fable in the latest *Star Wars* movie. Activities she didn't do with friends, activities that were so sweetly foolish, she would have felt too lonely doing them by herself.

This time spent watching, doing, eating, was not particularly intimate. Sabra knew this and didn't care. She could not handle intimacy with these small alien people who hugged her so fiercely and left gum on the seat of her car.

Jewel was different. She was too fine-tuned and intense for distractions. Only once during their brief weekly visits had Sabra attempted to entertain them, taking Jewel to see Spielberg's popular *E.T.* From the time the small monster appeared on the screen, Jewel hunched in Sabra's lap with her hands clamped over her eyelids, faintly trembling.

"Come on," Sabra whispered, stroking her hair, "we can leave, if you don't like this."

"No," Jewel hissed, her eyes tightly closed. "It's *interesting*, Sabra. It's *interesting*."

They remained like that for an hour, Jewel intermittently peeking at the screen and shutting her eyes whenever E.T. appeared, but refusing to leave. Sabra kept her nose in the child's fragrant hair, enjoying the feel of her plump thighs, of the small head brushing against her breasts.

She remembered holding Jewel in the night, after her

parents had separated and Grace and Jewel had moved in with Sabra. Jewel had begun having nightmares then, sitting up wild-eyed in the dark while Grace, exhausted and grieving herself, slept on. During those nights, Sabra had been the comforter, and she felt oddly guilty at the movies, having carried Jewel into this world of new and unnecessary terror. Halfway into the film, Jewel opened her eyes and seemed to get into it. She clapped her hands when the children on bicycles rose to the sky with E.T. But when the movie was over, Jewel began crying inconsolably. "We had our afternoon, Sabra," she said over and over, "but I miss *you*." And even before the tears began, Sabra herself felt oddly lonely and cheated.

Aqua

Jess Wells

I'd never seen anyone looking so relaxed and content, her
cowgirl boots propped on a chair-back, face pointing up to
the blistering sky as if waiting for a kiss. Her jeans were
tight, her shirt unbuttoned to the middle of her chest, and
she was so long and stretched out that I didn't want to
disturb her, but I had car trouble and in the middle of the
desert you don't have many choices.

"S'cuse me," I said, stepping onto the wooden porch.
"Wouldn't you know this piece of junk'd be having problems and me in the middle of nowhere with no money and
nobody to call. I don't suppose you'd have any ideas, would
you?"

I didn't have any reason to be explaining my financial
business to this woman, but somehow my mouth forgot all
about privacy that day. I should have seen from the response I got that it was time to back off the porch and leave.
She slowly turned her head and opened her eyes, little green
slits in a face that had been taut for the sun, but was now
wrinkled and parched as it surveyed a sweaty traveler on the
steps. I know not to poke at spiders, even the harmless
ones, but I proceeded anyway.

"My car's acting up. Is there a station near here . . . or a
phone?"

"Nope. Neither of those, but you can sit down if you want. We got a birthday party here," and she turned her face back to the sun.

I crossed the eight-foot porch, stood at the wooden chair beside her.

"But don't sit on the hat," she mumbled.

I scowled at her.

"You know about cars?" I asked, picking up the cowgirl hat and, finding no place suitable for such a gem, snapped it into her lap. I sat. She turned, sensing the challenge, and plopped her hat on one of the railing posts.

"What's the trouble?"

"I'm losing power. She's not good for much, this car, but every few minutes she gets slower and more tired, then she picks up speed again."

"It's from the heat."

No joke, I thought. I considered leaving, trying to ignore how worried I was about the car or how much I hoped she'd offer me something to drink. Everything was from the heat, as if the sun were making us all water drops in an oily skillet. Everyone I had talked to today was irritable and short, things popping out of their mouths that belonged miles away from their minds. How she could sit there staring up at the sun was more than I could gather. I was ready to dash into her house uninvited and drink anything I could find.

"Park it behind the house to cool down. Relax. She'll be all right after the sun goes down a bit. Your radiator all right?"

"I don't know. I'd be surprised if it was. Whose birthday?"

She put her feet down and turned to me, stroking sun-blonde hair from her forehead. "Sorry, I'm not really unfriendly. I get like a lizard in this heat—just bake in the sun and forget everything. It's mine. My birthday." She got up and went into the house.

"Congratulations! So, do you live here year round?" I called after her.

"Yeah. You want some ginger ale? It's all the party favors I got."

"Love it. What is it today, 95, 100 degrees?" I asked, feeling the sweat running down my cleavage.

"Hundred and two." The refrigerator in the house moaned against the battle of being opened. She handed me a tall glass with ice and bubbly. The ice shattered and scurried around in my glass as I took a long swallow.

"You traveling alone?" She stretched out and looked straight ahead, the lines in her face deep and dry.

"Always."

She grunted her approval.

"My name's Jody. Thanks for this," I said, saluting her with the half-empty glass. "So where's all the party guests? Am I the first?"

"My name's Aqua," she toasted, without looking away from the sun.

"That's your name? I mean, aren't you a little far from home?" I laughed. I should have quit right then, I know that now, but the porch was shady where I was sitting and I would have pawed the ground for another glass of ginger ale.

"I was thinking about that just as you came up, actually." She turned to me. "Born in the sea. No point in staying."

"No point . . ." I muttered. Looking back on the day, I can see what I was doing: picking and poking, bearing down like the sun had been doing on me all day.

"I told you," she was getting annoyed. "I was born there. You know," her voice went low and conspiratorial, "it's like trying to stay in your momma forever."

Dyke, I thought. Our eyes met. Only a dyke calls a car "she" and talks about being born.

"I like the ocean, actually. The breeze, the smell of it, the constant pounding . . ." I said, confused, wishing the ocean would pour around my miserable body instead of this puddle of sweat sitting on the shelf of my belly and this sand chafing the back of my neck. "I'm talkin' about a nice cool dip in the water."

"I hate the ocean," she said brusquely. "Had enough of it, anyway, that's for sure." She leapt out of her seat, alive suddenly, her mind waking up, her energy running up and down her long body in a torrent.

"Think your car's cooled down," she said through clenched teeth. "We could check her radiator. Maybe tighten a few belts." She went into the house for another ginger ale. "Never mind. You still thirsty?" I followed her.

"Yeah."

"How about bourbon in this one?"

I nodded.

"Oh, now I'm coming alive. Christ, who can think in that sun. Besides, I don't get a lot of company—not many women travel alone and even fewer come through here." She handed me my glass and looked at me. "Not women like you, anyway."

"Like us, you mean?" I said. She just snorted, stared into her bourbon with a splash of ginger ale. "Whaddaya do out here—for work, I mean?" I said.

"I'm a dancer in Reno. One of the big clubs—not strip, mind you, I'm a dancer. I throw everything I've got into every piece of music, so I'm good."

"Sounds great, Aqua," I said in a lack-luster tone. There was something missing in the way she said it, like a birthday party with no guests.

"It's life to me, you know, the joy and beauty of it all, set to music. I tell 'ya, Jody," she said, with a dead-pan face, "there's nothing like it, Life just leapin' and jumpin' all over the place. Hey, bottom's up."

"To life," I said.

"Yeah. I'll go for that. And you? You gotta work?"

"I work with kids. Preschool in San Francisco."

"Oh, now, that must be something. Little ones. Damn'd if life isn't glorious, you know?" She smiled but her eyes never changed, still little green slits with no sparkle.

"Most of the time, I suppose," I said, looking into my glass.

"Ah, all the time, honey. Just when things get bad at work, somebody gives me attitude or the place gets so smoky it makes me sick, well, just then I'll be driving home, tied up in knots, and there's the sun rising and it looks so . . . so," and she blew a half-kiss to the air, trying to explain joy to me with the broken face of someone watching their only chance at love drive away.

"You know what I mean?" she said.

"It must be really beautiful around here," I said, following her back outdoors.

"Oh, it is. I love the dust and the sun and the way the wind smells so dry out here. People think just because the sun shines all the time that the weather's always the same but they're crazy. There's spring sun different from winter sun and the flowers—you really have to know where to look to see them. Cactus, birds, the clouds. And the hills? They're solid rock and they look different, too. Even the dunes— you saw them a couple of miles south, right?"

"Yeah. Beautiful."

"All the tourists go to the dunes. Well, even *they* have seasons and there ain't nothin' grows out there." She took a long swallow. "Flowers are just a lazy way to tell the seasons, anyway. Makes me happy to think all this grows without water."

I looked at her with a long and steady gaze until she turned to me and her face seemed to close up again. She reached down and pulled at my glass.

"Time for a refill."

I shrugged my shoulders and let her take my glass back into the house.

"We got us a little party goin' on here, huh?" she called, dropping in more ice. "Well, good," she kicked the screen door open and handed my glass over my shoulder. "I don't drink, really. I've had this bottle for a long time, but what the hell. Today's my birthday and . . . it's nice to have company."

"So Happy Birthday," I said, raising my glass. "How old are you?"

"Sixteen," she said, flopping into her chair.

I laughed. "So when did *you* stop counting?"

"I said, I'm sixteen," she leaned over the arm of her chair, grave and threatening.

"Well, you don't *look* sixteen," I said, trying to diffuse the situation by touching the deep crows-feet around her eyes.

"Hey," she pulled away violently. "I said there weren't many of you women traveling through, I didn't say there weren't *any*."

"Sorry," I said, setting my glass on the chair and holding up passive hands.

"Yeah, well, I'd say you should keep that glass between your legs, girl."

"Is that so? Well, I imagine you'd be as frosty if you were there."

"Oooh, now, I don't have to be this friendly. You could just get in your car and scald, you know." She plopped her feet on the railing, then sighed and turned back to me.

"Oh, I'm sorry," she said, shaking her head. "But dammit, it's my birthday. Sixteen years ago I was born from the sea."

"Aqua," I said, feeling brave from the drink.

"All right, all right. It's the anniversary of my mother's death," she said, lowering her voice. "You want another drink?" She got up, quite drunk now and groped into the house, came back with both bottles under her arms. "Save some energy and just bring 'um out here, hell."

"I'm sorry about your mother," I said softly, fearing thin ice.

"What for?" she asked, quietly, twisting open the ginger ale. "She had a choice."

"She killed herself?" I felt sick inside, knowing I was prodding a lizard that had hissed its last warning.

"Yep. She sure did. Nearly killed me and my little sister with her. Did kill my little sister."

She wiped sweat from her forehead with her sleeve. "I shouldn't be so hard on her, I suppose. She had a bad time of it. Two kids, one always sick—my sister was such a weak little thing—and no man around, though when he was, it was worse than when he wasn't, of course. She was a grill cook. We lived in a little town by the ocean. You know, same old story."

"Work to pay the bills but the ends don't meet so you work some more and they still don't meet?" I asked sympathetically.

"Yeah. Well, one day she couldn't do it anymore so she put on her best sweater and pants, strapped my sister to her chest with the tablecloth and grabbed me by the wrist. Marched us on down to the sea. You don't want to hear this."

"Well . . . I do if you want to tell it," I said cautiously.

"She stood there for hours, looking at the water and nothing could move her. Her face didn't change. Not once. I know 'cause I watched her. I think maybe she'd taken a bunch of pills or something because I've never seen anybody so unreachable, you know, their face miles behind their flesh. So, we're standin' on this cliff and I keep going, 'c'mon Mom, let's go home now. What's the matter, Mom? We better go—you gotta cook in the morning." She looked down at her boots, then out toward the desert.

"Well, Happy Birthday, Aqua."

"I guess I was about eight, ten. Anyway, she never looked at me, just all of a sudden hiked me onto her back and dove off the cliff onto the rocks."

"Jesus Christ," I said setting my glass onto the porch.

"Oh now, don't go all dramatic on me. It was a short cliff. Maybe about six feet up. Can you believe that? I mean, why'd she pick a place like that? My little sister, she died

right away. She didn't know what was going on and she sure
was too small to make up her own mind, but me, I clung to
the back of that sweater like it was the edge of the world. I
guess when we hit, I rolled off and I just lay there, on the
top of the rocks."

"Oh Aqua, I'm really sorry."

"Real flat ones, like shelves out into the water, with
crevices running through them. So I'm flat on my belly—I
didn't want to look towards Mom, and I was thinking, 'You
better hurry up and die before the tide comes in.' " She
snorted, taking another pull on her drink. "Pretty weird,
huh?"

Aqua got up from where she was slumped over in her
chair and walked to the end of the porch, leaning her
forearms on the railing and kicking at the sand piled up
around the posts. She finished her drink and poured another.

"I remember everything—every single thing—about that
night. It's like I can still feel the stone against my belly and
the coldness. Must be because it's my birthday but I can see
that water surging up, waving the green slime back and
forth, saying, 'get out'a here girl, leave now, you've seen
enough, now go!'

"It started gettin' dark so I got up and didn't ever look
over at my mother, I just went straight to the cafe and told
'em what happened and they took me in. Mrs. Miller put
me in her house behind the cafe and put me to work
washing dishes, but I don't remember much about being
there. It's like my mind went blank until the day I ran away
and swore I'd celebrate life always." Aqua strode across the
porch and clinked glasses with me. "Yes m'am. Celebrate."

"Oh hell, there, traveler Jody, don't look so sadfaced,"
she laughed with a crooked smile, quite drunk. "Everybody
makes their choices: she chose to die and I chose to live and
that's that. No regrets, goddammit," she said, pouring another drink into her half-full glass. "I say life's burden
enough without carrying around a lot of sadness. Here's to
it, honey—lightening life's burden. To dancing!"

The sun was finally going down and the desert was lit up behind her. As Aqua leaned on the railing, she looked on fire, like the sand.

"Mamba, rumba, salsa," she twisted and spun in her boots, laughing with her mouth, but her eyes still tiny and expressionless. "And of course square dancing and the two-step: I even know Czechoslovakian folk dances—pretty, real pretty. You should come see me dance, Jody."

"Great. I'd . . . like that a lot," I said, heavy and frightened.

She yanked open the screen door with a laugh and stumbled inside, turning on lights. I followed her into the tiny house and went to the sink to rinse out my glass. I'd had half the number that she had downed, but another drink and I'd never be able to drive; I was already counting on the freeway being a straight away through the desert. I turned on the water, feeling it cool and refreshing across my wrists.

"What are you doing?" Aqua said, alarmed.

"You don't have to play hostess, I can. . . ."

"Turn off the water!"

"What?"

"Turn it off!" she shouted, stumbling across the cabin towards me. "I don't like it . . . water . . . in my house. It . . . makes the place smell."

I turned to Aqua, who was deliriously drunk, leaning over the back of a chair, looking down at the plastic-covered kitchen table.

"Damp. I hate it. Everything was so damp, Jody, my little bed behind the cafe, the air every day. Every single fucking day was wet," she said, and I, parched despite the drinks, standing there gritty and sandy and covered with dried sweat, looked at her as if she were talking about the moon.

"The salt all over my body from lying in the water, the lichen . . . in my nose, on my cheeks, green and . . . wet. Little . . . things swimming in the tide pools." She turned her head in disgust and staggered backwards. I wiped my hands on my dusty pants and grabbed her by the shoulders, leading her to her iron cot against the wall where she slumped onto her side, face twisted and closed, knees to her chest, hands like dried claws. I grabbed one of her feet to take off her boots.

"I swear to you, I can still feel it, Jody. Her sweater."

I took off her boots, and as the sand poured out onto the floor I looked at this woman, all parched skin and rough hands, passed out in her dusty house. I thought of my own mother, baking cakes she never ate, wringing her hands while she stared out the windows at nothing, and I knew there was no running from the pain of knowing that your mother may never be happy. I set the boots beside her and fished in my pockets for the keys. Feeling helpless and withered, I quietly closed the screen door behind me and, touching the sand on the railing as if willing it to protect her, I got in my car and drove.

The Juliette Low Legacy

Judith McDaniel

When I looked around, the two women were wrestling on
the floor in front of the fireplace, wrestling with serious
intention, but not with anger. The woman whose back was
toward me was slowly losing her pants as her body strained
and bent over. I watched with fascination as her pants slid
down over her large, solidly built ass, revealing dimples on
either side of her crevice.

The women sitting at the table with me seemed not to
notice, and I wanted them to notice. "They're wrestling," I
said, nodding toward the two on the cement floor in front of
the fireplace. The three women at my table glanced over
quickly, then drew their eyes back, but they had lost the
focus of their conversation.

"*That* tends to happen here sometimes," said Gwen, the
woman sitting directly across from me. I wanted to ask her
what she meant by *that*, make her say it out loud, here in
this all-woman setting that seemed so safe to these married
women. But when I caught her gaze, she frowned, and I
knew I shouldn't ask. Not if I wanted to keep knowing her
better. And I did.

Gwen shifted uneasily and turned to the woman perched
sideways on the bench next to her. "Do you want to go out
with one of the canoe trips this summer?"

"If I can, but not a long one or I won't be able to do the first aid program for the main camp." The woman's words came out in a rush, as though she might not say them if she slowed to think. "I think I'll be able to stay the whole week this year—sleep over and all. My sister and I are swapping kids for a week. She'll take my girls . . ."

I let their voices drift away from me as I turned back to watch the two women wrestling on the floor. It was after midnight and the smoke from the fireplace had drifted into the old Girl Scout camp winter lodge and collected at the top of the stairs to the sleeping loft. Most of the women had gone to bed, but several of the wrestlers' friends were watching, giving quiet encouragement. It was not a rowdy match. They were breast to breast now, legs entwined, arms glued together, waving slowly in the air as the heavier woman tried to pin her friend's shoulders to the floor. They should be kissing, I realized, as I watched the nearly silent pantomime.

Maxine had come over to our group earlier in the evening. I liked her warm smile, butch cut, and diesel-dyke build.

"Max," Gwen had greeted her. "I'm glad you could make it. Any trouble getting away?"

"Naw. I took the kids to Barry's mother and he's off ice fishing with the boys. You know I wouldn't miss this weekend. It's the social event of the year."

We all laughed. I looked with surprise at Maxine's ring finger when she mentioned her husband. Sure enough, it was there. The wedding band was there for almost all of them. Two married ladies, I thought wryly, as I watched the woman-to-woman body contact on the floor in front of the fireplace. It puzzled me. It was what I sensed in Gwen—this desire that moved toward women, but stopped just within the safety zone.

When most of the women had finally wandered off to bed, Gwen and I propped our backs against the wall and stretched our legs out the whole bench length. This way we could see the entire room, be sure no one could hear our conversation, and talk openly without having to look closely at one another's eyes. At least I hoped we could talk openly. We had been talking in hints, raised eyebrows, silent questions, and innuendo for several months now. I was curious, but my patience for Gwen's elaborate ritual of self-revelation had about run out. I wanted an ally in this world, someone who would know who I was and not run scared from it. Being known was my hedge against insanity in the insane world I lived in. At times the charade of being "normal" seemed to turn on me, threatened to engulf me unless I could whip out a safety line that would reattach me to my own reality. It wasn't a lot I asked, I thought, my eyes wandering back to the two women wrestling. I just want someone who will acknowledge with me what this is really all about.

Gwen sat quietly across from me. The flesh on her face was heavier than on her trim athletic body. It was the only part of her that looked forty-three. Her left hand, slowly turning the wine glass in the center of the table, was firm and muscular. Nice hands, I smiled to myself, noting that her wedding band was small and unobtrusive.

"You look depressed, Gwen. Isn't the weekend going well?"

"Oh, yes," Gwen roused herself briefly to enthusiasm. "It's an excellent turnout. The council should be pleased. We've never had this many leaders who would do winter camping training before." Her voice slid back down into the lower registers of boredom or depression.

"So what's wrong?"

"I'll tell you after I've had another glass of wine."

"Tell me now or I'm going to bed."

And the story came out. Mary, the woman I had led a troop with for two years. Gwen. Other women from our area at an adult Girl Scout training session, learning a new scouting ceremony from another country. Standing in a circle. Told to turn and embrace the woman standing next.

Mary, embarrassed, awkward, hugging Gwen, muttering, "This is ridiculous. They'll think all Girl Scouts are lesbians."

I was silent when she came to the punch line. This is it, I told myself. I could hardly complain about her reticence if I couldn't say something now. I was scared.

"Yeah, well," I cleared my throat. Lie. Truth. Or silence. "Well, lots are." I paused again and looked away. The wrestlers were sitting quietly on a bench in front of the fireplace, talking, bodies touching from shoulder to ankle. "I am."

"I know," she said, turning forward on the bench and peering at me intently. "I mean, I had figured."

"You had?" I took a gulp from my Coke bottle. Why was I surprised? I'd been dropping hints for three months.

"I always think of it when two women live together." Gwen seemed quiet, calm. She was looking at me curiously now.

"You do?" I took a deep breath. This was ridiculous. I'd expected her to be o.k. about it, so why was my voice shaking? Talk normal, I told myself, just talk normal.

"Does Mary know?" Mary. That was the fear. We'd worked together for two years and never exchanged a single item of personal information. Mary loves the outdoors like I do, but I'd always known—at some level—how wary she was of unpremeditated human involvements. And her husband taught in my high school.

Gwen was silent for a moment, thinking about Mary. "I doubt it. I doubt if it would occur to her."

I nodded, calming. There, that hadn't been so hard.

"I thought you'd never tell me." Gwen was peering at me again. I looked away. "I tried to let you know. . . ." Her voice trailed off as though she didn't want to make the accusation.

"Gwen, for god's sake, your husband is on Jessica's school board. She's an elementary school teacher. I can hardly go around proclaiming it from the roof tops." I was angry, let my relief spurt out in anger. Gwen looked as though I had missed the point.

"Sure," she said. "Sure. I know."

The sun came up slowly the next morning, pushing against the resistance of a night that was below zero. I woke at seven and peered outside my sleeping bag. In the dim half-light several women were dressing, moving around. I sat up, pulled my warmed-up long underwear out of the bottom of the sleeping bag, took off my sleeping sweatshirt, and started to dress for an outside day. The latrine seat was covered with ice crystals when I lifted the lid. I squatted gingerly over the dark hole.

"Minus thirty degrees wind chill factor," said a short red-headed woman cheerfully as I came into the kitchen. "Glad I didn't have to sleep in a tent last night."

"Me, too," I agreed, wondering whether I had met her last night or if she had just arrived. "It will be cold out on the ice today, for sure."

We were scheduled for a training session on hypothermia, then a chance to learn how to ice fish out on the lake our lodge overlooked. Northern pike and lake trout, we were promised, and Gwen had brought the potatoes for fish chowder.

More women came in during breakfast, women who had not been able to spend the night, red-cheeked from the morning cold, boisterous about leaving their families for this single day of adult training. I wondered how many of these leaders had ever thought of taking their troops winter camping, how many came for themselves, the day away from home with friends.

"I had to find two baby-sitters," one woman complained loudly as she took off her heavy snowmobile boots. "One for the kids and one for my husband." She continued against the laughter. "Really, he won't cook his own lunch."

"Get him to eat out, Lorraine."

"Are you kidding? Who can afford that?"

"Well, we're catching dinner today," Gwen said briskly. "Stop undressing, Lorraine. Let's get out and get started."

I slid down the embankment to the lake and started
across the ice, my skates slapping awkwardly against my
shoulder. The lake was frozen deep, but still freezing from
underneath. As the freezing water expanded into ice, the
lake crust pressed against its own resistance, cracking, shifting, a chorus of moans and sharp grunts as our weight
moved across the smooth surface.

"Indians used to say it was the lake talking," Gwen reassured one nervous woman. "It's frozen o.k. Really." She
handed me the ice auger. "Dig a hole. Let's see how thick
the ice is."

I leaned over the tall drill and turned the handle. As the
bit caught against the ice, shavings started to mound around
the handle. I pressed down and the muscles in my left arm
strained as I pushed the auger into the ice. When it went
through, Gwen said, "Now pull it out and slosh the water
around to clear your hole." We could see that the ice was
over a foot deep.

I learned the language of the ice fishers. Auger. Sounder.
Line. Minnow-bait. Tip ups. I found the spot on the minnow's back under the dorsal fin and inserted the fish hook.
The minnow sank when I threw it down the ice hole, swam
down and down to get to the warmer water, pulling my line
with it. I leaned over the eight-inch-wide hole and watched
the slim silver body spiral gracefully down through the ice
into darker waters, apparently oblivious to the hook and
line attaching it to this surface world. When it had played
out the line to my marking knot, I hooked the knot over a
little flag. If a larger fish took the bait, it would pull the line
free and my flag would "tip up," telling me I had a fish.

Gusts of wind scudded across the ice. We set fifteen
holes, rushed to one when the flag went up and pulled out a
pile of weeds the minnow had gotten tangled in.

"Raise the level of the bait," Gwen told Mary. "It's best
to be just above the weeds. No tangles that way." She
grinned at me when I raised an eyebrow to question her
innuendo. "Walk me over to the other side of the lake and
we'll set up the group that's just coming out."

We walked away from the voices until the only sound was the wind. "How long have you and Jessica been together?" she asked.

"Oh, about five years." I looked over to see what her face was saying, but it was silent behind the sunglasses.

"There was no one living like you that I knew when I was younger," she said.

"Me neither," I agreed, then paused. "I mean, I guess there were, but not in my nice suburb." I didn't know how much else I wanted to say. I hadn't talked to anyone but Jessica about the two women who worked the maintenance crew when I was a freshman in college, how I laughed at them like the other kids, not understanding the discomfort in my gut, the fear. And I did not know Gwen well enough to talk about why I hadn't been able to understand my connection to those women—those protections that seem so obvious in retrospect—how I'd wanted so badly as a child to fit in, to find approval for who I was. "Some women know it without seeing it first, I guess, but I just never thought of it until I met Jessica."

"I knew it from the first," she said.

I was silent. Afraid to interrupt, afraid I would not know what to say.

"But no one was doing it. I didn't know how I would live. It was the fifties. So I got married. The kids. The youngest is ten, so I figure I've got another seven years to serve. Then I don't know what, but it will be something else." She was crying behind her sunglasses, but I could not put my arm around her, here in the bright glare of the sun on ice.

"Did you ever have a woman lover?"

She nodded. In a low voice. "Now."

I turned at the sound of steel blades coming up behind us.

"Hey, watch my tip up for me, will you?" Mary called out to me. "I'm going to get a skating lesson so we can teach the girls to skate backward next time."

"Sure," I hollered, "but anything I catch is mine."

Gwen nodded and I turned abruptly back across the ice,

not sorry to have this moment to myself. I walked from ice hole to ice hole, checking the minnows and resetting the flags, trying to understand what I had just heard. What did it mean, I wondered, to have a husband and a woman lover? I could not imagine it. But I had no children, was never married, and needed to ask no one's permission to love Jessica. Not that it had been easy, even then. I always heard the voices that said, you do what? oh, god, how disgusting. And when my sister finally met Jessica, she told me she was disappointed. "She's nice. We'd hoped she'd sort of look like a truck driver, so you'd get over this woman thing in a hurry."

I was feeling lonely and cold when the red-headed woman I'd met in the kitchen at breakfast trotted over from the other side of the lake.

"Let's jog from hole to hole," she suggested. "It's the only way we'll keep warm today."

"Do you fish often?" I'd noticed she had brought her own tip ups and set each reel with finesse.

"My husband and I fish all winter down on Lake George. We put them in the freezer and eat fish year round. It's a great budget helper." She laughed, half embarrassed at the admission.

"It must be," I agreed.

"Where did you and your husband buy your house?" she asked, turning toward the next hole.

"Me?" I asked, flabbergasted. "I'm not married."

"Oh." Silence. "I'm sorry. I heard you talking about renovating a house last night. Didn't you say we?"

"Yes." I smiled. Here goes. "I live with a woman. We bought the house together. It's out in Paulet, just before the Vermont border.

She was silent for a minute as we checked the next reel for freeze up. "Are you girls teachers?"

"Yes," I said, laughing inside. "Yes, in fact, we are." And she turned comfortably back to the minnow bucket.

"They don't pay you teachers much," she said, freeing

the line of lake weed and sending the minnow back down. I wondered if the bottom of the lake seemed familiar to this small fish raised in a stainless steel tank for bait, or whether it found itself a stranger swimming back into what should have been its natural habitat.

She brushed a strand of hair back and tucked it under her ski cap, then looked directly at me and smiled. "It must be hard to live alone on what they pay."

"Yes," I said. "It must be." Loneliness settled back down across my shoulders as we moved across the ice, trying to catch sight of each of the flags, shielding our eyes against the sun's glare.

At noon we left the reels set and headed back to the lodge for lunch. I put on my skates and let the wind push me across the ice, dodging the small drifts of snow that had accumulated.

The lodge was crowded. More women had arrived and were cooking lunch outside over fires. Inside, I took off my boots, put on dry socks, and went for some hot coffee. In one corner I saw Max, sitting with a woman I hadn't met. Curly dark hair framed the newcomer's face, a face that seemed to have crumbled or melted slightly. The mouth slid down, her cheeks were slack beneath her gray eyes. It was not an expression I could define, and my eyes drifted back to the two, deep in conversation, apparently isolated in this crowded room. Women just coming in from the lake waved and greeted the newcomer, then moved away.

"Who's that?" I asked Mary as she sat down on the bench next to me. Then I wondered whether I should have asked, remembering Gwen's story about Mary from last night.

"E.J." Her voice was matter-of-fact. "She's here from Hartford. She ran the waterfront program at the camp here for nearly ten summers." She dismissed my inquiry with a wave toward her dessert plate. "Try the dessert," she urged. "I know you don't like chocolate, but Gwen says our girls will love the chocolate fondue with marshmallows. I'm going for more." I made a face of pure disgust at her departing back.

Sitting in silence, I ate my soup and watched the movement of women around me as they wove in and out of tables and conversations. Across the room was E.J. My eyes went back again and again to her face. Her eyes met no one's. She sat at Max's side, staring straight ahead, spoke without turning toward the heavyset comfortable woman sitting next to her.

"I thought I could wait." Gwen's voice was small, whispering in my ear. I had not felt her sit down beside me.

"When I met HER something in me said, uh, oh. We were always together. Whenever I needed another driver to take my troop somewhere, she would go. We camped together. Bicycled somewhere for the day. It never mattered what we did, we had fun together."

I nodded, but did not look at her. I was beginning to understand this mode of communication.

"I'd known her about six months. I had a camp reunion party and she came. My husband was out of town. The kids were farmed out. I was supposed to leave the next morning at six to take the troop to a conference downstate. She was driving the other car." Her voice dropped even further.

This must be it, I thought, looking around nervously to see whether anyone was watching us as I had watched Max and her friend.

"When they all left, she brought in her sleeping bag. She asked me where I wanted her to sleep. Oh, god, can you imagine?"

I couldn't, but nodded my head astutely, eyes fixed on the soup bowl.

"I said I wanted her to sleep with me. *With me*, I said. I couldn't believe I'd said it. Neither did she, but she never gave me a chance to take it back."

There was silence. I turned to look at her profile, impressed now, willing her to go on.

She would not look at me. "Neither of us had ever done it—made love to a woman—before. I thought, this is going to be a mess. How are we going to figure this out? But it wasn't. It was simple." She paused again. "It was the most natural thing I had ever done in my life."

I realized she had finished speaking. "What will you do?" I asked in hushed tones, not moving my lips, "Live together?"

"Oh, no." Her voice was shocked and she sat up straight at the table. "Oh, no. I couldn't do that. I mean, there's nothing to do. I have the children. And him." She gestured vaguely, including the whole room.

"But what about your lover?" I pursued. "What does she want?"

"I don't know." Gwen looked puzzled. "We'll just have to go on as we are. She understands."

"Oh." I thought about that as I scraped the last bit of soup from the bottom of my bowl. Gwen was silent beside me. Could I have asked the same of Jessica? I thought not, but then neither of us had children, neither was committed to an earlier promise. Still, I remembered my first erotic realization, the knowledge I had possessed in that first moment of being with a woman, that nothing, nothing would ever be the same for me. I wondered why it had seemed so obvious to me, so inevitable, so exhilarating.

The room was beginning to stir around me as women prepared for the afternoon's activities. "Do you think it will make a difference?" I asked. "Loving her?"

"It can't," she said, her voice rising from behind me. "I won't let it. I can't afford to."

Gwen directed the afternoon activities and I listened with half an ear. When it was time for me to leave, I asked her to walk me to the car. I had fabricated a late afternoon dentist appointment that would free me in time to be at my own home for dinner. These women fought free of their homes for this single day. I had to fight to create my home, to move toward it rather than away from it, and I had known weeks before I registered for this event that I would want to leave before it was over.

"Tell me about E.J.," I said as we climbed the hill to the parking lot.

"Oh," she said dully, "she's in bad shape."

"I could tell. Why?"

"She was with the woman who ran this camp. They met here. Were together every summer. Lived together, too, for a while, I think."

"Lovers?"

"I was sure they were. Her girlfriend got married last spring. It's the first time E.J.'s been up to camp since."

I remembered her face, the fragile mouth, the eyes that wouldn't meet mine.

"It's real hard for her," Gwen continued. "They all know it's hard."

"But all of this is unspoken?" It seemed cruel. Suddenly I was tired and the wind chill seemed more noticeable.

"Of course. No one can talk about it. There's no support for that." She paused. "I'm sorry you're not staying for dinner. We got enough fish for the chowder."

I looked into her eyes, trying to understand what was not being said. If the message was there, I could not read it. I was angry and sad and did not know what else to say.

Gwen shrugged. "Well, have a nice dinner at home to-night." I tried to lean forward to embrace her and say good-bye, but I could not move against the resistance in the cold air between us.

"Good night," I said. "See you." And I watched her back as she turned and walked back down the path toward the lake.

My Lesbian Imagination

Leslie Lawrence

It is Thursday April 1, the twenty-seventh day of our twenty-eight-day cold turkey agreement, and I'm trying not to think about our reunion tomorrow (how you will greet me, what I will read in your eyes, your touch). Instead, I'm doing what I've been doing all month—looking back rather than ahead, searching for ways to blame and forgive myself.

That first night on my porch, we were drinking Jack Daniels and you held out your empty glass. Some kind of test, I thought, staring at the glass, then glancing at your face in the yellow bug light. Late August, your freckles were out, your lips chapped, your swampy eyes stern and sly. I took your glass, wondering why you were so intent on getting drunk.

When it got chilly we moved into my living room. Then around one, my housemate Bonnie came down in her robe, said a surprised hello, shuffled through the living room into the kitchen, then back again with her glass of milk, thinking (I decided): Fay and her lesbian friend sitting tight on the couch in the dark at one in the morning!

She's right, I decided. Something is up. Yet I'd always thought that if I ever had an affair with a woman, it would just happen; I'd close my eyes and—

"Marty," I asked. "What do you think we should do about this?"

"About what?" you said.

"This tension between us."

"What tension?"

"This sexual tension."

"I don't know," you said. "What do you think?"

"I don't know," I said. (This wasn't how I'd imagined it.) "I—I think I'd like to ask you to stay, but I'm not sure it's a good idea."

"Why not?"

"Well—maybe it's just curiosity, maybe I won't like it, maybe I'll never want it again. Besides, you've sworn off straight women and—"

You took my hand. The window behind the couch was open, the air cool, the neighborhood quiet.

Upstairs, you seemed as nervous as I. We undressed in the dark and didn't kiss much; touching each other seemed easier somehow. When you put your head between my legs I thought: I am prepared for this. I've pictured it many times, telling myself a tongue is a tongue, it has no gender. I came. So there, I thought.

Of course picturing my head between your legs took more imagination, and when it came time for that I wasn't as prepared. But I told myself not to be squeamish, to approach this thing with an open mind. And I thought I was doing quite well—the smell was like my own, you seemed to be getting excited. I listened to how your breathing changed. I felt earnest, attentive. I thought: This is how a man feels when he's doing this to me. I thought: Any second now, she will come. And when you didn't—wouldn't, I thought (not only): What am I doing wrong? (but also): Why is she being so stubborn?

The next morning, you had an eight o'clock haircut appointment. We woke by alarm. "You're a good sport, Fay," you said. Then you zipped up your jeans and added, "Don't worry, it will never happen again."

The authority on straight girls had decided I didn't have it in me. I was hurt. Relieved. As we continued to see each other nearly every day, I thought, this is fine, the way it's supposed to be. But there were moments when I admitted to myself that we weren't having quite as much fun as we had had before we had done what we would never do again.

Then that night as we were leaving Kay's pot luck supper you asked if I wanted to go dancing. (As usual you had been the life of the party; people gathered around you, belly laughing as you told your stories, expertly acting out every part.) We were standing by the trunk of my car now.

"Dancing?" I asked. "Where?"

"The Saints."

I opened the trunk, deposited the salad bowl. I'd heard about The Saints. You'd told me how you used to hang out there—pick up women. I had pictured a dark smoky basement smelling of piss and beer; a pool table; enormous women with leather jackets and hardly any hair. But surely I was way off. Times had changed. *This will never happen again.* You'd said it so resolutely I supposed I was safe—safe enough to go dancing with you at The Saints.

"O.K." I said, slamming the trunk closed.

The place resembled my fantasy more than I expected it to. I threw myself into dancing—dancing fast. When you got tired I took other partners. I danced until everything ached and then collapsed beside you on a bench at a booth. Somehow you maneuvered us so that I was leaning back against your chest and your hands were combing through my soaking hair and stroking my dripping face. Were those tears mixing with my sweat? I could feel my face contorting. I knew I was no longer safe.

Back at your house, we sat close together on your dilapidated couch on your rickety porch. We were silent until suddenly you took hold of my shoulder and looked into my eyes, "Fay, I want you."

"What does that mean?" I asked, stalling, I guess.

"It means I want to sleep with you, to eat with you, to take care of you when you're sick. It means I want to be there for you if someone you love dies and I want you to be there for me, and I want us to go to the movies, to the

country, running, hiking, skiing . . ." Did I kiss you then? I
was moved by your simple words.

And when we made love, we were less like two stalwarts
marking out a minuet. I realized that trying to imagine how
a man felt making love to me was not the way, so I let my
tongue meander and frolic. And when you came, I felt
triumphant. I thought: I shouldn't have been feeling sorry
for all those men who had to do that to me.

We slept until one and then went out for brunch. When
the waiter gave us the best table I wondered how he knew.
We brought along a *New York Times* and tried to act a little
bored—like we'd been doing this for years.

How quickly our lives came to resemble the vision you'd
summoned that night on the porch. And how little trouble I
had learning how to love being your lover. I dove in like a
porpoise—jovial, articulate in a new subterranean language
. . . lips, nose, fingers, hips—grunting, snorting, whooshing,
whimpering, fluttering—the new music, the old, ballads,
ditties, scat, psalms, the blues. No pitch, no rhythm, no
modulation or syncopation was too subtle for me. Chimps,
cheetahs, hyenas . . . no creature in the animal kingdom too
exotic. Not that I'd been shy with men, but with you—what
pluck I had. I wanted us all the time. My dreams grew
bounteous and wild.

And in the daylight hours? Well, my boyfriends had always been nice guys—attentive, gentle, considerate. But
you—you were immersed in me. If I started coughing, there
you were with a glass of water. You relished hearing about
every twinge in my knee, throb in my elbow. You wanted
my every thought, observation, fear.

It was sometime the following spring, I think, that the
nightmares started:

My father kisses me hello and smells you on my face.

I get an anonymous package in the mail. A new product
to comb through your hair: "Anti-Lesbian Powder."

And during the day, you'd catch me looking gloomy.

"What's the matter, honey?"

"Nothing."

"Don't tell me nothing, I can see that Talmudic po

So I'd tell you: At Passover with my family, my eyes travelled around the table from Aunt Edith to Uncle Jacob, to cousin Denise, her husband Roger, my brother Adam, his wife Judy, their daughter Celeste, my mother Jane, my father Max. True, Jacob's an infamous womanizer, Roger a goy, Celeste dyslexic, and my mother a chronic depressive; nevertheless, it pained me that I could not find a place for you, Martha Rappaport—arch-Jew that you are. My first. (Hey Mom, hey Dad, guess what? At last a Jew. There's just one thing . . .)

"Het-er-o-sex-u-al priv-i-lege, Fay" (you almost hissed), "that's what you're afraid of losing." And later, you pointed out that when we were in our honeymoon phase my parents were touring China. And my decline in sexual interest happened to coincide with their approaching return to the States. And when they called saying they were back in Cleveland—wasn't that the start of my headaches, my backaches, my papers to grade, my just-too-pooped stage?

We started couples' therapy.

Barbara had us act out little scenes. For example, our ideal greeting. Your job as director was to make sure the lilt in my Honey-I'm-Home, the press and length of my kiss, the ideas I had for the evening, all matched your picture of heaven.

What a genius I was—embracing you from behind, kissing you on the ear, suggesting we take Doolittle for a walk. You had to search hard for something to pick on. I guess I was just a natural—marvelous me.

Poor you. Under my direction you could do no right. I stopped you every two seconds. Something was wrong. Your voice? Your lips? Your walk? I kept making adjustments, searching for one that would make it all right, but somehow nothing did the trick. Finally I looked up at Barbara with pleading eyes and blurted: "This is very difficult for me."

"Why's that?"

"All my fantasies are heterosexual."

"Well!" She took a deep breath, thought fast, "Marty, you've just been transformed into Martin. Now let's proceed."

What a sport you were, strutting into the kitchen, suggesting in a husky voice that we go to the Peacock for dinner. With this I perked up. We both laughed. "See," you said, slipping out of your role, "it *is* their money and clout that you want."

I didn't argue, or ask where their veiny hands fit in their small muscular asses. It wasn't that I liked them more than your soft hands, your generous ass; but I liked them—I did.

"Fay," Barbara said, "*you* need to work on developing your lesbian imagination."

One of your favorite expressions. You nodded. And nodded. And later helped me build scenarios to counter the millions I had that featured men: you and me hiking in the Andes, jeeping across the Kalahari, rocking on some porch somewhere—our hair gray, our bodies firm.

Still, you were always buttoning my coat, pulling the collar up around my neck. "Stop mothering me," I'd shout.

And at night I'd lie next to you believing that if I could just summon an image of our lovemaking in those early days when I'd enjoyed it so, that picture would draw my hand to your skin. Sometimes an image would jet by (my fingers on your belly, your thigh), but I could never hold it down and my hand wouldn't budge. Eventually, I'd roll over and grunt goodnight.

"So what *do* you find sexy?" you'd ask after another week of that.

"I don't know. Maybe Barbara's right. We need more distance. If I have lunch with a friend, you're jealous. If I want an hour to myself, you're hurt. You want us to dress alike—preppy, butch; to eat the same foods—ice cream and cake; to fight the same causes—lesbian/feminist. When you had your gum surgery you were always opening your mouth insisting I look in and gaze upon the artful stitches so that they, too, might be shared."

"Fay, wearing skirts is your way of keeping one foot in the straight world. You refuse sweets just to make me feel like a pig. There are millions of liberals in Lexington to stand up for the whales, but how many of them will don pink triangles when they start rounding up the dykes? You're always thinking of Fay first. A little intimacy makes you claustrophobic."

I thought you were onto something there. "More air," I was always shouting. "I can't breathe under all these blankets." We kidded about patenting lesbian bedding with portholes at hip height. We kidded about how perhaps I should have worked up to you more slowly—started with a *shiksa* into botany, rather than a Jew into literature like myself.

In private, I tried to remember my chemistry. *Bonding occurs when one molecule has what the other lacks. The bigger the gap, the bigger the spark.* Oh Marty, I don't think you know how much time I spent searching for a metaphor that would explain why I could no longer make love to you.

We had terrible fights:

"I suppose you find that tall, skinny Ingrid sexy?"

"I think I'd better leave now."

"Or maybe you prefer beards, the Jake Marcus type?

I snatched up my coat.

"No, I think you're more into house painters."

I headed toward the door.

"Fay . . . if you walk out that door . . ."

I stopped walking.

"I see the way he's started lounging around your porch."

I reached for the door knob, thinking, "Lounging?" He sat on the steps and drank a beer—shirtless and tanned, but he's eighteen and has nothing to say. "Lounging?" It's the kind of word the moral majority uses when they really mean fucking or sucking.

"Fay, if you dare walk out . . ."

So I turn around and I'm stalking towards you, with an odd feeling in my nose, like I'm on the bottom of the ocean. My body's shaking and I'm heading toward you as if I'm going to strangle you, and then, at a pitch that stuns even me, I shriek, "Lounging?" I shake your shoulders. "Lounging?" I hurl my body against the wall again and again until my knees give in. And it's as if the fight—the months of fighting—have all been designed to bring us here to this corner of the kitchen floor where I cry like a baby in your arms.

"When couples, gay or straight, are too merged, they have three major ways of reestablishing their individual identities." That's what Barbara said during one of our earlier sessions.

"And what are they?" I asked.

"Well, they fight" (we nodded), "they stop having sex" (we nodded), "they have affairs" (we looked up at the ceiling).

"Maybe I'll just go out and have myself an affair," you said a few sessions later, looking first at Barbara and then at me.

Go ahead. Did I say that? I think I did. You'd just finished talking about how attractive you'd been feeling lately—how the world seemed full of possibilities and sex was in the air. I'd been feeling dull and ugly and hadn't felt a sexual stirring for you or anyone in months.

I remember the night you first had dinner with her. That afternoon you had your third round of oral surgery and I picked you up at the clinic as usual. You held the ice pack while I drove and we stopped at the drugstore for your painkillers. After the first two rounds we'd indulged you with naps and ice cream, but we'd come to realize you were capable of more, so this time we spent the afternoon at Frameworks matting some Victorian prints we'd bought at a flea market.

I'd never been good with my hands—"Crab Claw" you often called me—and I had to do my framing job over and over. You were patient—I remember noting that. Could I have already known? My gratitude felt excessive. I wanted so much to please you.

I remember kissing you good-bye at the door. We'd lost track of the time. You had a dinner date at six and it was already quarter of. I gave you an especially nice kiss—on the lips, even though we were in a public place. Maybe because of the high color in your cheeks or the swelling on one side, or because your step seemed especially springy. "I'll call when I get back," you said.

At nine you hadn't yet phoned. At ten, still no call. At five to eleven the phone rang. "You sound funny," I said.

"I'm a little high," you said. "I didn't know what to say. You weren't supposed to drink for a week after the surgery. After the first two quadrants—when you were with me— you'd always obeyed. Did I ask you if you had a nice time? I know you asked if I wanted to go skiing the next day. I remember hemming and hawing, mumbling about student conferences and laundry. That wasn't like me. There was always time for fresh air.

The next morning I felt sure I could manage to find time for skiing. I called you from school at nine a.m., and called you every twenty minutes after that but no one answered and it was Wednesday and your first class wasn't until noon and I felt my panic grow. At eleven twenty I finally got you. "Where were you?"

"Shopping," you said, sounding casual, but not suspiciously so. We arranged to meet at the golf course at three.

You were on time. That increased my suspicion. But you were slow at waxing your skis and getting them on and that was typical so I felt reassured. You were overconcerned about Doolittle—were her paws too cold? That was typical too. Still, something was off. You were quiet, distant, pre-occupied, more like a man—more like me.

"Ready?" you said, gently whacking Doolittle's shaggy tan flank. Then, without looking at me, you pushed off and headed down. Doolittle stood for a moment and turned to me with unbearably compassionate eyes, and then sprinted down to you. I stuffed the blue wax into my jacket, yanked my zipper, and pushed off. At the bottom of the hill—and you know that hill, it's short—I saw you weren't waiting for me but were already heading toward the pine grove.

Something has changed in her, I thought, flashing on all those moments in our past. Skiing, swimming, hiking, biking, skating, running—it was always the same: Fay ahead, Marty behind; Fay looking back every once in a while just to make sure Marty hadn't twisted an ankle or drowned; Fay the navigator, the trailblazer always ready to give a few pointers; Fay feeling Marty's eyes on her stalwart back, trying to imagine what they saw, how Marty felt watching Fay speed ahead; Fay knowing that if *she* were the one behind she would not have felt too great—but reminding herself that Fay and Marty were very different people, she wondered if maybe Marty felt simply proud to have such a fierce and fearless girlfriend, with such energy and verve, such strong calves and lungs, such a nose for the right trail.

Now, watching your green vest getting smaller and smaller, I was sure I'd been mistaken: you hadn't felt proud, you'd felt as bad as I felt now—wanting to be near you, to talk to you, to feel your breath on my cheek—knowing that you preferred to be out ahead, alone. I could have made my own tracks but I decided to follow in yours. When you switched your course I switched mine. I would take the hypotenuse of the triangle leading to you. You switched again. And again. I can still feel my astonishment, my fury. I'm the better skier, I told myself. I have better form, more strength and endurance. How can it be that my breathing's so heavy and my thighs are aching and I'm sweating into my parka and she's still so far ahead of me. This defies all laws of muscle and motion. This is more than Wheaties or a good night's sleep.

I wasn't sure until a few weeks later. A Saturday. We hadn't seen each other since Wednesday. Susan and Marcia were down from New Hampshire and I was supposed to meet you all after my dance class. I walked into your kitchen; you were wearing a new sweater. A week before you'd bought new button-fly Levi's and a few days before that, a pink man-tailored Ralph Lauren, and when I saw this new sweater—a white cotton pullover with three leather buttons at the throat—I was sure.

We hugged for the sake of Susan and Marcia. "Lunch is all ready," you said proudly, cheerily. The kitchen was unbearably sunny, your white sweater blinding.

"Great," I said, "but I stink from dancing and need a shower first."

I took it very hot, wondering whether I might actually be burning my skin, imagining you riding with me in the ambulance and then offering a piece of your thigh to be grafted onto mine. I wondered if, at the very least, when I opened the shower curtain, you'd be standing there, a towel stretched out in your wide arms.

Your minestrone was perfect. The beans in the salad, bright and crunchy. I'd taught you to cook and you'd always kidded about how lucky your next girlfriend would be.

That evening, in a dark Beacon Hill bar, we told our friends the story of how veteran dyke (you) and thoroughly ho-hum straight girl (me) became lovers. We went off on a million tangents, exaggerated shamelessly, basked in the illusion that in telling the story of our love in those early days, we could make it still true.

When the evening was over and we got into bed, I started crying and wouldn't stop. You seemed surprised. "It's just an affair," you said.

Tears streaming the whole time, I made love to you that night—the first time in months—and so avidly, with the passion I had in our early days. In the morning I asked how it had been for you.

"Frankly," you said, "my sexual appetite is elsewhere."

It was a Sunday. We decided to call Barbara anyway.

"Is it an emergency?" her answering service asked.

I looked at your locked-up face, at the flutter in your jawbone. "Yes," I said.

When Barbara called back a few hours later she said she could squeeze us in on Tuesday.

"Tuesday?"

"Tuesday."

Sunday, Monday, Tuesday—I went around chanting *affair, affair*, as if the maharishi himself had assigned it to me.

"Marty's having an affair!" I told everyone I knew. Their faces fell. Male or female, gay or straight, it was as if they'd all been schooled in the proper-expression-to-wear-when-you-hear-your-friend's-lover-is-having-an-affair. In the seventh grade I stood in the schoolyard and made myself watch Dickie Fassberg talking close and steamy to Sally Mattes and I'd hardly felt jealous since. Now, I wandered the streets of Cambridge reeling with pain, fury, humiliation—knocking into words like "cuckolded." (Did it apply in the case of a semi-straight woman's lesbian lover having an affair with another woman?)

Barbara was big on choosing between alternative, time-limited contracts. Marty can stop seeing her affair. Marty can stop seeing Fay. Or Marty can continue to see both. I sat in the rocker crying demurely into dainty tissues I plucked from a square box decorated with deer and pines. Our hour was up before we had time to settle.

The next evening we sat on my couch with our calendars and counted out four weeks. When you walked down the stairs, at first Dolittle didn't follow. She stood very still on the top step, turning her sweet terrier face from me to you, twice, three times. "She's a little ambivalent," you said.

I was crying before I heard the door close. How had this happened? We'd agreed that seeing us both was out. But why hadn't I pushed for you to stop seeing her? Looking for a way out? I considered the possibility, then dismissed it. Your "sexual appetite was elsewhere." That was why. I had my pride—and I banked on you tiring of her soon.

Your birthday was two days after that. I'd already made dinner reservations. In a year and a half we'd never been apart for more than a Thanksgiving weekend. You'd never last more than a couple of days. You would call. You would repent. We would eat fish and drink wine for your birthday and we would hold hands across the table and I would not envy the woman seated across from her dark-haired man with strong jaw and sensitive hands. I would concentrate on the sheen on your green silk blouse, the vast lissom "V" of flesh that had always disturbingly reminded me of my Great-aunt Rose. I will imagine my face burrowed between your breasts. I will take a bite of fish and chew it slowly and uncross and recross my legs. I will refill your glass. Our waiter will be gay, the vegetables *al dente*.

You would call. *I* was the one with respect for rules. I could sit at a desk longer, force myself to run one more lap, pass on rich desserts.

At seven I cancelled the reservation and sat with every memento I could find. That photograph of you wearing raggedy cut-offs, nothing on top. You're bent at the waist; your breasts shade the patch you're weeding. I remembered my surprise when you first gave it to me: *You had a body before it was known to me!* And looking at it now, admiring the sunlight on your back, I told myself: *She will have those same arms and legs and breasts this April no matter whose garden her head is in.* I summoned every happy memory intending to say: *This will never be again.* Instead, I said, *It WILL!* There will be a time when I will make love to her as if my parents are in New Guinea. Oh Marty, you used to want to hear all my fantasies. But now? Tomorrow? What shall I tell you? How fervent they are? What fantastic positions I have us in? How I've suffered these twenty-seven days?

Better stick to lighter stuff. The Harvard Trust story?

Last Friday, the twenty-first day, I was starting up my car to go to the bank, when it occurred to me that I might run into you there—into both of you—together. I turned off the engine to think: There are many branches of Harvard Trust and I am not obligated to go to the Porter Square one which you also use—there's always Davis Square and Inman Square and Fresh Pond Parkway and . . . (I started the engine.) But it doesn't make sense, isn't *right* for me to go out of my way to a bank I wouldn't ordinarily go to, just to avoid you.

After all, if this were Shakespeare or *I Love Lucy,* you would also reroute, and in the end, we'd bump into each other at . . . the Kendall Square branch! And besides, if I spot your car parked in front, I can always decide to drive on.

By the time I'm halfway there, I'm convinced you're heading to the bank too. It's Friday, 3:48, there's nowhere else you could be. I step on the gas. And that's when I start chuckling—when I catch myself speeding because you're at the bank waiting for me! I'm amused by the tricks the mind plays and I'm pleased that now, only three weeks since I fell apart, I'm capable of being amused and I think that I *will* live and some day I'll tell someone—maybe you—this amusing story and the proper ironic twist will be that you actually *do* turn out to be at the bank.

But you don't.

Still, I took it as a good omen—that flash of amusement; I took it as a sign that I'd passed this month-long test and would be rewarded with your love.

But now, looking out this window at the tight little buds, I dread the coming spring. It's April Fool's Day, I just realized that, and I have this feeling my reward might not come in the form I'd most love. Or it *will*. We will meet at the appointed spot and right away I will see it in your eyes—you *do* love me; but moments later, something will tell me it's not going to work. We have changed too much? Not enough? No. I won't think like that. I'll think back—to how you'd take my hand, say, "What is it Fay? You're so silent." That probing of yours didn't always feel like a trespass; often it helped me find a way to the source of my sadness and fear. I'll remember those nights we'd wake from dreams, command each other to chase after those renegade images, no matter how fractured or strange, to follow them down. Our minds as well as our legs intertwining—how brilliant we were in those dark hours, how close to home.

Trespassing

Valerie Miner

Exhausted from four hours of traffic, Kate and Josie almost missed seeing the two doe and their fawn drinking at the pond. The women waited in the car, cautious lest the noise of opening doors disturb the animals. The deer lingered another five minutes, then stepped gracefully into the wings of sequoias. Last sun settled on golden hills. Night noises pulsed. Frogs. Crickets. Mallards. Wind whispered across dry grass. Jays barked from the top of the hill. As the sky grew roses, Kate and Josie watched Jupiter blaze over the eastern mountains.

They unloaded the Chevy quickly and sloppily, eager for the comfort of the compact wooden cabin they had built with their friends over five summers. Josie opened the gas line outside the house. Kate lit a fire, reflecting on the joys of collective ownership when the rest of the collective was absent. She could hardly believe it—two whole days away from Meredith High School; forty-eight hours of privacy and peace.

Suddenly starving, they decided to eat right away. Afterward they would sit in front of the fire and read to each other. Kate chopped salad while Josie made pasta and whistled. The sky got redder and then, abruptly, the cabin was dark. With heavy reluctance, Kate walked around and lit the lanterns.

"Oh," Kate said.

Josie turned and caught a flick of brown before her, like an insect crashing on a windshield.

"Damn bats," Kate shook her head and picked up the broom.

"Bats!" Josie screamed. "I thought Iris got rid of those gruesome things last month."

"Must still be some holes in the sun porch," Kate shook her head.

A dark object dropped beside Josie, like a small turd falling from the eaves. It disappeared. She fretted the wooden spoon through the pasta, watching another tiny brown mass cut its fall in mid-air and swoop across the room. It was too much. "Bats!"

Josie ran outside. She felt safer in the dark.

Kate stayed in the house, sweeping bats out of the windows and back door.

Staring up at the stars, so benign in their distance, Josie considered vast differences between Kate and herself. Rational, taciturn Kate was probably calculating the increasing velocity of wing movement as the bats ignited to wakefulness. Josie, herself, still cringed at Grandma's tales about bats nesting in little girls' hair. And raised as she was in a willful family where intentionality was more important than action, where danger didn't exist if one closed one's imagination to it, Josie was given to the substitution of "good thoughts." Let's see, she forced herself to concentrate on a pleasant memory: how she and Kate met. It was a miracle if you thought about it; *who* would have expected romance at the school Xerox machine? But there was Kate copying quark diagrams for her physics students while Josie waited to copy a new translation of "La Cigale et La Fourmi." If Kate hadn't run out of toner, they might never have become acquainted.

"All clear," Kate called. There was no disdain in her

voice, for she had always envied Josie's ability to show fear. She should tell Josie this.

Josie craned her neck and stared at the sky. "Glorious night," she called back. "Wanna see?"

Ducking out the front door, Kate ran through the pungent pennyroyal to her friend. Josie took her hand. Together they stood quietly until they could hear the frogs and the crickets once more.

They slept late and spent the next morning eating eggs and fried potatoes and rye toast. Josie noticed some wasps dancing around the table, so they cleaned up and went outside to lie on the warm deck.

Later they spent an hour fitting moulding around the edges of the sun porch's glass door, sealing the house seams against nocturnal trespassers.

At noon the women drove five miles to town for forgotten country necessities—ice, water, and flashlight batteries. Josie secretly checked the grocery shelves for bat killer, but she didn't find any, and she knew Kate wouldn't approve.

As they drove back to the land, Josie tried to renew her enthusiasm for the weekend. She stopped in front of the cabin. Kate, now completely restored by country air, bounded into the house with the grocery bag.

Josie moved the Chevy into the shade of an oak tree which was being gradually occupied by Spanish moss. As she locked up the car, she saw a fat man with a rifle, waddling out of the forest. He wore a yellow cap, a striped t-shirt, and blue jeans.

A giant bumblebee, she thought. Then she warned herself to get serious. The land was clearly posted, "No Trespassing. No Hunting." A shiver ran along her collarbone. They were half a mile from the highway here. It could be weeks before anyone investigated.

Josie decided to be friendly and waved.

"Hello there." He was winded, hustling to meet her.

Josie closed her eyes and hoped Kate would stay in the house until it was all over.

"I got lost," he said, nodding his whole body. "How do you get back to the highway?"

"That direction," Josie tried to calm herself. "Up the road there."

He looked her over. "You got any water? A glass of water? I've been walking for hours."

Biblical tales filled her head. The Woman at the Well. The Wedding at Cana. The Good Samaritan. "Sure," she said as noncommitally as possible. "I'll be right back."

"Who's that?" Kate greeted her.

Josie tried to be calm. "Water man. I mean, a lost man who needs water." She watched Kate's jaw stiffen. "Now let me handle it. He just wants a glass of water and then he'll be on his way." Josie poured water from a plastic jug into an old jam jar they used for drinking.

"Water, my foot, what is he doing on the land? It's posted 'No Trespassing,' for godsake."

"Listen, Kate, he was hunting and. . . ."

Kate took the glass and poured half the water back into the jug. "Don't *spoil* him. He may return."

She stalked out to the man, who was leaning on their car, his gun on the ground. Josie stood at the door, watching.

"Thanks, Mam," he reached for the water.

"No shooting on this land," Kate said as she released the glass.

"Sorry, Mam. I was hunting up there on the North Ridge and I hit a buck. But he got away. I followed, to make sure I got him good. Then I got lost and I guess I wound up here."

"Guess so," Kate said. She held her hand against her leg to stop it from shaking.

"I'll be off your land soon's I finish the water," he promised.

"That's right," she kept her voice even.

"But I'll need to be coming back to get the buck. See, I

finally did get him. But since I was lost, I couldn't drag him all over tarnation."

"We don't want a dead buck on the land," Kate conceded. "When're you coming?"

"Tomorrow morning?" he asked. "About eight?"

"Fine, and no guns," she said.

"No mam, no guns."

"Right then," she held her hand out for the jam jar. "Road's that way."

"Yes, mam."

Kate watched him climb the hill and walked back to the house, shaking her head. Josie reached to hug her, but Kate pulled away. "Goddamned hunter." She was on the verge of tears.

"How about some coffee or lunch?"

"Naw, are you nuts, after all we ate this morning? No, I think I'll just go for a walk. See if I can find the buck. If there *is* a buck."

Josie nodded. "Want company?" She wasn't keen on viewing a dead animal, but she didn't care to admit being afraid to stay in the house alone, not after her melodramatic performance with the bats last night.

"Sure," Kate was grateful. "Let's go."

Josie locked the ice chest and dropped the jam jar in the brown paper garbage bag on the way out.

It was hotter now, about eighty-five degrees. The pennyroyal smelled mintier than last night. The day was dry and still—bleached grass, golden hills scumbled against teal sky. A turkey vulture glided above the oak grove. As they walked around the pond, they could hear frogs scholop into the water. Kate stopped to inspect the eucalyptus trees they had planted in the spring. Four out of five still alive, not bad. Farther along, a salamander skittered across their path. Josie felt cool even before she entered the woods. In a way, she hoped they wouldn't find the buck. But if there were no buck, who knows what the bumblebee man really wanted?

The woods were thick with madrone and manzanita and

poison oak. It was always a balance on the land, Kate thought, pleasure and danger.

Josie wished she had worn sneakers instead of sandals. But Kate didn't seem to be bothered about her feet as she marched ahead. Right, Josie reminded herself, this wasn't a ramble. They continued in silence for half an hour.

" 'Round here, I guess," called Kate, who was now several yards ahead. "See the way branches have broken. Yes, here. Oh my god, it's still alive. Goddamned hunter."

They stared at the huge animal, its left front leg broken in a fall, panting and sweating, blind fear in its wide eyes.

"I told Myla we should keep a gun at the house." Kate cried, "What are we going to do?"

Josie didn't think about it. She probably wouldn't have been able to lift the boulder if she had thought about it. But she heard herself shouting to Kate, "Stand back," and watched herself drop the big rock on the buck's head. They heard a gurgling and saw a muscle ripple along the animal's belly. Then nothing. There was nothing alive under the boulder.

Josie stared at the four bullet wounds scattered up the right side of the buck. The animal's blood was a dark cinnamon color. She noticed sweat along the hip joints.

Kate walked over to her quietly and took her hand. "Good, brave," she stuttered. "That was good, Josie."

"Yeah, it seemed the right thing."

Kate hugged Josie and gently drew her away from the dead buck and the broken bush.

They walked straight out to the trail. Neither one seemed to want to stay in the woods for their customary ramble. Kate watched her friend closely, waiting for the explosion. This silence was so uncharacteristic of Josie. Soon, soon, she would erupt with anger and aggravation and guilt and a long examination of what she had done in the woods. For her own part, Kate could only think of one word. Brave.

"Let's go swimming," Josie said, trying to focus on the trail. It'll cool us off."

The two women stripped on the makeshift dock and lay in the sun beside one another. Kate was slim, her legs long and shapely. She didn't think much about this body which had always served her well. She never felt too thin or too plump. Josie, in contrast, fretted about her zoftig breasts and hips. Her skin was pinker than Kate's, a faint pink. Kate curled up beside Josie, her legs across Josie's legs, her head on Josie's shoulder.

Josie closed her eyes and told herself it was over. They were all right. She had never killed anything before and she felt terribly sad. Of course, the animal had been dying. It was a humane act. Still, her chest ached with a funny hollowness.

"What's that?" Kate sat up.

They listened, Josie flat and Kate leaning forward from her waist.

The noise came again.

A loud whirrr.

Like an engine.

Whirrr.

"Quail," Kate relaxed back on her elbow. "Come on, let's wash off the feeling of that creepy guy."

She lowered herself into the water from the wooden ladder, surprised as Josie jumped in.

"Freezing," Josie laughed, swimming around her friend and noticing how Kate's blond curls sprang back the minute she lifted her head from the water. "Freezing!"

"You'll warm up," Kate said, herself breathless from the cold.

"You're always telling me to stop daydreaming, to stay in the present. The present is freezing." Josie giggled and splashed her friend.

Kate laughed. She ducked under the water, swimming deep enough to catch Josie's feet, which were treading earnestly.

"Hey, watch it." But Josie called too late. Now she was

below the surface, tangled in Kate's legs and the long roots of silky grass. It was green down here and very cold.

They dried out on the sunny dock and dressed before starting toward the house. Often they walked naked across the land, especially after swimming when they didn't want to wear sweaty clothes. Today that didn't feel safe.

Back at the cabin, the afternoon grew long and restless. Both women felt fidgety. Kate put aside her equations and washed all the windows in the house. Josie couldn't concentrate on her translation, so she worked up lesson plans for the following week.

About five o'clock, she glanced at Kate, stretching recklessly to the skylight from the top of a ladder.

"Careful up there."

"Sure, hon."

"What did we bring for dinner?" Josie's mind was blank.

"That beef chili you made last week. And rye bread."

"Why don't we go out?" Josie paced in front of the wood stove. God, she wished Kate would be careful on that ladder.

"Out. But the whole point of being here, oops," she tipped precariously and then straightened. "Hey, just let me get one more lick in here and we can talk. There." She started down the steps. "But the whole point of being in the country is to retreat together in solitary bliss. And what's wrong with your chili? I thought this batch was perfect?"

Josie shrugged and looked out the big bay window across the grass. She told herself to watch the horses ambling along the ridge or the hawk hovering over the pond. Instead she was caught by a line of lint Kate had left in the middle of the frame. "I don't know. Not in the mood. Guess I'd like vegetarian tonight." Her eyes stung.

Kate stood behind her; still Josie could sense her nodding.

"Why not," Kate said. "Be nice to take a ride this time of evening."

Edna's Cafe was practically empty. But then—Kate checked

her watch—it *was* only 5:30. Edna waved menus from behind the counter. Josie and Kate said yes.

"Coffee, girls?" Edna carried the menus under her arm,
pot of coffee in one hand and mugs in the other.

"Thanks," Josie said.

"Not just yet," Kate smiled. Edna reminded her of Aunt
Bella who worked in a coffee shop back East.

While Kate studied the menu, Josie excused herself to the
rest room.

Kate breathed easier when Josie returned to the table
looking relaxed. She felt a great surge of affection as her
companion intently appraised the menu.

"I think I'll have the chef's salad with jack cheese," Josie
decided.

"Sounds good," Kate nodded. She was relieved to see
Josie looking happy. "Two chef salads, with jack cheese,"
she called over to Edna.

They talked about plans for the following summer when
they could spend four consecutive weeks on the land.

"You two girls sisters?" Edna served the enormous salads.

"No," laughed Kate. "Why?"

"Don't know. You kinda look alike. Course when I stare
straight at you like this, there's not much resemblance. I
don't know. And you always order the same thing."

"In that case, I'll have tea," Kate laughed again. "With
lemon."

They ate silently, self-conscious of being the only ones in
the restaurant. Kate could hardly get down the lettuce.
She'd feel better after she made the phone call. She wouldn't
tell Josie, who would get nervous. But it was responsible to
report the intruder to the sheriff. "Excuse me. Now I've got
to use the bathroom," she said to Josie. "Don't let Edna
take my salad."

"I'll guard it with my life," Josie grinned.

The sheriff's number was posted beneath the fire station
number. She dialed and heard a funny, moist sound, as if

the man were eating or maybe clicking in his dentures. She concentrated on the sturdy black plastic of the phone.

"Hello," he said finally.

She began to report the incident.

"Listen, you're the second lady to call me about this in twenty minutes. Like I told the other one, there's nothing I can do unless the man is actually trespassing on your land. Since you've invited him back tomorrow, he ain't exactly trespassing."

"We didn't exactly invite him."

"Okay, if it makes you feel easier, I said I'll swing by about eight a.m. That's when the other lady said he'd be coming."

"Thank you, sir."

"Sir," she shook her head as she walked back to the table. She hadn't said "sir" in fifteen years.

Josie had finished her salad and was doodling on a paper napkin. Definitely signs of good mood. Kate sat down and stared at her until she looked up. "So I hear you have a date with the law tomorrow morning."

Josie smiled. "Hope you don't thinking I'm stepping out on you."

By the time Kate finished her salad, the cafe was getting crowded.

"Refills?" Edna approached with a pot of coffee and a pot of hot water. "No thanks, just the check," Josie said.

"Guess you girls didn't mind my asking if you was sisters?"

"No, no, not at all," they spoke in unison.

It was a warm, richly scented evening and they drove home with the top down. Jupiter came out early again. Josie thought how much she preferred Jupiter to the cold North Star.

They were both worn out as they collapsed on the couch together. Their feet on the fruit crate coffee table, they watched pink gain the horizon. It was almost pitch dark when Josie reached up to light the lanterns.

She hesitated a moment, remembering last night, and then proceeded. Light, voila, the room was filled with sharp corners and shiny surfaces. Kate picked up her book, but Josie drew it away, cuddling closer.

"Here?" Kate was surprised by her own resistance. After all, they were alone, five miles from town.

"Where then?" Josie tried to sound like Lauren Bacall.

Kate sighed with a breath that moved her whole body, a body, she noticed, which was becoming increasingly sensitive to the body next to her. "Mmmmm," she kissed Josie on her neck, sweet with late summer sweat.

When Josie opened her eyes, she thought she saw something. No, they had sealed off the sun porch this morning. She kissed Kate on the lips and was startled by a whisssh over her friend's head. "Bats," she said evenly, pulling Kate lower on the couch.

"Don't worry," Kate said. "I'll get rid of him."

Worry, Josie cringed. She wasn't worried; she was hysterical. Calm down, she told herself. Think about the invasion of Poland. This was her mother's approach to anxiety—distract yourself by thinking about people with *real* problems. Worry is a perversion of imagination.

Kate opened the windows and set forth again with the broom, but the bat wouldn't leave. Eventually it spiralled upstairs into the large sleeping loft. Kate shook her head and closed up the house against further intrusion. She shrugged and returned to the couch, where Josie was sitting up, considerably more collected than the previous night.

"It'll be okay," Kate said. "It'll just go to sleep. You know they're not really Transylvanian leeches. They're harmless little herbivores. And rather inept."

Herbivores. Josie thought about eating salad for absolution after she murdered the buck.

Kate reached over and brushed her lover's breast, but Josie pulled away. "Not now, sweetie. I can't just now."

Kate nodded. She picked up her book. Josie fiddled with a crossword puzzle. About ten o'clock, Kate yawned, "Bed?"

"OK," Josie was determined to be brave. "I'll go up first."

"Sure," Kate regarded her closely. "You light the candle up there. I'll get the lantern down here."

They settled comfortably in the double nylon sleeping bag. Kate blew out the light. She reached over to rub Josie's back in hopes something more might develop. Suddenly she heard a whissh, whissh, whissh.

"Looks like our friend is back." Kate tried to keep her voice light.

"Just a harmless little herbivore." Josie rolled to her side of the bed, putting a pillow over her head.

That night Josie dreamt that she had become mayor of Lincoln, Nebraska.

Kate slept fitfully, hardly dreaming, and waking with the first sun.

She lay and watched Josie breathing evenly, blowing the edges of her black hair, her body ripe and luscious in the soft light. If she woke up early enough, they could make love before Mr. Creepo arrived. And the sheriff. Had they made a mistake in phoning the sheriff?

The loft grew lighter. Kate lay on her back with her head on her palms, wondering where the bat had nested, about the reliability of her research assistant, whether she would go home for Christmas this year. Then she heard the noise.

Her entire body stiffened. No mistaking the sound of a car crawling down the gravel road toward their cabin. She checked her watch. Seven a.m. Shit. The sheriff wouldn't arrive until their bodies were cold. Maybe Josie would be safer if she just stayed in the house; maybe she wouldn't wake her. Yes, Kate pulled out of the sleeping bag. She was grabbed by the nightgown.

"Not so quick, brown fox," Josie said sleepily. "How about a cuddle?"

She was adorable in the morning, thought Kate, completely "dérangé" as Josie herself would admit, before two cups of coffee.

The noise outside grew closer and Kate tightened.

"Don't you even want to hear how I got elected mayor of Lincoln. . . ."

"Not now," Kate couldn't stem the panic in her own voice.

Josie sat up. "What is it?" Then she heard the truck's motor dying.

"I'll just go check in with him," Kate said nonchalantly. "You wait here and I'll come back to snuggle." She pulled on her clothes.

"No you don't, Joan of Arc." Josie stood up and tucked her nightshirt into a pair of jeans.

The two walked downstairs together.

The fat man was approaching the house empty-handed. His friend, also bulky and middle-aged, stayed behind, leaning against the red pickup truck.

Kate called out to him when he was three yards from the house. "Back again."

"Sorry to bother you, mam. As you can see we didn't bring no guns. We'll just get that deer and then git offa yer property as soon's we can."

His friend shuffled and looked at his feet.

"Okay," Kate said gruffly. "We don't want dead animals on the land. By the way, we finished him off for you yesterday."

The man opened his mouth in surprise. His friend moved forward, tugging him back. They closed up the truck and headed into the woods.

Josie watched until they were out of sight. Kate went inside to make coffee.

Half an hour later, as they sat down to breakfast, another vehicle crunched down the hill. Josie looked out at the black and white sedan. "Our hero, the sheriff."

They walked over to greet the sheriff, a solid man, who looked them over carefully.

"You the girls who called me yesterday?"

"Yes, we did," Josie smiled.

"Yes," Kate nodded, the "sir" gone as quickly as it had come. She didn't like his expression.

"Only *ladies* listed on the deed to this land, I see. Looked it up last night. All schoolteachers. Some kind of commune? Something religious?"

"Just friends." Kate stepped back.

"Edna says she thought you were sisters." He squinted against the bright sun. "One sort or another."

"Just friends." Kate's voice was more distant.

"Soooo," the sheriff held his ground. "You want to run through the nature of that problem again?"

As Kate talked with the sheriff, Josie inspected the hunters' pickup truck. The bumper sticker read, "I live in a cave and one good fuck is all I crave." Inside dice hung from the rearview mirror. On the seat were a parka and two empty cans of Dr. Pepper. The dashboard was plastered with several iridescent signs. The sun glared so that she could read only one. "Gas, Ass or Grass—No one rides for free."

The sheriff noticed her and observed, "Leon's truck. Just as I figured. Leon Bates, a local man. He's, well, he's strayed off the hunting trail before."

"Isn't there something you can do about him?" Josie felt the heat rising to her face. "He might have killed one of us. On our property. With a gun."

"Today," the sheriff's voice was cool, "today your friend tells me that he has no gun. That, in fact, you said he could come back here to get his buck. That right?"

Josie closed her eyes, feeling naive for imagining this man might protect them. Now bureaucracy seemed the only recourse. "Right. Can't we make some kind of complaint about what he did yesterday?"

"Sure can," the sheriff nodded. "If that's what you want."

"What do you mean?" Kate's back tightened.

"You're weekend folks, right?" He lit a cigarette.

"We work in the city, if that's what you mean," Kate spoke carefully, "and don't live here year around."

"None of my business what you all have going on here. None of Leon's business either. But if you file a complaint and we take it to court, well, he's bound to do some investigating and. . . ."

"There's nothing illegal about our land group," Josie snapped.

"Miss, miss, I never said anything about legal, illegal, but you know there are natural pests the law can't control. And it's better maybe not to get them roused."

Kate and Josie exchanged glances. "Well, perhaps we'll check with Loretta; her sister's a lawyer. We'll get back to you."

"Yes, mam," he grew more serious. "That about all for today, mam? I mean you said they didn't bring no guns with them. You feel safe enough on your own?"

"Yes," Josie said. "We're safe enough on our own."

"Then if you'll excuse me, it's almost eight and services start early around here," he stamped out his cigarette and softened. "Church is always open to outsiders and weekend people, by the way. Just three miles down, on the road by the gas station."

"I know where it is," Josie said. "Good-bye, sheriff."

They watched him roll up the hill, then returned to the house for breakfast. They were both too furious to talk. Kate hardly touched her food, watching out the window for the trespassers.

About ten o'clock, she saw two pregnant-looking men pulling a buck through the dust by its antlers. Her first thought was how powerful those antlers must be. She tightened and Josie looked up from her book. "At last."

It took the men ten minutes to reach the truck. They were huffing and sweating and Josie had to resist the urge to bring them a pitcher of water. She followed Kate out on the front porch.

Leon Bates glowered at them, as if weighing the value of

wasting breath for talk. He and his friend heaved the buck into the truck. On the second try, they made it.

Leon's friend wiped his hands on his jeans, waiting with an expression of excruciating embarrassment.

Leon straightened up, drew a breath and shouted. "That'll do it."

"Good," called Kate.

"Gotta ask one question," Leon leaned forward on his right leg. "What'd you have to go and bust his head for? Ruined a perfect trophy. Just look at the antlers. Would of been perfect."

"Come on, Leon," his friend callèd.

Kate stood firmly, hands on her hips. Josie tried to hold back the tears, but she couldn't and pivoted toward the cabin.

"The road's that way." Kate pointed. "Only goes in one direction."

Kate stamped into the house. "Damn them. Damn them!" she screamed.

"Hey, now." Josie reached up to her shoulders and pulled Kate toward her. "Hey now, relax, love."

"Don't tell me to relax. This man comes on our land, shoots living things, threatens us. And you tell me to relax." She banged her hand on the table.

Josie inhaled heavily and pulled Kate a little closer. "They've gone now." She looked over Kate's shoulder and out the back window, which gleamed in the mid-morning sun. "See, they're over the hill."

"Out of sight, that's what you think, you fool," Kate tried to draw apart.

Josie held tight, hoping to melt the contortions from her friend's face.

Kate pushed her away. Josie lost balance, hitting her head against a pane of glass in the sun porch door.

The glass cracked, sending a high-pitched rip through the room.

Josie ducked forward, her eyes tightly shut, just in time to avoid most of the showering glass fragments.

Drenched in sweat, Kate shook her and shouted, "Josie, Josie, are you all right? Oh, my god, Josie, are you all right?"

"We'll never keep out the bats this way," Josie laughed nervously, on the verge.

"Josie, I didn't mean it." Tears welled in Kate's eyes. "I love you, Josie, are you all right?"

Josie nodded. They held each other, shivering.

Josie stepped forward, "Okay, yes, but I feel a little like Tinkerbell. Scattering all this glitter."

"Tinkerbell!" Kate laughed and cried and choked. The room seemed to be closing in on them. Hot, tight, airless. She could feel herself listing.

"But you, hey," Josie frowned, "Let's go upstairs and have *you* lie down."

They sat on the bed, holding hands and staring out at the land. The day was hot, even dryer than yesterday, and the golden grass shimmered against the shadowy backdrop of the woods.

"We really should go down and clean up the glass, put a board over the shattered pane." Kate whispered.

"Yeah, if we don't head home soon, traffic's gonna be impossible."

Kate rested her head on Josie's breast. She smelled the musk from the black feathers beneath her arms. Her hand went to the soft nest at the bottom of Josie's generous belly. Josie slipped off her clothes. Kate followed. They sank down on the bed, swimming together again, sucked into the cool sleeping bag.

"Home," Josie murmured.

"Hmmm?" Kate inhaled the scents of Josie's sweat and sex. Forcing herself to be alert, she pulled back. Was her friend delirious? Maybe she had a concussion.

"Home," Josie kissed her with a passion so conscious as to take away both Kate's concern and her breath.

"Yes," Kate moved her fingers lower, separating the labia, swirling the honey thicker. "Yes."

Josie crawled on top of Kate, licking her shoulders, her breasts; burying her nose in her navel; kissing her thighs. Then she was distracted by a slow fizzzz, as if their air mattress were deflating.

Josie looked up. Two wasps hovered over them, bobbing and weaving and then lifting themselves abruptly out of vision. Maybe if she just continued Kate wouldn't notice. But it was too late.

"They always come out in the middle of the day," Kate said drearily. "For food. For their nests."

Josie shook her head, staring at the unsteady, fragile creatures.

"What the hell," Kate shrugged, inching away from Josie.

"What the hell," Josie whispered seductively. They returned to the pleasures between them. When they finished making love, Josie curled around Kate. She explained how she had been elected mayor of Lincoln, Nebraska.

The wasps wove over and around the two women. Even as they fell asleep.

Letting Bode

Kristina McGrath

Where's Bode? She stands right there in winter sunlight on hard Rosanna ground. With an ax, by the portable tree stump, in her overlarge clothes. All the plain pieces of her cut so clear in the sun you can't miss her, not ever, it's done, she's there.

What she's tossed off, I've stacked up perfect. I stand here by the finished part of the woodpile where the air is sweetest from newly cracked wood. I stand here doing arithmetic with Bode's body, counting the length of the ground and sky between us. Bode stands about one quarter high of the sky, straight up and down as the pines, four yards off in three-quarter profile, one quarter of her turned away to a place I'll never know. Singular, apart from me and pine shade, apart from fences, clouds, or what I feel about her, she stands there, teaching me about solitary.

Sharp winter sunlight tells her for a minute. Ohio sunlight snaps Bode and three acres into focus. It snatches out from behind the clouds, comes like the sound of something metal, and traps Bode, her running, into stillness. It gives Bode her edges back, her hips, her legs carved out against the land. She stands there, nowhere near anything but Bode. She starts and ends like a better time of our lives, so clear you could put it on a map: this was good time, this was Bode. This oblong of her body.

Ax head to the earth, she stands without leaning. The ax is just an extra forgotten thing. The hills behind her are extra. The grass white with frost under her boots is extra, too. My love is extra, and what I feel about her. It falls from me, it flies off into the somewhere of the bushes. She stands apart from me. And every true thing she is flies back into Bode without my business of loving her. It's settled, that's final, it's pure Bode. She stands there like I never knew her, touched her, said one word about her childhood, like I never crossed her path, like I never took her by the shoulders and turned her to me, like she never let me.

The whites of her hands swim out pure like the tips of newborns from the bunches of her overlarge sleeves. Bode was, is, and will be. It's just my eyes that change her with the sunlight and the shade. She stands at the land's center, and when the sunlight fades, the center of the land sweeps out, the margins of the land wash out, blending into Horry Cornby's property. The out and in sunlight lets her go and takes her back. It fades again. Shade sweeps across her as if she were some final tossed thing. She quivers out like candlelight, blending into pine shade and what I feel about her. It's more me now than Bode. Her soft scrubbed boots lost in brown February grass, her body lost in gray clothes against the sky. My eyes can't unmix her from the backdrop of the road and what I feel about her.

That's her cousin's thin ribbed sweater, gray, overlarge, bunched at the sleeves. Her body, what's narrow and made of bone, unknown underneath it. Turned away, she seems one-armed, the other hooked around her back by her thumb in a belt loop. I know it's that way from memory, from all the practice I had of looking at her. Bode's left arm near always had a crook in it, like it was broken once, but it never was; I asked. My mind fills it in. My eyes adjust to a darkness so deep that most of what I love is invisible.

Bode is the hardest part of darkness. Nothing stops her from being such a mystery, least of all my eyes. I try to know her in her own bones, apart from me and what I feel about her. But her bones are the saddest part of shadow I just can't touch. I'll never know her. With the sunlight hidden, the day is colored like glaciers. Snow-covered fields stretch out, big and gray as Erie, with the point of Bode somewhere in the middle, then gone, to the left, then gone, to the right, then gone, like a sorrow I am sure of that knows no east or west, no north or south, only motion. She blends, continuous as a steam. What I know of Bode is like a shadow; I accept it like a stream, I accept its journey. Maybe that's most of what you can know of someone, how they pass by, in full motion. You watch them if you're willing to see them go.

If I can't think of Bode today, I do away with motion, with the world at a slant from the window, a road rising into sunlight. And in the wind, stirring up Ohio, that rises like something I would like to know for all time, I do away with tassels out of nowhere, or the swing of a metal bucket on its hanging post, the metal sure call of it against the stud. I do away with chickweed through the cracks of snow, or a single deer come evening. Yes, I'm glad you were there in Rosanna, Ohio, twenty-four years ago. Otherwise, I might have missed some sensation like ice or honey; and in the touch of your cool damp skin coming in from the air of the field, I might have missed remembering in the mix of time, my mama hanging laundry in the new air, her hands pink and red like wet blossoms. I might have missed the colors of your house before they paled, or never heard the gate's creak before it quieted. Yes, I was glad to listen to what you had to tell me once, just because it meant you spoke, though nothing fell silent for months afterward but me, and nothing held still, but burst forth in all its color and sound, with its place in time, its loss. Pines held, then swept to their own motion. The water boiled. The pots and pans spoke in their loud voices. The glories shut. The straw chair baked dry in the sun. Snow fell and was taken by the scruff of the neck down the road under the wheels of trucks. The rains came. Yes, I was glad to have seen you once across a table, a field, or bed. Otherwise, I might have missed telling him in my mind, where he stood all dressed in meeting clothes, O daddy you look so pretty, and I took him in my arms. And in the night, I might have missed waking up laughing because I was sneaking as a child around the borders of mama's backyard, taking you along by the hand, leaving everyone behind but you, who was all that mattered in that particular dream, and you didn't even exist then, Bode.

Or now in Creek. Though you stand right there where snowfall trails its light and makes its mark in air. You've been here all along, in the slant of the road, in the tassels out of nowhere. The eyes inside me stared at you for twenty years when I didn't know I saw.

Now my eyes get used to Bode, to what I am given in light or shade. I let her slip. I let her be. I stand right here in Creek and she's clear again. Our aloneness seems like such an ancient thing, like the rocks, or sky, and the way things are. My eyes adjust. She starts and ends in the half-hearted light. She's there in her always found place on earth, in the country of her own bones. Though my feet cannot change from leaving, and her eyes cannot change to see me, and our hands cannot hold. The sunlight breathes us in and out.

Causes

Jacqueline Woodson

Some damn caseworker come by here today wantin' to
know how well I knowed Lisa. Yeah, we was tight. Shit,
Lisa and me go back so far I don't even try to remember no
more. She saying I had some sort of 'fluence on Lisa's life,
talkin' 'bout how Lisa lay there and yell my name all the
time. I guess I'd be yellin' somebody's name too if my ass
was strapped to a bed all day.

This damn caseworker talkin' 'bout there must of been
somethin' sexual 'tween the two of us. I'd of knocked some
fire out of her head if my cousin weren't sittin' there. I let
her know right off that we wasn't practicin' nobody's freak
innercourse. Let her know right off I could show her in the
Bible where the Lord destroyed a whole city for committin'
those acts! I ain't let on that she had hit a soft spot that
made me start 'memberin 'bout the time my mama said she
gone send me away to meet some boys 'cause all I ever talk
'bout is Lisa this and Lisa that. Ain't let her know neither
that it'll be a cold day in hell 'fore someone 'cuse me of
being in love with Lisa 'cause my mama ain't raise no dykes!

Me and Lisa go back so far I can still 'member us gettin'
our bloods somethin' like a week apart. First Lisa come
runnin' to my house screamin' "SaraMae! SaraMae! I got
my friend! I got it! I got it!". She just was smilin' and

carryin' on. And then the two of us ran into the bathroom to take a peek into her panties to see if there really was blood comin' outta her body. I kissed her on the cheek to let her know I was proud, weren't jealous or nothin'. Let her know I respected her, wishin' *my* friend would hurry up and come. But that ain't near none of that nastiness that caseworker talkin' 'bout!

Shit, I wouldn't a let that ol' woman in my house had it not been that I was throwin' somethin' out the window for Joe to catch. See, I wanted him to go buy me one of those real coconut pops they makin' now. And me standin' in the window countin' change see this woman all prissy wit' her hair all straightened and pulled tight in a bun like my grandmother's grandma would of wore.

"Kin I help you wit' somethin'?" I asked her real neighborly. See, I thought she was one of them undercover cops and if she was, I was gonna run to the back of the stairs and let Charlie know there was cops aroun' so he could hide his stash in my 'partment till the coast was clear. But this lady look up wit' her hands hidin' the sun from eyes; lookin' like she too scared to be outside let alone outside in this neighborhood, talkin' 'bout "Are you Mrs. Ferguson? I'm from the Belldaire Psychiatric Center. I want to ask you a few question about your friend Marilisa Paigne."

I told her to come on up the stairs and stop yellin' up and down the block about psychiatrics 'fore someone think *I'm* the one gone crazy.

Now I don't live in the nicest part of Brooklyn but I got a big living room that I keeps real clean. I like to let people come in and tell me how nice it look with everything all polished and all. So even though I saw this lady was dressed in a fine expensive-lookin' suit, I wasn't the least bit shy to invite her up and let her see what I got.

I tell her to sit down in the blue cushion chair. That's the one my mama left to me. I guess it's a antique. I asked her if she'd like a cup of tea but she looking all nervous and squinchin' up in my chair like it got lice in it and all and I guess she was just too good to say yeah. I seen the way she looked at the cup I was holdin'. It's a old plastic cup that's gotten yellow in its old age but I refuse to drink tea outta anything else. It gives it just the right flavor, you know? But she sittin' lookin' at the cup talkin' 'bout how she had lunch and was tryin' to watch her weight and all. Lookin' at her skinny body, I know she better be watchin' somethin' before it disappear. It didn't bother me that she didn't want no tea though because it's a pain makin' a fresh pot anyway. I just as well drink what I had made that mornin'.

So Miss Diet Lady sits there and start takin' out all these papers 'bout Lisa. I told her if she think I'm the cause of Lisa tryna do herself in, she was wrong. Me and Lisa was tight but when she got involve with that ol' no good Johnnie Ray, I told her she was on her own. See, Johnnie Ray thought he was a real lady's man. He come boppin' down the streeet all scrubbed up for Saturday night with that conked hair tellin' me it ain't conked, it's "relaxed." I just know when you put lye in your naturally kinky hair, it's conked! But I told Lisa that man wasn't no better for her than chitlins for high blood pressure. Ol' Lisa had to find out for herself though. Caught her right in the act at that party. I was watchin' Lisa 'cause I hadn't seen her in a long time. Saw she had let her hair grow out pretty, put some makeup on and bought a new dress. I looked at her across the room and had to squeeze my man's hand to keep from callin' out to her. You see, my ol' man didn't like me callin' ladies across the room, said it made it seem like they was *my* lady or somethin'. Well, I told this to the caseworker and she come pipin' up 'bout how they may be some s'pressed feelings of homosexuality or somethin'. That's when I was gonna knock those pinch-nose glasses from her head 'cause my mama ain't raise no dykes! I got two kids, one four and one six to tell anybody I ain't s'pressin' no feelings for a woman.

Lisa and me, we was just tight, that's all. Ain't nothin' wrong with two women bein' tight. Just like it probably ain't nothin' wrong with Lisa. She was fine till she seen that no

good Johnnie Ray slow grinding with ol' crater-face Alice.
That's when she asked me to take a walk with her 'round
the block, help her think things out a little bit. My ol' man
wasn't likin' it a bit neither but I let him know he *would* get
over it!

So me and Lisa went on outside and shared a joint in the
park. Since it was September beginnin', it was real nice out,
the leaves smellin' like fall and the night real warm. Then
Lisa starts in 'bout how she don't feel the things she should
for Johnnie Ray and how she like him 'cause the other women
do and she wants to show women that she can get a good-
looking man like him. I don't think Johnnie Ray is anything to
write home to the boys about but that was Lisa's ol' man
and it wasn't none of my business how he look. Lisa was
going on about how her feelings for him weren't right and
how she needed someone to be soft like I was that time I
kissed her. I told her she should have some babies because
babies are soft. But she kept goin' on and on' 'bout how she
needs a special some kind of love that a lot of people can't
understand. I didn't know what she was talkin' 'bout and
figured it was the reefer talkin' so I just said "Uh huh" and
"Yeah baby, I know what you mean" when I was s'poze to.

We got back to the party and Johnnie Ray and his grind
partner had split. Lisa looked like she didn't even care.
Looked a little bit happy about it if you ask me. So I
took my ol' man home 'cause he was near drunk and actin'
crazy. I told Lisa to get in touch wit' me and we could talk
some more. But she was lookin' at her drink and not really
listenin'. Lisa and me was tight though, so I know she
heard. I ain't tell all this to that damn social worker 'cause
what she know about growin' up tight in Brooklyn. Growin'
up tight meant tellin' Lisa what it felt like when you did it
with someone for the first time. I ain't like some people and
say it didn't hurt, because it sure did. Felt like a train was
tryna knock out its own tunnel 'tween my legs or somethin'.
Lisa said she ain't want to feel no pain like that if she could
help it. But then I showed her how to kiss for the first time

so that spit didn't come out of the edge of your mouth and she liked that. We kissed together a lot, but that was only for practice. That's what I should have told her that night in the park when she said she wanted to feel the softness like when we used to kiss. I should've told her that was just for practice until the real thing happened. Then she wouldn't be all mixed up about everything. I should have told her men make women feel different things. Then she wouldn't be crazy now.

I guess I'm the cause for all her craziness. I ain't 'splain things the right way. But that caseworker woman got on my nerves so bad, I was sorry I even thought about throwin' that change out the window. No one tol' me to be all showoffy wantin' someone to see the little bit I got. My ol' man say that's gonna always be my downfall.

I had to shoo that woman outta my house quick. Seem to me, she was tryna get me in that crazy hospital with Lisa. I showed her pictures of the kids and my ol' man. Showed her my Bible and tol' her if she want, I'd show her where Sodom and Gomorrah was destroyed for the likes of the kinds of peoples she was talkin' 'bout. Ain't nothin' wrong wit' bein' tight though and that's what we was.

We was real close and went way, way back. But I ain't crazy and I ain't no dyke. Lisa just got a little mixed up 'bout the way things s'pozed to be. Now she laying strapped down in some crazy hospital talkin' 'bout "SaraMae! SaraMae!" but she don't understand I got these two kids now and can't be playin' those girl-games anymore. I done teached her all I could 'bout kissin' and such. I can't tell her nothin' 'bout softness though 'cause my mama ain't raise no dykes!

A Letter to Harvey Milk

Lesléa Newman

for Harvey Milk 1930–1978

I.

The teacher says we should write about our life, everything
that happened today. So *nu,* what's there to tell? Why
should today be different than any other day? May 5, 1986.
I get up, I have myself a coffee, a little cottage cheese, half
an English muffin. I get dressed. I straighten up the house a
little, nobody should drop by and see I'm such a slob. I go
down to the Senior Center and see what's doing. I play a
little cards. I have some lunch, a bagel with cheese. I read a
sign in the cafeteria. Writing Class 2:00. I think to myself,
why not, something to pass the time. So at two o'clock I go
in. The teacher says we should write about our life.

Listen, I want to say to this teacher, I. B. Singer I'm not.
You think anybody cares what I did all day? Even my own
children, may they live and be well, don't call. You think
the whole world is waiting to see what Harry Weinberg had
for breakfast?

The teacher is young and nice. She says everybody has
something important to say. Yeah, sure, when you're young
you believe things like that. She has short brown hair and
big eyes, a nice figure, *zaftig* like my poor Fannie, may she

rest in peace. She's wearing a Star of David around her neck, hanging from a purple string, that's nice. She gave us all notebooks and told us we're gonna write something every day, and if we want we can even write at home. Who'd a thunk it, me—Harry Weinberg, seventy-seven-years old—scribbling in a notebook like a schoolgirl. Why not, it passes the time.

So after the class I go to the store. I pick myself up a little orange juice, a few bagels, a nice piece of chicken. I shouldn't starve to death. I go up, I put on the slippers, I eat the chicken, I watch a little TV, I write in this notebook, I get ready for bed. *Nu*, for this somebody should give me a Pulitzer Prize?

II.

Today the teacher tells us something about herself. She's a Jew, this we know from the *Mogen David* she wears around her neck. She tells us she wants to collect stories from old Jewish people, to preserve our history. *Oy*, such stories that I could tell her, shouldn't be preserved by nobody. She tells us she's learning Yiddish. For what, I wonder. I can't figure this teacher out. She's young, she's pretty, she shouldn't be with the old people so much. I wonder is she married. She doesn't wear a ring. Her grandparents won't tell her stories, she says, and she's worried that the Jews her age won't know nothing about the culture, about life in the *shtetls*. Believe me, life in the *shtetl* is nothing worth knowing about. Hunger and more hunger. Better off we're here in America, the past is past.

Then she gives us our homework, the homework we write in the class, it's a little *meshugeh*, but alright. She wants us to write a letter to somebody from our past, somebody who's no longer with us. She reads us a letter a child wrote to Abraham Lincoln, like an example. Right away I see everybody's getting nervous. So I raise my hand. "Teacher," I say, "you can tell me maybe how to address such a letter?

There's a few things I've wanted to ask my wife for a long time." Everybody laughs. Then they start to write.

I sit for a few minutes, thinking about Fannie, thinking about my sister Frieda, my mother, my father, may they all rest in peace. But it's the strangest thing, the one I really want to write to is Harvey.

Dear Harvey:
      You had to go get yourself killed for being a *faygeleh?* You couldn't let somebody else have such a great honor? Alright, alright, so you liked the boys, I wasn't wild about the idea. But I got used to it. I never said you wasn't welcome in my house, did I?
      Nu, Harvey, you couldn't leave well enough alone? You had your own camera store, your own business, what's bad? You couldn't keep still about the boys, you weren't satisfied until the whole world knew? Harvey Milk, with the big ears and the big ideas, had to go make himself something, a big politician. I know, I know, I said, "Harvey, make something of yourself, don't be an old *shmegeggie* like me, Harry the butcher." So now I'm eating my words, and they stick like a chicken bone in my old throat.
      It's a rotten world, Harvey, and rottener still without you in it. You know what happened to that *momzer,* Dan White? They let him out of jail, and he goes and kills himself so nobody else should have the pleasure. Now you know me, Harvey, I'm not a violent man. But this was too much, even for me. In the old country, I saw things you shouldn't know from, things you couldn't imagine one person could do to another. But here in America, a man climbs through the window, kills the Mayor of San Francisco, kills Harvey Milk, and a couple years later he's walking around on the street? This I never thought I'd see in my whole life. But from a country that kills the Rosenbergs, I should expect something different?
      Harvey, you should be glad you weren't around for the trial. I read about it in the papers. The lawyer, that son of a bitch, said Dan White ate too many Twinkies the night before he killed you, so his brain wasn't working

right. Twinkies, *nu,* I ask you. My kids ate Twinkies
when they were little, did they grow up to be murderers,
God forbid? And now, do they take the Twinkies down
from the shelf, somebody else shouldn't go a little crazy,
climb through a window, and shoot somebody? No, they
leave them right there next to the cupcakes and the
donuts, to torture me every time I go to the store to pick
up a few things, I shouldn't starve to death.

Harvey, I think I'm losing my mind. You know what I
do every week? Every week I go to the store, I buy a bag
of jelly beans for you, you should have something to *nosh*
on, I remember what a sweet tooth you have. I put them
in a jar on the table, in case you should come in with
another crazy petition for me to sign. Sometimes I think
you're gonna just walk through my door and tell me it
was another *meshugeh* publicity stunt.

Harvey, now I'm gonna tell you something. The night
you died the whole city of San Francisco cried for you.
Thirty thousand people marched in the street, I saw it on
TV. Me, I didn't go down. I'm an old man, I don't walk
so good, they said there might be riots. But no, there
were no riots. Just people walking in the street, quiet,
each one with a candle, until the street looked like the
sky all lit up with a million stars. Old people, young
people, black people, white people, Chinese people. You
name it, they were there. I remember thinking, Harvey
must be so proud, and then I remembered you were dead
and such a lump rose in my throat, like a grapefruit it
was, and then the tears ran down my face like rain. Can
you imagine, Harvey, an old man like me, sitting alone in
his apartment, crying and carrying on like a baby? But
it's the God's truth. Never did I carry on so in all my life.

And then all of a sudden I got mad. I yelled at the
people on TV: for getting shot you made him into such a
hero? You couldn't march for him when he was alive, he
couldn't *shep* a little *naches?*

But *nu,* what good does getting mad do, it only makes
my pressure go up. So I took myself a pill, calmed myself
down.

Then they made speeches for you, Harvey. The same
people who called you a *shmuck* when you were alive, now

you were dead, they were calling you a *mensh*. You were a *mensh*, Harvey, a *mensh* with a heart of gold. You were too good for this rotten world. They just weren't ready for you.

Oy Harveleh, alav ha-sholom,
                                                Harry

III.

Today the teacher asks me to stay for a minute after class. *Oy,* what did I do wrong now, I wonder. Maybe she didn't like my letter to Harvey? Who knows?

After the class she comes and sits down next to me. She's wearing purple pants and a white T-shirt. *"Feh,"* I can just hear Fannie say. "God forbid she should wear a skirt? Show off her figure a little? The girls today dressing like boys and the boys dressing like girls—this I don't understand."

"Mr. Weinberg," the teacher says.

"Call me Harry," I says.

"O.K., Harry," she says. "I really liked the letter you wrote to Harvey Milk. It was terrific, really. It meant a lot to me. It even made me cry."

I can't even believe my own ears. My letter to Harvey Milk made the teacher cry?

"You see, Harry," she says, "I'm gay, too. And there aren't many Jewish people your age that are so open-minded. At least that I know. So your letter gave me lots of hope. In fact, I was wondering if you'd consider publishing it."

Publishing my letter? Again I couldn't believe my own ears. Who would want to read a letter from Harry Weinberg to Harvey Milk? No, I tell her. I'm too old for fame and glory. I like the writing class, it passes the time. But what I write is my own business. The teacher looks sad for a moment, like a cloud passes over her eyes. Then she says, "Tell me about Harvey Milk. How did you meet him? What was he like?" *Nu,* Harvey, you were a pain in the ass when you were alive, you're still a pain in the ass now that you're dead. Everybody wants to hear about Harvey.

So I tell her. I tell her how I came into the camera shop one day with a roll of film from when I went to visit the grandchildren. How we started talking, and I said, "Milk, that's not such a common name. Are you related to the Milks in Woodmere?" And so we found out we were practically neighbors forty years ago, when the children were young, before we moved out here. Gracie was almost the same age as Harvey, a couple years older, maybe, but they went to different schools. Still, Harvey leans across the counter and gives me such a hug, like I'm his own father.

I tell her more about Harvey, how he didn't believe there was a good *kosher* butcher in San Francisco, how he came to my store just to see. But all the time I'm talking I'm thinking to myself, no, it can't be true. Such a gorgeous girl like this goes with the girls, not with the boys? Such a *shanda*. Didn't God in His wisdom make a girl a girl and a boy a boy—boom they should meet, boom they should get married, boom they should have babies, and that's the way it is? Harvey I loved like my own son, but this I never could understand. And *nu*, why was the teacher telling me this, it's my business who she sleeps with? She has some sadness in her eyes, this teacher. Believe me I've known such sadness in my life, I can recognize it a hundred miles away. Maybe she's lonely. Maybe after class one day I'll take her out for a coffee, we'll talk a little bit, I'll find out.

IV.

It's 3:00 in the morning, I can't sleep. So *nu*, here I am with this crazy notebook. Who am I kidding, maybe I think I'm Yitzhak Peretz? What would the children think, to see their old father sitting up in his bathrobe with a cup of tea, scribbling in his notebook? *Oy, meyn kinder*, they should only live and be well and call their old father once in a while.

Fannie used to keep up with them. She could be such a *nudge*, my Fannie. "What's the matter, you're too good to call your old mother once in a while?" she'd yell into the phone. Then there'd be a pause. "Busy-shmusy," she'd yell even louder. "Was I too busy to change your diapers? Was I too busy to put food into your mouth?" *Oy*, I haven't got the strength, but Fannie could she yell and carry on.

You know sometimes, in the middle of the night, I'll reach across the bed for Fannie's hand. Without even thinking, like my hand got a mind of its own, it creeps across the bed, looking for Fannie's hand. After all this time, fourteen years she's been dead, but still, a man gets used to a few things. Forty-two years, the body doesn't forget. And my little *Faigl* had such hands, little *hentelehs*, tiny like a child's. But strong. Strong from kneading *challah*, from scrubbing clothes, from rubbing the children's backs to put them to sleep. My Fannie, she was so ashamed from those hands. After thirty-five years of marriage when finally, I could afford to buy her a diamond ring, she said no. She said it was too late already, she'd be ashamed. A girl needs nice hands to show off a diamond, her hands were already ruined, better yet buy a new stove.

Ruined? *Feh*. To me her hands were beautiful. Small, with veins running through them like rivers, and cracks in the skin like the desert. A hundred times I've kicked myself for not buying Fannie that ring.

V.

Today in the writing class the teacher read my notebook. Then she says I should make a poem about Fannie. "A poem," I says to her, "now Shakespeare you want I should be?" She says I have a good eye for detail. I says to her, "Excuse me, Teacher, you live with a woman for forty-two years, you start to notice a few things."

She helps me. We do it together, we write a poem called "Fannie's Hands":

Fannie's hands are two little birds
that fly into her lap.

Her veins are like rivers.
Her skin is cracked like the desert.
Her strong little hands
baked *challah,* scrubbed clothes,
rubbed the children's backs.
Her strong little hands
and my big clumsy hands
fit together in the night
like pieces of a jigsaw puzzle
made in Heaven, by God.

So *nu*, who says you can't teach an old dog new tricks? I read it to the class and such a fuss they made. "A regular Romeo," one of them says. "If only my husband, may he live and be well, would write such a poem for me," says another. I wish Fannie was still alive, I could read it to her. Even the teacher was happy, I could tell, but still, there was a ring of sadness around her eyes.

After the class I waited till everybody left, they shouldn't get the wrong idea, and I asked the teacher would she like to go get a coffee. "*Nu*, it's enough writing already," I said. "Come, let's have a little treat."

So we take a walk, it's a nice day. We find a diner, nothing fancy, but clean and quiet. I try to buy her a piece of cake, a sandwich maybe, but no, all she wants is coffee.

So we sit and talk a little. She wants to know about my childhood in the old country, she wants to know about the boat ride to America, she wants to know did my parents speak Yiddish to me when I was growing up. "Harry," she says to me, "when I hear old people talking Yiddish, it's like a love letter blowing in the wind. I try to run after them, and sometimes I catch a phrase that makes me cry or a word that makes me laugh. Even if I don't understand, it always touches my heart."

Oy, this teacher has some strange ideas. "Why do you want to speak Jewish?" I ask her. "Here in America, everybody speaks English. You don't need it. What's done is done, what's past is past. You shouldn't go with the old people so much. You should go out, make friends, have a good time. You got some troubles you want to talk about? Maybe I shouldn't pry," I say, "but you shouldn't look so sad, a young girl like you. When you're old you got plenty to be sad. You shouldn't think about the old days so much, let the dead rest in peace. What's done is done."

I took a swallow of my coffee, to calm down my nerves. I was getting a little too excited.

"Harry, listen to me," the teacher says. "I'm thirty years old and no one in my family will talk to me because I'm gay. It's all Harvey Milk's fault. He made such an impression on me. You know, when he died, what he said, 'If a bullet enters my brain, let that bullet destroy every closet door.' So when he died, I came out to everyone—the people at work, my parents. I felt it was my duty, so the Dan Whites of the world wouldn't be able to get away with it. I mean, if every single gay person came out—just think of it!—everyone would see they had a gay friend or a gay brother or a gay cousin or a gay teacher. Then they couldn't say things like 'Those gays should be shot.' Because they'd be saying you should shoot my neighbor or my sister or my daughter's best friend."

I never saw the teacher get so excited before. Maybe a politician she should be. She reminded me a little bit of Harvey.

"So *nu*, what's the problem?" I ask.

"The problem is my parents," she says with a sigh, and such a sigh I never heard from a young person before. "My parents haven't spoken to me since I told them I was gay. 'How could you do this to us?' they said. I wasn't doing anything to them. I tried to explain I couldn't help being gay, like I couldn't help being a Jew, but that they didn't want to hear. So I haven't spoken to them in eight years."

"Eight years, *Gottenyu*," I say to her. This I never heard in my whole life. A father and a mother cut off their own daughter like that. Better they should cut off their own hand. I thought about Gracie, a perfect daughter she's not, but your child is your child. When she married the *Goy*, Fannie threatened to put her head in the oven, but she got over it. Not to see your own daughter for eight years, and such a smart, gorgeous girl, such a good teacher, what a *shanda*.

So what can I do, I ask. Does she want me to talk to them, a letter maybe I could write. Does she want I should adopt her, the hell with them, I make a little joke. She smiles. "Just talking to you makes me feel better," she says. So *nu*, now I'm Harry the social worker. She says that's why she wants the old people's stories so much, she doesn't know nothing from her own family history. She wants to know about her own people, maybe write a book. But it's hard to get the people to talk to her, she says, she doesn't understand.

"Listen, Teacher," I tell her. "These old people have stories you shouldn't know from. What's there to tell? Hunger and more hunger. Suffering and more suffering. I buried my sister over twenty years ago, my mother, my father—all dead. You think I could just start talking about them like I just saw them yesterday? You think I don't think about them every day? Right here I keep them," I say, pointing to my heart. "I try to forget them, I should live in peace, the dead are gone. Talking about them won't bring them back. You want stories, go talk to somebody else. I ain't got no stories."

I sat down then, I didn't even know I was standing up, I got so excited. Everybody in the diner was looking at me, a crazy man shouting at a young girl.

Oy, and now the teacher was cryin. "I'm sorry," I says to her. "You want another coffee?"

"No thanks, Harry," she says. "I'm sorry, too."

"Forget it. We can just pretend it never happened," I say, and then we go.

VI.

All this crazy writing has shaken me up inside a little bit. Yesterday I was walking home from the diner, I thought I saw Harvey walking in front of me. No, it can't be, I says to myself, and my heart started to pound so, I got afraid I shouldn't drop dead in the street from a heart attack. But then the man turned around and it wasn't Harvey. It didn't even look like him at all.

I got myself upstairs and took myself a pill, I could feel my pressure was going up. All this talk about the past— Fannie, Harvey, Frieda, my mother, my father—what good does it do? This teacher and her crazy ideas. Did I ever ask my mother, my father, what their childhood was like? What nonsense. Better I shouldn't know.

So today is Saturday, no writing class, but still I'm writing in this crazy notebook. I ask myself, Harry, what can I do to make you feel a little better? And I answer myself, make me a nice chicken soup.

You think an old man like me can't make chicken soup? Let me tell you, on all the holidays it was Harry that made the soup. Every *Pesach* it was Harry skimming the *shmaltz* from the top of the pot, it was Harry making the *kreplach*. I ask you, where is it written that a man shouldn't know from chicken soup?

So I take myself down to the store, I buy myself a nice chicken, some carrots, some celery, some parsley—onions I already got, parsnips I can do without. I'm afraid I shouldn't have a heart attack *shlepping* all that food up the steps, but thank God, I make it alright.

I put up the pot with water, throw everything in onc-two-three, and soon the whole house smells from chicken soup.

I remember the time Harvey came to visit and there I was with my apron on, skimming the *shmaltz* from the soup. Did he kid me about that! The only way I could get him to keep still was to invite him to dinner. "Listen, Harvey," I says to him. "Whether you're a man or a woman, it doesn't matter. You gotta learn to cook. When you're old, nobody cares. Nobody will do for you. You gotta learn to do for yourself."

"I won't live past fifty, Har," he says, smearing a piece of rye bread with *shmaltz*.

"Nobody wants to grow old, believe me, I know," I says to him. "But listen, it's not so terrible. What's the alternative? Nobody wants to die young, either." I take off my apron and sit down with him.

"No, I mean it Harry," he says to me with his mouth full. "I won't make it to fifty. I've always known it. I'm a politician. A gay politician. Someone's gonna take a pot shot at me. It's a risk you gotta take."

The way he said it, I tell you, a chill ran down my back like I never felt before. He was forty-seven at the time, just a year before he died.

VII.

Today after the writing class, the teacher tells us she's going away for two days. Everyone makes a big fuss, the class they like so much already. She tells us she's sorry, something came up she has to do. She says we can come have class without her, the room will be open, we can read to each other what we write in our notebooks. Someone asks her what we should write about.

"Write me a letter," she says. "Write a story called 'What I Never Told Anyone.' "

So, after everyone leaves, I ask her does she want to go out, have a coffee, but she says no, she has to go home and pack.

I tell her wherever she's going she should have a good time.

"Thanks, Harry," she says. "You'll be here when I get back?"

"Sure," I tell her. "I like this crazy writing. It passes the time."

She swings a big black bookbag onto her shoulder, a regular Hercules this teacher is, and she smiles at me. "I gotta run, Harry. Have a good week." She turns and walks away and something on her bookbag catches my eye. A big shiny pin that spells out her name all fancy-shmancy in rhinestones: Barbara. And under that, right away I see sewn onto her bookbag an upside-down pink triangle.

I stop in my tracks, stunned. No, it can't be, I says to myself. Maybe it's just a design? Maybe she doesn't know from this? My heart is beating fast now, I know I should go home, take myself a pill, my pressure, I can feel it going up.

But I just stand there. And then I get mad. What, she thinks maybe I'm blind as well as old. I can't see what's right in front of my nose? Or maybe we don't remember such things? What right does she have to walk in here with that, that thing on her bag, to remind us of what we been through? Haven't we seen enough?

Stories she wants. She wants we should cut our hearts open and give her stories so she could write a book. Well, alright, now I'll tell her a story.

This is what I never told anyone. One day, maybe seven, eight years ago—no, maybe longer, I think Harvey was still alive—one day Izzie comes knocking on my door. I open the door and there's Izzie, standing there, his face white as a sheet. I bring him inside, I make him a coffee. "Izzie, what is it," I says to him. "Something happened to the children, to the grandchildren, God forbid?"

He sits down, he doesn't drink his coffee. He looks through me like I'm not even there. Then he says, "Harry, I'm walking down the street, you know I had a little lunch at the Center, and then I come outside, I see a young man, maybe twenty-five, a good-looking guy, walking toward me. He's wearing black pants, a white shirt, and on his shirt he's got a pink triangle."

"So," I says. "A pink triangle, a purple triangle, they wear all kinds of crazy things these days."

"*Heshel*," he tells me, "don't you understand? The gays

are wearing pink triangles just like the war, just like in the camps."

No, this I can't believe. Why would they do a thing like that? But if Izzie says it, it must be true. Who would make up such a thing?

"He looked a little bit like *Yussl*," Izzie says, and then he begins to cry, and such a cry like I never heard. Like a baby he was, with the tears streaming down his cheeks and his shoulders shaking with great big sobs. Such moans and groans I never heard from a grown man in all my life. I thought maybe he was gonna have a heart attack the way he was carrying on. I didn't know what to do. I was afraid the neighbors would hear, they shouldn't call the police, such sounds he was making. Fifty-eight years old he was, but he looked like a little boy sitting there, sniffling. And who was *Yussl*? Thirty years we'd been friends, and I never heard from *Yussl*.

So finally, I put my arms around him, and I held him, I didn't know what else to do. His body was shaking so, I thought his bones would crack from knocking against each other. Soon his body got quiet, but then all of sudden his mouth got noisy.

"Listen, *Heshel*, I got to tell you something, something I never told nobody in my whole life. I was young in the camps, nineteen, maybe twenty when they took us away." The words poured from his mouth like a flood. "*Yussl* was my best friend in the camps. Already I saw my mother, my father, my Hannah marched off to the ovens. *Yussl* was the only one I had to hold on to.

"One morning, during the selection, they pointed me to the right, *Yussl* to the left. I went a little crazy, I ran after him. 'No, he stays with me, they made a mistake,' I said, and I grabbed him by the hand and dragged him back in line. Why the guard didn't kill us right then, I couldn't tell you. Nothing made sense in that place.

"*Yussl* and I slept together on a wooden bench. That night I couldn't sleep. It happened pretty often in that place. I would close my eyes and see such things that would make me scream in the night, and for that I could get shot. I don't know what was worse, asleep or awake. All I saw was suffering.

"On this night, *Yussl* was awake, too. He didn't move a muscle, but I could tell. Finally he said my name, just a whisper, but something broke in me and I began to cry. He put his arms around me and we cried together, such a close call we'd had.

"And then he began to kiss me. 'You saved my life,' he whispered, and he kissed my eyes, my cheeks, my lips. And Harry, I kissed him back. Harry, I never told nobody this before. I, we . . . we, you know, that was such a place that hell, I couldn't help it. The warmth of his body was just too much for me and Hannah was dead already and we would soon be dead too, probably, so what did it matter?"

He looked up at me then, the tears streaming from his eyes. "It's O.K., Izzic," I said. "Maybe I would have done the same."

"There's more, Harry," he says, and I got him a tissue, he should blow his nose. What more could there be?

"This went on for a couple of months maybe, just every once in a while when we couldn't sleep. He'd whisper my name and I'd answer with his, and then we'd, you know, we'd touch each other. We were very, very quiet, but who knows, maybe some other boys in the barracks were doing the same.

"To this day I don't know how it happened, but somehow someone found out. One day *Yussl* didn't come back to the barracks at night. I went almost crazy, you can imagine, all the things that went through my mind, the things they might have done to him, those lousy Nazis. I looked everywhere, I asked everyone, three days he was gone. And then on the third day, they lined us up after supper and there they had *Yussl*. I almost collapsed on the ground when I saw him. They had him on his knees with his hands tied behind his back. His face was swollen so, you couldn't even see his eyes. His clothes were stained with blood. And on his uniform they had sewn a pink triangle, big, twice the size of our yellow stars.

"*Oy*, did they beat him but good. 'Who's your friend?' they yelled at him. 'Tell us and we'll let you live.' But no, he wouldn't tell. He knew they were lying, he knew they'd kill us both. They asked him again and again, 'Who's your friend? Tell us which one he is.' And every time he said no, they'd crack him with a whip until the blood ran from him like a river. Such a sight he was, like I've never seen. How he remained conscious I'll never know.

"Everything inside me was broken after that. I wanted to run to his side, but I didn't dare, so afraid I was. At one point he looked at me, right in the eye, as though he was saying, *Izzie, save yourself. Me, I'm finished, but you, you got a chance to live through this and tell the world our story*.

"Right after he looked at me, he collapsed, and they shot him, Harry, right there in front of us. Even after he was dead they kicked him in the head a little bit. They left his body out there for two days, as a warning to us. They whipped us all that night, and from then on we had to sleep with all the lights on and with our hands on top of the blankets. Anyone caught with their hands under the blankets would be shot.

"He died for me, Harry, they killed him for that, was it such a terrible thing? *Oy*, I haven't thought about *Yussl* for twenty-five years maybe, but when I saw that kid on the street today, it was too much." And then he started crying again, and he clung to me like a child.

So what could I do? I was afraid he shouldn't have a heart attack, maybe he was having a nervous breakdown, maybe I should get the doctor. *Vay iss mir*, I never saw anybody so upset in my whole life. And such a story, *Gottenyu*.

"Izzie, come lie down," I says, and I took him by the hand to the bed. I laid him down, I took off his shoes, and still he was crying. So what could I do? I lay down with him,

I held him tight. I told him he was safe, he was in America. I don't know what else I said, I don't think he heard me, still he kept crying.

I stroked his head, I held him tight. "Izzie, it's alright," I said. "Izzie, Izzie, *Izzaleh*." I said his name over and over, like a lullaby, until his crying got quiet. He said my name once softly, *Heshel*, or maybe he said *Yussl*, I don't remember, but thank God he finally fell asleep. I tried to get up from the bed, but Izzie held onto me tight. So what could I do? Izzie was my friend for thirty years, for him I would do anything. So I held him all night long, and he slept like a baby.

And this is what I never told nobody, not even Harvey. That there in that bed, where Fannie and I slept together for forty-two years, me and Izzie spent the night. Me, I didn't sleep a wink, such a lump in my throat I had, like the night Harvey died.

Izzie passed on a couple months after that. I saw him a few more times, and he seemed different somehow. How, I couldn't say. We never talked about that night. But now that he had told someone his deepest secret, he was ready to go, he could die in peace. Maybe now that I told, I can die in peace, too?

VIII.

Dear Teacher:

You said write what you never told nobody, and write you a letter. I always did all my homework, such a student I was. So *nu*, I got to tell you something. I can't write in this notebook no more, I can't come no more to the class. I don't want you should take offense, you're a good teacher and a nice girl. But me, I'm an old man, I don't sleep so good at night, these stories are like a knife in my heart. Harvey, Fannie, Izzie, *Yussl*, my father, my mother, let them all rest in peace. The dead are gone. Better to live for today.

What good does remembering do, it doesn't bring back the dead. Let them rest in peace.

But Teacher, I want you should have my notebook. It doesn't have nice stories in it, no love letters, no happy endings for a nice girl like you. A bestseller it ain't, I guarantee. Maybe you'll put it in a book someday, the world shouldn't forget.

Meanwhile, good luck to you, Teacher. May you live and be well and not get shot in the head like poor Harvey, may he rest in peace. Maybe someday we'll go out, have a coffee again, who knows? But me, I'm too old for this crazy writing. I remember too much, the pen is like a knife twisting in my heart.

One more thing, Teacher. Between parents and children, it's not so easy. Believe me, I know. Don't give up on them. One father, one mother, it's all you got. If you were my *tochter*, I'd be proud of you.

Harry

Fruit of the Loom Athletic Undershirts

Cathy Cockrell

Washed and folded athletic undershirts, stacked on open shelves, offer fantasies and facts of you, them, us and me, skin and shoulder blades and bone, angles of flesh and dominance control and freedom. On city streets, July middays, men sit on milk crates, eating lunch and drinking. With particles of sweat caught along their brows, in faded denim jeans and white athletic undershirts, they talk; wear their vulnerable weapons pressing the insides of their pants; claim the space stretching from this leg to that, spread wide. They stand, sit, curse and shout and shove, bear hidden miniature piles of colored fruit on the label flat against each neck, give a recognizable form to the formlessness of athletic under-shirts. They claim the space stretching from this knee to that, spread wide, and the rectangles of pavement where women pass rapidly, eyes averted.

Running vertically from the yoke below their neck chains to the bottom machine-stitched edge below the waist are high, then low, ridges of cotton along whose parallels the body carves shapes of youth and power. We wear these undershirts too—either boldly, barely hiding our breasts, or prudently, under other shirts. Your silver labyris on the delicate chain falls near the shirt's top edge; the vertical ribs follow the contours of your breasts, your bones, your solid muscular body. By the end of the day, or the next, depend-ing on humidity and heat, the shirt will stretch, lose tone, fall away in places where it once hugged close and comfort-ing. Then it must be thrown into a limp heap with the others, unusable, until their next journey through the suds, water, and heat of the laundry, the motion of your hands flicking and folding, smoothing and stacking the still-warm white shells, thin garments trailing streams of meaning and desire like the misty veils of teenage brides.

At the local laundromat, where we did our clothes together, the brand of detergent flakes became a contest of wills. You refused the box I'd bought on sale, would use only the particular brand you've sworn by for years. Later we cooperated, pooling our dimes to get everything dry. And I watched, aware, catching details suffused with meaning: the way the hair pushed back from your brow and temples, the sinews visible in your neck, nothing extra between your bones and skin. Hauntingly androgynous, unique but universal, you were the promise of something undefined and inaccessible I wanted and awaited as you handled your Fruit of the Loom shirts with a care that should have told me, from the onset, of their importance in our wardrobe of possibilities.

On the laundromat's public counter you took a long time folding the undershirts, denim bell bottoms, soft worn work shirts. Then we stacked our double load into the squealy-wheeled cart. Later, once we got it home, we would climb into your fresh sheets, our limbs tangled, fingers tentative, filling our hands with each other's bare breasts, or not—you grew reluctant to shed the undershirt, the power and protection of that last thin molt before the skin.

"It's OK," I'd keep on telling you, being the accommodator, paralyzed in my fear to push back, to know you naked, equal, bare of the vestments of importance and toughness you choose, I clothe you in to make you larger, powerful. I don't remember you asking about my life. You were telling stories about your past, times I need and needed to imagine, years when I was still new in the world, in tiny child's oxfords. While you, a seventeen-year-old, would go to the dance hall, you tell me, decked out in a suit, brimmed felt hat and blue suede shoes. We look at photos of Paula, a femme in a taffeta gown and nearly twenty years your elder, who leaned toward you at the door to ask: "Kid, you wearin' your father's shoes?" You nearly fell off your feet, you say. You describe the proportions of your humiliation.

You were passionately in love with Paula, or about to be, you've told me. And I've entered that time, that emotion. Late into the night we sit up in bed, eating cookies from the box between us, thumbing through the photo album, as you point things out: Paula seated at the edge of the dance floor, tipping a beer bottle; you in your sharp suit, doing the lindy. One night in a dream she turned to you and said "You're the best friend I've ever had." You shuddered as you told me in the morning, wondering at the distance that forever separated you two, despite your two-year affair; what she made of you; whether she's still alive. Your eyes follow the curve of her skirt against the chair. "Some of us," you say, "are afraid to wear our dresses." And I look, stalking significance. But you've shut the book. You reach and turn off the light. My hands touch your back through the night, reading your vertebrae for affection.

Or I hold the fierce lavender dragon tattoo, high on your thigh, the tattoo discussed by your various ex-lovers at parties all that year we spent together. I supposed you knew this when you walked in, to a hero's welcome, the sisters screaming hellos across the room to you, a superdyke among us. We greeted each other against the wall, for that moment shy and cautious with each other. I was wearing a formal tux, a bow tie, and a blue carnation, my hair combed back like Elvis—an outfit that seemed almost to astound you. You literally fell back a step, I thought, as if I grew close and blurry; as if crowded by new facts, and their wild shadows, truth. Asking me "Whenever did you get that idea?" Though it clearly is an old one, older by far than you.

We took a winding staircase to the apartment's overhanging second floor, do you recall, where the woman in the "Come Out!" t-shirt cut cocaine into lines on a mirror. We were aware of each other; our affair was new then; there was a wildness in us. We started throwing underwear from the chest of drawers over the railing, as if the party upstairs were really getting hot, and socks still in pairs in wide, high

arcs onto the women dancing below. Then women began
stripping and you ripped off your shirt. And my startling tux
came off—it felt like freedom and a submission to you,
both—and the leather boots. Underneath I wore girls' socks,
the undershirt, my panties. "Just lucky," you told me, playing
naked cop: two articles of women's clothing were required
by law, or I would have been thrown in jail. I could feel one
of your tales of the old days coming on.

Women came to tell you goodbye at the door as we left
the party. We walked home slowly through the streets,
singing silly songs:

A sailor went to sea sea sea
To see what he could see see see
But all that he could see see see
Was the bottom of the deep blue sea.

I know that sailor. You have described him to me. He had
grey eyes—steel-grey and thoughtful. He gave you money.
You knew what you'd have to give him in return. But with
him you were surprised: all he wanted was to offer up his
worries, things he'd seen that he needed to tell on solid
ground, objects steady around him. "Your money or your
life," they say. He gave you both. The bills were in the
drawer beside the bed and he kept talking, in his pants and
socks.

This life being crazy, I recognize this story. And will hear
it again and again, till the night turns thick. And then, if you
must, you just keep on talking, to the wall. I—or someone
else I recognize—will be there sleeping, one arm thrown
around you, fingers searching the ridges and furrows of your
undershirt, covering your breasts.

Our Life in Iowa

Margaret Erhart

> *The road is so long, and all of it uphill, and we're two of the lucky latecomers who at least have a road to walk on, where before there were only wagon tracks, and before that, nothing, no indication of human change and passage across the prairie.* Where will we find our home, Gussy? With each other.
>
> *—Maude*

Like Herself, I used to call her Maude. The presence eternally missed.

She gave me the three white geese. She brought them out to the farm in a hatbox and let them loose in the driveway. They were cornmeal-colored goslings then and they followed her up to the door. She lived about fifteen houses away at the time, which in country distance comes out to an equal number of miles. We saw each other at parades and around voting time each year, but that was all. She sometimes walked in town wearing a hat the shape of the Eiffel Tower. Her partner wore the Chrysler Building. Together, in their hats, they publicly tap-danced.

One spring she had a simple plumbing problem which I took care of, and shortly after that she brought me the goslings.

"Hello, Maude. Who are these?"

"Gussy, I'm so happy to see you this morning! You've been in my thoughts ever since the toilet stopped running. I suddenly feel we must have some sort of spiritual connection, isn't that odd?"

The goslings fled behind her skirt and stamped their little feet and wheezed.

"They sound congested," I said.

"Gussy, we may be *soulmates*! Do you know?"

"Mmm. . . ."

I was taken by Maude's skirt, a fluttery red and black calico, and I remembered one of the first conversations we ever had was on the Coe River bridge, four or five Fourth of Julys ago, when Maude, in her Eiffel Tower hat, had come up to me out of the blue and asked whether I'd ever seen a prairie.

"I have one in my yard," she told me. "It may be the only prairie in the world that's taller than it is wide. I'm wondering if I'll have to stake it because the end grasses have nothing to hold them up."

The parade was passing. I heard someone laugh. It was me, at the thought of this stranger's yard flopping over.

"Do you know why the pioneer women wore skirts?" was the next question. I shook my head. "They were their bushes," said Maude. "On the long walk there was nothing to squat and pee behind, so they brought the bushes with them."

Gosling day she'd brought her bush with her, but only the little birds squatted and peed behind it. We stood together for a short time. Maude went on to tell me about a clairvoyant brother of hers in Japan, about the absence of cutworms in her garden, and about a boat trip she took as a child to Wakulla Springs.

"Gussy, it was a nightmare. We rode around in a glass-bottomed boat that made it seem our feet were squashing all the tiny, pearly and rose fishes."

Life Herself. The goslings were her gift to Platypus Farms,

the land I live on. She came and lived here too after the Chrysler Building gave up on country life, and Maude, and relocated to Cleveland. "Which is a long shot from heaven," was all she would say about it, shaking her head as if trying to clear it of the need to say anything at all. I gave her the garden where she worked some sort of spell on the cutworms. (They all went over to Tam Gregorio's place and as far as I know he's still planting double to get half the tomato crop he used to.) I gave her the cherry tree and the kitchen, and every summer night that summer and the next, we quartered pies and promised each other to leave a half for breakfast, and never did. The goat's milk was just too sweetly cold not to pour over something warm and tart.

In the winter I worked construction on a downtown hotel and Maude collected cans on the road. She was a genius of loving and giving, and to see her bundled figure blown to the ditch by a passing semi, unnerved me. "Why do you do it?" I'd come to pick her up on the stretch of F46 where it widens past the hog buying station. She closed the car door and hid her frozen hands in her armpits.

"Because I don't like disorder. Because the intolerance of others makes me feel generous. These winter drivers are very intolerant, Gussy. I think a few of them would like to run me over just for being a woman with a bag of cans."

We got a cow, a red cow, Martha, who didn't give milk. When I wanted to trade her for something younger and fresher, Maude accused me of being a nasty old woman. I'm not old, though it has long been one of my ambitions, and nasty, I imagine, is something I learned from Martha who spent her last days with us moaning her childlessness into a bucket. Or eating everything we brought her, including two of my hats and Maude's new mittens. It was about to be spring and Life Herself rented a trailer to haul her cow and cans to town. The $35.90 in nickels covered the cost of the trailer, and she put the cow money into chocolates and a secondhand unicycle for herself.

"But we don't like chocolates," I reminded her.

"Oh yes, Gussy, we love chocolates! You're confusing us with Ruth and Ellen."

Ruth and Ellen despised chocolates, just as they despised everything melty and sweet. They were the names we'd given our alter egos, and we pictured them, two tinsel-haired ladies tottering around inside our bodies, armed with umbrellas and rolled up newspapers. They were vigilant, cranky and prudish. Their shoes were the color of gunpowder, slightly greener than their hair. They kicked and swatted at any softening or surrender. They hated generosity, and tried and failed two summers and a winter to beat back the lovers in us. "I spit on them!" Maude used to cry out whenever the chill of Ruth came over her or Ellen came over me. They had long fingers and a suffocating grip, and one part of us knew it would take our life to be free of them.

Maude is free of them now, as she is free of everything except how much I hold her in my heart. I hated to see her go. Friends who have hearts but no real understanding of these kinds of things told me, Better quick like it was than long and drawn out, Gussy. I needed a little longer, thank you. Maude did too. We were in our late thirties together and just discovering that if you wait long enough, life gives you something holy. Life herself.

Leaving the hospital the day she died, I had her overnight things in my hand. A toothbrush, her wooden comb, the bag balm she used to soften her hands. Also some clothes, that red and black calico skirt, whatever she'd thought she'd put on in the morning. I laughed and wept at this, sitting in a small square of grass in the parking lot.

I pulled her skirt on and pulled off my pants, and for no reason I thought of *soulmate*, the word I'd gotten wrong for a long while before Maude set me right about it. "Nothing ta-da-ta to it at all, dear Gussy. Just a poor little word that will never live up to people's notion of it. We don't have to use it, you know. We can change it. Let's never say it again. Instead let's say, *the one who before you meet her has already arrived.*" I did up the zipper. I fastened the waist. Whose waist, whose hips, whose skirt am I wearing? I wondered. Whose skin?

Your own, Gussy. Now go on. Fly up! Dance up! I remembered Maude's last words, two of them: "Brilliant medicine!"

I was the only one in that parking lot and I exhausted myself with high kicks and spins and the gyrating rhythm of jazz, coming from my deepest heart—my legs' heart, arms' heart, heart of my shoulders and head and hands. And when I got done it wasn't dark. There were doctors passing. There wasn't a tree or car to pee behind. Not even a grassy hump. My faith in the living wouldn't let me go back into that hospital, and my faith in the dead reminded me that years ago when this pavement was prairie, wide open, bushless, boundless prairie, women walked upon it in skirts as I did now, walking to the bull's eye of the parking lot, and they squatted as I did now, surrounded by the bushes they brought with them, and they scowled out from their weary faces, sorry to lose the friends they'd left behind, or lost over and over again on their journey, and a few in those resting moments between wagon tracks could shout out to the backs of the men and horses and noise of children ahead of them, "The whole difficult, pointless endeavor is worth it only now. Come back to me my life, on the hard arcs of the swallows sweeping upward!"

From *The Gloria Stories*

Rocky Gámez

Every child aspires to be something when she grows up. Sometimes these aspirations are totally ridiculous, but coming from the mind of a child they are forgiven, and given enough time, they are forgotten. These are normal little dreams from which life draws its substance. Everyone has aspired to be something at one time or another; most of us have aspired to be *many* things. I remember wanting to be an acolyte so badly I would go around bobbing in front of every icon I came across whether they were in churches or private houses. When this aspiration was forgotten, I wanted to be a kamakazi pilot so I could nosedive into the church that never allowed girls to serve at the altar. After that I made a big transition. I wanted to be a nurse, then a doctor, then a burleque dancer, and finally I chose to be a schoolteacher. Everything else was soon forgiven and forgotten.

My friend Gloria, however, never went beyond aspiring to be one thing, and one thing only. She wanted to be a man. Long after I had left for college to learn the intricacies of being an educator, my youngest sister would write to me long frightening letters in which she would say that she had seen Gloria barreling down the street in an old Plymouth honking at all the girls walking down the street. One letter said that she had spotted her in the darkness of a theater making out with another girl. Another letter said that she had seen Gloria coming out of a cantina with her arms hooked around two whores. But the most disturbing one was when she said that she had seen Gloria at a 7–11 store, with a butch haircut and what appeared to be dark powder on the sides of her face to imitate a beard.

I quickly sat down and wrote her a letter expressing my concern and questioning her sanity. A week later I received a fat letter from her. It read:

> *Dear Rocky,*
>
> *Here I am, taking my pencil in my hand to say hello and hoping that you are in the best of health, both physically and mentally. As for me, I am fine, thanks to Almighty God.*
>
> *The weather in the Valley is the shits. As you have probably read or heard on the radio we had a hurricane named Camille, a real killer that left many people homeless. Our house is still standing, but the Valley looks like Venice without gondolas. As a result of the flooded streets, I can't go anywhere. My poor car is under water. But that's all right. I think the good Lord sent us a killer storm so that I would sit home and think seriously about my life, which I have been doing for the last three days.*
>
> *You are right, my most dearest friend, I am not getting any younger. It is time that I should start thinking about what to do with my life. Since you left for school, I have been seeing a girl named Rosita, and I have already asked her to marry me. It's not right to go around screwing without the Lord's blessings. As soon as I can drive my car I'm going to see what I can do about this.*
>
> *Your sister is right, I have been going around with some whores, but now that I have met Rosita, all that is going to change. I want to be a husband worthy of her respect, and when we have children, I don't want them to think that their father was a no good drunk.*
>
> *You may think I'm crazy for talking about being a*

father, but seriously Rocky, I think I can. I never talked to you about anything so personal as what I'm going to say, but take it from me, it's true. Every time I do you-know-what, I come just like a man. I know you are laughing right now, but Rocky, it is God's honest truth. If you don't believe me, I'll show you someday. Anyhow it won't be long until you come home for Christmas. I'll show you and I promise you will not laugh and call me an idiot like you always do.

In the meantime since you are now close to the University library you can go and check it out for yourself. A woman can become a father if nature has given her enough come to penetrate inside a woman. I bet you didn't know that. Which goes to prove that you don't have to go to college to learn everything.

That shadow on my face that your sister saw was not charcoal or anything that I rubbed on my face to make it look like beard. It is the real thing. Women can grow beards, too, if they shave their faces every day to encourage it. I really don't give a damn if you or your sister think it looks ridiculous. I like it, and so does Rosita. She thinks I'm beginning to look a lot like Sal Mineo, do you know who he is?

Well, Rocky, I think I'll close for now. Don't be too surprised to find Rosita pregnant when you come in Christmas. I'll have a whole case of Lone Star for me and a case of Pearl for you. Till then I remain your best friend in the world.

Love, Gloria

I didn't go home that Christmas. A friend of mine and I were involved in a serious automobile accident a little before the holidays and I had to remain in the hospital. While I was in traction with almost every bone in my body shattered, one of the nurses brought me another letter from Gloria. I couldn't even open the envelope to read it, and since I thought I was on the brink of death, I didn't care at all when the nurse said she would read it to me. If this letter contained any information that would shock the nurse, it

wouldn't matter anyway. Death is beautiful insofar as it
brings absolution, and once you draw your last breath,
every pecadillo is forgiven.

"Yes," I nodded to the matronly nurse, "you may read my
letter."

The stern-looking woman found a comfortable spot at the
foot of my bed and, adjusting her glasses over her enormous
nose, began to read.

> *Dear Rocky,*
>   *Here I am taking my pencil in my hand to say hello,*
> *hoping you are in the best of health, both physically*
> *and mentally. As for me, I am fine thanks to Almighty*
> *God.*

The nurse paused to look at me and smiled in a moth-
erly way. "Oh, that sounds like a very sweet person!"
"I nodded.

> *The weather in the Valley is the shits. It has been raining*
> *since Thanksgiving and here it is almost the end of Decem-*
> *ber and it's still raining. Instead of growing a prick I think*
> *I'm going to grow a tail, like a tadpole. Ha, ha, ha!*

The matronly nurse blushed a little and cleared her throat.
"Graphic, isn't she?"

I nodded again.

> *Well, Rocky, not much news around this asshole of a*
> *town except that Rosita and I got married. Yes, you heard*
> *right, I got married. We were married in St. Margaret's*
> *Church, but it wasn't the type of wedding you are proba-*
> *bly imagining. Rosita did not wear white, and I did not*
> *wear a tuxedo like I would have wanted to.*

The nurse's brow crinkled into two deep furrows. She
picked up the envelope and turned it over to read the return

address and then returned to the letter with the most confused look I have ever seen in anybody's face.

Let me explain. Since I wrote you last, I went to talk to the priest in my parish and confessed to him what I was. In the beginning he was very sympathetic and he said that no matter what I was, I was still a child of God. He encouraged me to come to mass every Sunday and even gave me a box of envelopes so that I could enclose my weekly tithe money. But then when I asked him if I could marry Rosita in his church, he practically threw me out.

The nurse shook her head slowly and pinched her face tightly. I wanted to tell her not to read anymore, but my jaws were wired so tight I couldn't emit a comprehensible sound. She mistook my effort for a moan and continued reading and getting redder and redder.

He told me that I was not only an abomination in the eyes of God, but a lunatic in the eyes of Man. Can you believe that? First I am a child of God, then when I want to do what the church commands in Her seventh sacrament, I'm an abomination. I tell you, Rocky, the older I get, the more confused I become.

But anyway, let me go on. This did not discourage me in the least. I said to myself, Gloria, don't let anybody tell you that even if you're queer, you are not a child of God. You are! And you got enough right to get married in church and have your Holy Father sanctify whatever form of love you wish to choose.

The nurse took out a small white hanky from her pocket and dabbed her forehead and upper lip.

So, as I walked home having been made to feel like a turd, or whatever it is abomination means, I came upon a brilliant idea. And here's what happened. A young man that works in the same slaughter house that I do invited me

*to his wedding. Rosita and I went to the religious cere-
mony which was held in your hometown, and we sat as
close to the altar rail as we possibly could, close enough
where we could hear the priest. We pretended that she and
I were the bride and groom kneeling at the rail. When the
time came to repeat the marriage vows, we both did, in our
minds, of course, where nobody could hear us and be
shocked. We did exactly as my friend and his bride did,
except kiss, but I even slipped a ring on Rosita's finger and
in my mind said, "With this ring, I wed thee."*

*Everything was like the real thing, Rocky, except that we
were not dressed for the occasion. But we both looked
nice. Rosita wore a beautiful lavender dress made out of
dotted swiss material. Cost me $5.98 at J.C. Penny. I
didn't want to spend that much money on myself because
Lord knows how long it will be until I wear a dress again.
I went over to one of your sisters' house, the fat one, and
asked if I could borrow a skirt. She was so happy to know
that I was going to go to church and she let me go through
her closet and choose anything I wanted. I chose something simple to wear. It was a black skirt with a cute little
poodle on the side. She went so far as to curl my hair and
make it pretty. Next time you see me, you'll agree that I do
look like Sal Mineo.*

The nurse folded the letter quietly and stuffed it back
inside the envelope, and without a word disappeared from
the room, leaving nothing behind but the echoing sound of
her running footsteps.

After my release from the hospital, I went back to the
Valley to recuperate from the injuries received in the accident. Gloria was very happy that I was not returning to the
University for the second semester. Although I wasn't exactly in any condition to keep up with her active life, I could
at least serve as a listening post in that brief period of
happiness she had with Rosita.

I say brief because a few months after they got married,
Rosita announced to Gloria that she was pregnant. Gloria

took her to the doctor right away, and when the pregnancy was confirmed, they came barreling down the street in their brand-new car to let me be the first to know the good news.

Gloria honked the horn outside and I came limping out of the house. I had not met Rosita until that day. She was a sweet-looking little person with light brown hair, who smiled a lot. A little dippy in her manner of conversing, but for Gloria, who wasn't exactly the epitome of brilliance, she was alright.

Gloria was all smiles that day. Her dark brown face was radiant with happiness. She was even smoking a cigar and holding it between her teeth on the corner of her mouth.

"Didn't I tell you in one of my letters that it could be done?" She smiled. "We're going to have a baby!"

"Oh, come on, Gloria, cut it out!" I laughed.

"You think I'm kidding?"

"I *know* you're kidding!"

She reached across Rosita who was sitting in the passenger seat of the car and grabbed my hand and laid it on Rosita's stomach. "There's the proof!"

"Oh, shit, Gloria, I don't believe you!"

Rosita turned and looked at me, but she wasn't smiling. "Why don't you believe her?" she wanted to know.

"Because it's biologically impossible. It's . . . absurd."

"Are you trying to say that it's crazy for me to have a baby?"

I shook my head. "No, that's not what I meant."

Rosita got defensive. I moved away from the car and leaned on my crutches, not knowing how to respond to this woman because I didn't even know her at all. She began trying to feed me all this garbage about woman's vaginal secretions being as potent as the ejaculations of a male and being quite capable of producing a child. I backed off immediately, letting her talk all she wanted. When she finished talking, and she thought she had fully convinced me, Gloria smiled triumphantly and asked, "What do you got to say now, Rocky?"

I shook my head slowly. "I don't know. I just don't know. Your woman is either crazy or a damn good liar. In either case, she scares the hell out of me."

"Watch you language, Rocky," Gloria snapped. "You're talking to my wife."

I apologized and made an excuse to go back into the house. But somehow Gloria knew that I had limped away with something in my mind. She went and took Rosita home, and in less than an hour, she was back again, honking outside. She had a six-pack of beer with her.

"Alright, Rocky, now that we're alone, tell me what's on your mind.'

I shrugged my shoulders. "What can I tell you? You're already convinced that she's pregnant."

"She is!" Gloria explained. "Dr. Long told me so."

Yes, but that's not what I'm trying to tell you."

"What are you trying to tell me?"

"Will you wait until I go inside the house and get my biology book. There's a section in it on human reproduction that I'd like to explain to you."

"What are you trying to tell me?"

"Will you wait until I go inside the house and get my biology book. There's a section in it on human reproduction that I'd like to explain to you."

"Well, alright, but you better convince me or I'll knock you off your crutches. I didn't appreciate you calling Rosita a liar."

After I explained to Gloria why it was biologically impossible that she could have impregnated Rosita, she thought for a long silent moment and drank most of the beer she had brought. When I saw a long tear streaming down her face, I wanted to use one of my crutches to hit myself. But then, I said to myself, "What are friends for if not to tell us when we're being idiots."

Gloria turned on the engine to her car. "Okay, Rocky, git outta my car! I should've known better than come killing my ass to tell you something nice in my life. Ever since I met you, you've done nothing but screw up my life. Get out. The way I feel right now I could easily ram up one of them crutches up your skinny ass, but I'd rather go home and kill that fucking Rosa."

"Oh, Gloria, don't do that! You'll go to jail. Making babies is not the most important thing in the world. What's important is the trying. And just think how much fun that is as opposed to going to the electric chair."

"Git outta the car *now*!"

I did.

Cruz

Ida Swearingen

"You're really watching her, aren't you?" Deb asked as we rounded the storage tank. She nodded toward the woman standing just ahead of us—a small Hispanic woman wearing a bandana over her black hair. As we drew closer the woman turned toward us and caught my eye. I started to look down, but as I did she smiled at me. Involuntarily, I smiled back.

"She's a whore," Deb said once we'd rounded the corner.

I was still thinking about that smile. This was the second time she'd smiled at me and both times I felt like I'd just had a drink of cool water that cut to the back of my throat where the dust of the beet plant settled.

"Gimme a break."

"The women on the pack line say it. Everybody in the plant knows." Deb's short blonde curls bounced in the air above me. She was so tall that one of her strides equalled two of mine and I hurried to keep pace with her.

"They probably say I'm a whore, too."

"No, they say you're a communist." Deb opened the door to the lunch room. "And I'll tell you what else she is." seating herself on a stool and folding a paper napkin to mark her place at the lunch counter. "She's straight." She paused drawing herself together and arranging her face in a

215

helpful expression. "Kate, if you want to date I can always fix you up."

"You don't know anything about her."

We drank our coffee in silence and by the time we left the lunch stand, the woman was gone.

I didn't know her name. All I knew was that she was a Chicana and had the blackest hair I'd ever seen. Her features were delicate, but there was a strength and certainty in her movements. From the crease in her jeans to her crisp bandana she stood out in the filth of the beet refinery. And then there was that smile—oh God, that smile.

The beet plant had a nightmare quality of gloom and noise that made you long for the sight of something clean. The worst thing was the smell. Every morning, when I walked from the parking lot, it settled on me and made a dry spot in the back of my throat. It clung to my clothes and hair so that even after I left work, the beet plant stayed with me.

Beets were harvested in the fall. We unloaded them from trucks into block-long piles outside the plant. All winter we worked inside the plant changing them from pale, football-sized tubers into neat, blue-and-white packages of sugar. My job was in the washhouse. That meant spending my days knee-deep in filthy water digging beet tailings from a drain beneath a two-story cylinder where the beets were tumbled. It was like working in a sewer. Every fifteen minutes the water flushed, sometimes throwing me off balance so that I fell in. When I rose, I stood dripping muck, banging my shovel against the wall and yelling "motherfucker" loudly enough to be heard all the way up to the loft and bringing Billy, the washhouse boss, to warn me, "We better be careful. Some people might not like that kind of talk."

"Who's we, Billy?" I asked. "There's no one here but me and you."

Once they left my pit, the beets were spun and mashed and pounded until every bit of sugar was extracted. The company sold the dry pulp for cattle feed.

"What ever happened to hay?" I asked Deb as we watched her lover, Karen, load bags of pulp on a flatbed truck. Deb launched into a ten-minute discourse on beet pulp and nutrition as I traced the course of Karen's bobcat ripping back and forth carrying the huge brown bags.

Three times a day the women from the sugar-packing line passed by the ramp over my pit. They wore long white coats and little white hats that made them look like a flock of geese. Mabel Whiznant, the eldest of the group, took the lead with the rest of the women arranging themselves behind her. Once I found them gathered on the ramp gazing at me as I groped in the muck trying to retrieve a lost shovel. I was singing a song about going back to New York City. I looked up and met Mabel's gaze. Her stern face with its chiseled features froze me and I stood, transfixed, caught in the power of her disapproval. Mabel stared me right into that muck. I stooped to resume my search and when I looked up again, the women had vanished.

In my own mind I called the woman Linda—the Spanish word for beautiful. Deb said she worked in the pumphouse directly behind the washhouse. The washwater drained through the pumphouse to a steaming, fetid holding pond behind the plant. Billy told me if the pit weren't kept clean the water would back up and cause the pumphouse to explode. It made me feel connected to Linda and I wondered if she knew my work kept her safe.

The more I thought about Linda, the more I started watching her to see if she was coming on to anyone else. If she were really turning tricks, I figured I'd see her coming on to the men in the lunchroom, but I never saw her smile at anyone else. Just me.

"So, Deb, if she's a whore, why's she smiling at me?" I asked as we were riding in my old Chevy pickup. I leaned across Karen, who sat in the middle, to look at Deb crunched against the passenger door. She stared off into the distance as if she hadn't heard me.

"I don't suppose you know that some woman might go

after you for the farm," Karen answered for her. "You never think of those things." Her long brown hair blew slightly in the draft from an open window. Karen's gold, rimless glasses reflected the sunlight so it looked as if she had no eyes.

"Right, chase me for my money." I laughed. Karen and Deb exchanged one of their significant looks.

"Does she know I even have a farm?"

No one answered.

I chafed under Karen and Deb's concern. They'd moved in with me just after my relationship broke up—in the time when I was falling apart. They were buying the eighty acres adjoining mine, so it seemed like a good idea for them to trade work for rent and live with me until they could get a house built. It was a good arrangement except that I'd stopped being a mess awhile back and neither Deb nor Karen had caught on yet.

It was one thing to tease Deb, but it was another to actually find out the woman's name. The easiest thing would've been to ask the women in the pack line because they probably knew all about her, but I didn't want any of them to know I was interested. I got too much attention as it was, and I didn't want them talking about me—not for my own sake, but because Deb and Karen were in the closet and wanted me to be careful. There was more than that though, I was afraid. I mean, she might be just playing around with me—maybe it was all a big joke. She'd smile at me till she got a reaction and then everyone would have a good laugh at the dyke in the washhouse pit.

I knew Deb and Karen were worried about Linda when we started having guests out to the house for dinner—women guests. Marlys Engstrom was the first. She sat at the end of the table in a silent lump with her face hidden in her straight brown hair, rarely looking up from her plate as she ate.

When she did, her gaze was of such blue innocence that I felt constrained to watch my language. Through dinner she said little more than, "Yup," "Pass the potatoes," and "That was a good pie." I could feel Deb watching me anxiously as I sat at my end of the table.

"Marlys, tell Kate about your experience working at a sawmill."

Marlys put her cup in the saucer deliberately. She took a deep breath and, without raising her eyes, said, "Yup, I used to work in a sawmill." I waited, but the story was over.

"Tell her about what you did there," Deb prompted.

"Stacked lumber," Marlys replied.

I excused myself and went to the kitchen. Karen was drawing water from a bucket.

"What is this shit?" I whispered.

"Give her a chance, Kate. She'd be a lot of help around here."

"So would a chainsaw."

I stomped out to the woodshed and spent the evening splitting wood.

The next one was Polly Anderson. Polly talked. Oh God how she talked. She came out on a Sunday afternoon wearing a football jersey and carrying a case of beer. We sat in front of the television and watched football while Polly drank and recited statistics about the team and the players. Something about rushing champions of the NFL. She and Deb talked about the Vikings. Karen sat by a window working a crossword puzzle and I stared silently into the fire.

"I want you guys to knock it off." I told Deb and Karen the next morning when we were all crowded into the seat of my pickup driving to work.

Karen looked out the window. Deb cleared her throat. "Kate, I know it's lonely for you around here. It's not easy living with us. Three's an unstable number."

"Why now?" I asked.

No one had to answer.

*   *   *

I tried timing Linda's breaks, watching for her to pass just
to see her walk. She had a steady, even gait—like a woman
who knew where she was going.

But I still didn't know her name.

One morning I waited around for her to punch the time
clock. Her smile almost distracted me but I managed to
keep my eye on the card until she was out of sight and I
could pull it up. The name on the top was ORTEGA,
CRUZ. Cruz Ortega. I spent the rest of the morning repeating it to myself. It felt silky and soft on my tongue. Cruz
Ortega.

I started practicing my high school Spanish standing in
front of my bedroom mirror repeating *"Buenos dias. Que tal
con su vida? Aqui se prohibe fumar. Como esta usted?
Como se llama?"* After a couple of weeks I was ready. I saw
her in the lunchroom and positioned myself by the cash
register so she'd have to pass me on her way out. When she
came by, I said *"Buenos noches."*

"Buenas noches," she paused by my stool. *"Tu hablas
espanol?"*

"Si, un poco," I answered. She blasted me with a barage
me of rapid Spanish and, when I couldn't reply, she fell
back against the counter laughing.

"Where did you learn your Spanish?" she asked. "Did a
woman teach it to you or did you learn it from a man?"

I felt myself begin to blush like I used to when I was
fifteen. I couldn't bring myself to say it had been a woman
and she was Sister Mary Perpetua from St. Scholastica in the
Bronx, so I just looked down at my coffee cup. Cruz leaned
close to me and said *"Hasta luego."* And left me dazed and
fumbling.

The women from the pack line never took their breaks in
the lunchroom. They set up a table in one corner in the
women's dressing room where they could eat in private. At
a silent signal from Mabel they all sat down and unfolded

their lunches, making little cooing sounds of approval as they examined and commented on each other's offerings.

"Try some of my new hot dish, Mabel."

"Grace, let me give you some of this Jell-O."

As leader, Mabel Whiznant opened her lunch first, took the first bite, and stood up to signal the end of the meal. I never knew I wasn't supposed to sit with them, so when I wandered in one night and saw food being passed around, I pulled up an empty chair. I told funny stories in return for cookies and Hello Dolly bars. They tolerated my grease and filth because I was an exotic from "out East." With the exception of occasional visits from Deb and Karen, none of the other women from the plant ever came to that table.

We'd just started a week of working night shift. I took my break about 3:00 a.m. Just before I left the pit, a rush of water had swept me down so I was soaked and my T-shirt clung to me. I was afraid that if I went to the lunchroom all the boys would start yelling, "Wet T-shirt time," so I decided to join the ladies in the dressing room and dry out.

They were unfolding their lunches and laying out the paper wrappings. Grace Jorgenson was telling everyone about her husband, Elmer's, cold. I was looking over the array when I glanced up and saw Cruz standing in the doorway. She paused for a moment before walking to the table and sitting opposite me. Grace stopped in mid-sentence and the sounds of foil and wax paper ceased. The room became silent.

I said hello to Cruz. She gave me a tight little smile and then looked down at the table without replying. Alma Jordan's hand froze in the air on its way to pick up a piece of Edith Rolvaag's nut bread. Mabel Whiznant's eyes were narrow and cold. She stared silently at Cruz.

"How's life in the pumphouse?" I asked, fishing for something to break the silence. "Working hard?" Every woman at the table seemed suspended on my words.

Cruz looked at me without replying. The smile lost its spring and became artificial. The silence was overwhelming me.

"Have you eaten?" I asked.

"No," she replied and stood up. "No, I'll go eat now." And she turned to leave. For a full moment no one spoke. Then Mabel set a cup down with an abrupt thump.

"Well," she said regarding me. For a second time her eyes trapped me. I sat looking down at the table. As if on a signal the table came alive as the ladies resumed their unwrapping.

Everyone was talking, but no one looked my way. Finally I stood up and, without a word, pushed my chair up to the table and left.

By the time I got back to the pit I was shaking. I waded into the water and started throwing beet tailings everywhere. Finally I stopped and began banging my shovel against the wall, shouting "fuck" as loud as I could. Billy stood off to one side shaking his head.

At about 4:30 Deb appeared on the ramp. She shouted over the roar until I looked up and she caught my eye to motion me out.

"The whole place is talking. Kate, you've got to be more careful."

"More careful about what?" I was shaking tailings off my shovel.

"You know what. Look, we've got to live here. You can't just let this thing go on. People won't stand for it."

"You go fuck yourself." I threw the shovel to one side and left Deb standing on the ramp. I didn't know where I was going, so I was surprised when I got to the pumphouse. I paused and opened the door. The steam and the throbbing of the pumps made it impossible to see or hear. Finally I saw Cruz standing by a bank of dials writing on a clipboard.

"Hey Cruz," I yelled. I crossed a catwalk to get to her. She looked surprised. "Would you want to have breakfast with me after work?"

She looked confused. She hadn't heard me. I repeated myself, shouting over the noise of the pumps. I pointed at her and pounded my chest to show her what I meant. She nodded. She understood.

"I can't today. I'm busy."

I turned to walk away, but stopped myself and went back. "Well, would you like to go out for a beer Saturday night?"

"Sure."

It wasn't until I was riding home that the weight of my action hit me. As far as I knew she was straight and I'd never asked a straight woman out before. I didn't know where to take her and what in the hell was I doing asking straight women out on dates anyway?

On Saturday I picked her up at 8:00. I'd bathed in our old galvanized washtub, washed my hair, and put on my best jeans. I'd borrowed a clean turtleneck from Karen and talked Deb out of her bright green sweater. Just before leaving the house I found the black polish and shined my shoes. As I got out of the truck I checked myself in the rear-view mirror. I sighed. My hair needed cutting and the coat was getting threadbare.

"Who do you think you are anyway?" I asked the reflection.

Cruz lived in a shabby trailer in West Fargo. When I knocked, a woman who looked as if she could be Cruz's sister opened the door. I peered inside the door and saw two men sitting on a couch watching television. They looked up at me but said nothing. One man lifted a bottle of beer to his lips. Cruz appeared from the back of the trailer. She took her coat but said nothing to anyone present and didn't offer to introduce me.

She was wearing a red silk shirt and black pants. I'd never seen her hair without a bandana. It was long and slightly curly and she wore it loose. I wanted to touch it to see if it was as soft as it looked.

"Where would you like to go?" I asked as we got in my pickup. I'd had two days to think about where to take her and that was the best I could come up with.

"Let's go to Cisco's."

We drove through the treeless, icy streets. Snow banked the road way and glistened in the headlights. I reached down to the dashboard and pounded my heater to make it churn out some heat. The truck's condition had never bothered me before, but for this night I wished the rust holes in the body didn't let in so much cold air.

Neither of us seemed to know what to say so we limited ourselves to the directions and let the noise of the engine fill the empty space between us.

The barroom was small and nearly empty. The bartender was a short, dark man with a handlebar mustache.

"Hola!" he said as we entered. Cruz stopped and spoke to him in Spanish. I shuffled around till she joined me and we sat opposite each other in a booth. She was quiet. I didn't know where to start so I asked questions. Lots of questions.

"Where are you from?"

"Texas"

"How long have you been here?"

"A year," she pronounced it "jear."

"How do you like the beet factory?"

She looked at me with a kind of amusement. The soft light in the bar made shadows on her cheeks. "How do you like the beet factory?" She asked me back laughing. "Everybody says you say bad words and throw your shovel. They say you got a terrible mouth."

So she'd been watching.

Two men stood up from a table and began a game of pool. We observed their game in silence. I sipped my beer and thought about what to do next.

"Would you like to go someplace and dance?" I put my glass down on the table. Beer spilled and started to run toward the edge. I mopped it up with my napkin. When it was saturated, I took Cruz's. Taking a deep breath I started again.

"Would you like to go someplace and dance with me?" I repeated, braced for her refusal. When she said no, I'd apologize and order another beer. Then we could shoot some pool and I'd take her home. And that would teach me to go out with straight women.

Cruz returned my gaze without blinking. Never taking her eyes off me, she stood up and put on her coat.

There was only one gay bar between the Twin Cities and Winnipeg, and it was always packed with men. I expected Cruz to take one look and ask to leave because I didn't think she'd really understood what I'd asked. When we entered, she stopped and surveyed the room, smiling at the men dancing. For a moment she stood and seemed to let her body pick up the beat of the music. She moved slightly to follow it. She began small dance movements as she took off her coat. She handed it to me to put on a table.

"Let's dance," she said and took my hand and led me to the floor.

Cruz's dancing was like her smile, and it cut straight to my heart. I've never danced well, but I found myself following her, caught in her rhythm and movement. I'd never danced so freely in my life. We danced song after song. I was afraid to stop, afraid she'd leave. I didn't want to break the movement, not even for a moment. They played a slow number. I'd meant to sit out the first slow dance so that way she wouldn't know how much I wanted to touch her, but I opened my arms to her and she moved in. I held her a little back from me, but she pulled me close to her. I felt her hands on my back, just under the shoulder blades. Her cheek was so close that I could have kissed it with only the slightest turn of my head.

After the song ended, I suggested we sit down. All the dancing had left things easier between us. I sipped a beer.

"So, why are you up here so far from Texas?"

"There was no work for me down there. I came up here because my sister said there was work, but I don't want to stay at that factory. That Shorty, he puts his hands all over me. He asks me to go out to his truck with him and when I say no he tells everyone I'm a whore." She stopped and looked at me. "Does he do that to you?"

"No, he took one look at me and put me in the wash-house pit."

"Yeah, we all wondered why you were there. It's the worst job in the place. They usually give it to Spanish."

"He says he doesn't like my attitude, whatever the hell that means. I've asked the supervisor, I even asked the union, but it doesn't look like I'll ever get out of that place, at least not while Shorty's boss."

"I'm gonna get out of that damn pumphouse. I'm studying English. I want to get a job in an office where I can be clean and wear something besides jeans."

"Your English sounds okay to me."

"No." She shook her head." I can't spell for shit."

"Maybe I could help you."

Cruz looked at me as if I might be teasing her.

"I mean it. I used to teach English. I'll help you with it."

"You got time for that?" she asked very softly.

"I've got time."

We danced some more, slow and fast, and with each slow dance I wanted to touch her more. When we sat down again, she sat close beside me put her hand over mine. I rolled my hand over and held hers.

"So tell me how you got here" she asked.

"I've got a farm outside town. Eighty acres. It's not much, but we grow some vegetables."

"Are you alone out there?

"No, two other women live with me. They help out with the chores. They're buying the land next to mine."

"Those two in the beet plant?"

"Yeah"

"Those two don't like me. I can tell. They don't like any of the Spanish." She was silent for a moment.

"They don't even like people from New York." I was embarrassed for Deb and Karen.

"That's where you're from?"

I nodded.

"Did you really teach English?"

I nodded again.

"So how come you're shoveling beets?"

"Farm's not self-supporting and I need something to keep the place going."

Cruz nodded. "But how come you're not teaching?"

I swallowed hard, "Well, it's tough for a lesbian to be a teacher. Schools don't like us much." I waited for her reaction, but she didn't miss a beat.

"So how're they gonna know?"

"People know. You did, didn't you?" Cruz nodded thoughtfully. She knew all right.

"But you should be a teacher." She persisted. "You got an education. You can make good money teaching."

"Well," I stretched back and laughed, "the only thing I want now is enough money to buy a couple of pigs."

Cruz thought for a moment and shook her head.

"You should buy chickens. You don't lay out as much and you'll get more meat. And you can get eggs."

"How do you know about that stuff?"

"I used to live in the country."

"With your folks?"

"I used to have a husband." She looked at me quickly, biting on a straw. "I left him down there in Texas." She stood up. "Let's dance some more." And she led me back to the floor.

On the way home Cruz sat close to me on the seat of the pickup. Outside her trailer, we sat for a moment. She was pressing against my arm. I turned to ask her something and she moved closer and I forgot what I wanted to ask. I took her face in my hands and kissed her very slowly. We kept on kissing until our coats got in the way and we stopped to look at each other for a moment. Cruz pulled back and got out of the pickup. I followed her and took her arm as she started to unlock the door. I put my arms around her.

"You're shaking," she said.

"I thought it was you."

She took my hand and held it to her cheek. Then she kissed it slowly and gently.

"No, it's you," she said showing me my hand.

We went inside. The trailer was narrow and long with a single light showing from the back. The floor was strewn with ashtrays and beer bottles.

Someone was snoring. Cruz took off her coat and walked to the back of the trailer and I turned on a lamp by the couch and looked around. Someone had set a card table up and covered it with the pieces of a jigsaw puzzle. I picked up a piece and tried fitting it first in one place, then another. The picture on the puzzle box showed a lake shimmering in moonlight.

Cruz came back into the room. I continued fooling around with puzzle pieces, stacking and pushing them in little circles. She picked up some empty bottles and an ashtray and carried them to the kitchen.

"Look," I said as she returned, "I've got a long drive. Thanks for everything. I'll see you Monday."

Without giving her a chance to respond, I turned and opened the door.

The next morning I slept late. Karen was in the kitchen when I got up and I went to the stove and poured myself a cup of coffee. I started back to my bedroom so I wouldn't have to talk to her.

"How was your date?" she asked with elaborate casualness.

"Okay."

"Did you have a good time?"

"Yeah." I was almost to the bedroom door.

"What time did you get home?"

I was just about to turn and tell her to fuck off when Deb stomped in from the cold and announced that our ancient hand pump was frozen.

I pulled on longjohns, two pair of jeans, two sweaters, and a battered wool shirt the previous owner'd left hanging on the porch. Out in the pumphouse I felt in my pockets for a kitchen match, lit the torch, and squatted beside the pump listening to its steady hiss, and thought about calling Cruz. I

tried to picture what she might be doing. Sighing, I turned
the torch off, set it down, and stood in the door to the
pumphouse looking back at the house. It wasn't much of a
place—a tarpaper shack with rooms jutting out in every
direction. I tried to imagine her inside, in my bedroom. I
shook my head and went back to the pump. Later I went to
the woodshed to split wood and stack it. By the time I'd
finished it was sundown and too late to drive to Fargo. I
checked the phone directory, but there was no listing for an
Ortega.

The pit was steaming and a big wave of water had just hit
when I looked up and saw Cruz on the ramp. She was
walking quickly, glancing neither right nor left. I threw my
shovel down, waded through the muck, and scrambled up
the ladder.

"Hey! Cruz."

She kept on walking.

"Cruz!" I shouted this time and started running after. The
water sloshed in my boots. She turned, frowning, just as I
caught up with her. I wiped my hands on the bottom of my
shirt.

"I just wanted to thank you for Saturday night." I kept on
wiping my hands and brushing my hair back out of my eyes.
"It was great being with you. I really had a great time."

"Is that why you ran away?"

I shook my head.

"I thought maybe you didn't like me."

For a moment I reached over to touch her cheek. She
softened and put her hand on top of mine pressing it closer.

I heard a sound and turned to see the women from the
pack line approaching, their white coats and caps gleaming
in the darkness. Mabel led them past us until they vanished
in the gloom. I dropped my hand and gave Cruz an apolo-
getic smile. She smiled back.

"So you still want some help with your English?"

"Sure."

"Wednesday night okay?"

"Sounds good." Her voice was so soft I could barely hear it.

I turned away to climb back down to the pit. Cruz started back on her way.

"Cruz," I called out, "what time is your lunch break?"

She turned back and gave me the smile.

"Noon."

"So, I'll see you then."

As I waded through the water to find my shovel, I saw Billy watching me. I kicked around the muddy water, but couldn't feel it, so I stooped over and searched with my hands. My shirttails fell in the water.

"Shit," I said.

"Lose something?" Billy asked sweetly.

I took a deep breath and decided not to tell him to go fuck himself. I smiled at him and I touched my shovel handle and pulled it out.

"Not now, Billy."

And I started back to work.

Upstate

Naomi Holoch

As Sarah stepped inside the store, a hoarse buzzer sounded briefly in the back. She circled a large rectangular table checkered with cellophane-wrapped flannel shirts and made her way along a wall of refrigerators to the back. On the counter, facing her, a cardboard man dressed in blue coveralls held a can of motor oil over his head and smiled into space. His teeth were very white; his words, which ballooned comic-book style above his head, promised her car a cleaner engine and better gas mileage after the very first quart.

A young heavyset woman in a blue ski jacket stood next to the counter, joggling a quiet snowsuited baby in one arm as she leafed through a catalogue. She smiled at Sarah briefly, then went back to turning the pages.

"Maybe I should get us one of these," the woman said still studying the catalogue. She tapped at a picture of electric blankets piled neatly one on top of another in a rainbow of pastel colors. "Already feels like it's gonna be a hard winter."

"You're right there, Flora." Sarah looked up as another woman came through the doorway behind the counter. "See you got Jim Jr. all decked out to go snomobilin'." The woman put down a long rectangular package and chucked the baby under the chin.

"Soon as there's snow you can bet Jim'll be giving him his first lesson. He'd carry him off tomorrow to go huntin' with the boys if I'd let him."

The other woman laughed. "I'll go pull out the receipt." She turned and went back through the doorway.

The woman with the baby slapped the catalogue shut and smiled at Sarah again.

"Big day tomorrow. First day of deer season."

Sarah smiled back. "Yeah, I know."

"You from up around here?" There was mild surprise in her voice.

"No, not really. I bought a house over the summer up on Hollow Hill Road."

"You mean the old Holbrook place?"

Sarah nodded.

"That's a real nice place. Not too big, not too small. 'Least not unless you got a whole army o' kids."

"No. No army of kids."

"Used to be a real showplace. Sure needs a lot o' work now, though. Hope you got a lot of patience."

Sarah blinked under the other woman's gaze. "That's about all I've got. I just hope I haven't gotten in over my head." She reached out and pulled the catalogue toward her.

"Oh sure, you'll do o.k. Houses know when they're loved, at least that's what I think." The woman moved closer to Sarah. "I'm Flora Maynard. This here is Jim Jr. We live out on Route 11, about three miles from you."

"I'm Sarah Harrison." She touched the baby's head lightly, brushing the delicate silkiness of his hair with the tips of her fingers.

"Here's your receipt, Flora." The other woman pushed it toward her across the counter and handed her a pen.

"This here is Sarah Harrison, Mary. She just bought the old Holbrook place."

The saleswoman raised her eyebrows. "Did you now.

Glad to hear it. Shame to have such a handsome house standing empty all this time."

Flora Maynard settled her son against her shoulder and balanced the package under her other arm. "Well, I'll be goin' now. Ma and Dad are stoppin' by later, so I'd better get on home." She turned towards Sarah. "Don't forget. We're on Route 11. A big blue house with white trim, if you need anything. And don't let that house get you down. It's a good sound house."

"Thanks. I'll remember that."

Back behind the counter, the saleswoman tapped her pencil on a pile of papers. "So you're the mattress. We been wonderin' who it was who ordered it. Been here for over a week now. Thought maybe it was some kind of mistake or something."

"I'm sorry. Was it in your way?"

"Well no, not exactly. Just wondered why all of a sudden this mattress showed up here. Would be better next time if you order direct through us instead of through the warehouse. That way, we can keep track of what's goin' on."

"Sorry, I didn't know."

"No matter." She put her pencil down and turned her attention back to the papers. "Double mattress, wasn't it? Four-inch foam?"

Sarah nodded. "That's right."

"Guess you're parked out on the street." Sarah nodded again. "Well, you gotta pull around to the side. That's where you pick up bulky items. You drivin' a station wagon maybe?"

"Just a small car."

The saleswoman frowned. "Have to be tied to the roof then. I'll get my husband to give you a hand."

Sarah pulls the door shut behind her and closes her eyes for a moment against the bright sun. It is noon and the tree-lined street is very still. The shadows of the two gas pumps across the way fall in clean-edged angles onto the buff-colored sidewalk. Then a gust of wind breaks the silence as it raises circles of dead leaves from the pavement. She steps into the road and watches an old American car driven by a very small thin old man in a peaked wool hunting cap drift slowly past. He comes to a halt at the crossroads under the yellow blinking light, then turns left and disappears between the clapboard buildings. As Sarah opens the door to her car, she is startled by the noise of a large milk truck, silver-colored and cylindrical. She waits for it to pass, waits for the hissing noise of its airbrakes to diminish. It hesitates a moment by the light, then snakes off in the same direction as the old man. Sarah sits in her car for a moment, feeling the trapped heat of the sun, then starts the engine and drives around to the side of the store.

In the back, a short man with a florid face dressed in dark green coveralls was flapping his arms across his chest.

"Cold day, Mrs. Harrison. Cold day to pick up a mattress. Sure hope you and the mister haven't been sleepin' on the floor."

"No, I haven't," Sarah responded carefully.

"Well, that's good." He looked doubtfully at the plastic-wrapped package sagging slightly against the side of the building, at the roof of the car, then back to Sarah. "Well," he rubbed his head. "How're we gonna do this? Your husband didn't come along, huh?"

"No." Sarah pulled at a corner of the plastic cover. "I'm not married," she added.

"Oh well, we'll manage just fine." He patted the mattress and smiled at her. "Mary'll be along in a minute."

"You could just run it from bumper to bumper," Sarah said to the man as he circled the car, a loose coil of rope hanging over his arm.

"That's what I was figurin' to do. Just want to make sure it's not gonna go slidin' down on you so as you can't see."

He flipped a length of rope across the car roof. "You all alone up there, are you?"

"Some friends are coming up soon." Sarah walked around to the back of the car and took hold of the rope.

"I don't mean that there's them kind of problems up here, you understand. Not like down in the city. Why, there was a woman up here, lived for years on her own way outside of town."

The man moved next to Sarah and took the rope from her hand. He bent down, wrapped it around the bumper, and pulled the knot tight.

"Now, Ben, you be careful of your back, you hear."

Ben straightened up slowly. "You remember the Sergeant, don't you, Mary?"

Mary turned away without answering.

"Rita Kendall. She used to go bowling with you girls every Wednesday, don't you remember?" Ben stood still, looking at his wife expectantly for a moment, then went on. "You used to say she could have been a regional finalist, easy. Maybe even state."

Mary walked up to Sarah's car and examined the mattress. Then she turned to face her husband. "Instead of standing there gossiping, wouldn't it be a sight better if you finished up here so this lady could be on her way?"

Ben shrugged and came up beside Sarah, rubbing his hands together. She had pulled the rope taut around the front bumper and was about to loop the end into a knot.

"Here now, let me do that." He took the end of the rope from her and continued talking to his wife. "Don't you remember? Only one of you girls ever even came near her score. That's what you told me. Helen McGovern, wasn't it?"

Mary shook her head. "No. It was Nancy Cooper."

Ben nodded. "Nancy. That's right." He finished tying the knot and turned toward Sarah. "We all always told Rita to give it a whirl, but she'd never compete. Said she just played for a good time, ain't that right, Mary?"

Mary tugged at one of the cords. "This here rope could be tighter, Ben." Sarah followed it to the bumper and began to work on the knot.

Ben squatted down next to her. "I'll fix that in a jiffy. You'll have work enough getting this thing into the house." He frowned at me. "How're you gonna do it all by yourself?"

"I'll manage. I've moved things before."

Ben shook his head, and, resting his hands on the bumper, pushed himself slowly upright. "Sounds just like Rita, don't she?"

Mary snorted. "Except that you'd never of dared talk to Rita like that." She flapped her arms around herself. "We're all gonna end up like Frosty the Snowman if we don't get on inside. I'm gonna go heat up the coffee." Mary turned toward the door. Sarah shoved her hands into her jacket pockets and watched as Ben circled the car testing the ropes one last time.

"All set. Come on in and warm up before you go."

She followed him inside.

"She was somethin', though." Ben spooned sugar into his cup. "She worked over at the high school in the principal's office. His assistant sort of, though she was really his secretary at first. Boy, I tell you, she ran a real tight ship. Dressed the part too. Wore suits to work that looked like a uniform, and outside of school she always wore them gray pants."

Mary held out a large bottle of dairy cream to Sarah. "Not gray. They were tan."

Ben shrugged and went on. "Had real dark short hair. Would a' thought she was Spanish or Italian or somethin' except for her name." Ben laughed. "Wouldn't of taken her for a man though. Not the way she was built, if you know what I mean." He made curves in the air with his hands. "After a while, she had everybody shakin' in their boots . . . kids, teachers, even parents. Once some kids let the air out of her tires. Well, the next day, you should of seen the

school parkin' lot. All the most souped-up cars, flat as a
pancake, every single one of 'em. They mouthed off for
days, those tough kids did, but nothin' ever happened again,
not to her car, anyway."

"The truth is they was all afraid of her. A woman who
was no nonsense."

Ben moved away from the wall. "I wasn't afraid a' her.
No reason to be. That is," he laughed, "as long as you
didn't cross her. And anyway, she was a real card. She
could just sit around and drink beer and tell jokes with the
rest of us, real jokes." Ben winked at Sarah.

"She have a big house?" Sarah asked.

Ben nodded. "Big enough. An old house. I remember it
from when I was a kid. Don't think too many people seen
the inside as long as Rita was there, though. Mary there
used to complain that the girls was never invited in. And
seemed like she didn't have much family. I don't recollect
anyone coming to visit, not in all the time she was here.
Five years, wasn't it?"

"Something like that."

Sarah looked from Ben to Mary. "She didn't have any
friends at all?"

Mary shrugged. "Oh, people liked her all right, and she
was friendly enough, but no one ever seemed to think to
drop by her house, and she never did neither." Mary fell
silent.

"You remember Alice?" Ben asked. "How she got when
Rita was around?"

"She just didn't like her, that's all. A person's allowed
her likes and dislikes."

Ben laughed. "Hardly anyone Alice does like, but with
Rita, you'd have thought she'd been bit by her. Started
complaining that the Sarge was a bad influence on the kids.
Couldn't hardly talk about anything else. Said she wasn't
ladylike enough for the girls and that she horsed around too
much with the boys. But I tell you, she was a real discipli-
narian underneath it all. No harm in a few laughs if you

know what I mean. Not if you know when to get 'em to toe
the line. That's what I say, anyway."

Mary went over to the small, stained sink and picked up a
sponge. "You say a whole lot too much. What makes you think
these old stories gonna interest someone who can't even
know who you're talking about?" She turned away and
began cleaning the countertop.

"There was Shirley Caine, too." Ben's voice flowed on
unchecked. "Remember how all of a sudden she just stopped
goin' bowlin' with you girls?"

"She got tired of bowlin' is all."

Surprise wrinkled Ben's forehead. "Ain't what you said
then. Said she wouldn't go nowhere where she knew Rita'd
be. Like she got allergic or somethin'. That's what you told
me."

"Maybe I did, maybe I didn't. How can I remember every
little thing I said over two years ago."

Ben laughed. "Well, I sure remember it. It was dinner
talk for near on to a month."

Mary didn't answer. The only noise was the hum of the
electric heater in one corner.

Mary reached for the cups. "You should make sure the
stockroom is in order before we close up. I want to go give
Pam a hand with dinner."

Ben winked at Sarah again. "I got my own mini-sergeant."

"She been gone long, Rita Kendall I mean?" Sarah asked.

Ben wrinkled his forehead, calculating. "Just about two
years. It was all kind of sudden. One day, she just upped
and joined the army. It was a real joke, her having been
called the Sergeant all that time. We threw her a party.
Biggest party this town ever seen."

"Drank yourselves right under the table, you boys did.
You'd a thought a war was just over the way everyone was
carrying on." Mary snapped out her dishcloth and hung it
next to the sink. "I'll go see to the stockroom or we'll be
here all night." Ben nodded.

"Anyway, we organized this real big party. Open bar,

dancin', the whole thing. I still remember, it was cold like today, but rainin' buckets. And I got there with my wife kind a' late. People already drinkin' and dancin'. I didn't see the Sergeant nowhere. I was on my way to the bar when I see this incredible dish of a blonde. Hair all piled up on her head. Never saw her before, and you sure would of noticed her around town, I tell you . . ." Ben shook his head, his gaze fixed. "So there I am. I don't know who she is. The guys next to me don't know who she is. She walks right by, real close, perfume to knock you dead, low-cut dress and all." Ben scooped his hands over his chest. "She was wearin' this tight, shiny green dress. If my wife hadn't a' been there, I'd a grabbed a key to one of them rooms upstairs and bingo . . ."

Ben's stocky body swayed slightly. Then he looked at Sarah, a puzzled frown pinching his face. "And you know who that gorgeous dish was? The Sergeant. Would you believe it? She fooled all of us in that getup. Had the whole pack of us droolin' after her. And then you know what she does? She goes over and unplugs the phonograph, every-body starts hootin' and hollerin', and she just walks over to the door as cool as can be, turns around, whips this wig of blond hair right off her head, and says in her real loud voice somethin' like: 'Thanks for everythin'. You've all been swell. So long.' And out she walks. Can you beat that? I can't even remember if the party went on or not."

Ben stood in silence for a few moments then seemed to shake himself. "And that was it. I don't think anyone here ever saw her again. No one ever heard from her neither. Least not as far as I know." He sighed. "Well, it takes all kinds I always say. But a girl who could look like that. She could a' had any man she set her sights on. And all she does is show up like that just that once and walk out." Ben raised his hands and let them fall back against himself. "I sure don't understand."

Mary stepped back into the room, telling her husband to hurry up. Ben straightened up slowly and in silence checked that the gas and water were off. Then he waved the women to the door and pulled the metal chain hanging from the light bulb in the center of the room.

Sarah goes out with them, thanking them for their help and the coffee, and waits while Ben locks the rear door. As he slips the keys into his pocket, she asks him if Rita Kendall's house is far. Ben tells her where it is and that now it's painted yellow. He tells her that the family who lived there after Rita just moved across the road. Mary calls him to remind him about an order she promised to drop off. Her voice is impatient. Sarah says good-bye, waving to Mary as she gets into the car. Almost immediately, she is out of the village following the road through patches of sun and shadow. Right after the old stone bridge, Sarah slows down. Although Rita Kendall's house is a few miles out of her way, Sarah turns onto the road that will take her to it.

As the mattress catches the wind again, slapping noisily against the roof of the car, she thinks about the empty house and wonders if the cord will hold.

The Swashbuckler

Lee Lynch

Frenchy, jaw thrust forward, legs pumping to the beat of the rock-and-roll song in her head, shoulders dipping left and right with every step, emerged from the subway at 14th Street and disappeared into a cigar store. Moments later, flicking a speck of nothing from the shoulder of her black denim jacket, then rolling its collar up behind her neck, she set out through the blueness and bustle of a New York Saturday night.

She stripped the cellophane from her pack of Marlboros, hit the base of the pack against her fist and drew a cigarette out with her lips. Though the summer breeze was light, she stopped in a doorway, tapped the cigarette against her fist and used her Zippo. She lengthened the stride of her short, exaggeratedly bowed legs and found her rhythm again, diddy-bopping downtown.

Silently singing Brenda Lee's "I'm Sorry," she eyed the people around her on the street as she settled more into her walk. She knew she angered straight people, provoking merciless taunts and threats, but it was her own natural walk. She would walk as she wanted on Saturday nights.

The hell with them all, she thought, straightening proudly, dragging deep on her cigarette. Yeah, she walked like a man, or better still, she walked like a butch, lighter and more graceful than a man. All 4'11" of her was in the tough, bouncing walk. It said who she was. When guys on the street menaced her, she just got cooler, throwing herself into it more, dipping and weaving and dancing down the street. Yeah, she was a bulldyke, and every Saturday night she loved being a bulldyke in a bulldyke's world.

A breeze ruffled her pompadour and she smoothed it back, walking down a line of stores lit from within as if by magic lamps, their goods gleaming. At one window she stopped to pull a long black comb from her rear pocket. When she was satisfied her jet black hair had slid neatly back into a d.a., she began walking further into Greenwich Village, surveying her turf, easing her way into the gay world. She sang a few lines from "Will You Still Love Me Tomorrow?," feeling good. She was twenty-one, good-looking, and wearing her best clothes: black denim jeans with the jacket, light blue button-down shirt, sharply pointed, black ankle-high boots. She felt the edge of her garrison belt buckle. Those knife-carrying butches were dumb, she thought. Even if it really was a femme weapon, her belt was nearly as sharp, and she couldn't be arrested in a raid for concealment. So far she had not had to use it, but she was ready if any of those old deisel dykes crossed her, tried to take a woman from her.

Frenchy entered the last block before Campy Corner, the drugstore where everyone hung out until nightfall came and darkness, or the cops, pushed them into the bars. Would she stay at the Corner tonight or visit a few places before she went to the Sea Colony Bar several blocks away? The grand excitement of Saturday night swept over her, tinged with the fear which accompanies a secret life. She slowed to savor it. Here in her own world she was handsome and funny. Women liked her, wanted to dance with her, wanted to make out with her. The other butches, those not too busy protecting their femmes, joked with her, talked baseball with her. It made six days of standing behind a checkout counter melt away. Her straight clothes, her meekness before the boss and shyness with the other girls—all were bearable because down here she was a prince, a sharp dancer, a big tipper.

She saw the Women's House of Detention on the corner of 6th and Greenwich. This was her landmark, and she felt as if she was at home. Inmates called from windows to their lovers on the street. The flower shop across 6th blazed with color which spilled onto the sidewalk. She filled her small chest with air smelling sweet from the perfumes of a thousand passing femmes. An orchestra of rock-and-roll musicians played in her head.

A few early fags stood against the drugstore window. They weren't hustlers; she'd seen them before in the bars. They just wanted to find boyfriends for the night to take them drinking and dancing, then home. Wallflowers, she thought. The only place I've ever seen guys be the wallflowers.

A butch and her femme came out of the drugstore and Frenchy nodded to the butch, avoiding the femme's eyes. They had seen each other a few times, Frenchy and the femme, and the femme wouldn't want to let on to her new girlfriend. Frenchy tried to remember her name. "Hey, Frenchy," she heard a bass voice call from the curb.

"Hey, Jessie, how you doing?"

"Okay. I'm doing okay."

"Where's Pat?"

Jessie shook her head. The big soft face seemed to sag with sadness. "We broke up, Frenchy. She found somebody else."

"Hell, Jess. And you were together a long time."

"We were going to go for Chinese dinner on our six-month anniversary," Jessie said, her hands in her chino pockets. A light summer jacket was open over an unironed plaid men's sport shirt; her roughly cut brown hair was combed wetly back from her forehead in a wave. "I swear I thought this was it. I thought we had it made, me and Pat would last forever. But," she sighed, "I guess it's like that song, It's All in the Game.' "

"Yeah, love is some game," Frenchy agreed. "I'm sorry it had to happen, Jess, but lookit, you and me can have a good time tonight, how about it? Want to go to the bars with me?"

"Sure. I was hoping I'd see you around. You're not meeting no one?"

"Maybe. It's hard to tell. I said I'd be down here, but I don't know if Donna's going to cooperate, you know what I mean? We haven't been getting along any too good."

"You ready to split up with this one too, Romeo?"

"I really love her a lot, Jess. I don't know. She wants to get a place together. Or stay at a hotel Saturday nights. You know I don't go for that."

"Still don't want to settle down? Boy, if I could just find a girl who would." Jessie sighed again, watching a group of women round the corner.

"I'd get itchy feet. No. I don't want that. And you know I'd like to spend the night with her, but I can't get away with it. If I gave in once she'd be expecting it every week."

"I know. You're not made like that. Better to keep it light."

Frenchy smiled, a large winning smile, and leaned back against the plate glass window, hooking her thumbs into her belt. She mused, "That's how I like it, Jess, light. A new girl every few weeks would suit me fine."

Jessie poked at her with her elbow, chuckling and nodding. "That's you, Frenchy."

"Where do you want to go tonight?" Frenchy asked.

"It's kind of early. How about PamPam's?"

"Yeah, I could use some coffee. I worked all day." They started walking across 6th Avenue.

"You still up at the A&P in the Bronx?"

"Sure thing." Frenchy said as she stopped outside the Women's House of Detention to run the comb through her hair again. "How about you? Still typing for that insurance company?"

"Yeah." Jessie made a face as she borrowed Frenchy's

comb to prop up her wave and flatten the hair cut straight across her thick neck. "Still sitting all day typing forms. Wish I could get a job loading trucks or something. All I do is listen to the girls gossip. Talk about getting itchy, I can't take it much longer."

"I know what you mean. The other cashiers never shut up. There's a cute new girl, though, Marian. A little blonde. Wears these tight black sweaters. Winks at me," Frenchy confessed to Jessie. "Wish I could make her." She grinned lasciviously.

Jessie stretched her arm across Frenchy's shoulders. "Listen, if I didn't know you're called Frenchy from that long French names of yours, I'd say it fits you anyways. You never think of nothing else, you know that?"

Frenchy's smile was smug as they entered PamPam's and looked for a booth. She stopped and narrowed her eyes as she looked around, half-posing, half-looking at the women scattered among the gay men. They found seats at the counter. "Sometimes I want to break my own rule."

"About mixing work and fun?"

"Yeah. She's really something else. Something special. I dream about her all day." She broke into a smile again.

"And you count money like that? With your head in the clouds?" The door opened and they looked stealthily in the mirror at the women who entered. "Nobody," whispered Jessie.

"Yeah, I've got to make the right change so's I can teach the little blonde. The boss gives her to me to teach because I'm the best he's got," Frenchy boasted. "And believe me, she needs all the help she can get." She laughed, pointing to her head. "She may be cute, but she's got confetti for brains."

"If she's that dumb, maybe she thinks you're a guy."

"Not the way I dress at work."

"So ask her out already. Since when are you shy?"

"I don't want to lose my job. And I don't want to fool with girls in my own neighborhood. You know that. But I sure am in love," Frenchy sighed, glancing at herself in the tarnished mirror behind the counter and pressing her pompadour higher. Suddenly she stopped, hand in the air. Her expression changed to an almost sultry look that narrowed one dark eye and lifted one side of her upper lip off her teeth. She made a clicking sound in the corner of her cheek and nudged Jessie. "Donna's here. And look at what she brought you."

Jessie looked into the mirror as Frenchy's current girlfriend walked in with another woman. They could have been twins— both with teased hair piled high on their heads, tight black pants, tiny white pointed sneakers. Donna wore a chartreuse angora sweater with a high neck, her friend a lavender cardigan buttoned low. "What a body," Jessie said admiringly to Frenchy as they swung their stools in unison and stepped off.

Donna quickly kissed Frenchy on the cheek, one eye on the man behind the counter who was ever vigilant of affection between queers in his place. Frenchy asked, "How you doing, chickie? Who's your friend?"

"What do *you* want to know for?" teased Donna, unsmiling, snapping her gum at Frenchy. "This here's Marie, my cousin. The one I was telling you about?"

"Yeah, from the Island, right, Marie?" Frenchy bowed slightly to her and winked.

Marie was at least 5'7" and looked down at Frenchy and Donna. "You didn't tell me how cute she was, Donny."

Donna laughed, finally. "I didn't want you to know. This one's mine," she said, sliding her arm possessively under Frenchy's.

"Okay, girls, that's enough," the counterman said. "Order or have your meeting outside, understand?"

"Sure, Charley," Frenchy sneered. "Anything you say." She shrugged to her friends. "Let's get out of here and go someplace nicer, huh, Marie?"

Marie dropped her eyelids half-shut and began to snap

her fingers and sway. "Where's the dancing? I just turned twenty-one, you know."

"That's why I never brought her down here before, Frenchy. She was too young. And too scared to fake it."

"Well, I'm glad you finally got to twenty-one," Jessie interjected, butting with her blunt body into the closed group the three had made, an embarrassed smile on her face. "I've been waiting for you all my life."

"Oh, hey, Jess. Marie, this is my best friend, Jessie."

"Pleased to meet you," Marie said, then giggled.

"I'm really glad to meet you too, Marie," Jessie said with a glance at the open cardigan. She stepped back and took out her Marlboros. She offered them to Marie, then to Donna and Frenchy. Each took one, and they went outside.

On 6th Avenue Frenchy turned to light Marie's cigarette, but Jessie already had, so she lit Donna's and her own. Their eyes met and Donna cupped her hand around Frenchy's to shield the flame. She was just slightly taller than Frenchy and leaned very close to her. "Going to take me dancing, lover?"

A thrill went up Frenchy's arm from the touch and she inhaled the scent of Jean Naté. She stood there smiling a moment before she answered, savoring the girl and the people thronging around them, gay couples and tourists mixed. "Sure thing, babydoll," Frenchy answered, still touching Donna's hand and holding the unlit Zippo.

"You sure are looking handsome."

Frenchy allowed a smug expression to cross her face. "So are you, angel baby. Real pretty. I like that sweater," she said, touching it lightly on Donna's breast.

"Hey," Donna objected, pulling back. "You want us to get arrested?"

"I wouldn't mind a night locked up with you, beautiful," Frenchy smirked.

"In there, bigshot?" Donna asked, pointing over her shoulder with her thumb at the Women's House of Detention. Its windows were empty now and the building looked heavy,

looming over the intersection where they stood. "The House
of D isn't my idea of a good time. How about it tonight,
though? You got a place we can go?"

Frenchy smoothly took a drag on her cigarette. "No, I
couldn't come up with any place."

"Did you try?" Donna asked sarcastically.

"Sure I did, babe."

"Well, *I did*," Donna said proudly, patting her hair back
where the warm city breeze had pushed it. She raised her
penciled eyebrows. "What do you say, lover?"

"Where is it?" Frenchy asked, coughing on her smoke,
her poise shaken.

"Marie's got a friend with an apartment in the city. He's
out of town. All we've got to do is make sure Marie's got a
date. And it looks like you made sure of that when you
brought Jess along."

Frenchy silently cursed Jessie for breaking up with her
girl. "Donna," she began, leading the way along the sidewalk toward the bar, glancing back to make sure Jessie and
Marie were following. "Donna, I can't tonight."

"How many times are you going to give me that?" Donna
whispered angrily. "I finally got us a place, something you
say you can't do. It doesn't cost any money. It's private and
away from our neighborhoods and you're telling me you
can't?"

"Donna, honey, you know I love you," Frenchy said,
tossing away her cigarette and placing a hand on Donna's
arm. "I just didn't know. How could I know you'd have a
place tonight?"

"Sometimes I'd swear you've got another girl, Frenchy. I
don't know why the hell I bother with you."

"I don't, Donna, you got to believe me." Frenchy's brow
was creased and her eyes had the look of a trapped animal.
"Come on, girl, you can believe me," she said, shaking
Donna's arm.

"Stop it, Frenchy, don't make a scene. I brought Marie

down here for a good time. She's never been with girls before. Except me, when we were kids."

"You two? That's a laugh. You're both femme!"

"Hey, we were only kids. It was a few years ago. We were experimenting. We both liked it, but we were scared to talk about it till a few months ago. Then when I told her I'm gay she wanted to do it again. I told her how I'm femme and all. Besides, we're cousins. It wouldn't be right for us to do it together now we're older."

"No," Frenchy agreed thoughtfully, "it wouldn't be." She glanced around at Marie who smiled brilliantly toward her. Frenchy turned back and hitched up her jeans again, bowing her legs more and swaggering.

"You have your eye on her?" Donna asked suspiciously.

"No, angel. What are you so jumpy about? I'm just making sure Jess is showing her a good time." Frenchy was thinking about how sexy Donna's tall cousin was. She really ought to bring her out herself, not Jessie. There was something clumsy about Jessie. What did the femmes see in her? She was a great pal, but still, if it was the girl's first time out with a butch, someone more skilled ought to do it. Donna's fooling around with Marie didn't count, they hadn't known what they were doing. She needed an expert, somebody with a lot of experience. Somebody talented—like Frenchy. One of her girls had told her that. What was Donna complaining about, she wondered. She gave her a good time even if they couldn't stay together all night. She'd probably be ugly in the morning anyway, she thought, remembering her mother making breakfast all those years, her hair still in pincurls, no pencil on her eyebrows yet, her shapeless nightgown hanging sloppily on her body. No, she preferred her girls all spiffed up on a Saturday night, looking their best. She remembered to put more spring in her diddy-bop. Marie might be watching her.

"Hey, you coming in?" Donna asked, stopping.

"Sure, I was thinking."

"I thought I heard wood burning," Jessie quipped as she halted next to Donna and Frenchy.

Marie laughed and looked excitedly at the door to the bar. "I've never been in a gay bar before."

"Don't worry, beautiful, we'll protect you, right, Jess?"

"I'll protect you from Frenchy, is more like it, ain't it, Donna?"

"Hey, I thought you were my friend." Frenchy playfully punched Jessie, and held the door for Donna.

She and Jessie paid the bouncer and the group walked the length of the bar. Frenchy half-wished she were sitting at the bar cruising all the women who went by. If she wasn't with Donna and wasn't Jessie's friend, she wouldn't have to keep her hands off Marie. I'm falling in love, she thought, then smiled over at Donna as they reached the back room.

They sat at the last empty table. Frenchy looked around the small room. She waved at a few women and nodded distrustfully to the man who sat with his arm around his bleached blond girl friend. Potbellied and middle-aged, he was one of the owner's friends. Every week some man like him sat surveying the dykes. It made Frenchy mad. She could imagine what the men thought. More than once she'd been approached to accompany a straight couple home. The men acted like they had a right to be there, in her bar, just like out on the street they thought they had the right to humiliate her. "Pervert," she hissed low, wishing she didn't even have to dance in front of this week's grinning man.

"Okay, girls," the waitress said. "What'll it be? How you doing, Frenchy? Still got the shackles on Donna, huh? Let me know when you're free, Donna." She winked.

"You live around here?" Donna asked the waitress. Frenchy turned to stare at her.

"Over on the East Side, hon. Got my own place. You come up any time at all." She turned to Frenchy. "Just kidding, lover. I wouldn't touch her."

Frenchy eyed the waitress's slicked-back hair and the white turtleneck she wore under her black shirt. She was competition, Frenchy decided. "Give me a seven and seven," she ordered sullenly, throwing a five-dollar bill on the table.

"Jealous?" Donna asked.

"Let's dance," Frenchy said roughly, pulling Donna from the booth with her. Little Anthony and the Imperials sang "Tears on My Pillow." She walked bowlegged onto the floor, holding Donna's hand and scowling at the waitress's back. She told Donna harshly, "I don't want you fooling around like that."

"Why not? It's a free country."

"Yeah, but you're my girl."

"Not hardly." Donna yanked herself away from Frenchy.

Frenchy pulled her back. "Keep your voice down." She looked around and deliberately took her jacket off, still moving to the music. She leaned off the dance floor to lay it neatly on the back of her chair, then returned to Donna and looked into her eyes. "You don't want to be my woman any more?" She neatly rolled her blue sleeves up toward the elbows and took Donna into her arms once more. "Don't you remember the good times we've been having?" She knew she sounded half-hearted, her uncertainty about wanting Donna in her voice. But if Donna was going to give her a hard time, better to get out now.

Another woman caught her eye. Her long blond hair was in a flip and she was wearing a straight light green skirt and a silky white blouse, the collar wide open and flat against her throat. Such pretty blue eyes, Frenchy thought as she brought herself back to Donna.

"I want someone who'll hold me all night, Frenchy. Don't you understand that I want a girl who'll take me home?"

"You want a woman who'll *keep* you home. You want a husband," Frenchy accused.

Donna's dark eyes flashed anger and she pulled away. Frenchy grabbed at her arm, looking around to see if anyone had noticed. The other couples were either pressed against one another, dancing, sweatily erotic in the dim smoky light, or stared unseeingly at the dancers from their crowded tiny tables. "And what's wrong with wanting that?" Donna asked loudly. "I'm twenty-three. I want to settle down. I thought . . ." Her voice broke and she chewed her gum for a moment as she let Frenchy lead her into the dance again. "Tears on My Pillow," Little Anthony sang. She raised her head and looked wistfully at Frenchy. "I thought you might want to settle down too. I mean, you have a steady job, but no place of your own. I thought maybe we could get together."

"I ain't the marrying kind," Frenchy said, remembering the dream she'd once had of having a woman to come home to.

She'd never quite figured out how to do it, how to hide her gayness and live with a lover; how to be a butch and look the way she needed to when she was with her femme, yet pass for straight otherwise. How to figure out the dozens of other details about a split life.

"No." She shook her head. "You were wrong. I'll never settle down. I like the gay life, the bars. I like having a good time."

"I'm tired of it!" Donna pushed Frenchy aside. She struggled through the crowd to her seat. Whispering something to Marie, she picked up her purse and walked around the dancing couples and out of the back room.

Frenchy watched her, sadness welling up. She was going to miss Donna, she thought as she finished rolling up her sleeves. She shrugged when she reached the table. "Easy come, easy go." She picked up her drink and swallowed it in three gulps, grinning down at Marie.

"You drink *fast*," Marie said, impressed. "Doesn't that get you drunk?"

"I can hold my liquor," Frenchy bragged, slipping her hands into her pockets, feeling the hot alcohol press down on her sadness. She shrugged again. "How are you two doing? You look like you're getting along like a house on fire."

Jessie blushed to the roots of her wave. Then she smiled

toward Marie. "Want to dance?" Marie grinned across at her and gave her hand to Jessie. Frenchy could see their excitement about each other. "What happened to Donna?" Jessie asked Frenchy.

"It's over."

Jessie looked sad. "Tough break."

"Love 'em and leave 'em," Frenchy said, standing. "You two have a good dance. I'm going to see who's here."

"She always bounces back fast," Jessie explained to Marie.

Frenchy moved from table to table, greeting almost half the women in the back room. By the time Jessie and Marie had danced their third slow dance, to "Exodus," bumping and grinding as close as the bar owners would allow, Frenchy was dancing too—with the blue-eyed woman. She held the woman loosely and they talked as they danced. Afterward they pushed their way to the table. "This is Edie," Frenchy said to Jessie and Marie.

"Hiya, Edie." Jessie smiled, shaking her head in wonder at Frenchy.

Soon after that the two couples separated for the night. Edie and Frenchy walked hand in hand along Greenwich Avenue past the male hustlers leaning against buildings.

"I better be getting home pretty soon," Frenchy sighed. The Village was difficult to leave. Even in darkness it seemed to glow, to light up the sky out of sheer Saturday night energy. The streets were still crowded, but now with young straight couples nervously visiting the bohemian coffee houses in their shiny shoes and pastel dresses. Beatniks shuffled beside their guitar cases to join other folksingers in their many gathering places. A few bars flashed neon signs, restaurants were still full.

They walked all the way to the East Side to catch Edie's subway. Washington Square was quiet as they passed, though in one corner a classical guitarist played for some straight lovers. From Fifth Avenue on, New York University seemed to dominate the streets, silent and empty of its students. The streets narrowed, and warehouses began to appear.

"It seems awfully early to go home," Edie said as her station came into view.

"By the time I take you home and go back to the Bronx it'll be a lot later."

Edie's face brightened. "You're going to take me home?"

"At least as far as the subway goes. You think I'd let a beautiful woman like you walk the streets of the City alone at this time of night?"

"That's sweet of you. Somehow I imagined if I could ever meet a woman my first try tonight we'd go back to her place or I'd go home alone. I never thought of being escorted home."

"Queers are just like anybody else, baby. Got respect for a woman, treat them politely. Why," Frenchy drew herself up to her full height, "it wouldn't be gentlemanly of me to let you go all the way out to Queens alone." She was proud of the way she had skirted the issue of spending the night with Edie. "Just like I'd never ask a girl to—you know—go against her principles the first night."

"You're adorable." Edie laughed affectionately as they descended the subway stairs. "I just never imagined myself with someone like you," she said when Frenchy insisted on putting a token of her own in the turnstyle.

They walked past the blue and white tiling which lined the walls of the small station. "And I never imagined I'd have such a good time with a college girl. Or that a college girl would be interested in me," Frenchy said modestly.

"Why wouldn't I be interested? You're cute. And interesting. And sexy."

Frenchy leaned against a dark green iron column. "You think so?"

"I never dated a *boy* as good-looking as you. They don't go for my type: too studious."

Frenchy saw her reflection over Edie's shoulder in a mirror on a gum machine. She smiled and took Edie's hand. "I'm just glad I got to you on your first night downtown before someone else did. Were you nervous, comding down to the bars by yourself?"

Edie flushed. "I was," she said, her blue eyes seeming to search Frenchy's for sympathy and comfort. "But you rescued me," she said, laughing.

"How'd you know where to go?" Frenchy asked, moving slightly closer to her.

Edie stepped back a bit, as if afraid. Her warm laugh had turned to a nervous giggle. "My aunt is gay. She lives in the Midwest, but I wrote her a letter hoping she would know where I could go to see if I was gay. She said there used to be a place—The Sea Colony—and told me how to find it. She wished me luck." Her eyes twinkled with confidence again. "I guess her wish came true."

Frenchy had leaned closer, and Edie's eyes glittered. She seemed to have lost her breath while she spoke. Frenchy leaned up and kissed her, a fugitive kiss taken in fear that someone would come through the turnstyle, but Edie re laxed into Frenchy's arms as if in relief. When they leaned back to look at one another Frenchy could tell Edie had found her answer. Edie grabbed her and returned the kiss, knocking Frenchy slightly off balance. "Hold it, hold it," Frenchy said gently, gaining control. "Somebody might come," she whispered against Edie's lips. She was a little taken aback by Edie's aggressiveness.

Edie didn't seem to care who came. "I've waited for a long time to be here, to be doing this," she said, tossing her hair back and straightening the white cardigan. "Isn't there somewhere we can go?"

Frenchy joyously sang more of "Will You Still Love me Tomorrow?" in her head. She looked toward the women's bathroom. Edie had too much class, she thought, to want to make out in a bathroom. But Edie had seen where she was looking and tugged at her until Frenchy led her inside. The floor was littered and the tiny room smelled strongly of disinfectant. They leaned against a graffiti-covered stall, kissing each other lightly, then more and more hungrily

until Frenchy began to pass her hands across Edie's body
and over her breasts, creating sparks on her sily blouse.
Their breathing was so loud in the silence of the white tiled
room that they barely heard their train in time to catch it. In
an empty car they leaned on each other breathlessly, laughing and straightening their clothes. "You're pretty wonderful," Frenchy said, squeezing Edie's hand one last time as
they pulled into 23rd Street and other passengers filed sleepily on.

They changed trains at Grand Central, staring into one
another's eyes as they waited under the stairs, out of sight of
the platform. Frenchy was glad she had broken up with
Donna. The excitement had pretty much left that relationship, and she had almost forgotten how exhilarating it was
to start a new affair. Especially when she was bringing
someone out. Her heart pounded until it seemed as if her
whole body must pulsate with it. Her hands were like ice,
she shook inside. She was as excited as a kid going to a
party, at moments so excited that a cold sweat broke out all
over her body and she was almost overcome by a wave of
nausea. This was living. This was the gay life. This was what
made it all so worthwhile. It was a high better than any
liquor could bring. The woman she was with became a thousand movie stars rolled into one—the most beautiful woman
in the world. The subway became the most romantic of
places, its trains rushing to exotic parts of the city, its
passengers mysterious in their Saturday night finery, its
promise of new destinations and new women. The Village
truly was lined with magic lamps to lead her to all this.

Frenchy's life had become adventurous once more. She
was swashbuckling. She stood tall in her black pointed boots
and gazed romantically at Edie and felt herself melt in
Edie's adoring, desiring gaze. When the train came they
huddled on a double seat at the end of a car and Frenchy
grinned at everybody who stared at them. She wasn't afraid
of anything. She remembered once riding out to the end of
the Flushing line with another woman and stopping at Wil-

lets Point; it had been big—and empty. She pulled Edie off
the train there and led her to a high-backed wooden bench
with seats on both sides. They went around to the side that
faced the express tracks, empty this time of night.

"I love you, Edie," Frenchy breathed as they sat. "I don't
want to leave you yet."

"Let's just sit here awhile."

Frenchy kissed Edie's hair and held her close. She could
feel a wave of warmth rise through her body and began
again to tremble. "Are you cold?" Edie asked.

"No," Frenchy answered in her deepest, huskiest voice.
"I just want you so bad."

Reckless of being in the open, they began to kiss again.
The summer air seemed to sit around them still as a wall
and they could see stars, the moon over the track. The
pillars and roof of the station hovered protectively over
them and the wooden bench curved around them like an old
grey hand.

Frenchy made love to Edie as if they were sitting on a
living room couch, except that she went under her clothing
instead of removing it. She was protective against possible
discomforts for Edie to the point of painful discomfort for
herself. When she touched Edie's breast she knew they
would finish right there on the subway platform, college girl
or no college girl. "Edie, Edie," Frenchy sighed as she
spread her little hand across the flesh inside Edie's thigh.

"Frenchy," Edie said wondrously, digging her fingers into
her shoulders. "I don't know why it took me so long to do
this," she whispered.

"To come out?"

"Is that what you call it?" Edie asked between kisses.

"Yeah," Frenchy said, "and this is how you do it." Her
hand reached under Edie's nylon panties. They were bikinis
and she imagined them, black and sexy against the white of
Edie's skin. Then she felt the matted pubic hairs, parted them
with her fingertips, kneaded the soft flesh beneath and slipped
to the cavity of the panties' crotch. She felt Edie's wetness

where it had soaked through the nylon against her knuckles. She felt her own vagina tighten and loosen involuntarily and reached for Edie's softer parts as if to find release for herself.

"Ohh," Edie moaned, twisting against Frenchy's slowly stroking thumb. She let her legs fall more widely apart as her skirt rode up her legs. Frenchy parted her inner lips with her index and middle fingers and stroked her swelling clitoris. "Baby," Edie breathed, tightening. Frenchy began to kiss her face, tiny loving kisses all over, when the train she'd barely been aware of thrust a hot gust of wind against them and stopped behind their bench.

They held onto one another, not breathing, afraid someone would get off the train and come to their side of the bench. The train pulled out. Footsteps descended the steps at the end of the platform. They breathed in relief, looking at one another, falling onto each other's lips, desperate to retrieve their passion.

Although they went through the motions again, Frenchy could tell their lovemaking had a pallid end for Edie. Disappointed, they waited for the next train, Frenchy still touching Edie with passion.

"Will you be at the bar next Saturday?" Frenchy asked, her mouth nibbling on Edie's neck.

"Oh, yes," Edie replied as if there had never been a question about it. "Will you?"

"There's no place I'd rather be if you're going to be there, sweetheart."

"There are plenty of other bars, Frenchy, I'm sure. And girls," Edie said, pulling away to pat her hair into place. "Now stop kissing me and let me fix myself. I might know someone on the train!"

Frenchy stepped back, grinning. "Sorry, angel baby. I just can't keep my hands off you."

"No kidding." Edie smiled back, combing her hair and renewing her lipstick. "Why don't you come pick me up next week?"

"Come all the way out here? I don't get out of work till four. Think of all the time we'd waste travelling when we could be together downtown."

"It was being together I thought was important."

"Sure, Edie. You're right," she said, already missing her walk downtown. "I'll pick you up. Tell me how to get to your house."

"I'll show you. Take me there tonight," Edie tempted.

Frenchy looked eagerly at Edie's hips, thrust forward with her hands splayed on them. She shook her head. "I can't, I just can't tonight."

"Why? Do you have another girlfriend waiting for you in the Bronx?"

"No, Edie, no way. I only got eyes for you, honest. I wouldn't two-time you. I just got to get home. It's late already." She shouted as Edie's train came in, "Tell me where you live!"

"Never mind. I'll see you at the bar. Call me. I'm in the book under my father's name: Aaron Marks. What's your number?" Edie cried as she stepped onto the train.

Frenchy hesitated. She didn't want to lose Edie, but she couldn't have her calling her house. "I don't have one," she shouted into the train's closing door.

The night had cooled. Frenchy pulled her jean jacket tighter across her chest and buttoned it. She crossed to the other platform, aware of the huge dark sky over her, over the whole city that was settling into the night. She whistled a bar of "In the Still of the Night." At the edge of the platform she breathed deeply, lifting her chin, admiring the stars.

The magic had not yet left the night. Wasn't she, Frenchy, still out on a Saturday night? Wasn't she beloved of Edie who would soon be dreaming of her? Couldn't she go right back downtown and find another girl, give her just as much? She thought briefly of Donna at the waitress's apartment. She bet it wouldn't be as good as if Donna had stayed with her. Yes, Donna would miss her. She glanced up at the stars once more, hitched up her jeans and threw her cigarette on the platform where she ground it hard under her heel as the train stopped and opened its doors for her. The long ride to the Bronx began. It was with effort that she kept the spring in her diddy-bop as she changed trains.

By the Yankee Stadium stop Frenchy had unbuttoned her jean jacket and checked her collar for lipstick. She pulled a locket out from under her shirt and buttoned the shirt's top button, settling the necklace outside it. She rolled down the collar of her jacket and flattened it. At 167th Street she removed her pinky ring and ID bracelet. At 170th she slid her Marlboro box, almost empty, under the seat, glancing around to make sure no one noticed, then took out a stick of Juicy Fruit gum and stuffed it in her mouth. Her face changed as she chewed—from the bold arrogant look she had worn all night, to a wary expression. She clenched her jaw and looked, above the tightly buttoned collar and locket, almost old maidish, like a girl who'd never had a date and went to church regularly to pray for one.

At her stop Frenchy got off the train demurely, remembering the time she met her next-door neighbors coming home from their evening at Radio City Music Hall. She walked up the subway steps, pulling the comb from her back pocket. The cigar shop on the corner was still open, selling Sunday papers, and she used its window to take the point out of her d.a. and to dismantle her pompadour. She whistled "I'm Sorry" softly as she wound small spitcurls in front of her ears. She walked past her building and glanced up, relieved that no one was at the window. How often she had wished the apartment was at the back. Behind the stairs on the first floor was a cubbyhole, a small hiding place she had discovered as a child, just low enough for her to reach. Her heart raced with the anxiety she always felt here, afraid someone might have discovered and taken her plain brown slipons. She removed them, and squeezed her black boots into their space, patting them good-bye for a week.

Then, Sunday paper in hand, she flattened her hair one last time, chewed her gum more vigorously before throwing

it out, and gingerly ascended the stairs, key in hand. Each
step creaked beneath her feet. The four-story walkup needed
repairs; even the banisters creaked. There was no way, it
seemed, not to make noise. She opened her third-floor door
quietly. The little hallway was empty except for the light left
burning for her. She slipped quickly out of her jean jacket
and headed for her room. Then her mother called, in French,
"Is that you, dear? You're very late tonight. I guess the girls
wanted to play rummy all night this week, no?"

Frenchy stood frozen, remembering that she still smelled
of Edie. "Yes, Maman, I'll be in to say good night in a jiffy.
I need to use the little girl's room." She heard nothing more
from her mother and slipped into the bathroom.

"Dear . . ." her mother called as Frenchy let the water
from the tap wash away the remnants of her self.

From *Dead Heat*

Willyce Kim

Trajectory

Cody Roberts first had the dream the day after she had made it with Mary Lou Thomas, the senior prom queen.

"The horses appear through the mist. There's a bay, and a black, and a chestnut. Several big grays bring up the rear. Moving slowly in a line, they circle the field once, twice, no, three times. It begins to rain. And then I notice . . ." Cody's voice always trailed off here. If there was a window she gazed out of it. If there was no window she invented it. *"They have no eyes."*

"What?" said the therapist.

"They have no eyes."

"They have no eyes?"

"You're repeating me," said Cody, taking a long drag off her cigarette. "I don't like it when people repeat me."

"Okay," said the therapist, a sharp-featured man, in a low, well-modulated voice. "Go on."

"I grab the mane of the largest gray and pull myself up on her back. Steam rises from her flanks as I dig my heels in . . . Jesus, how we move. I'm a god!" Cody roared.

"A god?" *Shit*, thought the therapist, shifting in his chair, *seven on a scale of ten and rising.* "Go on."

263

"The rain is falling hard now. The horse is blind and I can hardly see. I can *feel* the other horses behind us. Flesh is buckling all around me. We're going down. We're all going down. I hear the loud roar of a crowd. Then everything goes black."

"Anything else?"

"One more thing," Cody said, stubbing out her cigarette. "I win the Kentucky Derby."

"The Kentucky Derby?"

"I'm not paying you *shit* if you do that one more time!" Cody yelled.

"How do you know you win the Kentucky Derby?"

"The horse told me."

"What horse?"

"The filly. The gray filly."

Nodding thoughtfully, the therapist scribbled "lunar trajectory" next to Cody Roberts's name and closed his appointment book.

Cody

The night Cody Roberts was born, the lights went out in Omaha. Her mother insisted that this was nature's way of punctuating the birth of her newest star.

The truth was: a series of thunderstorms jitterbugging across the Great Plains decided to rest a while and shoot the works over the placid city of Omaha.

"Whoa! Whoa! Whoa!" the good citizens of Omaha cried, as the herd of cumulo-nimbus mash-potatoed across the midwestern sky. Sticks of lightning flew like javelins. Thunder smashed from door to door, as rain blew over the city in wagon loads.

"Push!" the delivery nurses exhorted as young Jenny Roberts bore down for the fiftieth time.

"This is the first, and this is the last," panted Cody's mother. "No sex in the afternoon, no sex at the drive-in, no

sex in the kitchen, and goddammit no sex at Look-Out
Point after wine and cheese on a Sunday afternoon!" she
yelled.

"That's right!" the nurses screamed in unison. "Harder!
Harder!"

Jenny Roberts rolled her eyes, and thought of the summer of '62, and how she slipped in and out of love with
Jimmy Baker, the fireman's son, and Dusty Roberts, a shy
young drifter.

Jimmy bought her chocolates and some Elvis Presley
records.

Dusty brought her marijuana and poetry by men with
twisted names like Ferlinghetti and Ginsberg.

"Come marry me, and be my wife," said Jimmy Baker,
the fireman's son.

"Come live with me, and be my life," said Dusty Roberts,
the shy, stoned drifter.

"That's it, hon," urged the nurse to her left, shaking
Jenny loose from her memory bank. "One more time."

"For Mother," said the nurse to her right, and the sky
rocked and the table rolled.

"Fuck Mother, I can't do this any more."

"Yes you can," chanted the delivery nurses.

"No, I can't," Jenny Roberts shot back as all the lights in
Omaha went out.

And a great cry filled the room.

Seduction

"I desire you," said the voice trailing off into the warm
evening air. "My heart sings whenever you walk by, and I
can't keep my eyes off you, not for a second. I've strolled
past your house and smelled the flowers in your front yard
while hoping to catch a glimpse of you." Cody shook her
head and stared across the Platte River. That's what she had
meant to say. She had rehearsed those words for days. And

now sitting there with Mary Lou Thomas, the senior prom queen, the hard-on of every young male at Lincoln High, the moment Cody had waited for rushed over her, drowning those thoughts like a flash flood in July.

"Mary Lou," Cody said, taking the most beautiful hand she had ever seen, "trust me. Nothing's wrong here, but so help me, I'm wild about you. I eat my breakfast in the morning, and I see your face swimming in my cereal bowl next to the berries and nuggets—and I want a second helping. I see you in the hallway at school and I want to climb those long white legs and . . . Jesus, it's bad at night. I can't sleep without . . . wanting you. I want to push my face into your hair and breathe all the flowers of the universe. I want you," choked the flustered Cody.

"And I, you," said the most beautiful voice in the world.

"Wait," said Cody, blinking wildly. "I must be brain dead."

"No," whispered Mary Lou Thomas, the senior prom queen. "This is Omaha. The North Star is overhead, and I'm going to take you for all the nights you've ever come alone in your bed."

Cody Roberts fell back into the tall grass of summer and pulled Mary Lou Thomas down beside her. "You smell like horses," she whispered excitedly.

"Well, come on, Cody," said Mary Lou slowly, unbuttoning her shirt, "let's ride, Cody, ride."

Hound

Five years and four hundred therapy sessions could not alter Cody Roberts's dream. It had a life of its own. It followed Cody from Nebraska to Louisiana. Like a faithful hound, it bounded along after her. It nestled under her pillow and lay in wait for her. Cody tried meditation. And bio-feedback. And, of course, sex. And valium. But she couldn't lick it. The dream became her nightmare. She was going to be crushed by a ton of horseflesh. The burning question in Cody's mind was: was this before or after she won the Kentucky Derby?

Armageddon

Jack Tucker was the first horse trainer in Nebraska to give Cody a mount. She was nineteen years old and weighed ninety-five pounds with her boots on. "Hell, to this day I don't know what made me give her the mount," he would say in later years. "I liked the way she galloped the horses in the morning, and I seen she had a way with them. She had good strong arms and a nice set of hands. She was spunky and always trying to chase down a mount, going from barn to barn introducing herself to the different trainers. She worked twice as hard as some of the boys. So I give her a shot, and I guess made a little history. She was the first girl jockey to ride at Ak-Sar-Ben. Hell, *now* it's nothing. We got three. But then, Cody Roberts was the first. She rode a big bay colt named Armageddon that day, and I'll never forget the stretch run. Cody had the horse on the rail and nailed the leader at the wire. In the winner's circle, she took off her cap and shook her hair down. The fans went wild and the press went crazy. It's a shame she left. She rode as good as any boy."

Grit

Cody Roberts with her dog Gypsy said goodbye to the state of Nebraska, said goodbye to Ak-Sar-Ben. Left her mother with her news clippings, her scrapbooks, and a soggy handkerchief; left Jack Turner and his stable of horses; left Dr. Michael Irving, psychotherapist, pondering the hidden meaning of Cody's endless nightmare; and left Frankie Tucker, daughter of Jack, in a stall, lying naked under a blanket of hay, to pursue her career at other tracks. Did she have the grit to go up against the other jockey colonies, especially the ones situated in the West? "Like the song says," she whispered in Frankie Tucker's ear, "I want to be the best in the West."

"Why, Cody," Frankie Tucker murmured, "you already are."

"I'm talking about riding," Cody replied, clearing her throat.

"So am I," Frankie Tucker coyly answered.

"If your daddy only knew."

"I know what my daddy knows."

"And what's that?" asked Cody, panting as Frankie nibbled on her ear.

"That you have the softest hands since Shoemaker," Frankie Tucker whispered.

"Well," Cody said, gliding her hand over familiar terrain, "Daddy's always right."

Gumbo

Cody Roberts, on her migration west, stopped one evening at Louisiana Downs, a race track located east of Shreveport, to share a pot of gumbo with several of Jack Tucker's old stable hands. The evening ripened into several years. Cody stayed, a willing victim of Cajun cooking, reluctant to travel in mid-winter and itching to re-enter the winner's circle. She tossed her whip onto the track, encouraged by her old friends and a sweet-talking agent named Billy Bluestone.

Book

"I seen you ride in the Oaklawn Stakes on Memorial Day. You were on a filly named Khartoum, and you come out of the one hole, got shut off in the backstretch, took her wide at the top of the lane, and win the race going away. I'd

never seen a girl jockey pump like that," said Billy Bluestone, shaking his head and smiling shyly at the ground.

"I remember that race," replied Cody. "That was my first
stakes purse. Did you bet on me?"

"No," Billy said sheepishly. "I should have, but I wasn't
going to bet no girl jockey in a stakes race. See what I
know?"

"You know better now," said Cody, staring at Billy's
brown eyes and the scar that creased the right side of his
forehead.

"I do," laughed Billy, "and I'd like to prove to you how
much I've learned, by being your book if you ride here at
the Downs."

Cody scratched her head and looked over at the long lines
of shed-rows and the horses walking to and from their stalls.
If she stayed, she'd need an agent to work the backstretch
for her. "Can you get me live mounts? I need good horses."

"I can get you the best," said Billy, sucking in his breath.
"I know most of the local trainers, and it helps that you
rode at Ak-Sar-Ben."

"How long you been in the business, Billy?"

"Ten years," said Billy, crossing his toes. "I booked my
first mount at Bay Meadows in California."

"California," murmured Cody, tapping her chin thoughtfully. "I think your stock just tripled in value."

"Then," continued Billy, "I worked my way up the coast
to Washington, stayed a while until I couldn't stand the rain
anymore, and ended up here."

"Well, partner," said Cody, extending her hand. "I have
many plans. The first is to win the Kentucky Derby. The
second is to ride out west. And Billy," she called over her
shoulder as she turned to walk away, "you can bet on that."

Poker

Cody Roberts was in third place in the jockey's standings,
five wins out of first place, when a horse she was mounting

in the saddling paddock reared up and flipped over on top of her. Cody's right leg was broken in three places and put in a cast for six months. Billy Bluestone drew a pair of boots with wings on Cody's cast and signed his name.

"We were heading for a helluva year," he said, spitting out his toothpick. "I think you just about had them other guys by the balls."

"I can't talk about any of this right now," Cody replied glumly. "Frank Crawford, the head clocker, has offered me a job as his assistant until I'm able to ride again. At least that will keep Gypsy and me in food. "Won't it, girl?" she said, leaning over to pat a red, short-haired pointer.

"How is that old Goulash dog of yours? Number Five, if I remember rightly," said Billy, snapping his fingers.

"Very good, Billy," laughed Cody. "Hungarian Vizsla. Hungarian Vizsla. Someday you'll remember the name, and we'll both love you for it. Number Five here doesn't mind in the least, though," smiled Cody, lifting Gypsy's ear and waving it at Billy.

"I'll never get over that tattoo in the ear. But I guess it's just like the identification numbers in each race horse's mouth."

"Not quite. All it really means is Gypsy was the fifth pup born in the litter. Jesus Christ, Billy, this is going to be a long summer on the bayou," said Cody, slamming her fist down on the table. "Here's the keys to my car. Take five from my wallet and buy us a deck of cards, a couple of Cokes, and a six-pack of beer. Did I ever tell you what a great poker player I am."

"Hey," grinned Billy, "you are looking at the king of five card stud."

"Billy," said Cody, tapping her fingers along the heel of her cast, "as someone before us said, 'I have the feeling this is going to be the start of a long and wonderful friendship.' "

Excerpt from *Dead Heat* by Willyce Kim published by Alyson Publications.

The Penis Story

Sarah Schulman

The night before they sat in their usual spots. Jesse's hair was like torrents of black oil plunging into the sea. Ann watched her, remembering standing in the butcher shop looking at smoked meat, smelling the grease, imagining Jesse's tongue on her labia. She was starving.

"I'm just waiting for a man to rescue me," Jesse said.

"Look, Jess," Ann answered. "Why don't we put a timeline on this thing. Let's say, forty. If no man rescues you by the time you're forty, we'll take it from a different angle. What do you say?"

"I say I'll be in a mental hospital by the time I'm forty."

Jesse was thirty-two. This was a realistic possibility.

"Jesse, if instead of being two women, you and I were a woman and a man, would we be lovers by now?"

"Yes." Jesse had to answer yes because it was so obviously true.

"So what's not there for you in us being two women? Is it something concrete about a man, or is it the idea of a man?"

"I don't think it's anything physical. I think it is the idea of a man. I want to know that my lover is a man. I need to be able to say that."

Ann started to shake and covered her legs with a blanket

so it wouldn't be so obvious. She felt like a child. She put
her head on Jesse's shoulder feeling weak and ridiculous.
Then they kissed. It felt so familiar. They'd been doing that
for months. Each knew how the other kissed. Ann felt
Jesse's hand on her waist and back and chest. Jesse reached
her hand to Ann's bra. She'd done this before too. First
tentatively, then more directly, she brushed her hands and
face against Ann's breasts. Ann kissed her skin and licked
it. She sucked her fingers, knowing those nails would have
to be cut if Jesse were to ever put her fingers into Ann's
body. She looked at Jesse's skin, at her acne scars and
blackheads. She wanted to kiss her a hundred times. Then,
as always, Jesse became disturbed, agitated. "I'm nervous
again," she said. "Like, *oh no—now I'm going to have to
fuck.*"

Suddenly Ann remembered that their sexual life together
was a piece of glass. She put on her shirt and went home.
This was the middle of the night in New York City.

When Ann awoke the next morning from unsettling dreams,
she saw that a new attitude had dawned with the new day. She
felt accepting, not proud. She felt ready to face adjustment
and compromise. She was ready for change. Even though
she was fully awake her eyes had not adjusted to the morning. She reached for glasses but found them inadequate.
Then she looked down and saw that she had a penis.

Surprisingly, she didn't panic. Ann's mind, even under
normal circumstances, worked differently than the minds of
many of those around her. She was able to think three
thoughts at the same time, and as a result often suffered
from headaches, disconnected conversation, and too many
ideas. However, at this moment she only had two thoughts:
"What is it going to be like to have a penis?" and "I will
never be the same again."

It didn't behave the way most penises do. It rather seemed
to be trying to find its own way. It swayed a bit as she
walked to the bathroom mirror, careful not to let her legs

interfere, feeling off balance, as if she had an itch and couldn't scratch it. She tried to sit back on her hips, for she still had hips, and walk pelvis first, for she still had her pelvis. In fact, everything appeared to be the same except that she had no vagina. Except that she had a prick.

"I am a prick," she said to herself.

The first thing she needed to do was piss and that was fun, standing up seeing it hit the water, but it got all over the toilet seat and she had to clean up the yellow drops.

"I am a woman with a penis and I am still cleaning up piss."

This gave her a sense of historical consistency. Now it was time to get dressed.

She knew immediately she didn't want to hide her penis from the world. Ann had never hidden anything else, no matter how controversial. There was nothing wrong with having a penis. Men had them and now she did too. She wasn't going to let her penis keep her from the rest of humanity. She chose a pair of button-up Levis and stuffed her penis into her pants where it bulged pretty obviously. Then she put on a t-shirt that showed off her breasts and her muscles and headed toward the F train to Shelley's house to meet her friends for lunch.

By the time Ann finished riding on the F train she had developed a fairly integrated view of her new self. She was a lesbian with a penis. She was not a man with breasts. She was a woman. This was not androgyny, she'd never liked that word. Women had always been whole to Ann, not half of something waiting to be completed.

They sat in Shelley's living room eating lunch. These were her most attentive friends, the ones who knew best how she lived. They sat around joking until Shelley finally asked, "What's that between your legs?"

"That's my penis," Ann said.

"Oh, so now you have a penis."

"I got it this morning. I woke up and it was there."

They didn't think much of Ann's humor usually, so the

conversation moved on to other topics. Judith lit a joint. They got high and said funny things, but they did keep coming back to Ann's penis.

"What are you going to do with it?" Shelley asked.

"I don't know."

"If you really have a penis, why don't you show it to us?" Roberta said. She was always provocative.

Ann remained sitting in her chair but unbuttoned her jeans and pulled her penis out of her panties. She had balls too.

"Is that real?"

Roberta came over and put her face in Ann's crotch. She held Ann's penis in her hand. It just lay there.

"Yup, Ann's got a penis alright."

"Did you eat anything strange yesterday?" Judith asked.

"Maybe it's from masturbating," Roberta suggested, but they all knew that couldn't be true.

"Well, Ann, let me know if you need anything, but I have to say I'm glad we're not lovers anymore because I don't think I could handle this." Judith bit her lip.

"I'm sure you'd do fine," Ann replied in her usual charming way.

Ann put on her flaming electronic lipstick. It smudged accidentally, but she liked the effect. This was preparation for the big event. Ann was ready to have sex. Thanks to her lifelong habit of masturbating before she went to sleep, Ann had sufficiently experimented with erections and come. She'd seen enough men do it and knew how to do it for them, so she had no trouble doing it for herself. Sooner or later she would connect with another person. Now was that time. She wore her t-shirt that said, "Just visiting from another planet." Judith had given it to her and giggled, nervously.

The Central Park Ramble used to be a bird and wildlife sanctuary. Because it's hidden, and therefore foreboding, gay men use it to have sex, and that's where Ann wanted to be. Before she had a penis, Ann used to imagine sometimes while making love that she and her girlfriend were two gay men. Now that she had this penis, she felt open to different kinds of people and new ideas, too.

She saw a gay man walking through the park in his little gym suit. He had a nice tan like Ann did and a gold earring like she did too. His t-shirt also had writing on it. It said, "All-American Boy." His ass stuck out like a mating call.

"Hi," she said.

"Hi," he said.

"Do you want to smoke a joint?" she asked very sweetly.

He looked around suspiciously.

"Don't worry, I'm gay too."

"OK honey, why not. There's nothing much happening anyway."

So, they sat down and smoked a couple of joints and laughed and told about the different boyfriends and girlfriends that they had had, and which ones had gone straight and which ones had broken their hearts. Then Ann produced two beers and they drank those and told about the hearts that they had broken. It was hot and pretty in the park.

Ann mustered up all her courage and said.

"I have a cock."

"You look pretty good for a mid-op," he said.

His name was Mike.

"No, I'm not a transsexual. I'm a lesbian with a penis. I know this is unusual, but would you suck my cock?"

Ann had always wanted to say "suck my cock" because it was one thing a lot of people said to her and she never said to anyone. Once she and her friends made little stickers that said "End Violence in the Lives of Women," which they stuck up all over the subway. Many mornings when she was riding to work, Ann would see that different people had written over them "suck my cock." It seemed like an appropriate response given the world in which we all live.

Mike thought this was out of the ordinary, but he prided himself on taking risks. So he decided "what the hell" and went down on her like an expert.

Well, it did feel nice. It didn't feel like floating in hot water, which is what Ann sometimes thought of when a woman made love to her well with her mouth, but it did feel good. She started thinking about other things. She tried the two-gay-men image but it had lost its magic. Then she remembered Jesse. She saw them together in Jesse's apartment. Each in their usual spots.

"What's the matter, Annie? Your face is giving you away."

"This is such a bastardized version of how I'd like to be relating to you right now."

"Well," said Jesse. "What would it be like?"

"Oh, I'd be sitting here and you'd say 'I'm ready' and I'd say, 'ready for what?' and you'd say, 'I'm ready to make love to you Annie.' Then I'd say 'Why don't we go to your bed?' and we would."

"Yes," Jesse said. "I would smell your smell Annie. I would put my arms on your neck and down over your breasts. I would unbutton your shirt, Annie, and pull it off your shoulders. I would run my fingers down your neck and over your nipples. I would lick your breasts, Annie, I would run my tongue down your neck to your breasts."

Ann could feel Jess's wild hair like the ocean passing over her chest. Jesse's mouth was on her nipples licking, her soft face against Ann's skin. She was licking, licking then sucking harder and faster until Jesse clung to her breasts harder and harder.

"You taste just like my wife," Mike said after she came.

"What?"

Ann's heart was beating. The ocean was crashing in her ears.

"I said, you taste just like my wife, when you come I mean. You don't come sperm, you know, you come women's cum, like pussy."

"Oh thank God."

Ann was relieved.

Another morning Ann woke up and her fingers were all sticky. It was still dark. First she thought she'd had a wet dream, but when she turned on her reading lamp she saw blood all over her hands. Instinctively she put her fingers in her mouth. It was gooey, full of membrane and salty. It was her period. She guessed it had no other place to come out, so it flowed from under her fingernails. She spent the next three and a half days wearing black plastic gloves.

The feeling of her uterine lining coming out of her hands gave Ann some hope. After living with her penis for nearly a month, she was beginning to experience it as a loss, not an acquisition. She was grieving for her former self.

One interesting item was that Ann was suddenly in enormous sexual demand. More women than had ever wanted to make love with her wanted her now. But most of them didn't want anyone to know, so she said no.

There was one woman, though, to whom she said yes. Her name was Muriel. Muriel dreamed that she made love to a woman with a penis and it was called "glancing." So she looked high and low until she found Ann, who she believed had a rare and powerful gift and should be honored.

Ann and Muriel became lovers and Ann learned many new things from this experience. She realized that when you meet a woman, you see the parts of her body that she's going to use to make love to you. You see her mouth and teeth and tongue and fingers. You see her fingers comb her hair, play the piano, wash the dishes, write a letter. You watch her mouth eat and whistle and quiver and scream and kiss. When she makes love to you she brings all this movement and activity with her into your body.

Ann liked this. With her penis, however, it wasn't the same. She had to keep it private. She also didn't like fucking Muriel very much. She missed the old way. Putting her penis into a woman's body was so confusing. Ann knew it wasn't making love "to" Muriel and it certainly wasn't Muriel making love "to" her. It was more like making love "from" Muriel and that just didn't sit right.

One day Ann told Muriel about Jesse.

"I give her everything within my capacity to give and she gives me everything within her capacity to give—only my capacity is larger than hers."

In response Muriel took her to the Museum of Modern Art and pointed to a sculpture by Louise Bourgeois. Ann spent most of the afternoon in front of the large piece, an angry ocean of black penises which rose and crashed, carrying a little box house. The piece was called "Womanhouse." She looked at the penises, their little round heads, their black metal trunks, how they moved together to make waves, and she understood something completely new.

They got together the next day in a bar. As soon as she walked in Ann felt nauseous. She couldn't eat a thing. The smell of grease from Jesse's chicken dinner came in waves to Ann's side of the table. She kept her nose in the beer to cut the stench.

"You're dividing me against myself, Jesse."

Jesse offered her some chicken.

"No thanks, I really don't want any. Look, I can't keep making out with you on a couch because that's as far as you're willing to go before this turns into a lesbian relationship. It makes me feel like nothing."

Ann didn't mention that she had a penis.

"Annie, I can't say I don't love being physical with you because it wouldn't be true."

"I know."

"I feel something ferocious when I smell you. I love kissing you. That's why it's got to stop. I didn't realize when I started this that I was going to want it so much."

"Why is that a problem?"

"Why is that a problem? Why is that a problem?"

Jesse was licking the skin off the bone with her fingers. Slivers of meat stuck out of her long fingernails. She didn't know the answer.

"Jesse, what would happen if someone offered you a woman with a penis?"

Jesse wasn't surprised by this question, because Ann often raised issues from new and interesting perspectives.

"It wouldn't surprise me."

"Why not?"

"Well, Annie, I've never told you this before, actually it's just a secret between me and my therapist, but I feel as though I do have a penis. It's a theoretical penis, in my head. I've got a penis in my head and it's all mine."

"You're right," Ann said. "You do have a penis in your head because you have been totally mind-fucked. You've got an eight-inch cock between your ears."

With that she left the restaurant and left Jesse with the bill.

Soon Ann decided she wanted her clitoris back and she started to consult with doctors who did transsexual surgery. Since Ann had seen, tasted, and touched many clitorises in her short but full life, she knew that each one had its own unique way and wanted her very own cunt back just the way it had always been. So, she called together every woman who had ever made love to her. There was her French professor from college, her brother's girlfriend, her cousin Clarisse, her best friend from high school, Judith, Claudette, Kate, and Jane and assorted others. They all came to a big party at Shelley's house where they got high and drank beer and ate lasagna and when they all felt fine, Ann put a giant piece of white paper on the wall. By committee, they reconstructed Ann's cunt from memory. Some people had been more attentive than others, but they were all willing to make the effort. After a few hours and a couple of arguments as to the exact color tone and how many wrinkles on the left side, they finished the blueprints. "Pussy prints," the figure skater from Iowa City called them.

The following Monday Ann went in for surgery reflecting on the time she had spent with her penis. When you're different, you really have to think about things. You have a lot of information about how the mainstream lives, but they don't know much about you. They also don't know that they don't know, which they don't. Ann wanted one thing, to be a whole woman again. She never wanted to be mutilated by being cut off from herself and she knew that would be a hard thing to overcome, but Ann was willing to try.

A Lesbian Appetite

Dorothy Allison

Biscuits. I dream about baking biscuits, sifting flour, baking powder, and salt together, measuring out shortening and buttermilk by eye, and rolling it all out with flour-dusted fingers. Beans. I dream about picking over beans, soaking them overnight, chopping pork fat, slicing onions, putting it all in a great iron pot to bubble for hour after hour until all the world smells of salt and heat and the sweat that used to pool on my mama's neck. Greens. Mustard greens, collards, turnip greens and poke—can't find them anywhere in the shops up North. In the middle of the night I wake up desperate for the taste of greens, get up and find a 24-hour deli that still has a can of spinach and a half a pound of bacon. I fry the bacon, dump it in the spinach, bring the whole mess to a boil and eat it with tears in my eyes. It doesn't taste like anything I really wanted to have. When I find frozen collards in the Safeway, I buy five bags and store them away. Then all I have to do is persuade the butcher to let me have a pack of neck bones. Having those wrapped packages in the freezer reassures me almost as much as money in the bank. If I wake up with bad dreams there will at least be something I want to eat.

Red beans and rice, chicken necks and dumplings, pot

roast with vinegar and cloves stuck in the onions, salmon patties with white sauce, refried beans on warm tortillas, sweet duck with scallions and pancakes, lamb cooked with olive oil and lemon slices, pan-fried pork chops and red-eye gravy, potato pancakes with applesauce, polenta with spaghetti sauce floating on top—food is more than sustenance; it is history. I remember women by what we ate together, what they dug out of the freezer after we'd made love for hours. I've only had one lover who didn't want to eat at all. We didn't last long. The sex was good, but I couldn't think what to do with her when the sex was finished. We drank spring water together and fought a lot.

I grew an ulcer in my belly once I was out in the world on my own. I think of it as an always angry place inside me, a tyranny that takes good food and turns it like a blade scraping at the hard place where I try to hide my temper. Some days I think it is the rightful reward for my childhood. If I had eaten right, Lee used to tell me, there would never have been any trouble.

"Rickets, poor eyesight, appendicitis, warts, and bad skin," she insisted, "they're all caused by bad eating habits, poor diet."

It's true. The diet of poor southerners is among the worst in the world, though it's tasty, very tasty. There's pork fat or chicken grease in every dish, white sugar in the cobblers, pralines, and fudge, and flour, fat, and salt in the gravies—lots of salt in everything. The vegetables get cooked to limp strands with no fiber left at all. Mothers give sidemeat to their toddlers as pacifiers and slip them whiskey with honey at the first sign of teething, a cold, or a fever. Most of my cousins lost their teeth in their twenties and took up drinking as easily as they put sugar in their iced tea. I try not to eat so much sugar, try not to drink, try to limit pork and salt and white flour, but the truth is I am always hungry for it—the smell and taste of the food my mama fed me.

Poor white trash I am for sure. I eat shit food and am not

worthy. My family starts with good teeth but loses them early. Five of my cousins bled to death before thirty-five, their stomachs finally surrendering to sugar and whiskey and fat and salt. I've given it up. If I cannot eat what I want, then I'll eat what I must, but my dreams will always be flooded with salt and grease, crisp fried stuff that sweetens my mouth and feeds my soul. I would rather starve death than myself.

In college it was seven cups of coffee a day after a breakfast of dry-roasted nuts and Coca-Cola. Too much grey meat and reheated potatoes led me to develop a taste for peanut butter with honey, coleslaw with raisins, and pale, sad vegetables that never disturbed anything at all. When I started throwing up before classes, my roommate fed me fat pink pills her doctor had given her. My stomach shrank to a stone in my belly. I lived on pink pills, coffee, and Dexedrine until I could go home and use hot biscuits to scoop up cold tomato soup at my mama's table. The biscuits dripped memories as well as butter: Uncle Lucius rolling in at dawn, eating a big breakfast with us all, and stealing mama's tools when he left; or Aunt Panama at the door with her six daughters, screaming, *That bastard's made me pregnant again just to get a son*, and wanting butter beans with sliced tomatoes before she could calm down. Cold chicken in a towel meant Aunt Alma was staying over, cooking her usual six birds at a time. *Raising eleven kids I never learned how to cook for less than fifteen.* Red dye stains on the sink was a sure sign Reese was dating some new boy, baking him a Red Velvet Cake my stepfather would want for himself.

"It's good to watch you eat," my mama smiled at me, around her loose teeth. "It's just so good to watch you eat." She packed up a batch of her biscuits when I got ready to leave, stuffed them with cheese and fatback. On the bus going back to school I'd hug them to my belly, using their bulk to remind me who I was.

*   *   *

When the government hired me to be a clerk for the Social Security Administration, I was sent to Miami Beach where they put me up in a crumbling old hotel right on the water while teaching me all the regulations. The instructors took turns taking us out to dinner. Mr. McCullum took an interest in me, told me Miami Beach had the best food in the world, bought me an order of Oysters Rockefeller one night, and medallions of veal with wine sauce the next. If he was gonna pay for it, I would eat it, but it was all like food seen on a movie screen. It had the shape and shine of luxury but tasted like nothing at all. But I fell in love with Wolfe's Cafeteria and got up early every morning to walk there and eat their danish stuffed with cream cheese and raisins.

"The best sweet biscuit in Miami," I told the counter man.

"Nu?" he grinned at the woman beside me, her face wrinkling up as she blushed and smiled at me.

"Nischt," she laughed. I didn't understand a word but I nodded anyway. They were probably talking about food.

When I couldn't sleep, I read Franz Kafka in my hotel room, thinking about him working for the social security administration in Prague. Kafka would work late and eat Polish sausage for dinner, sitting over a notebook in which he would write all night. I wrote letters like novels that I never mailed. When the chairman of the local office promised us all a real treat, I finally rebelled and refused to eat the raw clams Mr. McCullum said were "the best in the world." While everyone around me sliced lemons and slurped up pink and grey morsels, I filled myself up with little white oyster crackers and tried not to look at the lobsters waiting to die, thrashing around in their plastic tanks.

"It's good to watch you eat," Mona told me, serving me dill bread, sour cream, and fresh tomatoes. "You do it with such obvious enjoyment." She drove us up to visit her family in Georgia, talking about what a great cook her mama was. My mouth watered, and we stopped three times for boiled peanuts. I wanted to make love in the back seat of her old

DeSoto but she was saving it up to do it in her own bed at home. When we arrived her mama came out to the car and said, "You girls must be hungry," and took us in to the lunch table.

There was three-bean salad from cans packed with vinaigrette, pickle loaf on thin sliced white bread, American and Swiss cheese in slices, and antipasto from a jar sent directly from an uncle still living in New York City. "Deli food," her mama kept saying, "is the best food in the world." I nodded, chewing white bread and a slice of American cheese, the peanuts in my belly weighing me down like a mess of little stones. Mona picked at the pickle loaf and pushed her ankle up into my lap where her mother couldn't see. I choked on the white bread and broke out in a sweat.

Lee wore her hair pushed up like the whorls on scallop shells. She toasted mushrooms instead of marshmallows, and tried to persuade me of the value of cabbage and eggplant, but she cooked with no fat; everything tasted of safflower oil. I loved Lee but hated the cabbage—it seemed an anemic cousin of real greens—and I only got into the eggplant after Lee brought home a basketful insisting I help her cook it up for freezing.

"You got to get it to sweat out the poisons." She sliced the big purple fruits as she talked. "Salt it up so the bitter stuff will come off." She layered the salted slices between paper towels, changing the towels on the ones she'd cut up earlier. Some of her hair came loose and hung down past one ear. She looked like a mother in a Mary Cassatt painting, standing in her sunlit kitchen, sprinkling raw seasalt with one hand and pushing her hair back with the other.

I picked up an unsalted wedge of eggplant and sniffed it, rubbing the spongy mass between my thumbs. "Makes me think of what breadfruit must be like." I squeezed it down, and the flesh slowly shaped up again. "Smells like bread and feels like it's been baked. But after you salt it down, it's more like fried okra, all soft and sharp-smelling."

"Well, you like okra, don't you?" Lee wiped her grill with peanut oil and started dusting the drained eggplant slices with flour. Sweat shone on her neck under the scarf that tied up her hair in back.

"Oh yeah. You put enough cornmeal on it and fry it in bacon fat and I'll probably like most anything." I took the wedge of eggplant and rubbed it on the back of her neck.

"What are you doing?"

"Salting the eggplant." I followed the eggplant with my tongue, pulled up her T-shirt, and slowly ran the tough purple rind up to her small bare breasts. Lee started giggling, wiggling her ass, but not taking her hands out of the flour to stop me. I pulled down her shorts, picked up another dry slice and planted it against her navel, pressed with my fingers and slipped it down toward her pubic mound.

"Oh! Don't do that. Don't do that." She was breathing through her open mouth and her right hand was a knotted fist in the flour bowl. I laughed softly into her ear, and rocked her back so that she was leaning against me, her ass pressing into my cunt.

"Oh. Oh!" Lee shuddered and reached with her right hand to turn off the grill. With her left she reached behind her and pulled up on my shirt. Flour smeared over my sweaty midriff and sifted down on the floor. "You. You!" She was tugging at my jeans, a couple of slices of eggplant in one hand.

"I'll show you. Oh you!" We wrestled, eggplant breaking up between our navels. I got her shorts off, she got my jeans down. I dumped a whole plate of eggplant on her belly."

"You are just running salt, girl," I teased, and pushed slices up between her legs, while I licked one of her nipples and pinched the other between a folded slice of eggplant. She was laughing, her belly bouncing under me.

"I'm gonna make you eat all this," she yelled.

"Of course." I pushed eggplant out of the way and slipped two fingers between her labia. She was slicker than peanut oil. "But first we got to get the poison out."

"Oh you!" Her hips rose up into my hand. All her hair had come loose and was trailing in the flour. She wrapped one hand in my hair, the other around my left breast. "I'll cook you . . . just you wait. I'll cook you a meal to drive you crazy."

"Oh honey." She tasted like frybread—thick, smoked, and fat-rich on my tongue. We ran sweat in puddles, while above us the salted eggplant pearled up in great clear drops of poison. When we finished, we gathered up all the eggplant on the floor and fried it in flour and crushed garlic. Lee poured canned tomatoes with basil and lemon on the hot slices and then pushed big bites onto my tongue with her fingers. It was delicious. I licked her fingers and fed her with my own hands. We never did get our clothes back on.

In South Carolina, in the seventh grade, we had studied nutrition. "Vitamin D," the teacher told us, "is paramount. Deny it to a young child and the result is the brain never develops properly." She had a twangy midwestern accent, grey hair, and a small brown mole on her left cheek. Everybody knew she hated teaching, hated her students, especially those of us in badly fitting worn-out dresses sucking bacon rinds and cutting our names in the desks with our uncle's old pocketknives. She would stand with a fingertip on her left ear, her thumb stroking the mole, while she looked at us with disgust she didn't bother to conceal.

"The children of the poor," she told us, "the children of the poor have a lack of brain tissue simply because they don't get the necessary vitamins at the proper age. It is a deficiency that cannot be made up when they are older." A stroke of her thumb and she turned her back.

I stood in the back of the room, my fingers wrapping my skull in horror. I imagined my soft brain slipping loosely in its cranial cavity shrunk by a lack of the necessary vitamins. How could I know if it wasn't too late? Mama always said that smart was the only way out. I thought of my cousins, big-headed, watery-eyed, and stupid. VITAMIN D! I became a compulsive consumer of vitamin D. Is it milk? We will drink milk, steal it if we must. *Mama, make salmon stew. It's cheap and full of vitamin D.* If we can't afford cream, then evaporated milk will do. One is as thick as the other. Sweet is expensive, but thick builds muscles in the brain. Feed me milk, feed me cream, feed me what I need to fight them.

Twenty years later the doctor sat me down to tell me the secrets of my body. He had, oddly, that identical gesture, one finger on the ear and the others curled to the cheek as if he were thinking all the time.

"Milk," he announced, "that's the problem, a mild allergy. Nothing to worry about. You'll take calcium and vitamin D supplements and stay away from milk products. No cream, no butterfat, stay away from cheese."

I started to grin, but he didn't notice. The finger on his ear was pointing to the brain. He had no sense of irony, and I didn't tell him why I laughed so much. I should have known. Milk or cornbread or black-eyed peas, there had to be a secret, something we would never understand until it was too late. My brain is fat and strong, ripe with years of vitamin D, but my belly is tender and hurts me in the night. I grinned into his confusion and chewed the pink and grey pills he gave me to help me recover from the damage milk had done me. What would I have to do, I wondered, to be able to eat pan gravy again?

When my stomach began to turn on me the last time, I made desperate attempts to compromise—wheat germ, brown rice, fresh vegetables and tamari. Whole wheat became a symbol for purity of intent, but hard brown bread does not pass easily. It sat in my stomach and clung to the honey deposits that seemed to be collecting between my tongue and breastbone. Lee told me I could be healthy if I drank a glass of hot water and lemon juice every morning. She chewed sunflower seeds and sesame seed candy made with molasses. I drank the hot water, but then I went up on the

roof of the apartment building to read Carson McCullers, to
eat Snickers bars and drink Dr. Pepper, imagining myself
back in Uncle Lucius's Pontiac inhaling Moon Pies and R.C.
Cola.

"Swallow it," Jay said. Her fingers were in my mouth,
thick with the juice from between her legs. She was leaning
forward, her full weight pressing me down. I swallowed,
sucked between each knuckle, and swallowed again. Her
other hand worked between us, pinching me but forcing the
thick cream out of my cunt. She brought it up and pushed it
into my mouth, took the hand I'd cleaned and smeared it
again with her own musky gravy.

"Swallow it," she kept saying. "Swallow it all, suck my
fingers, lick my palm." Her hips ground into me. She smeared
it on my face until I closed my eyes under the sticky,
strong-smelling mixture of her juice and mine. With my eyes
closed, I licked and sucked until I was drunk on it, gasping
until my lungs hurt with my hands digging into the muscles
of her back. I was moaning and whining, shaking like a
newborn puppy trying to get to its mama's tit.

Jay lifted a little off me. I opened stinging eyes to see her
face, her intent and startling expression. I held my breath,
waiting. I felt it before I understood it, and when I did
understand I went on lying still under her, barely breathing.
It burned me, ran all over my belly and legs. She put both
hands down, brought them up, poured bitter yellow piss
into my eyes, my ears, my shuddering mouth.

"Swallow it," she said again, but I held it in my mouth,
pushed up against her and clawed her back with my nails.
She whistled between her teeth. My hips jerked and rocked
against her, making a wet sucking sound. I pushed my face
to hers, my lips to hers, and forced my tongue into her
mouth. I gripped her hard and rolled her over, my tongue
sliding across her teeth, the taste of all her juices between
us. I bit her lips and shoved her legs apart with my knee.

"Taste it," I hissed at her. "Swallow it." I ran my hands

over her body. My skin burned. She licked my face, growling deep in her throat. I pushed both hands between her legs, my fingertips opened her and my thumbs caught her clit under the soft sheath of its hood.

"Go on, go on," I insisted. Tears were running down her face. I licked them. Her mouth was at my ear, her tongue trailing through the sweat at my hairline. When she came her teeth clamped down on my earlobe. I pulled but could not free myself. She was a thousand miles away, rocking back and forth on my hand, the stink of her all over us both. When her teeth freed my ear, I slumped. It felt as if I had come with her. My thighs shook and my teeth ached. She was mumbling with her eyes closed.

"Gonna bathe you," she whispered, "put you in a tub of hot lemonade. Drink it off you. Eat you for dinner." Her hands dug into my shoulders, rolled me onto my back. She drew a long, deep breath with her head back and then looked down at me, put on hand into my cunt, and brought it up slick with my juice.

"Swallow it," Jay said. "Swallow it."

The year we held the great Southeastern Feminist Conference, I was still following around behind Lee. She volunteered us to handle the food for the two hundred women that were expected. Lee wanted us to serve "healthy food" —her vegetarian spaghetti sauce, whole wheat pasta, and salad with cold fresh vegetables. Snacks would be granola, fresh fruit, and peanut butter on seven-grain bread. For breakfast she wanted me to cook grits in a twenty-quart pan, though she wasn't sure margarine wouldn't be healthier than butter, and maybe most people would just like granola anyway.

"They'll want donuts and coffee," I told her matter-of-factly. I had a vision of myself standing in front of a hundred angry lesbians crying out for coffee and white sugar. Lee soothed me with kisses and poppyseed cake made with gluten flour, assured me that it would be fun to run the kitchen with her.

The week before the conference, Lee went from church to campus borrowing enormous pots, colanders, and baking trays. Ten flat baking trays convinced her that the second dinner we had to cook could be tofu lasagna with skim milk mozzarella and lots of chopped carrots. I spent the week sitting in front of the pool table in Jay's apartment, peeling and slicing carrots, potatoes, onions, green and red peppers, leeks, tomatoes, and squash. The slices were dumped in ten-gallon garbage bags and stored in Jay's handy floor-model freezer. I put a tablecloth down on the pool table to protect the green felt and made mounds of vegetables over each pocket corner. Every mound cut down and transferred to a garbage bag was a victory. I was winning the war on vegetables until the committee Lee had scared up delivered another load.

I drank coffee and chopped carrots, ate a chicken pot pie and peeled potatoes, drank iced tea and sliced peppers. I peeled the onions but didn't slice them, dropped them in a big vat of cold water to keep, I found a meat cleaver on the back porch and used it to chop the zucchini and squash, pretending I was doing *karate* and breaking boards.

"Bite-sized," Lee told me as she ran through, "it should all be bite-sized." I wanted to bite her. I drank cold coffee and dropped tomatoes one at a time into boiling water to loosen their skins. There were supposed to be other women helping me, but only one showed up, and she went home after she got a rash from the tomatoes. I got out a beer, put the radio on loud, switching it back and forth from rock-and-roll to the country-and-western station and sang along as I chopped.

I kept working. The only food left in the apartment was vegetables. I wanted to have a pizza delivered but had no money. When I got hungry, I ate carrots on white bread with mayonnaise, slices of tomatoes between slices of raw squash, and leeks I dipped in a jar of low-sodium peanut butter. I threw up three times but kept working. Four hours before the first women were to arrive I took the last bushel basket of carrots out in the backyard and hid it under a tarp with the lawn mower. I laughed to myself as I did, swaying on rubbery legs. Lee drove up in a borrowed pickup truck with two women who'd come in from Atlanta and volunteered to help. One of them kept talking about the no-mucus diet as she loaded the truck. I went in the bathroom, threw up again, and then just sat on the tailgate in the sun while they finished up.

"You getting lazy, girl?" Lee teased me. "Better rev it up, we got cooking to do." I wiped my mouth and imagined burying her under a truckload of carrots. I felt like I had been drinking whiskey, but my stomach was empty and flat. The blacktop on the way out to the Girl Scout camp seemed to ripple and sway in the sunlight. Lee kept talking about the camp kitchen, the big black gas stove and the walk-in freezer.

"This is going to be fun." I didn't think so. The onions still had to be sliced. I got hysterical when someone picked up my knife. Lee was giggling with a woman I'd never seen before, the two of them talking about macrobiotic cooking while rinsing brown noodles. I got the meat cleaver and started chopping onions in big raw chunks. "Bite-sized," Lee called to me, in a cheerful voice.

"You want 'em bite-sized, you cut 'em," I told her, and went on chopping furiously.

It was late when we finally cleaned up. I hadn't been able to eat anything. The smell of the sauce had made me dizzy, and the scum that rinsed off the noodles looked iridescent and dangerous. My stomach curled up into a knot inside me, and I glowered at the women who came in and wanted hot water for tea. There were women sitting on the steps out on the deck, women around a campfire over near the water pump, naked women swimming out to the raft in the lake, and skinny, muscled women dancing continuously in the rec room. Lee had gone off with her new friend, the macrobiotic cook. I found a loaf of Wonder bread someone had left on the snack table, pulled out a slice and ate it in tiny bites.

"Want some?" It was one of the women from Atlanta. She held out a brown bag from which a bottle top protruded.

"It would make me sick."

"Naw," she grinned. "It's just a Yoo-hoo. I got a stash of them in a cooler. Got a bad stomach myself. Only thing it likes is chocolate soda and barbecue."

"Barbecue," I sighed. My mouth flooded with saliva. "I haven't made barbecue in years?"

"You make beef ribs?" She sipped at her Yoo-hoo and sat down beside me.

"I have, but if you got the time to do slow pit cooking, pork's better," My stomach suddenly growled loudly, a grating, angry noise in the night.

"Girl," she laughed. "You still hungry?"

"Well, to tell you the truth, I couldn't eat any of that stuff." I was embarrassed.

My new friend giggled. "Neither did I. I had peanuts and Yoo-hoo for dinner myself." I laughed with her. "My name's Marty. You come up to Atlanta sometime, and we'll drive over to Marietta and get some of the best barbecue they make in the world."

"The best barbecue in the world?"

"Bar none." She handed me the bottle of Yoo-hoo.

"Can't be." I sipped a little. It was sweet and almost warm.

"You don't trust my judgment?" Someone opened the porch door, and I saw in the light that her face was relaxed, her blue eyes twinkling.

"I trust you. You didn't eat any of those damn noodles, did you? You're trustworthy, but you can't have the best barbecue in the world up near Atlanta, 'cause the best barbecue in the world is just a couple of miles down the Perry Highway."

"You say!"

"I do!"

We both laughed, and she slid her hip over close to mine. I shivered, and she put her arm around me. We talked, and I told her my name. It turned out we knew some of the same people. She had even been involved with a woman I hadn't seen since college. I was so tired I leaned my head on her shoulder. Marty rubbed my neck and told me a series of terribly dirty jokes until I started shaking more from giggling.

"Got to get you to bed," she started to pull me up. I took hold of her belt, leaned over, and kissed her. She kissed me. We sat back down and just kissed for a while. Her mouth was soft and tasted of sweet, watery chocolate.

"Uh huh," she said a few times, "uh huh."

"Uh huh," I giggled back.

"Oh yes, think we gonna have to check out this barbecue." Marty's hands were as soft as her mouth, and they slipped under the waistband of my jeans and hugged my belly. "You weren't fixed on having tofu lasagna tomorrow, were you?"

"Gonna break my heart to miss it, I can tell you." It was hard to talk with my lips pressed to hers. She licked my lips, the sides of my mouth, my cheek, my eyelids, and then put her lips up close to my ears.

"Oh, but think . . ." Her hands didn't stop moving, and I had to push myself back from her to keep from wetting my pants. ". . . Think about tomorrow afternoon when we come back from our little road trip hauling in all that barbecue, coleslaw, and hush puppies. We gonna make so many friends around here." She paused. "They do make hush puppies at this place, don't they?"

"Of course. If we get there early enough, we might even pick up some blackberry cobbler at this truck stop I know." My stomach rumbled again loudly.

"I don't think you been eating right," Marty giggled. "Gonna have to feed you some healthy food, girl, some *healthy* food?"

*   *   *

Jay does *karate*, does it religiously, going to class four days in a week and working out at the gym every other day. Her muscles are hard and long. She is so tall people are always making jokes about "the weather up there." I call her *Shorty* or *Tall* to tease her, and *Sugar Hips* when I want to make her mad. Her hips are wide and full, though her legs are long and stringy.

"Lucky I got big feet," she jokes sometimes, "or I'd fall over every time I stopped to stand still."

Jay is always hungry, always. She keeps a bag of nuts in her backpack, dried fruit sealed in cellophane in a bowl on her dresser, snack-packs of crackers and cheese in her locker at the gym. When we go out to the women's bar, she drinks one beer in three hours but eats half a dozen packages of smoked almonds. Her last girlfriend was Italian. She used to serve Jay big batches of pasta with homemade sausage marinara.

"I need carbohydrates," Jay insists, eating slices of potato bread smeared with sweet butter. I cook grits for her, with melted butter and cheese, fry slabs of cured ham I get from a butcher who swears it has no nitrates. She won't eat eggs, won't eat shrimp or oysters, but she loves catfish pan-fried in a batter of cornmeal and finely chopped onions. Coffee makes her irritable. Chocolate makes her horny. When my period is coming and I get that flushed heat feeling in my insides, I bake her Toll House cookies, serve them with a cup of coffee and a blush. She looks at me over the rim of the cup, sips slowly, and eats her cookies with one hand, the other hooked in her jeans by her thumb. A muscle jumps in her cheek, and her eyes are full of tiny lights.

"You hungry, honey?" she purrs. She stretches like a big cat, puts her bare foot up, and uses her toes to lift my blouse. "You want something sweet?" Her toes are cold. I shiver and keep my gaze on her eyes. She leans forward and cups her hands around my face. "What you hungry for, girl, huh? You tell me. You tell mama exactly what you want."

*   *   *

Her name was Victoria, and she lived alone. She cut her hair into a soft cloud of curls and wore white blouses with buttoned-down collars. I saw her all the time at the bookstore, climbing out of her baby-blue VW with a big leather book bag and a cane in her left hand. There were pictures up on the wall at the back of the store. Every one of them showed her sitting on or standing by a horse, the reins loose in her hand and her eyes focused far off. The riding hat hid her curls. The jacket pushed her breasts down but emphasized her hips. She had a ribbon pinned to the coat. A little card beneath the pictures identified her as the steeplechase champion of the southern division. In one picture she was jumping. Her hat was gone; her hair blown back, and the horse's legs stretched high above the ground. Her teeth shone white and perfect, and she looked as fierce as a bobcat going for prey. Looking at the pictures made me hurt. She came in once while I was standing in front of them and gave me a quick, wry grin.

"You ride?" Her cane made a hollow thumping sound on the floor. I didn't look at it.

"For fun, once or twice with a girlfriend." Her eyes were enormous and as black as her hair. Her face looked thinner than it had in the pictures, her neck longer. She grimaced and leaned on the cane. Under her tan she looked pale. She shrugged.

"I miss it myself." She said it in a matter-of-fact tone, but her eyes glittered. I looked up at the pictures again.

"I'll bet," I blushed, and looked back at her uncomfortably.

"Odds are I'll ride again." Her jeans bulged around the knee brace. "But not jump, and I did love jumping. Always felt like I was at war with the ground, allied with the sky, trying to stay up in the air." She grinned wide, and a faint white scar showed at the corner of her mouth.

"Where you from?" I could feel the heat in my face but ignored it.

"Virginia." Her eyes focused on my jacket, the backpack

hanging from my arm, and down to where I had my left hip pushed out, my weight on my right foot. "Haven't been there for a while, though." She looked away, looked tired and sad. What I wanted in that moment I will never be able to explain—to feed her or make love to her or just lighten the shadows under her eyes—all that, all that and more.

"You ever eat any Red Velvet Cake?" I licked my lips and shifted my weight so that I wasn't leaning to the side. I looked into her eyes.

"Red Velvet Cake?" Her eyes were friendly, soft, black as the deepest part of the night.

"It's a dessert my sister and I used to bake, unhealthy as sin and twice as delicious. Made up with chocolate, buttermilk, vinegar and baking soda, and a little bottle of that poisonous red dye number two. Tastes like nothing you've ever had."

"You got to put the dye in it?"

"Uh huh," I nodded, "wouldn't be right without it."

"Must look deadly."

"But tastes good. It's about time I baked one. You come to dinner at my place, tell me about riding, and I'll cook you up one."

She shifted, leaned back, and half-sat on a table full of magazines. She looked me up and down again, her grin coming and going with her glance.

"What else would you cook?"

"Fried okra maybe, fried crisp, breaded with cornmeal. Those big beefsteak tomatoes are at their peak right now. Could just serve them in slices with pepper, but I've seen some green ones, too, and those I could fry in flour with the okra. Have to have white corn, of course, this time of the year. Pinto beans would be too heavy, but snap beans would be nice. A little milk gravy to go with it all. You like fried chicken?"

"Where you from?"

"South Carolina, a long time ago."

"You mama teach you to cook?"

"My mama and my aunts." I put my thumbs in my belt and tried to look sure of myself. Would she like biscuits or cornbread, pork or beef or chicken?

"I'm kind of a vegetarian." She sighed when she said it, and her eyes looked sad.

"Eat fish?" I was thinking quickly. She nodded. I smiled wide.

"Ever eat any crawfish pan-fried in salt and Louisiana hot sauce?"

"You got to boil them first." Her face was shining, and she was bouncing her cane on the hardwood floor.

"Oh yeah, 'course, with the right spices."

"Sweet Bleeding Jesus," her face was flushed. She licked her lips. "I haven't eaten anything like that in, oh, so long."

"Oh." My thighs felt hot, rubbing on the seams of my jeans. She was beautiful, Victoria in her black cloud of curls. "Oh, girl," I whispered. I leaned toward her. I put my hand on her wrist above the cane, squeezed.

"Let me feed you," I told her. "Girl . . . girl, you should just let me feed you what you really need."

I've been dreaming lately that I throw a dinner party, inviting all the women in my life. They come in with their own dishes. Marty brings barbecue carried all the way from Marietta. Jay drags in a whole side of beef and gets a bunch of swaggering whiskey-sipping butch types to help her dig a hole in the backyard. They show off for each other, breaking up stones to line the firepit. Lee watches them from the porch, giggling at me and punching down a great mound of dough for the oatmeal wheat bread she'd promised to bake. Women whose names I can't remember bring in bowls of pasta salad, smoked salmon, and Jell-o with tangerine slices. Everybody is feeding each other, exclaiming over recipes and gravies, introducing themselves and telling stories about great meals they've eaten. My mama is in the kitchen salting a vat of greens. Two of my aunts are arguing over whether to make little baking powder biscuits or big buttermilk hogsheads. Another steps around them to slide an iron skillet full of cornbread in the oven. Pinto beans with onions are bubbling on the stove. Children run through sucking fatback rinds. My uncles are on the porch telling stories and knocking glass bottles together when they laugh.

I walk back and forth from the porch to the kitchen, being hugged and kissed and stroked by everyone I pass. For the first time in my life I am not hungry, but everybody insists I have a little taste. I burp like a baby on her mama's shoulder. My stomach is full, relaxed, happy, and the taste of pan gravy is in my mouth. I can't stop grinning. The dream goes on and on, and through it all I hug myself and smile.

Afterword

Joan Nestle

This anthology could not have happened without the courage and tenacity of a lesbian writing and publishing community that reaches back into the late fifties. When the women of Daughters of Bilitis, the first lesbian civil rights organization, started putting together a small journal called *The Ladder* in 1956, a new literary tradition was born. Mixed in with community news, reviews of books and plays, reports on police raids and psychological treatises, were short stories that spoke of love and loss, coming out and self-discovery. Sold in the sleazy sections of some big-city drugstores and mailed out in brown covers, this journal of lesbian culture was to last sixteen years, and one of its editors, Barbara Grier, would become co-founder of Naiad Press (1973), the largest and longest-running lesbian publishing house in the world with now over eighty-five titles in print.

In the seventies, lesbian periodicals, presses, and publishing houses appeared in large numbers, and for almost twenty years now there has been an alternate literary world of lesbian writing, publishing, and reading, a world that is alternate not just because the literary establishment acts as if it does not exist but because a different set of choices is at its heart. Born at the crossroads of three movements for

social change, lesbian publishing became a tool for the
liberation of a group of people—lesbians—who were still
considered criminals in many states of this country and for a
class of people—women—who many still thought of as aux-
iliary members of the human race. Inspired by the vision of
the civil rights movement, the women's movement, and the
gay liberation movement, lesbians created their own social
and cultural territories. In their presses and books, in their
periodicals and publishing houses, they tried to begin the
dismantling of the racist, heterosexist, gender-bound society
that surrounded them.

When *The Ladder* stopped publishing in 1972, a new
lesbian cultural journal called *Amazon Quarterly*, a lesbian-
feminist arts periodical, announced its intention to "explore
through its pages just what might be the female sensibility in
the arts." According to the editors, Gina and Laurel, lesbians, "freed from male identification," were to be the van-
guard voice of this new cultural perspective. Through the
seventies and into the eighties, lesbian periodicals flour-
ished, their titles suggesting their political and cultural
visions—*13th Moon* (1973), *Sinister Wisdom* (1976), *Conditions* (1976), *Quest, Focus, Chrysalis, Feminary, Heresies*
(1976), *Azalea,* a magazine by Third World Lesbians (1978),
off our backs (1970), *Lesbian Connections* (1982), and *Common Lives/Lesbian Lives* (1981). Often produced by collec-
tives, these publications were dedicated to being inclusive of
all lesbian experience and to keeping their prices as low as
possible. *Lesbian Connection*, a stapled multipage monthly,
was and still is distributed free through a network of wom-
en's and gay bookstores as well as through a huge national
mailing list. Contributions from a grateful community keep
this publication alive. Embodying the lesbian feminist spirit
of the seventies, these journals gave lesbian writers a chance
to develop a community of sympathetic readers.

Joining Naiad Press in the early seventies, two new lesbian publishing presses—Daughters, Inc., under the direction
of June Arnold and Parke Bowman, and Diana Press—

committed themselves to publishing writers who challenged the prevailing literary canon. With little money but with enough passion to build worlds, the presses and periodicals were reaching an estimated three hundred thousand readers by the mid-seventies. The commercial success of Rita Mae Brown's *Ruby Fruit Jungle* and *Plain Brown Wrapper* made even *The New York Times Book Review* consider for a moment this other face of writing and publishing, but mostly lesbian writers and publishers went about their work without fanfare or recognition from the patriarchal literary establishment.

Today, lesbian and feminist publishing houses and presses are thriving. No less committed to social change and artistic excellence, presses like Kitchen Table, Women of Color Press (1981), Firebrand Books (1984), The Seal Press (1976), Cleis Press (1980), Clothespin Fever Press (1986), New Victoria Publishers (1976), and Spinsters/Aunt Lute (1978) continue to give the lesbian writer the respect and audience she deserves. Because they take risks and seek out the historically silenced voices, these publishers and presses continue to keep alive the hope for a more just and humane national culture that will reflect the full diversity of our peoples. For those of us who live and work in this cultural community, the lesbian literary world is not marginal or temporary. On our pages live our dreams, our desires, our politics, our sense of another kind of world where money and power do not determine who will survive.

A more specific thank you is owed to three anthologies of lesbian short stories that have appeared previously: *The Lesbians Home Journal, Stories from the Ladder*, edited by Barbara Grier and Coletta Reid (Diana Press, 1971); *True to Life Adventure Stories, Vol. 1* and *Vol. 2*, edited by Judy Grahn, (Diana Press and Crossing Press, 1979 and 1981); and *Lesbian Fiction*, edited by Elly Bulkin (Persephone Press, 1981). In her introductory essay, "A Look at Lesbian Short Fiction," Elly Bulkin provided a brilliant overview of the development of the lesbian short story and its connection to community ethics. These books, well known to lesbian readers, were ground-breaking attempts to construct a people's literary heritage.

In addition, individual writers such as Maureen Brady, Sandy Boucher, Ann Allen Shockley, Jan Clausen, Carolyn Weathers, and Barbara Wilson have all published solid collections, marking this genre as their own.

We wanted to write this brief historical overview as a way of saying thank you to our community of writers and publishers. We wanted to commemorate the act of courage each of them took when they described themselves with the simple words "lesbian writer." Before the established presses were even willing to consider lesbian material, our publishers risked all they had in an attempt to keep us alive as a literary people, as a public community. We know, as other oppressed groups know, that silence, invisibility, help no one survive in the long run; we know that we must author our own stories because if we do not, our lives will be reduced to dirty jokes or simplistic summaries of deviant behavior. Literary fashions come and go, but lesbian publishers, in their commitment to the survival of a body of literature deemed peripheral by some, obscene by others, hold out the hope for a more enduring literary tradition—one that nourishes and gets life from a collective vision of new social and cultural possibilities.

Author Biographies

Dorothy Allison is the author of a collection of short stories, *Trash*, winner of the LAMBDA literary awards for best lesbian fiction, and a book of poetry, *The Women Who Hate Me*. Allison's fiction, poetry, and essays have appeared in *Conditions, The Village Voice*, and *The Advocate* and in numerous anthologies. She was born in Greenville, South Carolina, and now lives in San Francisco.

June Arnold is the author of *Sister Gin, The Cook and the Carpenter*, and *Applesauce*. She co-founded the feminist publishing house Daughters, Inc., with Parke Bowman. She died in 1982.

Becky Birtha is a black lesbian feminist poet and fiction writer and is the author of two collections of short stories: *For Nights Like This One: Stories of Loving Women*, and *Lover's Choice*. She is the recipient of a Creative Writing Fellowship Grant from the National Endowment for the Arts. She was born in Hampton, Virginia, and now lives in Philadelphia.

Beth Brant is the editor of *A Gathering of Spirit*, a collection by North American Indian women, and is the author of

Mohawk Trail. She is a Bay of Quinte Mohawk from Deseronto, Ontario, a mother and grandmother, and currently lives in Detroit.

Willa Cather (1873–1947) announced her arrival in Pittsburgh with the publication of *Tommy the Unsentimental* in the conventional family magazine *Home Monthly Magazine*. *Tommy* reminds us that Cather, fresh from Red Cloud, Nebraska, came fully equipped to combat narrow-mindedness with a westerner's sense of humor. At an early age, Cather earned a reputation as a tomboy by cutting her hair and signing her name as William Cather, M.D. In Pittsburgh, Cather met Isabelle McClung, with whom she lived until 1906 when she moved to New York as an editor for *McClures*. By 1908 Cather was living with Edith Lewis, a partnership that would last almost forty years until Cather's death in 1947.

Cathy Cockrell is the author of *Undershirts and Other Stories* and *A Simple Fact*. Her short stories have appeared in anthologies and in the journals *Croton Review* and *Hanging Loose*. She lives in San Francisco.

Margaret Erhart is the author of *Unusual Company*. She lives in Provincetown, Massachusetts.

Rocky Gámez has published fiction in *Cuentos, Politics of the Heart, Intricacies, Wicked Girls and Wayward Women*, and *Common Bond*. She was born and raised in the lower Rio Grande Valley of Texas.

Jewelle L. Gomez is the author of a collection of poetry *Flamingoes and Bears*, and a forthcoming novel, *The Gilda Stories*. She has reviewed books for *Belle Lettres, The Village Voice, The Nation*, and *The New York Times*. She lives in Brooklyn, New York.

Bertha Harris is the author of three novels: *Catching Saradove, Confessions of Cherubino*, and *Lover*. She is the co-author of *The Joy of Lesbian Sex*.

Naomi Holoch lives in New York City and has been teaching French at the State University of New York at Purchase for the past fifteen years. She is the author of several short stories and a novel, *Offseason*.

Willyce Kim is the author of two works of fiction, *Dancer Dawkins and the California Kid* and *Dead Heat*. Both books are published by Alyson. She has also written three books of poetry: *Curtains of Light, Eating Artichokes*, and *Under the Rolling Sky*. She has just completed a manuscript of poetry called *Declarations* and is currently finishing her third novel, *Gabriella, a love story*.

Leslie Lawrence received a master of arts in teaching from Brown University and a master of fine arts in fiction from Goddard College. A recipient of a Massachusetts Artists Foundation fellowship in fiction, her stories have been published in *The Massachusetts Review, Sojourner*, and *The Green Mountain Review*. She lives in Cambridge, Massachusetts.

Lee Lynch is the author of seven books, including *The Swashbuckler, Dusty's Queen of Hearts Diner*, and, most recently, *Sue Slate, Private Eye*. She writes "The Amazon Trail," a nationally syndicated column. She lives in southern Oregon.

Judith McDaniel is the author of *Sanctuary: A Journey* and *Metamorphosis, Reflections on Recovery*. She lives in Albany, New York.

Kristina McGrath is the author of both fiction and poetry and has been published in *The Paris Review, Harper's Mag-*

azine, and *Feminist Studies*. She has received the Pushcart Prize in Fiction and several grants for both fiction and poetry. She lives in San Francisco.

Valerie Miner is the author of *All Good Women, Winter's Edge, Movement, Blood Sisters*, and *Murder in the English Department*. Her reviews, essays, and stories have appeared in *The New York Times, Conditions*, and *Ms.*, and she has won the PEN Syndicated Fiction Award. She teaches at the University of California, Berkeley.

Joan Nestle is co-founder of the Lesbian Herstory Archives and the author of *A Restricted Country,* winner of the 1988 Gay Book Award of the American Library Association. She lives in New York City.

Lesléa Newman is the author of a novel, *Good Enough to Eat*, a collection of poetry, *Love Me Like You Mean It*, and a collection of short stories, *A Letter to Harvey Milk*. She was born in Brooklyn and now lives in Northampton, Massachusetts, where she teaches women's writing workshops.

Sherri Paris teaches writing and Third World politics at the University of California, Santa Cruz. She has worked as a fundraiser and coordinator for feminist organizations treating survivors of domestic violence, child abuse, and rape. She received her Ph.D. in philosophy and literature from the University of California and has done postdoctoral work at Yale University.

Camille Roy's writing has appeared in many small magazines, including *Mirage, Zyzzyva*, and *HOW(ever)* and has been anthologized in *Deep Down: The New Sensual Writing by Women*. She has been living and working in San Francisco for ten years.

Joanna Russ is a science fiction novelist and short story writer whose works include *Magic Mommas, Trembling Sisters, Puritans and Perverts, The Two of Them, We Who Are About To, The Female Man, And Chaos Died*, and *Picnic on Paradise*. She has won both of science fiction's most prestigious awards, the Nebula and the Hugo.

Sapphire is the author of *Meditations on the Rainbow*, a book of poetry. She is also a novelist and short story writer and her work has appeared in numerous anthologies and journals.

Taya Schaffer lives in Oakland, California, and often writes about the Old Country of New York.

Sarah Schulman is the author of four novels: *The Sophie Horowitz Story, Girls, Visions and Everything; After Delores*, winner of the American Library Association Gay Book Award in 1989; and *People in Trouble*. She lives in New York City.

Ida Swearingen is a family therapy trainer and psychotherapist. Her work has been published in *The Evergreen Chronicle* and in *Plainswoman*. She lives in Minneapolis.

Jess Wells is the author of several volumes of short fiction, including *Two Willow Chairs: Stories of Love and Courage*, and *The Dress/The Sharda Stories*. She lives in San Francisco.

Jacqueline Woodson is the author of *Last Summer with Maizon*. Her short stories and poetry have appeared in a number of magazines and journals.